To my beloved father who made the greatest sacrifice in his life to provide me with a secondary education, which triggered my entire future academic career.
I owe this much to him

To my dear loving uncles – Sam and Clifford – who have always encouraged me to, in their very own words, "read, read any piece ah paper you put you han'on." Their legacy lives within me.

THE CURSED VILLAGE

16th October, 2020

To My Dearest warm, charming,
loving, intelligent Rose.

It is with the greatest of pleasure &
utmost delight to present you with a
copy of the book now that it is published.
I thank you for helping me though it
wasting of it and for listening to my
stupidness when talking about it.
You have plenty of guts to put up with
me — more guts than a Corlabagh.
I always remember — "You if tact with
priest and common sense is not so
common ; But you are loaded with
common sense.

I sincerely thank you for all the
help in the entire process of the
book's production and coming out
to be a reality.

with Love & Plenty of it
from this

B.JA

16/10/2020

xxxx
xxx
xxxx

THE
CURSED
VILLAGE

HARRIPERSAD SAMAROO

Matador
9 Priory Business Park,
Wistow Road, Kibworth Beauchamp,
Leicestershire. LE8 0RX
Tel: 0116 279 2299
Email: books@troubador.co.uk
Web: www.troubador.co.uk/matador
Twitter: @matadorbooks

ISBN 978 1 83859 523 4

British Library Cataloguing in Publication Data.
A catalogue record for this book is available from the British Library.

Printed and bound by CPI Group (UK) Ltd, Croydon, CR0 4YY
Typeset in 11pt Minion Pro by Troubador Publishing Ltd, Leicester, UK

Matador is an imprint of Troubador Publishing Ltd

CONTENTS

Introduction

A FOUR-YEAR-OLD BOY, USATI, (U), describes his life as he sees and experiences it in a small remote sugar cane farming village in Trinidad. He charts his experiences over two decades in the 1940s and 1950s. The little village of Sunnyvale comprises two hills separated by a valley. There is a river in the middle of the valley cutting the village into East and West. There is a notorious and much feared silk-cotton tree along the river. The evil spirits live there and cause untold misery and deaths in the village. These spirits can, and do, transform themselves into cobos, squirrels, owls as well as human apparitions to lure victims to their deaths. Can anyone destroy this tree and rid the village of these evil spirits? The spirits act as soothsayers as they echo their premonition of impending deaths in the families of Sunnyvale. These are the firm beliefs among the families of these illiterate, peasant sugar cane farmers. For generations the villagers have believed that the spirits live in the silk-cotton tree. Usati lives in East Hill, which is the most picturesque section of the village. His grandparents, that is, his mother's parents, live in the valley but in the West section.

His parents' house is on the brow of East Hill, later called Cotton Hill. It is a simple mud dwelling. From the age of four he has to care for his two younger siblings while his parents go out to work in the garden in the bull cart. He must ensure that they have their food, which is left in the kitchen for them. He is supervised by their neighbour, Madam Daniel. He is warned by his parents every morning that if he misbehaves in any way he is severely and brutally beaten for being "too harden" (i.e. stubborn). He also witnesses regular domestic violence coming from the neighbours' house. On several occasions he has acted as a human shield to protect Madam Daniel from further beating from Mr Daniel. She seeks revenge on Mr Daniel by developing an intimate relationship with Alex and Gloria. Gloria becomes pregnant and both Alex and Gloria have brief lives. Madam Daniel, called Marj, turns her life around. She becomes the village Christian missionary and devotes her life to the Lord and to serve the community. Domestic violence in the village is a common practice. It is due to ignorance, mental illness, illiteracy, alcoholism and male domination. The war is taking its toll on the village due to the shortage of food and medicine. Water shortage is chronic. The villagers go to the shop with their ration cards to get foodstuffs. These cards are signed by the shopkeeper to confirm that the weekly supply is given to a villager. The shopkeeper cheats the villagers by giving them less than their scheduled quotas. Few supplies of medicine reach Sunnyvale because of its size and its remoteness.

Infectious diseases such as tuberculosis, measles and hookworms cause serious illnesses and early child deaths. The situation is made worse by the villagers seeking out witch doctors, because they believe that the evil spirits are bringing illnesses to their children, taking them away and causing bad luck within their families.

Following his mother's death, the grandparents, called Nanny and Nana, bring up the four siblings, thus depriving their father of any of the children. At Nanny and Nana's house there is plenty of everything – food, clothes, work and beatings. This last item of plenty is the most painful, severe and devastating to any adult, much more for a child to bear. Therefore, living at Nanny and Nana's house comes with a very heavy price tag on their heads. This grand English-style country mansion is the envy of not only many of the villagers but more so of Aunty Jenny.

Nana sees the two oldest boys (Usati and brother) as his permanent key workers in the garden while Rani is Nanny's worker in the kitchen, doing the washing, cooking and cleaning. By bringing them up together they are a long-term investment to foster Nana's empire. Child labour begins at the age of six. There is only one roadside standpipe to supply the village with water. One of the several jobs for Usati and his brother is to go and fetch water from the standpipe with the mule cart. The village pond is a handy water resource.

The boy, U, sees the fatal consequences of illiteracy and ignorance in the village. He also witnesses greed and exploitation within the family and the extent to which family members would go to exploit other family members to achieve their goal. As a result, there is gross brutality, murder, and severe corporal punishment.

He was refused to be sent to college by his Nana and Nanny and had to turn to his poor, and seemingly wayward, lazy and drunken father to get this educational opportunity. His whole purpose has always been to gain education. He knows that only education can help him and others make a difference to enhance their quality of life for the future. Nothing, or no one, not even B, would stand in his way to prevent him from gaining an education. Corporal punishment in school and in the home is rampant and savage and there seems to be no end to it. The boy has been a victim of this on many occasions. Yet he still fights his way to receive an education. Having gained his education, he takes on the village establishment to turn the table around 180 degrees. He aims to make every adult in the village of Sunnyvale a literate person. He boldly steps out to seek a total ban on all forms of punishment and oppression against children and women. This is a tall and ambitious order. Can he rise to these challenges? What are his chances of success in a village where attitudes and beliefs are deeply embedded among the villagers?

The beliefs in "Obeah" (witchcraft) and black magic are deeply entrenched in these peasant villagers' minds.

Hence, they quickly seek out the Obeah men (witch doctors) for help in solving their problems. Even the poorest in the village will do so, thereby spending their little hard-earned money on these witch doctors. These witch doctors, including the village Obeah man, Ganti, are engaged in a lucrative trade as a result.

Nana's money is stolen on three occasions and Rani is accused of the theft. The evidence according to Aunty Jenny points clearly to Rani. What will Nana do to the fourteen-year-old Rani? What will he, Nanny, Aunty Jenny and Uncle Jhan do to find out the truth whether Rani did steal Nana's money? How many Obeah men will they seek out to prove Rani's guilt?

Usati experiences disappointment in a loving, warm relationship with his teenage girlfriend. It manages to become an enduring one in a situation of loyalty and true love for each other. Usati goes abroad to further his studies. He is returning after fifty years and plans to marry B as soon as he arrives at her side. She is very ill and is eagerly waiting for Usati's arrival. She sings for him before he flies out. Is this an omen? In ten hours he will be there. How will these ten hours pan out?

The number "18" pops up throughout the novel. What is its significance? The drama is intense and emotive thus presenting a sordid and gruesome picture. Can the forces of good overcome the evil and the curse of the village? The novel also shows the strong will and determination of the boy, U, as he battles against serious hardships to achieve his goal.

Acknowledgements

I would like to express my sincere thanks and appreciation to the staff of Matador Publishing involved in the entire production process and marketing services of the book. I am extending my special thanks and appreciation to Hannah - Customer Services Assistant - for her help, advice and support throughout. She has always been kind and patient and very professional in her communication with me. Hannah has always been ready to answer my queries. My sincere and special thanks also go to Fern - Production Controller - in relation to the copy editing and the proof reading by the editors, and the typesetting. She has been very accommodating and understanding and helped me willingly in all my last minute amendments to the typeset proofs. I thank them heartily for their patience in labouring through the manuscript. I gratefully acknowledge the efforts and the contribution of the marketing team in getting the book out to the wider public. I thank Andrea, Digital Production Controller, and her team for the e-book conversion process to make the book available on-line. I thank the cover designer for a unique and attractive front cover.

I am very thankful to Anita Mercy, Senior Copyrights Coordinator of Elsevier publishers, for granting permission to use five excerpts from the book entitled -Integrating Conventional and Chinese Medicine in Cancer Care ISBN - 13; 9780443100635 by Tai Lahans (2007). The five excerpts are CA 125 on page 196, and CEA and CA 19 – 9 on page 231. I gratefully acknowledge your permission.

I am indeed very thankful to Jack Baker, Contracts Assistant, of Harper Collins Publishers for granting me permission to quote from the Holy Bible -English Standard Version (ESV), Psalms 1 and 23, the gospel according to St Luke Chapter 23, verses 39–43 and the Lord's Prayer. I sincerely thank you and appreciate the support and permission given.

I thank the publisher Oxford Publishing Ltd for granting permission to quote from the Bhagavad Gita by W.J. Johnson Chapter 9 Verse 26.

I sincerely thank Rose Weekes for painfully and assiduously reading through the drafts of the manuscript and giving helpful suggestions and comments. Much appreciated.

I sincerely thank my friend Habib Jahoor, artist and sculpture, for allowing me to take photographs of the ink well, the bull cart wheel, the okhree and moosarr, the copper for water, and the painting of a woman pounding cocoa beans in the okhree. I thank two of my cousins, Vishmati Roopchand for allowing me to photograph her 1950's scrubbing board which is still in use. Harriram Ramdin for preparing the calabash bowls and the bolee and gifting them to me. I gratefully appreciate them. The three of them are currently living in Trinidad.

Chapter I

"Doh fight, an doh hit your sister, nah, an look after dee chiren till we come home, you hear dat?" said Papa, looking sternly at me. He brought the bull cart to the front of the house and waited for Mama.

"You go gi dee chiren dey food. Dee roti and takari [a generalised term referring to various forms of cooked vegetables] on dee table and dee milk in dee bucket wid water so it eh go spoil," Mama said to me.

Every morning Papa and Mama tell me the same thing before they go into the garden to work in the sugar cane fields, and to grow their vegetables. I have heard their warnings and commands so many times over weeks on end. I have now memorised them, can sing them and can recite them as a nursery rhyme. Every morning these recurring decibels ring through my ears before they take leave and drive away in the bull cart. I am sure that Madam Daniel must also be sick of hearing them saying the same thing every morning because she is usually outside at this time with a toothbrush in her mouth.

"You go keep an eye an dem for me, eh gyul?" Mama would say to her while the bull cart is slowly moving away. Madam Daniel will reply to Mama with her toothbrush still in her mouth.

"A'right nah gyul."

Despite their daily warnings that I must not hit my sister, I do lose my temper with her and smack her. I will get a beating in turn when Papa and Mama come home from the garden.

Regarding toothbrushes and toothpaste, the entire Daniel family uses proper ones which are bought from the shop. Papa cannot afford to buy such toothbrushes or toothpaste because of the expense. We use our own type of toothbrushes, called "datwan", and they work very well indeed. Every morning, we break off a thin branch of guava stem or a hibiscus branch. We cut the stick about six to eight inches long. Then we chew up one end of this stick and it looks like a thick painting brush. Next, we rub the brush end on blue soap and use the soap as our toothpaste. We use this method every day. The blue and brown soap is used for washing clothes on the scrubbing board and for bathing. There is another type of datwan which Papa cuts from the bushes and brings home. It is called "soap vine". This vine is thick like my middle finger. Again, we cut off six to eight-inch lengths of this vine, and chew up one end to form the brush. This vine produces its own natural soapy toothpaste. Hence its name, soap vine. The saponin contained in the vine liquid is considered to be an antibacterial agent. After brushing our teeth with these various types of toothbrushes, we split the sticks in longitudinal halves, and use one of the halves as our tongue scraper. We then throw away our toothbrush as disposable items. Every month or two Madam Daniel will inspect our teeth and we look into her mirror to compare our teeth. She would comment, "Aal you teet lookin' nice foh so. Look, dey white like mine. Dem datwan an dem dah do a good jab foh you teet."

I told Madam Daniel, "Our datwan is cheap and cheerful and there is an abundance of it all around the house. Also, chewing up the ends of the datwan with our teeth, strengthens our teeth and gums. There is one more very important aspect to our very expensive datwan, Madam Daniel! It certainly prevents dental decay, and so, we can really go down and bite into our roti with ease."

The roti is always sada (plain naan) because it is quick and easy to make. It can go down well with any type of takari (cooked vegetable). Mama has a wide range of vegetables from which to choose. They are pumpkin, tomatoes chokha or fried, aubergine chokha, or curried with aloo, bodi, ochro, karailee and curried green mango. Some of them are grown in our garden and around the house, and others come from Nanny and Nana (Mama's parents). Today Mama has cooked roti and curry aloo and coconut chutney for us. Such a wide variety of vegetables to accompany the sada roti overshadows the monotony of this daily roti. In these very difficult times during the war, it is a great benefit for us to use what we have grown. It also means that we do not have to buy such foodstuffs as other people will have to do. Papa and Mama adhere to the government slogan "Eat Local, Buy Local". This is to encourage the people to help themselves by planting fruits and vegetables of their own, whether they are living in urban or rural areas. We do not have enough vegetables to sell in the market just yet. Papa says, "When we plant a lot more fruits and vegetables we will be able to sell some of them in the market for the town people to buy. Nana plants plenty of vegetables such as, tomatoes, aubergines, cucumbers, pigeon peas, eddoes, cassava, yams, corn and sweet potatoes. He hires several workers to work for him. Every week Nana sells one truckload of vegetables to the retail market in San Fernando.

Papa's bull is a young, strong, healthy-looking four-year-old black-and-white bull. The black is on the upper part while the white colour is throughout its under section. He looks a handsome creature from the Wild West although he is a born-and-bred Sunnyvale product. His horns have grown outwards and their pointed ends are now beginning to curve inwards. They are his weapons of defence and attack. Papa says that we must not go near the bull. He may turn round and butt us although he sees us every day. Papa said that last week, Mr Cooly's bull charged at him and butted him in his belly and he had to be rushed into hospital as an emergency.

Papa ties the bull at the back of the house to the calabash tree. There are several calabash fruits on the tree. All our bowls are calabashes cut in halves. Papa uses the large ones for water containers to take into the garden. He calls it his "bolee". This is a large globed-shaped calabash. A small hole about one-half to one inch in diameter is made in the calabash then gutted out and washed thoroughly. The flesh inside the calabash is soft and easy to dig out. When it becomes functional the bolee can contain two to three gallons of water. This is adequate for a day's supply of water for both of them. Papa puts a handle through the hole. The handle is made with two pieces of wood each about two inches long and tied together at their middle with a piece of wire about three to four inches long. When held up this figure looks H-shaped. One arm of the H-shaped wood is put into the calabash while the other end hangs out as the handle to carry the bolee of water. When Papa takes a full bolee of water in the garden he leaves the bolee under his marai [ajoupa]. The water remains cool in the bolee throughout the day despite the heat of the sun. Papa says, "Is me bless fridge." Musicians use the smaller calabashes for musical "shack-shacks". Although the bull and I are the same age I am certainly no match for this five-foot giant-looking beast. Papa said, "He can pull a ton of cane with ease in dee crop time. Every load ah cane I carry to dee factory does weigh over eighteen hundred weight." One hundred weight (CWT) is equal 112 pounds in weight. Twenty hundred weight (CWT) is equal to one ton in weight. This is how the cart loads of sugar cane are weighed at the factory.

Our village is made up of two hills on either side with a wide lowland valley between them. One hill is in the East, called East Hill, and later called Cotton Hill. The other in the West is West Hill. Through the middle of the village in the valley runs one section of the Guaracara River. It cuts the village into East and West. A strong, well-reinforced concrete bridge connects both sides of the village. We live on the brow of East Hill. From here we can survey the scene below. The breeze up here is strong, cool and unrelenting. This is particularly appreciable during the heat of the midday sun. Nanny and Nana live in the West part of the valley, about 500 yards away from the river. This river meanders through Nana's sugar cane fields thus watering the fields with a constant supply of water. Frequent floods in the village sweep through and drown the sugar cane field. When these floods subside, they leave behind them the much desired rich and fertile deposits of silt on the land. As a result, this section of Nana's sugar cane fields produces prolific yields of sugar cane annually. The river runs for several miles from its source in the mountains of the Central Range, and passes under the bridge. The Guaracara continues on its way to the Gulf of Paria where its delta is mangrove inhabited. The valley also has a special tree along the river in the middle of Nana's cane field. This is the reputed and feared "silk-cotton" tree. The evil spirits live in this tree. It stands on the riverbank, and is surrounded by a large bamboo patch. Welcome to the home of the evil spirits.

The silk-cotton tree is well over one hundred feet tall and approximately six to seven feet in circumference. It provides a welcome shade for its resident bathers. The evil spirits and the cobos live on this tree. Here cobos are vultures. This is a local dialect to refer to the vultures. The black colour is associated with evil. This is the belief of the villagers in Sunnyvale. The silk-cotton tree has a ten feet high arched hollow entrance at its root. This is where these evil spirits enter and leave the tree. Very often we hear noises and laughter coming out of the tree. We also hear the splashing of water and sounds of squealing coming out from the river near to the tree. When these noises are heard there is no one bathing in the river, nor anyone around the area at that time. The only person who is likely to be there is Nana or his workmen, since this tree is in the middle of Nana's cane field. No one cuts bamboos from that patch because they fear the spirits.

No one in the village is brave enough to go and cut down this tree. The villagers claim that if anyone were to cut bamboo or cut down this tree that person or his entire family will become ill and die. If anyone smacks at the tree or its bamboo they are asking for trouble. They refer to this tree as "real trouble". The weapon will rebound and give that person a very serious injury. Therefore, they do heed this warning which says, "Never trouble trouble." Everyone stays clear of the silk-cotton tree and its bamboo. Who planted this tree? How did this scourge of the village happen to grow up here? Above all, why did it have to grow in the middle of Nana's sugar cane field? These questions are puzzling me. No one seems to know the answers. Every month at around full moon the combination of squealing, squeaking, and splashing in the water becomes louder and more fearsome. Dozens of cobos would perch on the tree and flap their wings and squeak. The owls would join in the squeaking, and the squirrels would be running frantically from branch to branch. The tone is angry and fearsome if anyone should hear it for the first time. The villagers have grown used to these noises particularly around the full-moon period of each month.

When an infant is about to die from infectious diseases, such as *Mycobacterium tuberculosis*, (TB), or poliomyelitis, or measles, or hookworm, these cobos squeal and squeak incessantly for several days while they are on the tree. They will fly around the particular home of the infant or child in circular motion, like mini helicopters in search of a criminal from above. Further loud squeals are also heard coming from the tree even when the cobos have flown away. These squeals foretell when death is imminent, because such events have been observed on several occasions by villagers. The villagers argue that if it were only on one occasion such sounds followed a death in the village, this would be seen as a mere coincidence.

They claim that the jealous and spiteful people go to the Obeah men and work evil spells on their children causing them to become ill. I regularly hear them speaking in this manner: "Somebody wok Obeah an mee child." This belief is very strong indeed. It has become so widespread that it is generally accepted as the primary cause of their children's illness and death, and bad luck for their whole family. They say, "Dis grah [evil spell] could last for twenty years once the spell comes on you. And if you cross water you could break it." Therefore, the afflicted families' first line of help is to visit the Obeah man to cast out the evil spirits. It is difficult to readily obtain medical treatment in this remote rural village of Sunnyvale. In addition, the village suffers from overcrowding, poor sanitation and serious water shortage. We are told that there is a shortage of anti-TB drugs because of the war. Ships are in danger of being torpedoed if seen by the enemy in Caribbean waters. Sunnyvale has a high infant mortality rate. Therefore, families are large to compensate for any possible infant deaths they may experience. Another reason for the large families is that the girls are married at a very tender age of thirteen to seventeen. This gives them many years of childbearing age. For example, B had three children by the age of nineteen. Mama was having her fifth child by the age of twenty-three.

What the villagers fail to realise is that they are the ones causing more harm to their children. They are the ones responsible for and contributing towards the high infant and child mortality rates in the village. When they delay effective medical treatment by firstly seeking out the witch doctors, the bacterial and viral infections are allowed more time to multiply and proliferate within the individual. This worsens the child's condition as a result. At present, TB is the biggest killer in our village.

The majority of houses in the village are in the Valley. This section of the village has a huge pond, the White

Rose sports ground, and the Sunnyvale CM school. The school conducts church services and church activities. It is the only primary school for all of the surrounding villages. There is one roadside standpipe to supply the whole village with water. Water shortage is a continual chronic problem in the village. There is one grocery shop and it also serves as a rum shop. One villager uses his house as the village post office. Jasodra is the main member of the family who manages the postal services. She is B's personal and confidential friend. The Valley houses the one village witch doctor, named Professor Ganti. Villagers frequently visit him either for advice, or to cure an ailment, or to cast an evil spell on another person, or to drive out evil spirits from afflicted persons. The village standpipe serves as a meeting point for its residents. When water comes in the standpipe there are long queues of people with buckets, or kerosene tins, box carts or bull carts waiting their turn to fill up.

Papa goes with our bull cart to fetch one barrel of water at a time. Other boys go with their box carts carrying two to four ten-gallon kerosene tins of water per trip. Ladies and their daughters carry their buckets and tins of water on their heads. When there is no water in the standpipe, they go to the pond to fetch their water. At one time the pond provided water for the sugar cane factory, which is now relocated to the Reform district. It remains the community's backup water resource.

One end of the playground borders the pond. This end is lined with guava trees all along the edge. There are prolific yields of guavas every year and birds are always feeding on the ripe guavas. The toads spawn at the edge of the pond under the guava trees. Thousands of tiny tadpoles feed on the ripened guavas which fall into the water. Mama picks buckets of ripe guavas to make guava jam at home. Many villagers also do the same.

West Hill contains masses of bamboos, teak, mahogany, cedar, and carat palm trees. It prides itself as the only section of the village with a large cocoa and coffee estate. The locals call it the jaunty cocoa estate. This section provides building materials for the villagers. Our house roof is covered with carat palm leaves cut from here. The timber in Uncle Jhan's house was cut from West Hill forest. This quaint remote village of Sunnyvale is primarily a peasant sugar cane farming community. The two hills are like twin peaks with the valley keeping them apart. Illiteracy rate is high as most women like Mama and Madam Daniel never went to school.

Our house is a mud-walled, carat-roofed (palm leaves from West Hill), two-bedroomed detached bungalow. The veranda has one bench and a hammock. There is one bed, which is made as a low table. There is a home-made mattress filled with sugar cane arrow flowers. The pillows and cushions are cotton-filled. The mud walls and floor and the roof keep the house cool throughout the day and night. Our house stands out because it is built at the brow of the hill. The walls are made with bamboo wattle and daubed with mud mixed in cow's dung. When dry the walls look like recently plastered brick walls painted in an apple-white colour. The walls and floor tend to get defaced easily. Nevertheless, we are pleased to have a cool, refreshing and breezy house twenty-four/seven.

The Daniels live opposite us on the other side of the road. The Ding family lives halfway down on the same side as the Daniels. They are our closest neighbours. Madam Daniel comes over to us every day after Mama and Papa come from the garden. Papa would give her some ochra, tomatoes, or pumpkin to take home. At the front of the Daniels' house there is a large bushy croton hedge while there is a thick hibiscus hedge at the front of our house. On the left side of our house looking from the front is a croton hedge forming a thick wall. There is a large mango tree, an avocado tree, and a banana patch. Pink, white and red periwinkle flowers are all around our house. Ripe mangoes rain down on the house, then roll down to the ground and continue to roll down the hill. We have fun trying to catch the mangoes as they fall off the roof. Papa always beats us. Papa ties the bull at the back of the house onto the calabash tree, and has built a shelter for him next to the calabash tree. The best and prettiest feature of all is that the East Hill has an abundance of cotton trees. East Hill provides cotton for the entire village.

The cotton is brilliant white, and some of the fibres fly out in the breeze like swarms of bees in search of nectar. There are cotton trees all around our house. They line both sides of the road going down all the way to the bottom of the hill. The cotton trees extend for hundreds of yards behind the houses of East Hill. When you look out you see a sea of soft white fluffy cotton fibres covering the trees. The cotton forms a white canopy and it looks like freshly fallen soft snow on evergreen coniferous trees in English country gardens. Seen from a distance, these soft lily-white blobs of wool cover the trees like white sheets of women's washing which are spread out on the cricket field. However, our cotton field is a mere microcosm of the extensive cotton fields of the southern states of America, such as Alabama, Georgia and Mississippi.

All the residents of this quiet rural village of Sunnyvale benefit from the cotton harvest. They make pillows and cushions and mattresses with the cotton. However, Rani and I play games with the fibres by seeing whose fibres will fly away the furthest. Sometimes the young Daniels join in the game. This scenery makes our section of the village the most idyllic place in which to live. The villagers usually say that they are going to the hill to pick cotton, and so East Hill has been gradually renamed "Cotton Hill". From now on, I will use this adopted name whenever I refer to East Hill.

Mr Daniel blasts his saxophone so loudly that his music can be heard on West Hill on some days. He plays both his saxophone and trumpet every day for short spells before going to work. On weekends he plays this saxophone for several hours, simply relaxing and entertaining himself and the villagers. No one complains about the loudness of the music. It is the village way of life. He comes over to us to talk about the war with Papa and Mama.

One day, I told Mr Daniel that we saw two big balloons flying in the sky. Papa called them Zeppelins. He said, "Run, run and hide under dee bed before dey get you."

"What are Zeppelins?" I asked Mr Daniel.

He said, "They are aeroplanes without wings, and they don't make noise like aeroplanes. They are the enemy planes. They could destroy us."

"But we look out for them every morning, and they never do us anything," I said to him. "They are very nice and shiny in the sky. They move so gracefully over our house. I wish I could ride in a Zeppelin."

Mr Daniel said, "Maybe when the war is over and they have them for people to go in them."

He and Papa talk about how the war is going, and how food is getting scarcer in the shop.

He said, "The Americans have a base in Waller Field and the enemy is looking for it." He told Papa, "The Americans bombed the Japanese and that is what caused the war to end. Now we will be able to get more food, but this will still take a long time for that to happen. That bomb killed thousands and thousands of people," said Mr Daniel. "It was a terrible destruction. I read it in the papers," he said. My poor parents cannot read nor write a word of English.

Mr Daniel reads the paper every day, but he shouts loud and quarrels if any of the children makes noise or disturbs him. He gets so vexed that he starts beating all the children as well as Madam Daniel for not controlling them properly. He uses his belt or a stick. We regularly hear them crying and screaming. Madam Daniel and the children are all beaten at the same time. No one is spared when Mr Daniel starts to beat them. Madam

Daniel would bawl and run over to us and hold the baby and me tightly and stay close to us to prevent Mr Daniel from beating her. She often hugs and lifts me up first and shows me to him.

"Doh hit dis child nah," she would say to him. Mr Daniel does not hit her any more because he is afraid that he may accidently strike me instead of Madam Daniel. She would stay by us until Mr Daniel cools down or goes out. She would sit in the hammock with the three of us and swing and sing for us. She would give us our food and drink and eat with us. Before she goes back she would cuddle all of us and say, "Ah goin' now, you Mama and Papa go come soon."

Mama cleans the walls, floor and "choolha" (the curved mud fireside on the kitchen floor), with a cloth soaked in a mixture of mud and cow's dung in a soft runny consistency. She daubs it smoothly like a professional plasterer. The choolha can accommodate one or two pots at the same time. It is Mama's "ayk ailah" (single burner pot) and her "doowailah" (twin burner) cooker respectively. She takes great pride in maintaining it in superb condition. She "leepays" (plasters) the kitchen walls, fireside and floor every week, because the smoke from the fireside blackens the kitchen. When she is going to leepay the whole house, she would shout to us, "Ah goin' to leepay dee house. All you chiren go outside an play. Doh come in here till ah tell you to come. Ah doh want you to mess up dee house while I leepayin' it, caz you go gimme extra wok to do."

The choolhas are built of a mixture of mud and cow dung. The single choolha is about twelve inches high, twelve inches wide with the walls about four to six inches thick. At the top there are three projections, two at the front and one in the middle of this curved back structure. They are like three horns on which the pots and pans are placed. Mama uses a half inch (15mm) diameter iron pipe, twelve to fifteen inches long, to blow into the fireside when the wood is smouldering and smoking out profusely. By blowing into the smoking wood with this pipe, she gets wood ignited and the fire gets blazing. This pipe is called a "phooknee". She is often seen wiping the tears from her eyes due to the smoke from the choolha. She resorts to her phooknee frequently because the firewood is sometimes wet. It is an essential tool for her when she is cooking under these conditions.

We are usually very happy when Mama is going to leepay the whole house, because we can run over by Madam Daniel to play with Tom and Henrik and Gloria. She is bigger than us. She makes up all the games for us to play. Madam Daniel calls us inside and gives us her home-made cassava "pone" (a sweet sticky stuggy cake made with grated cassava), biscuits and orange juice. The biscuits are hard to bite so we soak them in the orange juice. Then she says, "You Mama is a very good cook too. Ah like she dahl-puri and chana and aloo for so with mango takari."

Their house is big and high. We climb up ten steps to get inside. They have nice chairs and a table, and a settee. The cushions are soft-green and very comfortable. The settee is covered with a large red flower-patterned sheet.

"All you chiren doh make no mess an dee settee, oh dee floor, you hear me?" shouted Madam Daniel from her kitchen.

"When you Mama and Papa get some more money from the cane crap [crop], you Papa go buy a settee like mine," said Madam Daniel.

"Where will we put it, because our house is cramped up already," I said to her.

"Well, we don' know, you Papa might have a bigger house too," she said. Although I did not see the prospect of such an event taking place in years to come, I did not say anything to Madam Daniel. We finished our snacks and ran off outside to play cricket in the yard. Across the road and at the back of our house, I could see Mama with the bucket of mud-and-cow's dung paste and her dirty hands. She was clearing up, having finished her leepaying. I could see Mama's face streaming down with sweat, and her clothes wet and muddy. Leepaying is a very tedious and messy job, but its effects are startling and dramatic. Our house always looks like a newly painted brick house when Mama finishes her leepaying.

Mama came to talk to Madam Daniel and to allow for the leepaying to dry out. "Gyul, ah just done make some pone, it still hot yes! Go an take a piece nah from dee kitchen," Madam Daniel told her. Mama helped herself to the hot cassava pone, fried ochra and bake. She made a cup of tea and sat at the table with Madam Daniel. Mama knows the kitchen very well, and usually helps herself as though it is her kitchen. Mama likes to cook in Madam

Daniel's kitchen because she can stand and cook when using the stove. There is no smoke so there is no need for her phooknee. Madam Daniel's kitchen is modern by the day's standards. She has wall and base units and a fridge. She regularly calls Mama over to cook in her (Madam Daniel's) stove. They would make a big cook-up together and then share the food between them. When Madam Daniel cooks in Mama's choolha Madam Daniel is continually wiping her eyes because the smoke gets into her eyes. Madam Daniel thinks that it is real fun to blow into the phooknee to get the fire going.

At the table Mama complemented her host. "Marj, gyul, dis pone come out really nice yea!" Mama said to Madam Daniel.

"Seeta, gyul, dis is fresh cassava ah root out from dee back ah dee house. Dis is the same set a cassava plant you dee gimme to go and plant," she replied.

"Gyul, you have a good han' for cassava yea," Mama said to her and went on. "Ah just finish leepaying dee whole house an ah tired for so. Ee go take ah hour or two to dry, den dem chiren go come home," Mama said to her.

"Gyul, you lay dong an dee settee an take a good rest. You wok so damn hard aready. Dem man an dem doh know how hard we does wok. An wen dey come home all dey want is good cook food. You, youself does see how Danny da beat me up wen dee food eh ready foh ye to eat wen ye come home."

"Dat is true gyul, Marj, ah da feel so sarry foh you eh gyul?" said Mama.

"You take a rest an ah goin' in dee kitchen to wash up dee wares," said Madam Daniel. The children were outside but quiet.

"Ah kyan hear dem chiren an dem, gyul," Mama said. Marj called out from inside her kitchen.

"We lost the ball in the bush over here. Henrik hit a big six and we can't find the ball now," I shouted back to Madam Daniel as she was looking through her kitchen window.

"All you look good an you go find it," she said. It took us at least half an hour searching for the ball until Henrik found it in the thick bush hooked up among some branches. As we restarted our game the ladies came downstairs. I called out to them. "Would you like to have a game with us? You have to field first before you get to bat, OK? Mama, you go behind the wicket, and Madam Daniel, you go in second slip."

"Wey dat secon' slip dey, near to your Mama?" she asked. I directed her to second slip position. The first ball came directly to Madam Daniel and she dropped the catch. "Oh gad, ah ley go dee dam baal, gyul," she bawled out, laughing and telling Mama. The game duly ended and Mama took us home.

"Marj, come nah gyul, come an see mee wok for dee day," Mama said to her. Everyone of us trotted across the road to our house. "Gyul, you is a real good painter! Dee house so clean an so nice everywhere, gyul. You know how to leepay good gyul, Seeta," remarked Madam Daniel.

Mama replied, "Gyul, ah dee larn to mix dee gobarr [cow dung] and mud from me moye. Ah know how much gobarr to mix wid dee mud good now. Dee mud from dee pond is blue, gyul. Dat is why it dah come out so nice. An ah doing dis leepaying since I was a child, gyul. Years an years ah practice dah make me get puffick [perfect], gyul."

"You dam right, gyul, we wok an wok aal we life, gyul, in we modder [mother's] house an now we wok in we own house. Seeta, gyu, I eh go stay caz ah have to go an cook dinner now, before Danny come from wok. You know how he does get on, an he always beatin' we up," said Madam Daniel.

"Mr Daniel have a good jab in dee oil refinery. He does wok for plenty ah money. He get dat jab caz he could read an write good," said Mama. Mr Daniel gets the previous day's paper from the waste-paper basket at work every day. He would sit in the veranda with his feet up while reading his newspaper. The hot topic is the progress of the war. What I do know about this war is that we have to use our ration card to get our foodstuffs from the shop. The shopkeeper sometimes robs us by weighing less than our required amount. He puts down the foodstuffs, all be it flour or rice, on the scale and quickly removes food before the scale can balance correctly. Mr Daniel complains bitterly about this and tells all the villagers about the thieving shopkeeper. Whenever he goes to the shop he has a big row with the shopkeeper. The shopkeeper knows that Mr Daniel is right about his thieving, and says nothing, to avoid aggravating the situation. The shopkeeper knows that Mr Daniel is an educated man, knows his rights, and can involve the police to investigate the shopkeeper. Most villagers will support Mr Daniel if the police step in.

We see the two Zeppelins flying over our house every morning. Since they don't make any noise we have to keep looking up in the sky regularly to see when they fly past. These are two very large shining oval-shaped balloons flying smoothly through the breeze. When Mr Daniel has a free time he would come over to talk to Papa and give him the latest news about the war. The scarcity of food and medicine is the biggest worry for the villagers in Sunnyvale. Mr Daniel earns a hefty salary from the oil industry. He can afford to pay extra for foodstuffs. "Dat is why he could buy nice table an settee for dey house. You Papa can't read an write like Danny," Mama said. "Me an Marj didn't go to school, dat why we can't read and write too," Mama said with sadness in her heart and tone of voice. "You Nanny and Nana didn't send me to school, caz ah had to help Nanny in dee house," she said. There was a sense of regret, anger and jealousy coming from Mama because Aunty Jenny can read and write very well. She tends to show off and look down on Mama. Aunty Jenny rivals Mama for Nanny's affection and attention. She seems oblivious to the fact that Mama is Nanny's own daughter, and that Aunty Jenny is her daughter-in-law. Nanny will always give Mama rice, flour, potatoes, garlic and onions and salt and sugar. Nana buys plenty of the foodstuffs through his good friend Mr Atta Roberto, a Portuguese overseer of a very large cocoa estate.

Nana says, "Dis is dee time wen it eh not who you is, but it is who you know. Atta know plenty ah dee high people an dem."

Mama has enough foodstuffs to make do at home and to take to work in the garden. One morning, Papa got up early and bathed. He kept on singing "bhajans" (devotional songs) all morning instead of getting the bull cart ready. He sang the Hanuman Chalisa while he faced the rising sun and slowly poured a "lota" of water with a marigold flower and a tulsie leaf in the water. A lota is a rounded brass jug with a lip broadening out from the neck of this water jug. It is also used in hindu prayers and functions. He recited one verse from the *Bhagavad Gita* as he continued to offer the water. It went like this: "I accept a leaf, a flower, a fruit, or water from the disciplined person who, with devotion, offers me that loving offering." (Bhagavad Gita, Chapter 9, Verse 26, by W J Johnson ,1994).

He and Mama were not going to work in the garden today. Mama was up early as usual, and was busy cooking. She got us all bathed and put on clean clothes. A little later on Nanny was here. This was a pleasant surprise to see Nanny so early at our house. Then Madam Daniel also arrived and picked us up one by one. She said, "Marning Seeta, dee chiren lookin' clean and nice, gyul."

Papa was preparing the "Beidi". It was almost finished. Madam Daniel went up to him and ruffled up his head of hair and said, "Saga boy, you doin' a masterpiece ah art dey, man. It looking good, boy. Dee pundit man go be glad to see it." The Beidi is decorated with marigold, hibiscus, red, yellow and white ixoras, white lilies, and tulsie leaves. He also put some paan and mango leaves and a lota of water. Varied colour rice and flour were used to draw diagonal, horizontal and vertical lines on the Beidi. A Beidi is a small rectangular earthen platform beautifully decorated with flowers and different colours of rice. The pundit uses it to carry out his hindu prayer during the ceremony or a religious function. Nanny was in the kitchen helping Mama with the cooking. Papa got up to look at his Beidi. The pundit arrived at the same time. "It looking good," he commented, pointing to the Beidi. "Are we all ready?" he asked.

The puja was about to start. Papa sat opposite the pundit. A puja or pooja is a hindu religious prayer. Mama, Nanny and Madam Daniel sat alongside Papa and we sat at the back. The pundit started the prayer with the chanting of "Om" several times followed by the Gayatri Mantra. Papa, Nanny and Mama joined in the singing as they know it well. Madam Daniel knows the tune very well but she does not know all the words. She sings some and hums some of the mantra together with Nanny and Mama. The pundit read passages from the holy scripture in Hindi and then explained it in English. During the procedure Papa offered food and drink to the various deities and to the fire. Other bhajans were sung and prayers said. The conch shell blared out loud, clear and sharp as the pundit summoned the presence of the deities. The "aarti" was the last procedure for the puja. The aarti is an offering made with a brass plate and a lighted deeya , that is similar to a tealight. A deeya is a small cup made of earth and baked or dried out. It is filled with oil and a cotton wick is used to light it. All of us sat down to eat. Nanny and Madam Daniel took home food with them. Next day it was work as usual.

Papa brought the bull cart to the front of the house and came up to me to carry out his daily sermon. As he held on to the hammock I raised my hand to him as he usually does to me every morning. He looked at me as I began, "Don't fight, don't hit your sister, and look after the children till we come back from dee garden, you hear me? You go give dee chiren dey food. The roti and takari on dee table and dee milk in dee bucket with water so it eh go spoil." Both Mama and Papa looked at me and laughed at my speech. Papa said, "You does larn fast." They climbed on to the cart and drove off slowly.

Madam Daniel was outside with a toothbrush in her mouth. "You go keep an eye an dem chiren for me, eh gyul, till we come back nah," Mama said to Madam Daniel.

"Ah right, gyul," she replied. Papa and Mama tend to raise their voices at the end of a statement as if they were asking questions. My caretaker role begins as Mama and Papa drive away to the garden.

Rani and I would come out to look and see when the two Zeppelins fly over the house. They do not make any noise so we have to look up frequently. I love to look up and admire these two quiet machines every morning. I wave to them as they fly over our house, but they do not wave back to me. At this time Rani and I would be competing with each other to see whose cotton fibre will fly the highest and furthest away. We try to see if our cotton fibres will reach the Zeppelins. Sometimes she will win and sometimes I will win. This depends on proper timing of the gusts of wind as they blow through the fields. I can hear the leaves rustling and see the branches swaying from side to side. I can also feel the breeze blowing through my hair. I tell Rani that when she feels the wind blowing through her hair it's the best time to let her cotton fibres go up into the sky. Sometimes we will send up handfuls of cotton fibres all at once when a strong breeze blows. It is a spectacular sight to see so many snow-white cotton fibres flying up into the sky, rushing along with the breeze, then swirling around like chunks of snowflakes before raining down to the ground. The mango tree is laden with ripe ones. When the strong wind blows the mangoes fall on the house and roll down to the ground. We try to catch them as they roll off the roof. I am better than Rani, but Papa is better than all of us. He catches the most number of mangoes.

Suddenly, a strong gust of wind blew several mangoes in one spell. They came tumbling down from the carat roof and on the ground. Rani got very excited, but did not catch any. She ran to pick them up from the ground, but they rolled down quickly on to the road, picking up speed as these mangoes went down the hill. Rani chased after them on the road. I got frightened and shouted at her, "Rani, Rani, come back here." I ran, grabbed her and pulled her into the yard. "I told you not to go in the road. Don't go there ever again," I rebuked her. I smacked her hard, and smacked her again. She began crying, and bawling loud as though all her guts were coming out.

Madam Daniel quickly ran across and Rani held on to her tightly still crying. In her sobs she said to Madam Daniel, "He hit me, he hit me." Madam Daniel cuddled her, and sat in the hammock with both of us. She swung and sang until Rani stopped crying. She asked what happened. I said, "Rani ran into the road to pick up the rolling mangoes. I told her not to go in the road."

"She smaal, an she eh know dat. It eh good to raise you han for nobady," Madam Daniel said. "Say sarry to she, an gi she a nice hug up. All you eat a'ready?" she asked. We both said "No." Madam Daniel went into the kitchen and took out three plates of roti and curry bygan (aubergine) and aloo. She gave the baby his milk. I told her that we like to look out for the Zeppelins as they fly over our house every morning. Madam Daniel said, "Wen you see dee Zappalin tomarrow marnin, caal me an ah go look an aal, a'right? Den aal ah we go look at dee Zappalin." She stayed with us, hugged up both of us and said, "Ah goin' now, you Mama and Papa go come just now." About ten minutes later, the bull cart pulled up in front of the house.

Mama came off the cart and Rani ran to her saying, "He hit me, he hit me today, Mama. Madam Daniel was here, and I told her."

Mama picked her up and came and hugged me up too. "You bad for so, you too bad. Wey you hit she for? You dee say dis morning, 'Don't hit you sister,' and you gan an do dee same ting. Ah doh know wat kind a buaye you goin' to come out, eh? Wen you fadder come he go gi plenty ah licks. You dissove [deserve] ah good cut ass," said Mama. When Papa came in, he would usually take out his leather belt, hold me with one hand and give me a couple of belts on my backside or on my legs. Then he tells me, "Doh hit she again, you hear dat?" He would hang up his belt and tell me to go and play in the yard. Every week I get this same treatment from Papa for hitting Rani. On this occasion, I expect the same dose of medicine from Papa when he comes in. I quickly put on two pairs of trousers so that the imminent belting would not make my bottom too sore.

Papa came in through the kitchen having undone the bull's yoke and tethered it to the calabash tree near the pen. Rani cried out to him, "Papa, Papa he hit me hard, yes Papa, he hit me this morning. Madam Daniel came to see us and she gave us the food." Papa looked at me seriously. I saw his eyes showing anger, and his face stern. He undid his belt, held on to me with one hand and belted me severely on my bottom. He hit me also on my hands, arms, and legs. I could not run away because he was holding me with one hand. Then he said, "Everyday ah tell you not hit you sister, everyday ah tell you dee same ting and you still gan an hit dee child, an you nah listen to me. You too dam harden [stubborn]. An you too damn bad. Come here, ah go larn you a good lesson today." I bawled and bawled from the beating Papa dished out to me. My arms and legs were paining me so much that I could hardly move them. I did not expect to receive so much of a walloping from Papa. The pain was excruciating on my bottom despite wearing two pairs of trousers. It was the quantity of the blows which fell on my bottom that caused so much pain. It was when I saw the rope being pulled out, that I started screaming louder and louder until I was exhausted.

Papa took the rope, tied both my hands, and both my legs. He tied me to the foot of the bed and left me there.

"No food for you today, you too damn bad." I cried and cried and bawled as though he was killing me. I could not move. Rani started crying too, feeling very frightened and sorry for me. She sat next to me, probably feeling guilty about reporting me for hitting her. She showed her love, loyalty and sympathy for me by sitting close to me and holding me. It was her way to comfort me and to demonstrate her support for me. Mama came with a cup of coconut water and a piece of cassava pone. She fed me, wiped my face and was going to untie me when Papa appeared. "Leave him there, don't loosen him, he too bad," he said. Mama obeyed him to avoid a quarrel. Rani went in the kitchen, got her coconut water and pone, and sat next to me. "Madam Daniel dee make the pone yesterday," Mama said.

"Yes, I know, because she gave us biscuit, pone and orange juice when we went there to play while you were leepaying the house," I told her.

My arms and legs were paining me and I continued crying and eating the cassava pone. The pain was worsening and I called out to Mama. Mama did not come, but Nanny appeared. She screamed out, "Barp re Barp!!" (literally meaning "Father oh Father" – equivalent to "Oh my God!"). "Who tie up dee childlike dis?" Mama ran in and said, "He hit Rani so he fadder beat 'im and tie ye up." Nanny quickly untied me, and shouted and quarrelled with Papa. "Wey you tie up dee child so? You eh go tie up a animal like dis. Dee child only four an a half and you go beat ye and tie ye up like dis? You mean to say, you eh have no shame to tie up dee child so?" Papa remained quiet and slowly walked away.

"Come, bayta [son or boy], ley me see you han' an foot. Bring dee coconut oil foh me nah gyal," Nanny told Mama. She looked at my hands and feet, pulled me close to her and said, "Ah go rub down you han an foot for you." Nanny said to Mama, "Ah go take dee child wid me. Put some clothes for 'im in a bag. An ah bring onion, garlic, and rice and flour on dee box. Wen you come you go get bygan [aubergine] and tomatoes. Dee man an dem dee pick dis marning. Dee buaye [brother] larning to wok now. Ye Nana dah show ye how to plant cane, an rice, an bygan and tomato. Ye dah larn dee wok fas' fas' fas'. Ye like dee buaye too bad."

Nanny was referring to our older brother. He lives with Nanny and Nana. Nanny took him away from Mama when he was six months of age and is bringing him up. Krish is the first grandchild and better still, he is their first grandson. Nana and Nanny are lucky, and are very proud to have him with them. He calls Nanny "Mama" and "Moye", and he calls Mama "Tanty". He does not accept

Mama as his mother. He and I can now play when I come down there with Nanny. Nanny brings him up to Cotton Hill by us only occasionally. Brother was surprised to see me. Nanny said that I must call him "Brother" and not by his name. None of us is allowed to call him by his name. We played marbles, cricket, and treasure hunt with our cousins. They are Uncle Jhan and Aunty Jenny's children. Uncle Jhan is Mama's brother. They live behind Nanny and Nana's house. Nana built their house and then built his in front of theirs. This house is close to the main road. This is the only road which passes through the village. It goes to Mayo in one direction, and to Tabaquite and Rio Claro in the other direction. Uncle Jhan and Aunty Jenny already have eight children and another one is on the way. They ended up having ten children apart from the two who died from tuberculosis in their infancy.

The best loved of all fourteen grandchildren, oh yes, undoubtedly, is Brother. He is their favourite. He gets away with everything. He has neither been slapped nor pinched by Nanny or Nana, never mind beaten. This is extremely rare to know that in this age, he has not been smacked. All parents and teachers punish children daily for almost anything they do that's wrong or appears to be wrong in their eyes. I am jealous of Brother for this height of favouritism shown by all the adults in the family. Whatever he asks for, Nana gets it for him. Nanny told him that Papa beat me and tied me up to the bed and that's why she brought me here. She did not say for how long I will be staying with them. It is fun playing with my brother and all my cousins as we have so many of us together. The yard is about twenty feet wide and more than one hundred feet long. We run races every day. Sometimes I win but most times Brother wins. I am happy when he does not run because I am the fastest among the rest of us. My stay with Brother did not last long.

Mama came to take me back home. She said, "Rani missing you and you must come home now." As usual Nanny would load up Mama with plenty of tomatoes, bygan, cucumbers, peas, and rice. Nana has two big boxes of rice. "Take some more 'dhaan' [rice grains] wid you. Dey go plant more in the rice season." Aunty Jenny only says hello to Mama and goes back into her house. She is always very nicely dressed, with high-heeled shoes and permed hair, and lipstick. She does not go in the garden to do any work, nor does she wear any "orani" to cover her head. An orani is a long head scarf. It is usually worn with a sari. Mama's dress is so different, wearing a loose bodice and a long flared dress. Sometimes Aunty Jenny wears trousers and Nana gets very vexed and goes and quarrels with her and makes her take them off. "Ah ole big ass ooman like you playing man?" he asks her.

She has to go and change into dresses or skirts. She can read and write very well and makes that point clear to Mama, who never went to school. Of course, she says that she is better and more beautiful than Mama. That is why Mama does not say much to her when she comes to see Nanny. I help Mama carry some of the foodstuff. Nanny said to Mama as we were leaving, "You go send dee scissors for me nah. Nana want to cut ye hair wid it."

As we reach the bridge Mama tells me that I must not stop and idle there. She said, "Dee spirits an dem dah come here and caal dee people in dee water. So, you mustn't stay here, waak fas' fas' fas' and go, a'right? You see dat big tree over dey by the bamboo patch? Nanny say the spirits dah live in it," Mama said to me. It seems to me that there is a symbiotic relationship existing between the spirits living in the silk-cotton tree and the villagers of Sunnyvale. These spirits sometimes act as soothsayers of imminent deaths in the village. When the villagers hear their unusual bleetings and wailings they become aware that someone is about to die. The cobos would also hover round and round. The villagers have got used to these occurrences. When I got home, I was happy to see Rani, Tom, Henrik and Alex. We would run in and out of each other's house freely, crossing the road several times together.

Mr Daniel said, "Seeta, just look at them running around and crossing the road like free-range chickens. They do get on very well with each other. Cotton Hill has very few cars passing by. One is more likely to get run over by a mule or bull cart than by a motor car."

Mama said, "Danny, boy you so dam right eh, caz ah dah always tell dee buaye [me] to mine dem kyart [cart] an dem wen ye waakin in dee road."

These are two whole oval shaped calabashes. The larger one is 33cm long and 45cm around the middle. They are tough. Usually they are spherical as those seen on the tree (following page). They are used as water containers to take water into the fields. A small hole is made in the stem site and the internal flesh is dug out cleanly to make the water container. These are called "Bollees". The water remains cool inside them. The larger ones can contain 8–10 litres of water. Usati's parents as well as other villagers in Sunnyvale use them to carry water every day when they go to work in the garden. The outside turns dark brown when dried out. It is smooth and silky.

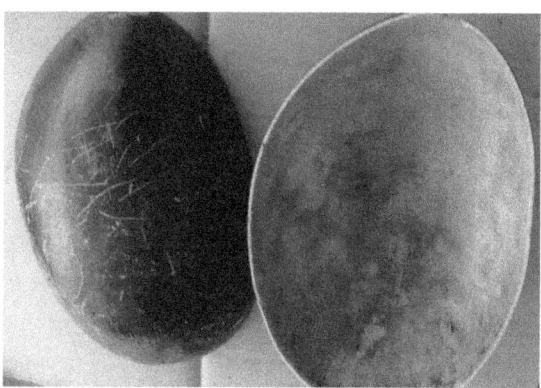

Two calabash bowls. The smaller calabash is cut in half and the internal flesh is cleaned out and used as a bowl. Usati used such a bowl every day to eat his food. It is commonly used by the other villagers in the same way. This oval-shaped bowl pictured measures 20cm by 15cm. Most calabash bowls are round in shape.

A similar tree to this calabsh tree grew at the back of Usati's house. That tree was about five metres high. His father tied the bull onto the tree. The small round calabashes were also used as musical shack-shacks in steel bands and orchestras.

The bull and mule carts were the most comon means of transport in the village of Sunnyvale because of the sugar cane farming industry. Indeed, Mr Daniel had commented that one was more likely to be run over by a cart than by a motor car. The wheel pictured is a 1940's bull cart wheel removed from the cart. The wheel was made of hard wood and the circumference was covered with iron. The iron enabled the wheel to last a very long time. The central axle was also of iron.

CHAPTER 2

ONE BEAUTIFUL SUNNY MORNING Rani and I were playing our cotton race. We were waiting to see the Zeppelins flying over our house as they do every morning. The baby was sleeping. We don't make too much noise to wake him up. Mr Daniel was playing his saxophone and the music stopped. *He is ready to go to work*, I thought. *Then we will call Madam Daniel to sort out the food for us.*

But Mr Daniel began shouting and banging the table. He was quarrelling with Madam Daniel. He got more angry, shouting at Madam Daniel to stop the children from making noise. He took out his belt and began walloping Madam Daniel. He was lashing out all over her body, head, back, legs, chest and belly. He kept on beating her. She was bawling and bawling and he continued beating her. "Oh Gad, Oh Gad, you go kill me today. Please Gad, please Gad, help me. Dis man go kill me today," she screamed out. His children ran outside because Mr Daniel would beat them also when he is in this mood. He ordered them to come back inside the house. They were crying for their mother, but they also got a belting one after the other. He spares no one, and blames Madam Daniel for everything that appears to go wrong.

Madam Daniel managed to escape from him. She ran across the road quickly, went directly into the bedroom, picked up the baby and held him close to her chest. She pulled me in front of her. "Doh hit dem chiren nah. Dey fadder go chop you up," Madam Daniel said to him. Mr Daniel paused, looked belligerently at Madam Daniel, and dropped his belt. Then he picked up a large stick and tried to hit her with it. He confronted her. Madam Daniel picked me up and showed me to Mr Daniel. I got very frightened. Madam Daniel said, "Doh hit dis child for Gad sake." Mr Daniel was taken by surprise at her decision to use me to defend herself. Every time Mr Daniel attempted to hit Madam Daniel, she pushed me in front of Mr Daniel. He attempted to lash out at her head. Madam Daniel raised me up above her head. I shielded her head. Then it was her chest and her back. I was frightened and was bawling as though Mr Daniel had hit me. Mr Daniel looked at me screaming in Madam Daniel's hands. He did not risk hitting her because I would be the first to receive the blow. He dropped his stick and walked away home.

Madam Daniel remained with us and said to Dewan and me, "Child you save me from plenty ah beating today.

Gad Bless you! Gad bless you, child!" Dewan is my baby brother who I also look after while my parents are out working. Madam Daniel picked me up, smiled with me, hugged tightly, kissed me on my cheeks and said, "Buaye, you is my saviour. Tank Gad foh you today. Gad bless you plenty child. Ah doh know wat would a happen to me today if you eh dah dey here." Rani was still trembling with fright. She was bawling too. Madam Daniel picked her up, and kept cuddling her. "Ye go be a'right, darlin', all ah we go be a'right," Madam Daniel said. All of us sat in the hammock and Madam Daniel swung and sang until Rani felt more relaxed. She was beginning to enjoy the ride in the hammock and Dewan was about to fall asleep. Madam Daniel stopped and said, "Ley we eat some food now nah. What you Mama dee cook dis marning. Ah goin' to see." She went into the kitchen and gave us the roti and tomato chokha. She gave the baby his milk. Madam Daniel took some food for herself and sat with Rani and me. She said, "Boy, dis tomato chokha tastin' nice foh so. You Mama is a damn good cook eh?" She gave us water and then played with us until Mr Daniel had gone to work. She left us and said, "Ah go come back later when you Mama and Papa come home." I remained in the hammock while Rani went out in the yard. I thought of all these beatings Madam Daniel and the children received from Mr Daniel. I also reflected on the amount of beatings I had received from Papa and Nana and Nanny in my long four years of life. I believe that Nana, Mr Daniel and Papa must have graduated with the highest distinction in beating women and children from some weird university. If there is a Nobel Prize to be awarded for beating women and children then all three of them will be at the top of the shortlist of candidates for this award. Madam Daniel shouted from across the road, "Aye, aye, ah see dee bull kyart comin' buaye."

They arrived about half an hour after Madam Daniel went home. We were in the yard and Rani ran to meet them. "Mama, Mama, Madam Daniel came and picked us up and Mr Daniel came to beat her. Yes, Mama, she picked up the two of us."

"Wey you saying, child, wey happen?" I briefly told Papa and Mama what took place and that Madam Daniel would come over later. Papa took the bull cart to the back of the house and tied the bull to the calabash tree. He gave it water and grass before coming inside. Mama took out food for themselves seeing that we had already eaten. Mama called out to Madam Daniel, "Ey gyul, Marj, wey you doin', come nah gyul."

Madam Daniel replied, "Gyul, Seeta, ah jus' finish cookin' a pot a soup, gyul. Ah comin' now, an ah go bring some foh dee two ah you." Madam Daniel came with two bowls of soup and a jug of soursop drink for us. Papa told Rani and me to go outside and play.

Madam Daniel told them how Mr Daniel beat her that morning. He was merciless and completely lost his temper. She showed Mama and Papa the bruises on her back and legs. She had a very bad headache from the blows to her head. "Gyul, dee child save me today, adderwise dee man would ah kill me wid licks. Ah doh know wah does go in ye head. Like dee man does get crazy when he start beating me. And he beat up aal dee children an aal. Gyul, ah so fed up eh, ah wan to leave ye ass an go somewhere far from here, wey he kyan't find me. I eh have nowhere to go caz none ah dee family doh wan to know. Dey eh want me by dey house. Dey does send me back here. Dey say ah have to live wid dee man. Gyul, Seet, ah does do everything in dee house. Ah doh go no wey. Dee only place ah does come is by you, an you does come by me. But Danny does wok for good money and ye does buy everything in the house. Any lil ting does upset ye, an ye go start to beat me an dee children up. Me can't understand ye at arl."

Mama said, "Gyul, ah doh know wat to say. Ah so sarry gyul to hear dis. Gyul, ah does see for meself how he does quarrel and beat all ah you from one side. Gyul, dee man have so much education. He does read dee paper every day and he does come here and tell we arl wey goin' an in the country and wid dee war. He say dee whole wol fighting. He dah tell we about dee war. It go finish soon, Danny say. Marj, gyul, Danny so nice wen ye does talk like dat eh? Dis one ah have here [i.e. Papa] doh know Bee from Bull foot. He does larn everything from Danny. Me too, gyul, ah does larn from he too." Papa was quiet all the while, as the two women were talking.

With a studied look, he said to Madam Daniel, "Why you eh tell him to go and see dee doctor, and tell dee doctor why he does behave like dat. Danny doh sound right in he head, gyul."

"Boy, ah does tell ye dat every time you know, but he doh listen to me. Ye is a man, ye ey go listen to nobady. Ye is dat kind ah man, you youself know 'im. Boy ah fed up tellin' 'im dat. Ah go carry 'im if he eh want to go by yeself." When she does suggest going to the doctor, Mr Daniel would turn to her and yell, "What's wrong with me? What do you think is wrong with me? You keep on at me to go and see a doctor. Are you a doctor? Only sick people go to the doctor. I am a strong, healthy working man. Stop nagging me to visit a doctor. Remember, I am the boss in this house."

Papa said to her, "When ah see him ah go have a good man-to-man talk wid him. Den ah go carry 'im wid me to dee DMO." That is the District Medical Officer, the local doctor.

Mama brought out the coconut oil and said to Madam Daniel, "Gyul, rub down you han' an foot wid de oil nah. Den ah go rub you back for you nah." Mama turned to Papa and said, "You go an see wey dee children doin' outside an leave we here." Mama counted twelve belt lines across Madam Daniel's back and another six across her chest and abdomen. Mama hailed out to her, "Barp re Barp! Gyul, Marj, look how dee man beat you up like dat. Like ye eh ha no mussy [mercy] for you." Mama gently massaged Marj's back, abdomen and chest with her coconut oil. She gave Madam Daniel half a bottle of the oil to take home and use on herself and on the children's skin.

Madam Daniel was in a vexed mood. She said to Mama, "Gyul, Seeta, ah make up me mind now. I ey go sleep in the bed wid 'im from now. He could do wat ye want, ah doh care. Ah get too much beating, and sometimes for notting. Ley me hear wah ye go say. Gyul, ah wish ah could run away from here. No man ey go want a woman wid six children. So ah have to bear it. But ah go get me own back on him one day."

"Wey you go do, gyul?" Mama asked.

"Ah doh know but we go see nah wen dee time come."

Mama got worried and was concerned about what Madam Daniel might do to herself. She did not pursue it any further. It was getting late and Madam Daniel went home. Mama remembered the pair of scissors to send down for Nana. She had taken the pair of scissors to cut and sew clothes for us. She called me.

"You go carry dis scissors for Nanny. She dee axe me for it dee edder day. Walk on dee side ah dee road, you hear me? You go watch dem kyart an dem comin' an goin', a'right? Go now."

I am pleased that I will see Brother again. We pitch marbles together, and pelt each other with his sponge ball. Brother gets more things than us. Mama had wrapped the pair of scissors in brown paper. While walking down the hill I opened the wrapping to look at the scissors. I put the paper in my pocket and started working the pair of scissors with both hands. It was interesting to see how the blades opened and closed. I tried cutting a few leaves from the roadside. I reached the bridge and paused for a moment. I looked down at the clear water in the river below. Although the water is about three feet deep, I can

Here is a section of the bridge over the river where the two fair-haired, fair-skinned and blue-eyed apparitions of the phenylketonuric girls were seen lying on the riverbed. They would call the onlookers to come and join them. Alex went down to meet them but he met his death. The silk-cotton tree lies at the back of the bamboo patch. Jenny and Ganti lived under the bridge for the rest of their lives after the silk-cotton village curse fell on them.

see the riverbed clearly. There are lots of small pebbles lining the riverbed. There are many tiny ripples on the surface of the water. On one side of the riverbank there are bamboo trees overhanging the river and providing a shady section. The other bank has tall grasses. I bent over the bridge and looked at the water to see if there are any fishes in the river. Instead, I saw my own reflection. I was surprised to learn that my head is rather large and my hair is long. I looked at the pair of scissors and then at my reflection in the water. Just as I had practised cutting the leaves, I would do the same to my hair and give myself a decent haircut.

This pair of scissors was very sharp as I found out with cutting the leaves. I looked down in my mirror, and using both hands as previously, I cut my hair almost to a skinhead all the way down the middle of my head from the front to the back. As my hair fell into the water it flowed away downstream. I continued to look at the clear water after my hair was washed away. There was no hair nor any fish in the water, but there was a very unusual occurrence taking place in the water.

The water became cloudy, murky, sent up splashes as though either someone had thrown a large boulder in the middle of the water, or someone was muddying the water. I thought it might have been a large fish or alligator jumping about in the water. The murky water gradually cleared and settled. I could see the pebbles on the riverbed once more as clearly as before. But, "Oh my God! Oh my God! Who's that?" I yelled out.

There they were, lying on their backs at the bottom of the river on the tiny pebbles. They were so pretty, so very beautiful, so young, and the two of them were smiling at me. They were about nine or ten years of age, I would imagine, but would be younger than Gloria. They resembled each other very much, perhaps twins, and were about the same size in length lying side by side. They were both fair-haired, fair-skinned and had Caribbean sky-blue eyes. Their fair straight long hair was flowing away from their heads. They were smiling and looking at me. They seemed so comfortable lying in the water. They did not surface to take in a breath of air. How could they hold their breaths for such a long time at the bottom of the river? They were still smiling and looking at me, and now they both raised their hands and their two index fingers. Now they were calling me with four fingers. They were motionless in the water except for their moving fingers. Now they were calling me with both their hands. I got very scared seeing them doing this. I could not take my eyes from them. My heart was beating fast. I could feel it beating against my chest, dup, dup, dup. I had goose pimples on my face and arms. I was very scared at that sight. I held on to the scissors tightly and ran as fast as I could until I reached Nanny. She was in the kitchen. I held on to her crying and frightened, and trembling. I could not speak for some time and would not let go of her. Nanny had not seen my face or head as yet since my head was in her skirt. She was holding me but now spoke. "Wey happen to you?" I pointed in the direction of the river.

Nanny suspected what might have happened. When Nanny saw my head she was shocked at what I did. "Wey you cut up you hair like dat for? Who tell you to do dat eh? You Nana go beat you if he see you cut up you hair like dat. When you go home you fadder go beat you an aal. You too bad," she said angrily. I was still trembling from the scene in the river. My body was feeling hot, and I felt sick. I began to vomit. Nanny came quickly, bent my head forward and only water came out. She put me to lie down and rest.

I cannot get those two girls in the river out of my head. I am seeing them all the time smiling at me and calling me with their fingers and hands. I am seeing their fair hair, fair skin and blue eyes. My eyes are transfixed on them as if being hypnotised. I cannot shift my gaze away from these two gorgeous-looking girls. I feel compelled to keep my eyes on them. These striking features are going round and round in my head. How could they be lying at the bottom of the river with their faces upwards and water not getting into their nostrils and not get drowned or asphyxiated? They keep on smiling at me as though they are enjoying themselves down at the bottom of the river. Is that stony ground on the riverbed not too hard for them to lie? I was sweating profusely. Nanny took a towel and wiped me. She took off my clothes and gave me one of Brother's shirts and a pair of trousers. I was beginning to feel weak. Nanny gave me a cup of water but the cup fell out of my hand. She called Nana.

Nanny said, "Dee buaye say ye see dem two gyal in de river. Ye get frighten, an now ye bring up, ye sweating and ye han' weak. Ye kyan't hole dee cup ah water self."

Nana said, "Dee spirit! Dee spirit come pan top 'im. Dee buaye go get sick now. Ah go take 'im by dee pundit straight away, ley ye see and 'Jhaaray' 'im. Ye go gi dee buaye a 'tabeej' to put an. Dah go drive away dee spirit from 'im, but ye go take time. Ah go send dee buaye [i.e. Brother] to get goat milk for ye, when ye come from dee gyarden."

"Dee pundit say dat a strang spirit gat apan 'im. It is a good ting ah come straight away to see 'im. Before the spirit could make dee child more sick dee pundit say ye dee able drive it out. Dee pundit make a strang strang 'tabeej' an tie it round ye neck. Ye go have to put it an for one month. Tank Gad for dat. Tell ye fadder to 'Jhaaray' 'im an aal in dee marnin' an evenin'. Ye fadder dah 'Jhaaray' good. Gi dee buaye dee goat milk three time a day. Make some fever grass tea for dee child. Put some coconut oil in ye head. Tie ye head wid the headache leaf." I felt as though Nana was a fully qualified practitioner to be issuing his medical prescription for me.

My fever persisted for several weeks. Nana took me to Dr Luo. He examined me. My temperature was 38.50C. "Give him these soluble aspirin tablets, one tablet every six hours for two days. Put it in a little water to dissolve it and give it to him to drink. I don't want him to take too much of this medication, because it will upset his stomach. Encourage him to drink plenty of fluids. Come back to see me in a week, OK? There is no sign of an infectious disease like measles or tuberculosis," he said to Nana.

Everyone in the family including the Daniels was worried about my health and this fever which did not seem to be coming down. Madam Daniel was thinking ahead and perhaps negatively. She said to Mama, "Ah hope dee spirit doh carry 'im away from we eh gyul." She reflected on how she lost two of her children before they were five years of age through contracting tuberculosis. She said that it was the Obeah that someone did on her children. That is what caused them to die. Then Madam Daniel said to Mama, "Gyul Seeta, me doh interfere wid no bady. Me doh hut no bady feelin', gyul. Me eh know who does wok this dam Obeah on me an mee children." Mama started to cry at such a thought that this would happen to me. Nana told her that I had got the evil spirits in me. Those spirits from the river followed me and came inside me. That is why I got this high fever. "Ley we hope an pray nottin' eh go happen to dee child, eh gyul?" said Madam Daniel. Nanny was looking after me while Papa and Mama carried on working in the garden. Aunty Jenny and Uncle Jhan came to see me every day. Aunty Jenny told me the same story every day. It was about an old lady who lived by the pond all on her own. That was an interesting story. I liked it very much. She told me other stories. They were all lovely stories. I like Aunty Jenny very much because she is so nice and she tells me all these wonderful stories. I call her the best storyteller in the whole world.

Aunty Jenny is very pretty with an infectious smile. She is light-skinned, has a slightly elongated face, high cheekbones, black eyebrows and long eyelashes, and brown eyes. She did have thick-set long, black and straight hair, but now it is shoulder-length in a light-brown colour. She is slim and tall. She wears red lipstick. She is the only one in the entire family who wears lipstick, high-heeled stiletto-style shoes, shoulder-length bobbed permed hair, tights and skin-tight knee-length dresses to reveal her bodily curves.

This is to Nana's disgust and disapproval but he stays quiet and he is holding his nerves for the time being. She is at most times wearing the latest ladies' fashion despite the hard times during the war. She has the latest fashion ladies' magazines, weekly and monthly ones. Aunty Jenny is treading a fine line apparently not recognising this. She tells everyone that she is a "town girl" and that Mama is a "country-bookie girl". Aunty Jenny is one of the better-read ladies in Sunnyvale. The villagers do make quiet unpleasant remarks about Aunty Jenny's dress style. For example, "She's such a show-off ooman", "Who dee ass she tink she is?", "She playing white lady", are some of these aspersions cast on Aunty Jenny. These uneducated, peasant sugar cane farm workers wear working clothes for most of the day. They are normally barefooted whereas Aunty Jenny is always wearing stylish shoes at home. She can afford this luxury because Uncle Jhan, like Mr Daniel, works in the oil industry. For a woman with ten surviving children Aunty Jenny prides herself on her attractive figure.

The women in the village do wonder how she manages to keep herself so elegant-looking. Therefore, it is no surprise to learn that there is this chorus of antipathy among them towards Aunty Jenny. Uncle Jhan and Aunty Jenny consider themselves a higher class than the farmers in the community. Nevertheless, Aunty Jenny does have a decent allotment-size kitchen garden at the back of their house. She appears to have a keen interest in growing the local herbs, and uses them in her cooking and salads. Aunty Jenny would call a few of the neighbours round on a sunny afternoon, and in true traditional English custom would say to them, "Girls, let's have some tea on the lawn, shall we?" with the accent to boot, to live up to her seemingly high lifestyle. These peasant women would giggle and chuckle in their throats at Aunty Jenny's choice of words and in the manner of her delivery.

The rest of the family are out in the fields, including Brother. Nanny finished cooking lunch and took it in the garden for Nana and all the workers. I would stay with Aunty Jenny until they return home.

Papa continued to "Jhaaray" me in the morning and evening but with no significant improvement. This is a treatment to drive out evil, to dispel abdominal pain, and to improve appetite and well-being. It is a non-invasive procedure. Papa takes five or seven coconut palm broomsticks, washes them, holds them together and measures them to be of the same length. He recites his Hindi prayers, while passing the broomsticks from the top of my head sweeping down all the way in front of me to my toes. Then he looks at the broomsticks. An unusual phenomenon is seen with the broomsticks. Sometimes one or two of the sticks become shorter than the others. Papa will break off the longer ones and make them to be of equal length once more. Papa repeats this process five or seven times, depending on the number of sticks he uses. Each time he sweeps me down and gets unequal lengths of sticks he says, "Look, you see, it wuking, it wuking good. You go get better soon," and he would smile lovingly. Nanny normally sits and looks on when Papa is "Jhaaraying" me. She seems relieved that Papa's treatment is responding positively.

Nana took me back to Dr Luo after one month. Dr Luo examined me again, palpated my abdomen, checked my lung and heart sounds. He asked me to breathe in deeply, hold my breath and breathe out. I did this a few times and he told Nana, "Everything seems clear. His temperature is now all right at 37.6^0 C. No more tablets, just plenty of fluids to drink. OK! The boy is on the mend."

I told Dr Luo about the two beautiful fair-haired, fair-skinned and blue-eyed girls who were lying on the riverbed face upwards and were calling me. Dr Luo said, "Oh I see, I have heard about them before. They were the two mentally handicapped girls bathing in the river. They were suffering from a condition called phenylketonuria. The cause is genetic and both parents had an abnormal autosomal recessive gene. One in four of the children usually get affected. It is an inborn error of metabolism.

They cannot metabolise a form of protein, phenylalanine, an amino acid in the body, because there is a deficiency of the enzyme phenylalanine hydroxylase. They must have a special protein-free diet once diagnosed. This condition can be averted if this special diet is given straight away for several years. If they are left untreated it would lead to this condition. They test all newborn babies for this condition. They used to do a urine test but it was not reliable so now they do a blood test. It's called a Guthrie test. They can also become epileptics and so they have grand mal fits."

He continued, "I understand that those girls had grand mal fits while they were bathing in the river and no one was around at the time. As a result, they were drowned. That happened several years ago. They do have the characteristic features of this condition." Nana said that he did not fully understand what Dr Luo was saying about the girls' condition. I simply told Nana that the girls were born mentally handicapped and had also suffered from having fits. That caused them to get drowned in the river as no one was around to rescue them. Nana told Dr Luo that the evil spirits live in the silk-cotton tree and come to the spot in the river where they were drowned. These spirits will always stay at the bottom of the river and lie on the tiny pebbles.

At home Brother was waiting to see me and to hear what the doctor had said. When he saw me he shouted out, "I bet the doctor said that you are going to live for 101 years without any fever knocking you out." I ran up to him and hugged him up. "Who say you could touch me, hot blood? Moye made soup today and I had a whole bowl full already. Boy, the soup is delicious and moreish. It has plenty of dumplings in it. And don't talk about the red and the white sweet potatoes. OK! Ready, steady, and make a race for the kitchen." Of course, he won again. He said, "Nanny took out two bowls of soup. Boy, I've got an appetite like a bull. This is my second bowl of soup I'm having. I'm strong, powerful and could work hard like Papa's bull. But you are thin and weak and need building up. You eat so little amount like a rabbit. You are meek and gentle like a rabbit. This seems to bear out our personality differences according to the traditional Chinese New Year. Do you know what that means? I was born in the year of the ox, showing my strength and power. You were born in the year of the rabbit, being calm and gentle."

"That's a rather interesting and intelligent analogy! How did you know this to come up with such a comparison?" I asked him. My brother's face brightened and gave the broadest smile you could ever see. He put his index finger to the tip of his nose, and gently kept on tapping it, indicating to me that I am too nosey and inquisitive.

"Ah! That would be telling. There are many things better not be echoed, but simply laid to bed." He continued, "These are not calabash bowls like those up at Cotton Hill. They are expensive cut-glass bowls Aunty Jenny bought for us, but with Nana's money. Moye gave her the money to buy bowls for the two houses. I don't have to read and spell for you. She loves dressing up, going to town and spending money like a big shot. That is why she went and bought these bowls for us."

The soup was very tasty and appetising. It helped to bring back my appetite. Nanny gave us orange juice, which she had made from freshly squeezed oranges. The two orange trees are covered with oranges of varying grades from very small young green ones to the larger greens and of course to the ripe oranges. Nana would soon be buying grafted oranges, grapefruit, tangerine, avocado and the new yellow "Chinese coconut" plants from St Augustine Agricultural Farm to make his own orchard on the side of the two houses. Nana said that the citrus plants would bear fruits in twelve to eighteen months, while the yellow "Chinese coconuts" will start bearing in two to three years. I had not realised that it would be Brother and me who would doing all the planting when that time would come.

I was feeling better steadily and so it was time to go back home to see Madam Daniel and her boys, and to resume my usual work of looking after Rani and Dewan. I was sorry to leave Brother as we had such a lovely time together. He said, "Nana and I will come up to Cotton Hill, and you can come and join us to pick a few bags of cotton. Moye will make pillows with it."

Madam Daniel quickly ran across when she saw me. She picked me up and hugged me and kissed me. She said, "You get a bit lighter, boy. We go have to fatten you up wid some good yam and cassava pone every day from now, you hear dat? You modder go send you by me nah, a'right?" Madam Daniel is so kind and sweet. She loves us as much as she loves her own children. It is rather a pity that Mr Daniel beats all of them so often and so severely. He is well educated, is such a talented musician, and blows his trumpet loud to entertain the whole village. He is the only musician in our village. He plays his trumpet and saxophone in church and in the village ceremonies.

He is seasonal in his choice of music and songs. The villagers are attuned to his music. For example, "Oh it's Easter time now," or "Oh it's Christmas time now," or "It's Carnival time now," they would comment as they heard his blend of music. The villagers see him as educated, articulate and fully updated with current affairs. He demonstrates a pleasant and charming outlook to all the villagers. He is a tall, well-built, muscular, handsome man with an athletic frame. He wears two gold teeth on both sides of his upper row of teeth. When he smiles or laughs these gold teeth are most prominent. They glitter and light up his face. He stands upright and aloof. However, despite this, even the illiterate and uneducated members of the community are puzzled at his violent and aggressive behaviour towards Madam Daniel and the children. Every parent in Sunnyvale beats his or her children, but not to the extent that Mr Daniel does. However, regarding highly inflammatory tempers, Nana is two or three streets ahead of everyone. This is well known throughout the village because there is hardly a secret kept in this village regarding family life.

Despite this, Nana is well respected in the community.

Nana and Brother came up with three large sugar bags to pick cotton. The Daniels were at home but Mama and Papa were still out in the garden. "Are you buaye lookin' after dee chiren good till you fadder come?" Nana asked me.

Mr Daniels hailed out to Nana, "Hello Boss, how are you doing these days? It's very nice indeed to see you. We'll all come up and help you." Mr Daniel, Madam Daniel and their children came over. All the kids were running around from tree to tree emptying out the cotton from them. It did not take long to fill one bag. "Danny, how much chiren you ha, buaye? Dee edder day one a dem dee get sick an ye dee dead nah?" asked Nana. Mr Daniel said, "Oh yes, Boss, she contracted *Mycobacterium tuberculosis* and the medical treatment was not available. When it became available, it was not possible for it to reach us in time to save her. Boss, living in this part of the country is a great disadvantage to us for many of the amenities we are supposed to receive. It's sad, but what can we do about it? Shall we move to somewhere else? No, Boss, I love our quiet village, especially Cotton Hill, which has such a picturesque and idyllic setting."

Nana, although he did not understand such language, replied, "Danny, buaye, you damn well right, eh!"

Madam Daniel was keeping quiet and said nothing up to this moment. She opened up, "Bass, ah see you an Danny hitting aff nice man? Ye aalways tink ah lat 'bout you eh. Danny does say how hard you does wok seven day ah week."

Nana replied, "Ah does aalways ha plenty wok for dem man an dem, gyal. Ah ha to go an check an dem aal de time caz dey eh go wok good."

Mr Daniel intervened, "Boss, that's quite true, you know, it's just as when the cats are away the mice are at play."

"Danny, buaye, you know dat dam good. Who tell you dat? Dem stray cat an dem dah make young one aal about in dee bush an in dee cane field," Nana replied.

"Boss I'm not referring to those cats in particular, but you are absolutely right, you've got to keep a close eye on your workers at all times," Mr Daniel said to Nana.

Nana told him, "Dee crap [sugar cane harvesting season] finish, dee rain fallin' an ah ha to start doin' dee kola to plant rice."

Madam Daniel came up to Nana, put her arms around his waist and said to him, "Bass ley we sit dong an have someting to eat nah man. Ah bring fry plantain, boil-an-fry breadfruit, an cassava pone. An we have soursop an barbadine drink to go dong wid it. Ley dem chiren play an pick dee cotton in dee mean time. Ah go gi dem dey food after we done eat, a'right? Wash you han' wid dis battle ah water nah. An look, ah gat dee towel here to wipe you han' wid it. While we eating we go taak bout dee rice plantin' nah."

"Dee man an dem start to cutlass dee kola a'ready. Nex week ah go plough up the kola and den level dee whole ting. Dee rice nussry ready to plant. Ah hope dee rain go come wen we plant dee rice," said Nana.

Marj was excited about rice planting. She said to Nana, "Bass, ah go come one day to see how you dah plant dee rice. Ah go gi you a good han' man."

Nana replied, "Dat is plenty hard wok, gyal."

Meantime, the kids were having a wonderful time playing hide and seek, and swinging round and round the cotton trees, but picking cotton as they went along. They had picked a further two bags, which Nana felt would be sufficient. Brother said, "Boy, we've got enough cotton here to make a nice soft sleep-easy mattress. I can dream all night long on it."

I said to him, "Listen to me, young man, you simply can't go on dreaming your life out all night long. This is a waste of valuable hours and poor time management. It's best that you keep away from that cotton mattress idea."

He turned round to me, looked into my eyes and belched out, "Let sleeping dogs lie, you got it?" Alex, Hendrik and Tom burst out laughing when they heard him. "Hey, hey, hey, let's have a toast to that, let sleeping dogs lie."

When I looked at these semi-naked cotton trees in their present state I felt guilty of robbing them of their clothing. They were now like the rough-skinned pond alligators basking in the midday tropical heat. There was a huge contrast in the appearance between the cotton trees which were stripped of their cotton and those fully laden with their snow-white soft woolly fibres. These ravaged trees also looked like the sheep farmer's sheared sheep versus the unsheared ones.

The children had their fill and we came home to see Mama cooking for every one of us. The bull was tethered to the calabash tree and was bawling as though he was hungry. Papa had gone to get a bundle of grass for him. Mr Daniel had pulled down a few lianas from the tall mahogany tree and used them as ropes to tie the bags of cotton. He bound two bags together as one bundle and tied the other bag. "Boss, Marj and I will carry these bags to your home for you. It is nonsense to have two young and strong people simply watch you struggling with three bags of cotton all on your own. That's why I made two bundles, one for Marj and the other for me. We'll take a leisurely walk down with you, and it's also good company for us. We need to go down to the shop anyway," Mr Daniel told Nana. When Mr Daniel flung the bulky load of cotton over his shoulder he was bending forwards with his head down and his eyes fixed to the ground. Nana looked at him and said, "Danny, buaie, you lookin' like dem donkey in Pay Shay carrying basket ah cocoa. But dee catten nah too heavy like the cocoa." Madam Daniel burst out laughing and said, "Wey! Papa yoh, Bass, man you dam funny wen you ready eh!"

"Poye [Papa], you go eat some food nah before you go? Ah jes finish makin' bodi takari an roti for aal ah you. An ah make some sillyment [cinnamon] tea. Come an wash you han' nah," Mama asked Nana.

He replied, "Gi dem buaye [i.e. Brother and I] to bring it home. Dem buaye an dem [i.e. Daniel and Marj] go help me carry dee catton. Me nah go stay." Nana continued, "You dee gaan to wok in the gyarden today? Wey you do dat foh? You eh see how big you belly dey? You go make child soon."

Mama replied, "No Poye, ah dah only go an watch ye [Papa] an keep ye company nah. Wen ah go dey, ah dah sit dong in the marai [i.e. a hut, or ajoupa] an watch ye. Me eh dah do no wok in dee gyarden now." She was heavily pregnant.

The Daniels came with Brother and me. They had filled their pockets with cotton and were flying the fibres as Rani and I did every morning.

"Look how many cobos are perched on the silk-cotton tree," said Henrik.

"No, they are not real, although they are looking like real ones. Those are transformations of the spirits living in the tree. They are out sunbathing. Very soon they will disappear," said Alex. He paused for a while looking at the cobos and said in a knowledgeable manner, "There are several other transformations of these spirits. They can appear as squirrels if you want to catch squirrels, or as opossum if you are out hunting at night, or as night owls flying in front of you. And of course, how about the two beautiful fair-haired, fair-skinned, blue-eyed girls lying on the tiny pebbles in the riverbed?"

As we approached the bridge, it came flooding back to me. I got scared and held on to Brother. We walked briskly across the bridge without looking sideways. I could feel my pulse racing at 100mph, and my heart hitting my sternum like a bass drumbeat. The fine hairs in my forearms were standing erect. Goose pimples propped them up. Brother looked at me and saw my drained face, devoid of blood, and beads of sweat were popping up on my forehead. He came out in his usual jocular, cryptic fashion, "I thought you told me that you are the 'finest ladies man' on this planet," and began laughing with the others when they heard him. That was the joke of the day, my take-home message. My fears were almost vanished as I had to join the others. Gloria came and hugged me up and kissed me on both cheeks. Alex said, "You see, you see, it's true what your brother said about you. Look how Glory loving you up." We reached home to find Nanny sitting in the wicker rocking chair relaxing, and gently rocking away. She was surprised to see this big gang strolling in with three bags of cotton.

Madam Daniel quickly ran in to see Aunty Jenny. She was doing a bit of crocheting in her veranda. "Ey gyul, Jenny, wey you doin' gyul? Ah waalk dong dee road wid dee Bass an Danny. We bring some catton for dee Bass. Dee chiren come dong wid we an aal. We goin' in dee shap to buy some rice an ting. Ey, wey you makin' dey, gyul. It lookin' pretty, gyul. Gyul, how you does do dat? Ye go take plenty ah time to sew dis kind ah ting, yes? Wey you call it, gyul Jenny?"

Aunty Jenny smiled and looked at her, "My darling Marj, this is called crochet. It is not sewing as such, but it is a form of fine artwork." She continued, "There are various designs you can make. I learnt to do this before I was married." Madam Daniel suggested to Aunty Jenny that she would like to learn how to crochet, but Aunty

Jenny pretended that she did not hear. Knowledge is power, and therefore, Aunty Jenny would like to maintain the status quo.

"Well a'right gyul, we ha to go in dee shap now. We go talk again nah, when we go ha more time." Mr Daniel was telling Nana about his job and that his Alex would like to become a policeman. The other one hadn't made up his mind as yet. Madam Daniel came up to Nana and put her arm on Nana's shoulder.

"Bass, we goin' to get a few ting from dee shap. You go an have a good rest, you must be dag tired now." The Daniel children took me home. We played "hit me, run and catch me" until we reached home. Nobody could catch Alex because he is the fastest runner. I jumped into the hammock and got a shock.

Papa was in the hammock eating his dinner. Half of his roti fell off his calabash bowl. I got a good smacking from Papa for my error. When he finished eating his roti and pumpkin he gave me some good news. Papa said, "You big now and you go make five years. You go have to go to school next week. Dem Daniel chiren go carry you wid dem."

"Who will look after Rani and Dewan when I go to school, Pa?" I asked.

"We go carry dem by Nanny for two days and Madam Daniel go come for three days an she go mine dem till we come from dee gyarden. Ah have to go an get a shut an pants for you to go to school. You go see you bredda in dee school. He been goin' to school two years now. He could read and write good. You go be like he soon when you start to go to school." I am excited and eager to see Brother in school. We can play together with Alex, Tom, Henrik and Gloria. Although I am very excited to go to school none of them tell me what it is like to be in school. They do not mention the word school. They appear to have forgotten all notion of school.

CHAPTER 3

It is Monday 18ᵗʰ. Mama dressed me, gave me pumpkin and roti and put coconut oil on my legs and on my head. At the same time four of the Daniel children ran across the road to meet me. "You ready?" they shouted. Gloria and Henrik held each of my hands and off we strode along to school. The school is very big. There are hundreds of children playing and shouting and enjoying themselves. I got frightened seeing so many children. There are small ones like myself, and lots of bigger children. They are all running in different directions like wild animals. It is very noisy in the playground.

The entrance to the school is lined with palms and periwinkle flowers in between on both sides. There are whitewashed stones in front of the palms and flowers also lining the entrance. The school building is on a mound overlooking the front flower garden. There are roses, ixoras, hibiscus, marigolds, and dahlias grown in neatly manicured garden beds. There is also a large vegetable garden at the back of the school. I wondered who is the school gardener. He must be a skilled professional gardener to maintain such a beautiful compound. I was shocked to learn that the gardeners and school janitors are the children themselves.

The main school ground has five straight white lines. These are for five days of the week. The first line represents Monday, then followed by Tuesday, Wednesday, Thursday and Friday. The children line up on these lines according to the areas from which they come. Brother came up to us. He took me to the Friday line. It is the last line of children to leave the playground to go to their respective classes. There are no janitors in the school. It is the children's job to clean the inside and outside of the school every day.

On each day of the week one line will have to clean the school premises inside and outside. For instance, on Mondays it is the Monday line children's responsibility for cleaning. Our cleaning day is on Fridays. The lines get points for the cleanliness of the place. Points are deducted if the compound is not cleaned properly. Points are also deducted for personal appearance at inspection times. The winners get a special treat at the end of the term. When the school bell rings at 9.00am and at 1.00pm all the children must line up in their respective lines. The teachers come out and start to inspect the lines with rulers and whips.

I was standing next to Tom. The others were further down the line. Alex and Gloria were at the other end of the line as they are the biggest and in the highest class. Tom and I are in the infant section of the line. One teacher started inspecting our line. Everyone has to put out two hands to show their fingernails. The teacher hits anyone seen with long fingernails or dirty nails. Our feet and clothes must also be clean. The teacher hits the children on their fingers, legs and buttocks if they are not clean. I see several children being beaten during this inspection.

It is a Monday morning at nine o'clock and I see teachers beating children in the lines. They may have dirty feet, long fingernails, or they may not have brushed their hair. It is interesting to note that they have not yet entered their classes and they start getting beaten by these teachers. *Is this what this school is for children?* I asked myself quietly. While standing in the line I repeated this question in my mind several times, *Is this what schooling is about for children?* How can I get to like school if the first thing I see is that children are being beaten in the public arena by the teachers for their appearance.

I have not seen a classroom as yet. I do not know anyone who might be in my class, because Tom is in a higher class than me. It's now time to go into our classes. The smallest ones start moving out in an orderly manner at one end while the eldest ones do the same at the other end of the line. Monday line goes first. This is followed by the Tuesday line until we reach the Friday line, that is our line. I was happy about going in last because I can see the entire school disappear before I eventually get into my class. I cannot say it's a classroom because the whole infant department stays in the open ground floor. At the far end I can see Tom in his class. His teacher is a lady teacher.

My teacher, Nick, is a young man not much older than Alex. He says that he is a monitor-pupil-teacher having recently passed his school leaving exams. The head teacher says that he is bright and hard-working. He would become an excellent teacher. He is under the guidance of the head of the infant department. He also has a whip in his hand. I have been debating silently whether *a whip or a ruler is an integral accompaniment, as a teaching aid, or whether it is a tool to demonstrate the teacher's authority over us minors.*

I have been concerned that those children who received whips and rulers on their fingers may not be able to write comfortably. Do these teachers care about what they are doing to the children's fingers? Surely, there must be an alternative way to have the children well groomed every day. The breeze blows right across the open ground floor department. This morning there is a strong gust of wind sweeping through. Blackboards and easels are tumbling over from the front of classes. Fortunately, no one is hurt. Our teacher ran quickly and propped up the blackboard and prevented it from falling over. He removed it until the wind died down. I am the only new child in class today but the teacher did not make an issue of it. We sat on long benches. There are six rows of benches. Six children sit in each row. This is the first lesson in class today. We learnt to count from one to ten. We repeated the counting many times. Teacher Nick allowed us to move around and count the number of children in each row. We counted the number of rows of benches. This practical activity led to a lot of movement and noise among the children. We continued the counting up to ten using strings of Coca-Cola bottle tops. Each string contains ten tops. This is a modified form of the abacus counting apparatus. The next class is separated from ours by a three-feet-wide aisle. Both teachers use this aisle to walk around their classes. We are told to call our teacher Nick "sir" whenever we need to talk to him.

One advantage of the open school is that we can see what is going on in the whole department at a glance. Another advantage is that one teacher can speak to all the children in the department at once. It is easy for the whole department to sing hymns and other songs together. The disadvantage is that we can be easily distracted by the other children in the different classes. Tom told me, "I like it like this, because I can mind the other people's business easily."

However, this open system causes much distraction and loss of concentration among the children, as I have already experienced. The wind subsided and the blackboards and easels went up once more. Our teacher shared out sand trays for all of us. These sand trays are twelve by ten inches in size, with a rim a half inch high. Sand is spread in each tray. We use these trays for writing the alphabet and words and for numbers and working out sums.

On my first day at school, I learn to write numbers one to ten. I also learn to write letters A to H. We repeated these several times until we are able to say and write them from memory. Rote learning is the method of teaching and learning in our primary school. We learn a song containing numbers one to ten, and letters A to H. These sand trays are easy for writing numbers and letters. Sir would walk round to see how we are writing. He checks our work and corrects it on the tray. We have to be careful not to shake our sand trays. The work would be easily erased if we shake it. I have found that I can deliberately erase my writing if I didn't wish my teacher to see it especially if I had wrong words or sums. We would have to rewrite it in his presence to confirm that we know our work.

There is one great health hazard in using these sand trays despite their easy use. There are plenty of gigger fleas in the sand. These would jump out of the sand trays onto the ground or from my tray on to the tray next to me. We find it quite funny to see these gigger fleas popping out of one sand tray and diving into another boy's or girl's tray. They are faster than the jack-in-the-box pop-up. These fleas do burrow in the corners of our fingernails, in the webs of our fingers, or in our toes. They would lay dozens of small white eggs within a self-contained capsular membrane. With care, Nanny would dig them out without bursting the membrane. Nanny would throw these into the fire. At the inspection of our fingers and feet, the teachers do look out for these fleas on us. Two of the female teachers would act as school nurses to remove any gigger fleas or fully grown giggers from the children's fingers or toes. The fleas are not infectious but they are terrible health hazards for all the children in the school.

The playground is of a red sandy soil. It is infested with these gigger fleas. In the heat of the midday sun it is amazing to see the hundreds and hundreds of these fleas jumping up and down because the sand gets too hot for them. This is a way of cooling themselves. Nevertheless, the children run around and play in the sand oblivious to these tiny mites. The sanitary inspection team, from the Infection Control Department, would come once a month and spray the entire school premises to kill off the gigger fleas. Within days of the spraying we would see the fleas popping up again. The gigger fleas bury themselves deeply into the sand to escape the effects of the pesticide. When the effects are worn out or washed away the gigger fleas reappear.

My teacher, Nick, tells us that the *Mycobacteruim tuberculosis* bacteria employ a similar escape strategy. As they enter the cell, they hide themselves in a comfortable vacuolar niche where some anti-TB drugs do not reach. In this way the bacteria can obtain nourishment, multiply and proliferate in vast numbers freely. They also have strategies to resist the effects of the drugs by pumping out the drug as the drug enters the cell. It is not surprising that with such resistance strategies tuberculosis is so difficult to treat. Teacher Nick says that many children die from this disease in our village.

One way to prevent it is to improve sanitation and reduce overcrowding in the home. Anyway, he says that the gigger fleas are not as harmful as TB. At lunchtime, Brother and I ran home. Nanny had cooked soup. I love the dumplings best, then the sweet potatoes and the cassava. We ran back to school but I could feel the food jumping up and down in my stomach as we ran. Brother wanted to show me how he plays "hold-it" with his friends and that I would join them on the next day.

At one o'clock the bell rang for the next line-up and inspection of hands and feet. Again, some children got smacked with rulers and whips by the teachers for dirty hands and feet. Some children could not wash their hands and feet because the other children were using the tap as the bell went. They had to leave and run for the line in order to be on time. We went into our classes in the same order as in the morning. Teacher Nick spoke to us very nicely and wanted to know if we all had something to eat for lunch. Two boys had nothing to eat because they did not bring any lunch to school. Their mothers did not have enough food to give them.

Teacher Nick felt very sorry for them. He sent a big boy from another class to go and get two crusty rolls with fried eggs and tomatoes for the two boys. He gave them water to drink. Sir told us that we all must eat something every morning and try and bring even a mango or banana for lunch if we did not have any food at home. He said that it is very important to eat some food every day, even if it is only some fruits. He understands that the war is going on and that food is very scarce in the whole country. He also said that he will not be able to buy food for other children as he himself has not got much money. He reminded us to tell our parents to plant vegetables around their houses as these can help to give us food especially in these hard times.

We went over the numbers one to ten and the letters A to H. Sir told us a lovely story about this thirsty clever crow. It saw a container with a little water but his beak could not reach it. It looked around and found little pebbles and threw them in the container one by one and saw that the water level began to rise. He added some more pebbles until the water level rose sufficiently so that his beak could reach it and drank as much as he needed. Sir said that this crow was a scientist because he applied science to get his water to drink. "You can all be scientists in some way too. You can all discover something yourselves, just as this crow did. When you get home think of something you can work out," teacher Nick told us. We joined the other classes to sing. They sang loud. I only listened. I saw Tom singing at the top of his voice at the far end. The teacher got the children to sing the same song several times so that everyone will learn it. It began, "Old MacDonald had a farm, ee ai ee ai oh."

It is a beautiful and meaningful song because everybody in the village has dogs, fowls and chickens at their homes. Nana is a big sugar cane farmer somewhat like Old MacDonald. This is only my first day at school and I have experienced a lot of different things. *Will every day be like this?* I asked myself quietly. I am already looking for more different experiences tomorrow.

What I found out is that some activities do not change and are the same every day. They are, bell rings at 9.00am and 1.00pm and the water bell rings ten minutes before 9.00am and 1.00pm. All teachers come out with whips or rulers to carry out inspection and children get beaten for dirty feet or long nails or general untidiness. The order in which classes leave for their respective classes is the same. Our line is always the last to go into our classes. Sand trays are our writing pads. The school children recite the Lord's Prayer before we are dismissed. I sang the number song, and the Old MacDonald song all the way home with Tom and Henrik. Brother only listened.

On Friday it is our line's turn to clean the school premises, outside and inside. Children broke branches from shrubs to use as brooms. They also used coconut palm brooms. These brooms are brought in as handicraft by children. I broke off small branches of the guava trees for my broom. We swept the long entrance from the road to the school. Others swept the oil sand court yard, and others cleaned the inside of the school. All the cleaning was finished by 8.30am. We washed our hands and feet, brushed our hair, tidied ourselves with shirts tucked inside our trousers. The girls were well groomed as well. At the 9.00am inspection our line was the best. No one got beaten for uncleanliness. We waited our turn to get into our classes.

Teacher Nick led us into our class. We all said our

prayers, sang hymns and set to work. I had learnt all the letters of the alphabet, and can count from one to thirty very easily. I asked Henrik and Tom to test me and to correct me as I said the alphabet and counted my numbers. By the end of my first week at school I was very pleased to learn so much. We had the soft drinks tops in strings of ten for counting and doing addition and subtraction. We also used our fingers. We learnt more songs, such as "Three Blind Mice", "Incy Wincy Spider", "Jesus Loves Me This I Know" and "He's a Jolly Good Fellow". Teacher Nick told us other stories such as "The Fox and the Grapes", "The Dog and the Bone', and 'Jack and the Beanstalk". It has been a very interesting first week of schooling.

Teacher Nick told us that we will be going on a school outing next week to visit the volcano at Piparo. He said that it is a dormant one. It only bubbles up and makes a gobbling sound when you poke the centre of the volcano with a long rod down into its crater. All of us are very excited and looking forward to this visit. None of us has ever seen a volcano. Teacher Nick said that he will tell us more about it next week. The one song that is continually spinning in my head, and I keep on humming it, is the "Old MacDonald" one. I do think of Nana at the same time as being Mr Old MacDonald. Over the weekend I have to tell all my cousins and Nanny about my first week at school, when we go down to see them and Brother. Papa said, "Dee bull cyart ready an aal ah we goin' dong by Nanny, come, come." I was so excited that I picked up my piece of roti and shataigne takari, stuffed it in my pocket and took my calabash bowl with me. I loved eating from my own bowl. Papa was quiet all the way and had a sombre look about him.

CHAPTER 4

BROTHER AND ALL OUR cousins surrounded the bull
cart in the yard. They were also thrilled to see us.
I immediately developed verbal diarrhoea and could not
stop yapping about my first week at school. I said, "Do
you all know that we have our very own Mr Old Mac
Donald here. That is our Nana for all you know," and we
spontaneously began singing it.

On Saturday evening all the cousins were sent into
Nanny's house. Nanny said that we all will be sleeping
there for the night. Aunty Jenny came over and gave us
our dinner. We had dahl and rice and curry chicken and
fried plantain. Fourteen of us ate in the sitting room, some
around the table and others on the floor. We were not
allowed to go outside. After dinner we made up games
and played inside, running through the whole house.

I told them about my first week in school. There are
hundreds of children in school and gigger fleas everywhere

around the school. We sang "Old MacDonald" several times, and switched to "Jesus Loves Me This I Know". Brother was leader and conductor of the group. Story time followed before we were told to go to bed. Brother gave up early and sat on the veranda but will not allow us to come there. Some of us slept on the beds and a few of us slept on the floor. Uncle Jhan came over to ensure that we were all inside the house. He said very firmly, "No one must come outside, do you all hear that? If I see anyone of you outside you are going to get a good beating from me." I was looking at Uncle Jhan while he was talking, his eyes were red, his face looked saddened but not angry, but his voice contained a very vexed tone. There was no smiling in his face, and his shirt looked roughened up and not his normal neatness. When we were ready to sleep, I spread a bag on the floor as my bed. Brother came and pulled me up and said, "Come, we four are going to sleep in my bed." Thus, four siblings, Brother, Rani, Dewan and I slept together, and our cousins scattered themselves in the other beds and on the floor until the following morning.

Sunday 18th June. It is a glorious sunny morning. It is the one day that I will always remember for the rest of my life. The morning sunshine has an unusual brilliance. The air is warm and fresh, and the sky is cloudless. It is all blue. Aunty Jenny came over to serve us breakfast. We had roti and fried plantain and bhaji and cocoa. "When all you finish eating stay right here. Uncle will come for you later. Don't go outside, all right?" she said in a stern voice. Aunty Jenny is at most times laughing and friendly.

When she sees us she always cuddles Rani and me. She calls me "fighter boy" since the incident with me being tied to the bedpost for hitting Rani. I wondered whether Uncle Jhan had quarrelled or shouted at her to upset her and put her in a vile mood.

Aunty Jenny is very serious. Her eyes are also red, seemingly from an endless bout of crying. She has no lipstick and no make-up. There are no smiles coming from her. She is wearing a long skirt and covers her head with a white "oorni" (a very long headscarf of very fine material). This is the first time that I am seeing Aunty Jenny wearing a head covering and such a long skirt. We are imprisoned in Nana's house since the last evening. We started hearing noises outside. We peeped through the jalousies and lots of people are already gathered in the yard. Men and women are pouring in and heading for the back house, i.e., Uncle Jhan's house. The men are standing in groups talking to each other quietly so we cannot hear their conversation. All the ladies are going inside Uncle Jhan's house while the men remain outside. Some of the ladies go up the front stairs, others go up the back stairs into the kitchen or into the sitting room. It seems like the entire village of Sunnyvale are here this early Sunday morning. The silent conversations are also unusual. The men are all serious-looking. There is no laughter among them. They are talking in a sombre mood. Nana is nowhere and Nanny is in the back house.

Uncle Jhan comes in, looks at all of us, and said, "All of you go by Kaki and Kaka to play." He held back Brother,

Rani, Dewan and me. "Nanny wants all of you," he said. But Nanny did not want us for quite some time. We could have also been playing with the others. I wanted to know why so many people are here but I am frightened to ask. We are not supposed to ask strangers anything. We are not allowed to question any of the adults because this will be seen as rudeness from us. I now see Nana. He is ordering men to make a long work table. He told Uncle Jhan, "Are you buaye get de hammer, an nail, an saah, an jack-plane." He went on, "Bring dem wood from over dey, and dee cedar bode from dat pile." Some men brought the 3" x 3" timber, and the ten-feet-long cedar boards. This activity is taking place under Uncle Jhan's house. "Plane dem bode. Measure dem six foot lang and saah dem," Nana ordered the men. The long workbench was duly completed, then the men started jack-planing the cedar boards.

Nana looked very angry and ordered the men in a rough manner. The men simply responded sympathetically to his orders. The shavings of the cedar boards smelled sweetly. It is genuine natural perfume. It's highly aromatic but it can be intoxicating. The planed boards are a rich reddish appearance. The two dogs, Bulla and Clara, were continually smelling the shavings. "Drive dem dag from dey. Doh ley dem eat dem shaving," shouted Nana from the other corner of the house. Men are standing in the yard and under the house. All the ladies are upstairs.

They have begun to sing bhajans. Suddenly, Madam Daniel came down with a large tray with cups of coffee and biscuits. She put down her tray and ran up to me and lifted me up and cuddled me tightly. She kissed me on both cheeks, and said, "You is me little man, you so good-looking eh. You is me little saviour. You stay dong here wid dem man an dem. Ah little busy dis minute, ah gi in dem man an dem some caffee an biscuit," she said. Two other ladies brought trays of coffee and biscuits for the men. Madam Daniel brought down a full tray of roti with pumpkin and mango takari. Three ladies followed her down with trays of roti and takari to serve all the menfolk.

I am curious to see what is going on upstairs where the ladies are singing. The kitchen is packed with ladies who are busy cooking, pouring out cups of coffee and wrapping up the roti. The ladies are eating and drinking. I tried to walk through the crowd. No one stopped me. The large sitting room is very crowded, all the bedrooms are filled with ladies, and the veranda is also packed with them. Some ladies were sitting and singing while the majority had to stand. As I was coming from the veranda, I saw a strange object in one corner of the sitting room. There are several deeyas lighted around and on the top of this object. Ladies are standing around it and blocking my view.

I got a bit closer but could not get near enough to see what it is. One lady helped me to go out of the sitting room. Aunty Jenny, Nanny and Madam Daniel were in the kitchen busy working. I came downstairs to see Nana supervising the men. At the far corner I saw Papa sitting quietly on his own. I went up to him and he immediately hugged me. He said nothing. He was very serious. I looked at him, saw his eyes were red and his face sad-looking. "Papa, why are you sitting here on your own? Why are you not helping Nana? Papa, has Nana quarrelled with you?" Papa did not answer. He simply kept shaking his head from side to side. I am wondering who may have upset Papa. Could it be Uncle Jhan? Did Nanny shout and quarrel with him as she did when Papa beat me and tied up to the bedpost? I want to ask Uncle Jhan but I fear that he will beat me. I will ask Madam Daniel if she knows. She is too busy in the kitchen, and the place is very crowded. Now, I am going to chance my luck to find out more about this mysterious object in the sitting room with the lighted deeyas placed all around it.

I went in quietly where the ladies were still singing. I slowly inched my way towards the object with the lighting deeyas. It is a very large object, covered with a white sheet. I went to lift the sheet to see what is under it. As I lifted one end of the sheet three or four ladies shouted simultaneously, "No, no, no, bayta. Doh do dat. You Mama sleeping. Ley she sleep nah. She want a rest. Leave she alone. Doh wake she up." Two of them pulled me away. They said, "Go below to see wey dem man an dem doin.'"

I am extremely disturbed at how these ladies treated me. They said, "Mama is sleeping. Doh wake she up." I sat on the step and was puzzled at what they told me. I asked myself, how can Mama be sleeping with all those deeyas

around her? Why would they be singing if she is sleeping?
Why would Mama be fully covered from head to toe with
a deeya lighted on top of her? If Mama is sleeping why are
so many people here this morning?

I looked on at the men making this lovely cedar
furniture. Nana is in full control of it. It is a box six feet
long, two feet wide and one and a half feet high. "Wey dee
cover," Nana asked. The men were working on it at the
other end. "Make sure it fit exact," Nana said. "Bring dee
sandpaper and make it smooth." With all that is going on
this morning, these ladies were lying to me. Why should
they tell me lies about my Mama? Did they think that I
believed them? Did they not think that I can think for
myself and reason things as they unfold before my eyes? I
hate them for telling such lies to me. The evidence is there
to prove that the ladies told me lies about Mama sleeping
and not to wake her up.

Papa is on his own, the whole village has assembled
this Sunday morning, Nana is busy making a six-feet-
long box. Their eyes are red, faces are sad, Papa is sitting
in his own and not talking. If Mama is sleeping, why will
the ladies be singing bhajans so loudly? Do they want to
disturb her and wake her up? Why will almost all the
villagers assemble here on this early Sunday morning?
Questions keep on ringing and recurring within me.

Mama is not sleeping. Mama is dead. I know it for
certain. I will never forgive the ladies for telling me lies.
It is the worst thing which they have done to me. Their
lies will remain in me for the rest of my life. How can

adults tell such gross lies to little children like me and assume that they have got away with it? There is so much clear evidence to prove that Mama is dead. She is sleeping forever.

Downstairs the cedar box was completed and Mr Daniel commented, "Boss you have made an absolutely beautiful coffin. It is a wonderful piece of furniture. She will rest comfortably in it. RIP Seeta."

Nana said to Uncle Jhan, "Bring a white sheet an make two pillow wid dee catton we pick dee adder day. We de pick three bag a catton las week." Nana covered the coffin with the sheet. The pundit arrived to carry out the last rites. He took a lota of water with a tulsie leaf in it. While he was saying his prayer, he sprinkled water over Mama with a mango leaf. He said to everyone, "If you know the 'Hanuman Chalisa' say it together with me." Nanny knows almost all of it, Nana and Papa know it very well. Several villagers also joined in reciting it.

The pundit sang a few bhajans and most of the crowd sang. It was time to carry Mama outside for a special ceremony. Papa, Uncle Jhan, Nana and few other men lifted Mama and placed her into the coffin. Her head rested on one of the cotton-filled pillows and the other pillow was placed by her side. Aunty Jenny, Madam Daniel and Nanny had bathed and dressed Mama in a white cotton sari, and a white "oorni" to cover her head and drape down her sides. Mr Daniel said, "Let's all sing 'Amazing Grace'." This was followed by "What a Friend we Have in Jesus". "Let us all recite the Lord's Prayer together," Mr Daniel said to the villagers. He continued, "God had sent this angel Seeta for us to be privileged for her company. Today, the 18th June, he is receiving her back in his arms in heaven. He had only lent us here for company. I will miss her as my very own. Friends, look at her, so serene and peaceful. She looks like Mother Mary."

The pundit came forward and said, "Yes, yes, she looks like Lakshmi Mata."

Papa went to Mama, kneeled down beside her and with tears raining down his cheeks, cried out, "Oh God, oh God, why you take she away from me?" He held on to both sides of the coffin and leant over Mama's face, sobbing incessantly. His tears fell on Mama's face as he cried over her. Mama's face was wet with his tears. He bowed closely over her face. He could not see her clearly because his tears blurred his vision. Papa stayed there for a while until he gradually regained his composure. He touched Mama's face while he recited the "Hanuman Chalisa." Mr Daniel had stopped Nana and Uncle Jhan from approaching Papa. "Allow him to have his last wish," he said to them.

Everyone was looking at Papa and Mama being together for the last time. Mr Daniel slowly walked up to Papa, gently placed his arms around Papa's shoulders and lifted him. He took Papa away from the coffin. Madam Daniel hugged Papa and remained by his side. Nana told everyone who wanted to see Mama must come in here. It seemed to me that the entire village of Sunnyvale queued up in an orderly manner. They came up via the front stairs, had a good look at Mama and went out via the back stairs. It was like a state funeral procession where Mama was lying in state. When the viewing was finished, Nana, Uncle Jhan, Papa and the pundit put the lid on the coffin. The white coffin with a white lid was draped with a white cotton sheet. Outside, the men had finished making the bamboo bier (a stand for the coffin). Suddenly, the weather changed. The glorious warm sunshine was replaced by darkness.

A thick black cloud came across the sun and blotted out the sunshine. It became very dark. A terrific storm blew across the house. The trees were swaying vigorously. The jalousied windows were opening and closing as the strong wind blew through the house. Drops of rain came and sprinkled over Mama. Uncle Jhan tried unsuccessfully to close the windows as the wind and rain continued to come in. The cocks began crowing steadily, the chickens were cackling ferociously, Bulla and Clara were wailing and wailing, not barking, and Tobago, the mule, was crying long and loud. It was not his usual "hee-haw" noise. He broke loose from his stable and stood outside the window where Mama was lying. He began a prolonged wailing and stretched out his neck in the direction of Mama. The rain was bucketing outside. All the animals assembled outside the window where Mama was lying. They looked up at the window while they were mourning. The cacophony of noises was deafening and continued all through the terrific storm and rain. In the midst of this another strange event occurred in the middle of the yard. From where it appeared, no one knows, from where it dropped, no one saw. The men and women were looking on in utter amazement. There it was.

A mighty long snake in the yard, strong, handsome, friendly. It coiled tightly, uncoiled and spun round and round trying to catch its own tail, spinning faster than the speed of a rotating centrifuge. It gradually and gracefully slowed down until it stopped. The snake had energised its tail. It stood erect on its tail like a ballerina standing on her toes. The snake was an eighteen-feet-tall lamp-post. It bent down its head, opened its mouth fully, stuck out its fangs in the direction of Mama. It stayed in that position for about five minutes, then squirted a few drops of its viscous creamy poison three times. The fluid landed on the jalousied window. The snake closed its mouth, bowed and nodded before straightening its head and looking up at the sky. It gradually lowered itself to the ground, coiling as before. Again, it spun round and round as it did in the first instance. This time it was equalling the speed of lightning, moving away and uncoiling with each revolution it made. It stopped and straightened its eighteen-feet length.

It slowly crawled towards the cocoa-house, which is eighteen yards long and eighteen feet wide. Before it had reached there it suddenly vanished. No one saw where the snake went although so many of us were looking at it. It was in the yard when it disappeared. The villagers were amazed. No one experienced any fear. No one wanted to strike at the snake.

At the same time the animals were still weeping and wailing in their own ways. The cacophony of noises was deafening but not intimidating. But the questions kept coming up. What kind of creature was it? Was it a real snake? Was it a spirit? If yes, well what kind of spirit was it? The pundit was in no doubt. "It is a good omen," he said. Mr Daniel said that the Spirit of the Lord God Almighty is in this house with us this morning.

"Where are the cobos?" someone shouted. "Why aren't they here also? They are spirits too!" Mr Daniel, emulating the priest, raised both his outstretched hands and said, "You have seen the Spirit of the Lord appeared before us in the shape of the celestial serpent to take away Seeta's soul, how can those evil black cobos dare enter?"

The two umbrella trees in the yard were heavily laden with brilliant red flowers. The strong wind and rain blew off the flowers. As they fell, they created a red carpet under the trees. I ran out to stand on this new carpet and put out my hands to catch flowers as they fell. My hands were filled with these lovely fresh flowers. The rain came down more heavily and the flowers continued to fall. Almost everyone shouted at me to come out of the rain. Even Nana shouted at me. "Dee buaye go get sick in dee rain," he said. I continued to put my hands out to catch flowers. I was dry throughout. The storm and rain subsided.

The snake disappeared. No one saw where it went. The animals' cries faded away. Tobago returned to his stable. I came under the house with two handfuls of red flowers, all dry. Nana was the first to feel my clothes. Every item of clothing on me was dry. No one was able to explain this phenomenon. Mr Daniel would give a biblical rationale for what we experienced this morning.

Nana came on the floral carpet. "Right here. Good. Right here," he said to Uncle Jhan and Mr Daniel. Two chairs were placed about five feet apart and facing each other. Mama was brought down and the coffin was placed on the two chairs. The four of us were dressed in new clothes, whites for all of us. Mama's coffin was draped in a white sheet. The pundit said his prayers and again sprinkled water over Mama with a mango leaf. Nana lined the four of us in order of our ages, Brother, me, Rani and Dewan. We were at the mid-section of the coffin. Nana shouted, "Seben time, seben time."

Four men raised the coffin one metre high. Nana took Brother to the coffin. One man lifted him and passed him across Mama to the other side. Another man received him and put him down. He told Brother to walk across underneath the coffin to complete the circle. Brother was lifted again, passed over to the other side and down under the coffin. This procedure was repeated seven times for each of us. On completion of this ceremony, Nana said, "Dat good, dat good, ye [i.e. Mama] eh go bodder dem chiren an dem now."

I never saw nor heard any more of the day's proceedings. No one spoke a single word of what happened to Mama. Mama's name was never mentioned in any of the two households. It was forbidden to mention Mama in the two houses. We were staying in the two houses without realising that we were not going back to Cotton Hill. We did not question why we were not going back to Cotton Hill. I had only gone to school for one week. I was so looking forward to the school outing to visit the volcano at Piparo.

On Monday morning, Nanny said to me, "No bayta, you eh go go school today. You go stay home wid me, an Rani, Dewan an dem chiren over dey. Only Bredda go go to school." I was happy to be playing with my ten cousins from the back house. Henrik and Tom came in to take me to school. They were disappointed that I was not going. At home we all ran around. We played hide and seek, merry-go-round, scooch, and role-playing carrying cane to the to the sugar cane factory. We ate in the front house.

The four of us (Brother, Rani, Dewan and I) are now living permanently together with Nanny and Nana. Nana built a house for Papa in West Hill. None of us will ever be going back to Cotton Hill to live. I am already missing Cotton Hill because of the natural beauty of the cotton fields up there. The Daniels are enjoying such beauty. From Nanny's house we can hear Mr Daniel playing his saxophone and trumpet. We would watch the children going to and coming from school every day. I help Nanny to sweep the yard every day. We will go in the back garden and dig up eddoes, sweet potatoes and pick peas. I help Nanny to feed the fowls every morning and evening. We also sit down and shell corn by the cocoa-house. When Brother comes from school he does not tell me what he has learnt or is learning. "When you start going to school you will learn for yourself," he says to me. I tell him, "You are mean." Instead he would bring out our bats and ball to play. There is so much activity at Nana's house, I had forgotten about Mama. Nanny treated us like Mama. She replaced Mama. Further, having ten cousins with whom to play, any thoughts of Mama were forgotten by me.

One day we were playing in the yard and I heard a chirping or tweeting sound coming out of the croton hedge. The hedge was very thick so it was not easy to see inside it. Everyone had run away. The tweeting was going on and on. I thought that it might be a little birdy missing its mother. I got closer to the hedge and moved a few branches and leaves to see if I can get a glimpse of this little birdy. As I moved another branch, the chirping was very loud. My face was inches away from the birdy's open beak. A snake had grabbed the birdy in its mouth and it was going to swallow the birdy. It was bawling for its life.

I screamed out in fright, "Nanny, Nanny, a snake, a snake over there in the hedge. It is swallowing a birdy." Nanny got a long stick. She listened to find out from where the birdy's cry was coming. Nanny smacked the hedge with as much force as she could muster. The snake, alarmed by the strike, dropped the birdy and disappeared. Nanny gently picked up the little fledgling. It was not fully covered with feathers as yet. The bird is still crying having escaped from death. Nanny fed it drops of water at first. She gave it a little morsel of bread soaked in milk. Nanny said that it may not live because of the bite it received from the snake. "Ley he have a lil res an ah go feed 'im again," she said.

It was one year later when Nanny said that I will start attending school. Throughout the past year no one ever mentioned Mama or talked about her. It was the biggest taboo subject in both houses. One day I inadvertently mentioned Mama helping Nanny when she used to come here. Nanny shouted at me in a vile temper, "Shut you mouth, doh say dat again. Ah doh want to hear you caal you Mama."

Nanny, Nana, Uncle Jhan and Aunty Jenny do not want Papa to come into the yard again since the fight with Uncle Jhan. Nanny, Mussy, Uncle Jhan and Aunty Jenny drove him out like a dog. Mussy is Mama's sister. Uncle Jhan threatened to chop him up if he ever crosses the yard to come here in future.

I have vivid memories of that fight. Papa had come to see us. We were in Uncle's house in the veranda. Everything was going well. Papa and Uncle had a few drinks of alcohol. A row developed, and Uncle Jhan blamed Papa for Mama's death. "You are the cause of Seeta to die. You make she work so hard even though she was pregnant. You make her go in the garden every goddamn day," he said to Papa. Papa was incensed by the accusation. He got up from his chair.

Uncle Jhan quickly kicked Papa and punched him in his face. They grappled together, and was about to come down the stairs. They exchanged several punches on the landing. Nanny, Mussy and Aunty Jenny were bawling at them to stop. Uncle Jhan leant on Papa and pushed him over the bannister. Papa fell on the ground and the three women shouted and quarrelled with him.

Then Nanny, Aunty Jenny and Mussy drove Papa out of the yard. Nanny shouted, "Doh come back here. Doh crass me yard again."

Uncle Jhan took up the sugar cane cutting cutlass, and brandished it at Papa. "If you ever cross this yard and I see you here I am going to chop you up into mincemeat." The glittering blade continued to be waved at Papa. Our Papa will not be able to see us again. We will not be able to see him as well. This is a devastating blow for Papa and us four siblings. He lost Mama and now he is about to lose his children. The horrible names they call Papa continued. None of them was thinking of us when they use these derogatory remarks against Papa. They kept saying these in front of us. I feel humiliated and ashamed when I hear such nasty remarks about Papa. We cannot open our mouths to say anything, because we will be beaten by them.

Whenever Nanny sees Papa walking along the road she would say, "Look at you fadder, he eh have no shame. He is a drunkard, an walkin' about like a beggar. Dee man doh go an do no wok in dee gyarden since you Mama gaan." This is what I have endured from Nanny for many years while living here. She would never say these things to Brother. They were always directed at me, and sometimes at Rani. The truth is a painful pill to digest for any adult, and even more so for young three- and five-year-olds like Rani and me respectively.

I sometimes wonder if Nanny doesn't think that we do have feelings too. We do get hurt when they say such things to us. Have they, that is, Nana, Nanny, Aunty Jenny and Uncle Jhan, ever sat back and considered the tumultuous psychological injury and hurt they are inflicting on us? Have they considered what permanent scars they are imprinting on us? Have they ever thought of Papa's inner feelings where he has lost Mama for ever and lost contact with his children as well? Have they ever thought that he is suffering immense bereavement and depression and this may take years to heal? He has to cope with it entirely on his own!

The village has no bereavement or counselling service. The midwifery and obstetric services are woefully inadequate in this remote village of Sunnyvale. Is Uncle Jhan not aware from his education that there is a high rate of infant mortality and maternal mortality here because of the difficulties in accessing what services are available to the community, and these may have contributed to Mama's death? Therefore, where can Papa turn for help? Is it any surprise to them that Papa wanders up and down the road aimlessly? Is it any surprise that he lacks motivation, and neglects himself? Have they considered how depressed Papa is at this critical phase in his life? No one has considered these painful issues which Papa is suffering, but they are quite ready to knock him down and treat him as an outcast. Uncle Jhan and his ten children are living as one big happy family. They are a unified lot. What about us four siblings? We are a broken and fragmented group. Papa is without Mama and us, his four children.

The wonderful opportunity we have is that Nanny and Nana have taken all of us. We must show our gratitude to Nana and Nanny for bringing us up. We must bear silently the insults they give Papa. Is it their motive for us to break our ties with Papa? These are very tough issues for us to handle.

When Papa is walking along the road sometimes all four of us will run to the roadside to meet him. We would surround him and hold on to him clinging on to him like bees on their honeycomb. He would give us the biggest, the broadest, the happiest smile we could ever dream of having. Simply, his smile and his touch meant so much for us. We could not get enough of each other. Sometimes, he would attend a puja (a Hindu prayer) in the village. When he gets his "prasad", he would not open his packet, but he would bring it for us to share among ourselves.

At the prayers, he usually helps the pundit to perform part of the ceremony. He is very knowledgeable in his religious work. The villagers are always pleased when he attends their pujas. They feel confident that the pundit will perform a full service, and not make any shortcuts during the service. According to the Hindu tradition, Papa's caste has prevented him from becoming a fully ordained pundit. The villagers are aware of this, but accept him for his degree of expertise and sincerity. As a result, he frequently brings prasad for us just as he received it at the prayer.

Nanny notices our love for Papa and the way we cling on to him at the roadside. She does not prevent us from meeting him at the roadside, but only allows it for a short moment. Within five minutes of our meeting Papa, Nanny would come in the middle of the yard and look at us. She says nothing at this moment. She simply wants to make her presence known and felt. She is in control of us, not Papa. Nanny will go in the kitchen and call us loud and sharp. "What aal you doin by dee road, come out of dey right now." The tone of her voice tells us that we have had enough time at the roadside with Papa.

He would say, "Go, go, you Nanny calling you. Ah go come back again." He goes away quietly with a cool smile on his face. He does not speak to anyone as he walks along the road, not even to his good neighbour Mr Daniel. The war may be coming to an end according to Mr Daniel, as foodstuffs are getting better in the shop, the Zeppelins have stopped flying across our village, the ration cards are being phased out, but our contacts with Papa are increasingly rationed. There are no indications that this will improve. Papa is not allowed to come in since the fight with Uncle Jhan. He continued to blame Papa for Mama's death. He was telling Nanny and Mussy, "Dat man mus pay for his deeds. He is the cause for Seeta, my sister, to die so young. She was only twenty-three years old with the fifth child in her belly. Dat is what hurt me so much today." Nanny said, "Nah taak like dat nah, dee chiren dah hear wey you say."

Yes, indeed it was a thunderbolt which struck

through my heart and my brain. It was very painful to hear this statement from Uncle Jhan. I will remember this for the rest of my life from the age of five years. I will always remember these numbers, five (me), twenty-three (Mama) and fifth child (zero, unborn). How did Papa cause Mama to die? What did Papa do to Mama? Is Uncle Jhan speaking the truth? Is he wrongly accusing Papa for Mama's death?

The fleeting moments of being with Papa are treasured on both sides, with Papa and with us. On occasions while we are playing and running around in the yard our cousins will see Papa walking along the road. They will say, "Look, your father is by the roadside. See how he is looking at all of you." They will come with us half way and stand up and wait for us. We will tell him briefly what game we are playing. Innocently, yes, innocently and spontaneously we will say to him, "Papa come and play with us." We will pull him into the yard but he will resist. Papa would simply say in a sympathetic and grieving manner, "Another time, not now." He will give us his very broad smile as he always does. He would slowly walk away before Nanny would be calling us.

This is the pattern of our relationship with Papa for many years while growing up by Nanny and Nana. Of course, our cousins view him as a stranger and do not talk to him. That is why they stay away when we go to meet Papa at the roadside. I can also feel the contempt which Nanny holds for Papa by continually casting aspersions on him. She and Aunty Jenny seem oblivious to the damaging effects of how these derogatory remarks are impacting on us. Needless to say, they continue and we have to absorb and digest these remarks without demonstrating any rebellious Stomach Qi. Instead of narrowing the gap, making amends, becoming more tolerant, their animosity towards Papa increases exponentially. At five years of age I can see this. Do you mean the adults, namely, Nanny, Nana, Aunty Jenny and Uncle Jhan, are unable to see this as well? They still bear it in their minds about the big fight Papa had with Uncle Jhan. It seems to me that they will never forgive Papa for that.

I do sit and reflect on many questions which are in my mind. Why have they become so hard against Papa? Why must Aunty Jenny, Uncle Jhan and Nanny tell me about Papa's conduct as a wanderer, a beggar, a lazy good-for-nothing, and a drunkard on the road. Do they want us to feel ashamed of our own father and break ties with him? Regarding Mama, no one is prepared to mention her name. Why? Why? Is she so quickly forgotten? Do they think that it will hurt us more if they mention her to us? Or, are they themselves so distraught and bereft in their minds that they cannot bear to mention or talk about Mama? Is this their coping mechanism for the loss of Mama? For how long will they suppress all thoughts of Mama? They behave as though Mama was never born on this earth.

It seems to me that their motto is: "Life must go on regardless and forget the past." Therefore, let us get on with the business of everyday life. Nana goes to the garden as usual. He has at least half a dozen men working in the fields. He has two permanent workers, namely, Sam and Stamford. Sam is east Indian like Nana and Stamford is Spanish. Both are very dedicated and loyal workers. They live approximately four miles away from Nana. They walk from their home to Nana's house every working day. This may include a Sunday sometimes. Sam is a polio victim with one foot affected. Therefore, he walks with a limp. He has his wife and two young children. Stamford is a well-built, muscular, tall and fair person. He is single. There are lots of fruit trees all around his house. Both of them are very friendly and easy-going. They are considered as an extension of Nana's family. The others are all ad hoc workers.

Nana has approximately twenty-five acres of sugar cane fields dotted around in small parcels. The largest block is a six-acre one. His workers are dispersed in the various fields but Sam and Stamford always work together with Nana. The home compound including the back house is approximately one acre. The yard is about seventy-five metres long. It extends from the road to the end of the cocoa-house at the back. At this point there is a long shed. Part of it is the mule's stable, called "the mule pen" or Tobago pen. The mule was brought from Tobago. The remaining part of the building is for shelling corn (dried maize). The cocoa-house (eighteen yards by eighteen feet) is used for drying corn, cocoa, coffee and rice. It runs on rails.

Nana built the two houses. Uncle Jhan's house was

first. It is a huge wooden building thirty feet by thirty feet with large hardwood posts and galvanised roofing. The largest post is six feet in circumference and ten feet high. This is in stark contrast to our cosy little carat-roofed mud house at Cotton Hill. There is a long croton hedge from the road to the cocoa-house spanning two houses. Uncle Jhan's house has flowering plants all around the veranda. Aunty Jenny loves flowers and she tends to the plants better than she cares for her ten children, Nanny would say to us. Nana's house is a large brick building with three sets of stairs to the front and back. The house is ten yards from the road. One of Nana's rules is that no one must go out of the house after 6.00pm. This rule is very closely monitored by Nana. He sits and relaxes outside and no one dares to pass by. Sometimes he will be on guard duty from 5.30pm sitting in the shade against the tall croton hedge. I am learning more of his home rules as the weeks and months pass by.

The next interesting rule is that all communication must be through a bureaucratic channel. If we want anything by way of clothes or toys or cakes we must ask Nanny who will tell Nana who will get them for us. He enjoys this style of leadership. Nana hardly ever speaks to us directly. The only time he does speak to us is when he is landing belts or sticks on our backsides or our limbs. The regular sentences go like this, "Are you buaye [i.e. me] nor dah listen," or "Are you buaye too harden [stubborn]," or "Are you buaye like to play too much." These coincide with the blows which sound like, "Whap! Whap! Tie!

Tie! Tie!" The sounds of the belts are far more terrifying on their own than the effects they have on my skin.

The pain from these blows is excruciating and burning like fire. It feels that it will last all day. My back or legs or buttocks become sore and tender to touch. It is difficult to sit comfortably because of the pain especially from my buttocks. Well, if you think Mr Daniel beats his wife and children severely, you simply need to multiply that by a factor of ten to grasp the severity of Nana's beatings. Although we are living here, I find it difficult to call it "home" or "my home" as Brother says. It is his home because he has been living here since he was six months of age.

Brother is the darling of the house. He is loved and adored by every one of the adults in the two households. I can see that there is a clear pattern of favouritism existing. Nanny's excuse, or her rationale, or her explanation for this is, "Well you see Bredda is big." Nanny expects us to simply accept this and live with it as one big happy family. Everything Brother has asked for, Nana gets it for him. Also, Nanny will give him money to go and buy sweet drinks or ice cream. We have been living here for a few months now and I see that this is the practice. When Rani or I ask Nanny for something similar we are told that she will tell Nana to get it for us. Brother does not see it this way, because his requests are granted to him almost straight away. I have decided to adopt a different strategy. From now on whenever we want something, I will ask Brother to get it for all of us. Nanny will be hard pressed to deny his request. Brother and I have made a pact to use this strategy at all times in future so we all can get the same things.

Nana's house is one with foodstuffs, fruits and vegetables and also plenty of work to do. There is also plenty of space to run and hide, especially when the work is too much to do. It is so different from our life at Cotton Hill. The villagers say that Nana is a big cane farmer. Nana is a trader in corn. He buys the dried corn when it is plentiful in the village, shells it, barrels the grains, sells the shelled corn at an opportune moment, at premium prices in the Port of Spain market when corn is a scarce commodity. Nana had bought a hundred steel barrels from the sugar estate when the factory closed down. The factory was close to the pond.

Those barrels were used for molasses, a by-product of the sugar cane industry. Nana also bought the land where the factory was situated on condition that he planted sugar cane there. He plants rice during the rainy season, vegetables are grown all year round. These ventures are profitable and rewarding except when severe blight strikes. At the back of the kitchen there is a nursery with tomato, peppers and aubergine plants for planting out in the fields. Every six to eight weeks another batch of seeds is sown and will be ready to plant out in the fields. There are two huge trees resembling each other at the back of the kitchen. I can hardly tell the difference between them when there are no fruits in them. One is a breadfruit tree and the other is a shataigne tree. A few branches of this tree lean on to the kitchen window. When it is bearing fruits we can easily stretch our hands out of the window and grab a shataigne to cook. Brother keeps Nana's company, and Nana teaches him about these gardening activities. Nana sees Brother as his protégé.

The corn-shelling activity takes place in the large shed and in the cocoa-house. There are two manually operated corn mills to shell the dried corn ears. Unfortunately, these machines leave grains of corn at both ends of the cobs. This is another painstaking manual procedure to remove all these grains. Nana and his two permanent key workers (Brother and I) made graters from kerosene tins. These tins were cut longitudinally in half, straightened, and hundreds and hundreds of holes made in them. The trio made twenty graters in the course of one week. These are invaluable and indispensable investment tools. They are strong and durable, comfortably outlasting a generation of Nana's grandchildren.

When the workers shell corn there is a mountain of corn cobs heaped up. The cobs are called "corn-hux" by Nana, Nanny and all the workers. I will use their terminology when referring to the corn cobs. Nanny organises all the grandchildren to grab a grater. We all sit in a semicircle so that Nanny can observe all of us. Interestingly, Aunty Jenny joins us when she feels like doing so. Nanny demonstrates how we must remove the remaining corn grains from the corn-hux.

"Waatch dee grater and you finger. Doh grate you finger. Take out aal dee grain ah carn from dee hux. An mine you finger, ah say." These are the instructions which we must follow in order to perform a safe job. As soon as one mountain of corn hux is almost cleared, the workers create another mountain for us. As I am at home with Nanny my job starts after Brother goes to school in the morning. Rani stays with Nanny to learn to cook, wash and clean the house. It is optional for my cousins to sit with me while I am at work. I cannot idle because Aunty Jenny monitors me from her kitchen window. She has the authority to come and give me a belting if I waste time. Nanny will come later to check on how much I have accomplished thus far. She praises me when she sees that I have done a big pile of hux. "Bayta, you goin' good. Ley we sit dong an eat something nah. Den you go start again. But ley me see you finger nah. Good buaye. You larnin dee jab good." There are no grater cuts or grazes on my fingers. The work is continuous for three to four months in the year. Sometimes Aunty Jenny calls away her children quickly if they are working together with me. Nanny gets annoyed with her, "Ley dee chiren do some wok nah gyal. Dee wok eh go kill dem. Ye good foo dem to larn a lil wok." Nanny overrides and makes them stay. "Ent aal you dah get cake an aal wen Nana dah bring?" Nanny would say to them. Some of the hux is used for firewood in cooking. The rest of it remains in the back garden to decompose into compost and is recycled as fertiliser for the vegetables.

The shelled corn is dried, aired and fanned in the cocoa-house. Nanny has taught me how to fan the corn so that it is free of particles. The corn is ready to barrel and store. The barrels have screw caps fitted to seal them. Nana made a hole in the floor of the cocoa-house through which he funnels the grains directly into the barrels below the cocoa-house. When each barrel is filled it is capped and rolled away. We pour the grains through the hole and the workers do the filling below. At the end of this activity, seventy to eighty barrels of grains are stored below the cocoa-house. The rainy season activity is rice planting and harvesting. This is also another onerous activity. In Trinidad lagoon rice is often grown, Nana has approximately six acres of flat lowlands. These contain water in the rainy season, which begins in June or July and ends in October or November. Nana's lowlands are divided into several small sections. These are the "kolas". They are separated by banks or small dams called "mayri". The mayri enables water to be retained in the kola to facilitate growth of the rice nursery.

Every kola is prepared before any rice planting takes place. Nana hires farmers with bulls to plough the kola, after it is cleaned by his workers. He also uses the mule to pull our plough. He gives Brother and me the job of guiding the plough while he drives the mule. This is very tedious because we cannot rest while Nana is driving the mule. We cannot tell him to stop so that we can have a rest. My arms ache while holding on to the plough while Nana drives on the mule. All the cut grass is heaped together to decay. It will be used as compost for the vegetables.

The other farmers seem to guide their ploughs and

bulls effortlessly and smoothly. As each kola is ploughed another bull will be pulling a leveller. This smooths the waterlogged soil. Following this, Nana's workers will plant the rice nurseries. Nana took Brother and me into the kola to see the entire process. "Ah go bring are you buaye again wen dee man an dem go cut dee rice. Ah you buaye go larn to plant rice an aal. You go see how dee man an dem da cut dee rice, an how dey da beat dee rice to get dee dhaan. Ah go cut dee rice wen ye ripe in November," Nana said to us. I am looking forward to seeing the harvesting being carried out. This is a muddy and messy type of work. The rice nurseries will be planted in bundles of ten to twelve about six to nine inches apart and kept in water. I am seeing and experiencing the activity first-hand in these water-filled lagoons. This on-site learning is real learning, and it is learning through the hard way. Although it is exhausting work, I am finding the experience to be a rather stimulating one. It will stick in my head forever.

CHAPTER 5

NANNY SAID TO ME, "You getting big now, an you go go to school nex week."

I asked her, "Will the Daniel boys be coming to take me to school, Nanny?"

Nanny said, "No, Bredda go carry you. Ye [Brother] been gwain in dee school aready."

I remember a few things about school – things like the teachers with whips, sand trays and gigger fleas in the playground. Old MacDonald and lots of children. I am glad that I will be getting away from sitting behind that grater every day grating off the remaining corn grains from the ends of the cobs. It is a very tiring job. It will be a big relief for me to be in school. Brother does not tell me much about school. Nanny had other plans for me when she said that I am big now. It meant that more work will be added on to our daily routine. Yes, indeed, I am coming out of the frying pot and landing inside her choolha (earthen fireside).

Nana bought four grass knives and two pairs of wellington boots for Brother and me. He took us to Floodie, the village tailor, who measured us each for a pair of khaki trousers to be of mid-tibial length. These trousers were ready to wear within forty-eight hours. When Dr Luo saw them he smiled, "This is the latest fashion: 'Tiao Kou to Stomach 38, and Fenglong to Stomach 40' length trousers. You boys are trendy." He seems to use a rather unusual form of measurement. These are two acupoints on the Stomach meridian.

At home, Nanny said to Brother and me, "From tomarrow maarnin' dee two ah you go get up befoh 6.00 a'clack, put an you new pants, an put an you taal boots. Dee pants go fit inside dee boots. Da go cover up you whole leg so you eh go get wet wid dee maarnin dew." We were each given one of Nana's old working hats. Those oversize hats almost covered our eyes, but Nanny insisted that we must wear them. I must say that we looked like two young Victorian work boys of the Charles Dickens era.

Nanny said to us, "You go go an cut a bundle of grass with dee grass knife. Put it an you head an bring it for dee mule." This is the first of our morning duties as from tomorrow. When I return with my bundle, I have to clean out the stable and wash it. I leave it to dry. We have breakfast and then go and shell two barrels of corn. Brother usually turns the handle of the mill and I feed the ears of corn into the nozzles of the mill. After finishing this we get ourselves ready to go to school.

After coming home from school, I have to spread straw in the stable as a bed on which the mule will sleep during the night. We must feed Tobago his oatmeal and molasses water, and give him a box of "chop-chop" [sugar cane tops in very small chips] for his evening meal. Lastly, his evening supper will be the two bundles of grass we had brought in the morning. Finally, we sit and grate off the corn grains for another half an hour. When this is done we bathe and get ready for our evening meal. Following this we sit down to do our school homework. Brother and I will be carrying out this daily routine for years and years to come while we are living with Nanny and Nana. I am now confident in walking to school all alone. I always remember the teacher's warning, "Please walk on the right side of the road and walk in Indian file."

At last I have come to realise what Nanny meant when she told me that I am big now. Our daily number of tasks before and after school is the worst recipe to study effectively. Completing our schoolwork has the lowest priority in this house. How can we sit down to study and retain any information when we are so physically and mentally tired? Brother and I are now viewed as two additional permanent members of Nana's work team. He has provided us with the necessary resources so that we are adequately protected to carry out our tasks. The time Nana had spent showing us how to grow vegetables and plant sugar cane and rice and nurture them while they are growing was his investment to prepare us for our long-term work and his gain.

Today is Monday and it is the first day of the new term. But there is no school because the teachers are having an inset day. I will be going back to school from tomorrow, the 18th.

"Wash you han'an foot," Nanny said. I was dressed in new school clothes. Nanny told Brother to hold my hand as we walked to school. Brother told me to walk in front of him and do not run. We arrived early. Tom and Henrik came and stayed with me. Brother went to play with his friends. The children were running and playing all over the playground. The nine o'clock school bell rang. Everyone adheres to the usual daily routine of lining up, inspection, which may be followed by beatings, and an orderly walk to the children's classes.

Teacher Nick is our teacher. I remember him, but he does not remember me. We are still using sand trays as last year. We learn to read and write on the sand trays. We learn the alphabet and to count up to twenty-five. We also learn how to add, take away, the times tables, and how to share. The gigger fleas are still popping up from one tray on to another or onto the ground. They continue to be a cause of discomfort for us while we are writing. We use our fingers to write in these sand trays. Teacher Nick said that I will be going to another class when we return after Christmas.

My new class is first primer. From now onwards I have had a meteoric rise to Standard 5, which is one of the examination classes. In order to reach there quickly, I skipped second primer, second standard and fourth standard. Interestingly, they are all even numbers. *"Am I the only odd one out?"* I asked myself.

Brother and I carry out our work at home as usual. It is our set routine. Sometimes we have work which is more like fun than work. For example, when we do not get any oil from the shop Nanny turns to making homemade coconut oil. This Saturday afternoon is one such fun occasion.

SATURDAY 18TH

We collected forty-five dry coconuts from under the trees. I used Nana's cutlass to cut open the coconut in three sections. It is easier to scoop out the copra by this method. We grated the dry kernels in a rather quicker time than I had anticipated. The great advantage for Nanny is that there is no shortage of manpower, and no shortage of graters – there are fourteen grandchildren and sixteen graters. Every one of us grabs a grater and we all sit in a circle under the red flamboyant shady tree. We sing along while we grate the coconut. We munch pieces of the kernels as we grate. We are quite good at using the graters because we use the same graters to grate off the corn grains from the ends of the corn-hux.

It is Nanny's orders which make us sit behind graters to grate the copra. When the grating is finished, Nanny gets a large fireside in the yard going. This is where Mama's coffin was placed and the four of us were made to go up, over and across, down and under the coffin seven times. On this occasion there is no red floral carpet. We use the large iron pot. This is usually lent to the villagers to cook large amounts of food at weddings and prayers. Nanny gets four of us to wash our feet thoroughly and go into the pot and massage the grated copra to help release the vegetable fat and speed up the process. The others have to massage by hand. It is good fun doing it both ways. We love dancing in the pot like Bacchus dancing on his grapes. We collect wood, corn-hux and dried coconut shell fibres for the fire. Water is added to the well-massaged grated copra and well stirred. This is now cooked for two to three hours stirring the mixture regularly.

It requires a great amount of heat to evaporate the steam and to leave home-made coconut oil and its residue. Nanny calls this tawny residue the "ghu-ghu-ree". These sediments are the burnt flakes of coconut. They taste sweet, and sweeter when sugar is added to it. When this operation is seen for the first time, there is a height of curiosity and expectancy about how the coconut oil is extracted from the grated nuts. Nanny shows us how to keep on turning the stew as it is cooking. The smell of coconut oil oozes out from the pot as the fluid changes from white coconut-milk cream to the tawny appearance. This is like carrying out a home experiment where a chemical reaction is taking place under intense heat. This is an advantage we have over the town children to carry out such home experiments. When the oil is cooled Nanny bottles it in clean sterilised bottles.

This learning serves me well throughout my future years. Again, I must say that this practical on-site learning is a lifelong experience. I can use this experience to make coconut oil at any time or anywhere in the future. If anyone thinks seriously about it, this can also become a lucrative start-up business for any budding entrepreneur. We have the knowledge, the skills, the machinery and the resources – the manpower and coconuts.

Nana's friend Atta came to visit Nana. He brought wild meat in the form of venison, wild boar and agouti, and cocoa beans. Nanny and Rani got busy in the kitchen to have some of the meat for dinner.

Nanny would dry and roast the cocoa beans and pound them in her "moosarr"or "ochree", i.e. mortar and pestle. The pounded beans eventually become very soft as a paste. Nanny makes small oval-shaped rugby ball versions with the cocoa paste and allows them to dry. They are then ready to be grated into granules for our cocoa drink. Whenever she pounds the beans, we would be elsewhere playing games in the yard. Therefore, I had not seen the entire process.

Nanny gave me the job of pounding the cocoa beans, while they were busy in the kitchen with the dinner. I filled the ochree with the freshly roasted cocoa beans. I chewed one of the hot beans to find out the taste. The bean was slightly bitter. This was followed by a sweet taste. It is not one that I would recommend as a delicacy. However, these hot freshly roasted dark brown beans are fragrantly aromatic. I began the manual labour of pounding the beans. If I pound them too forcefully, they pop out of the ochree unto to the ground. I put the

This is the mortar and pestle as we know it. It was used for pounding cocoa and coffee beans and boiled green plantain and rice. This okhree is made out of the solid hard wood poui. It was a similarly made okhree in which Usati was pounding the cocoa beans. When the beans were not getting moist and soft he had poured water into the okhree thus wrecking the beans. He received a thorough beating from his nanny when she saw what he did. He was six years old. This okhree pictured is thought to be more than one hundred years old.

This is a photo of an oil painting on canvas of an elderly woman pounding cocoa beans. The original painting is in colour and measures three feet by four feet. It is painted by artist and sculptor Habib Jahoor in Trinidad.

ochree on a clean sheet to prevent the beans getting on the ground. The pounding continues arduously until my arms begin to ache.

Nanny is not coming to check on my progress because she is very busy in the kitchen. Brother doesn't know anything about pounding cocoa beans as he is not around when Nanny does the pounding. I took a rest to ease my arms. I looked at the beans and they seemed to be as whole as when I put them in at the start. *Perhaps I am doing it wrong?* I thought to myself. *How else am I to use this mortar and pestle?* I felt the beans and they were slightly warm. Therefore, they are still emitting heat. I started pounding again, observing the beans rather closely to detect any changes. The beans began to break up. Encouraged by this I continued pounding. No further changes occurred apart from more beans being broken up. I asked myself, *how do these beans become moist and soft from their present dry state? How does Nanny get the beans to become so moist and soft? I know that to soften something I can add water to it.* Therefore, I half-filled the ochree with rainwater and continued the pounding the cocoa beans.

Ten minutes later, Nanny walked down the front kitchen stairs to check on the beans status.

"Dey saft, bayta?" she asked.

"No Nanny, the beans are not getting soft. I have been pounding them for such a long time that my arms are now aching," I replied. She held the ochree and looked at the beans. She turned around and grabbed a stick, held me, and started firing blows on my bottom. They seemed to

This was an absolutely beautifully designed and crafted white glazed ceramic ink container. It was filled with black ink. The top surface had a small hole in the middle and an extended ledge all around it. Each long desk had three holes into which the ink wells were housed. The extended ledge around it prevented the ink well from falling through the hole in the desk. The writing pens were in two parts. One was the pen shaft. At one end a metal nib holder was fitted. The tin nib would be fitted into the nib holder and there we had a fully writing pen. Blotting paper was used to mop up any surplus ink while writing to present neat, clean and tidy written work. Thus blotting paper was an essential accompaniment while writing with the pen and ink. The children started writing with a pen from Standard one. Invariably, the children's fingers were stained with ink while writing. The ink well pictured is taken from an original 1940's early relic.

be endless. Crying as loud as I could, she did not stop as the sticks fell on my baackside. I tried to pull away from Nanny but I couldn't. Then Nanny asked, "Who tell you to put waatar in dee bean an dem? You eh see how ah da do it? You gaan an spail aal dee bean now. If you Nana dee see dis ye go gi you more licks. You na da listen. You too harden. You too hurry to go an play," Nanny said. Nanny has not yet told me how these dry cocoa beans become moist and soft.

She poured out the water from the ochree, took the beans in the kitchen to dry them under very low heat since they were already roasted. Nanny said to me, "Go an pong dee bean till ye go get saft by yeself. Study pong it, den ye go get saft, you hear me dis time?" she commanded. Nanny made me pound those redried cocoa beans all on my own until my arms were aching me. All the beans were broken up so I pounded more quickly. I felt them and they were still warm. Suddenly, I actually saw magic. The beans were becoming moist and warm. It's fascinating, and interesting. The "Aha" principle struck me. The continuous pounding of the beans made them shed tears just like me. I forgot the beating I had just received from Nanny. I continued pounding until the smashed up cocoa beans were becoming a soft, sticky, moist paste. I did not want Nanny to help me to make the oval-shaped rugby balls with the moistened cocoa beans. When Nanny came this time, she saw an array of the balls of cocoa placed on the tray. She said, "Dat good, bayta. You dah larn ah good lesson today." Yes indeed, it was a good lesson for me in more than one way. The intriguing question in me has not been answered. How do these hot dry beans change from one texture to another by merely pounding them continuously? None of the adults in either house was able to give me a satisfactory answer. I was six years old at the time. More garden work continued through the years.

Teacher Preim is our Standard 1 teacher. Sir is very friendly. He has a whip but he does not beat any children with it. He uses it as his blackboard pointer. He is the only teacher in the school who does not beat any children. Instead, he hits his desk with a loud bang using a ruler. That quietens our class immediately, and everyone is attentive. Then he speaks in a very soft voice. This means that we have to pay close attention to hear what he is saying.

This is the first time that I am using a pen and ink. We have to dip the pen nib into an inkwell which is embedded in the long bench. Each bench contains three inkwells. These are on our students' desks. There are five children cramped in each bench. We are shown how to use blotting paper while we are writing. This is to prevent blotchy and messy work. Teacher Preim is softly spoken, calm, pleasant and very approachable. Sometimes he makes interesting jokes. He has a library of stories accrued in his head. He supports and encourages us to read. "You must read every day and do read aloud. Make it your habit to read every day. It will certainly improve your vocabulary and writing skills. Read loud and clear for your brothers, sisters and parents. This will give you confidence in public speaking later on."

In my case I cannot approach Nana to read for him, and Nanny does not want to hear a single word from me. Nanny repeatedly tells me her same beautiful phrase every time I approach her to read for her. She puts her hand to her lips and say, "kutch nah bole, kutch nah bole." I simply have to walk away to approach another member of the family. Brother is always very busy, Rani is in the kitchen with Nanny, and Dewan is too small to understand. My cousins ridicule me when I read aloud for them. I resort to my regular students, the fat mahogany posts in Uncle Jhan's house. These posts are passive listeners and silent recipients of my rather verbal diarrhoea. I do not expect any response from them whether it's good, bad or indifferent. That is how I practise my reading aloud every day. I also play teacher and beat the hell out of these posts following the beatings which I get at home and at school. These posts will remain standing as the rock of Gibraltar while I exhaust myself in beating them. Sweat will be streaming down my face and I feel relieved from this activity. This is my displacement of anger.

One day, teacher Preim stopped all work and asked us to pay attention. Everyone has come in today. He said, "I am going to ask all forty of you the same question. I am going to write down each answer on the blackboard. OK? We will start from the front here and work our way to the back. OK?" I am sitting at the back in the far right-hand corner of the class. In this corner there are two floorboards with rotted ends. These act like springboards of a swimming pool.

Teacher Preim began his survey. He called out to James and said, "James, what would you like to be when you leave school? Speak loudly so that all those at the back of the class can hear you. Do you understand?"

James replied, "Yes, sir," very loudly at the top of his voice. James stood up and turned around to face the class. He said, "Sir, when I grow up and leave school, I will be going to help my father work in the garden. Papa said he will buy a bull for me to take out the cane." Teacher Preim wrote down his answer on the blackboard – sugar cane farmer.

Teacher Preim continued, "Next, Marie, what would you like to be when you leave school?" Marie followed James and shouted out, "Sir, I have to help my mother to cook, wash, clean the house and sew my clothes. Mama said when I get big she will marry me to a rich man." Teacher Preim wrote on the blackboard – housewife.

The questions and answers swept through the class until it was my turn. I was the last child to answer. When we looked at the blackboard, we found that all the boys would be following in their fathers' footsteps. Some of them hoped to be working in the oil industry because their fathers were working there. Mr Daniel was one such person. The girls will be doing domestic work and learning to sew and may become seamstresses and eventually full-time housewives. Ninety per cent of the boys were heading for the sugar cane fields with their fathers. Such were the aspirations of the children in my class. They will be of the lower socio-economic class.

Teacher Preim continued, "Now, you at the back of the class and in the far right-hand corner. Every time I look at you I see that you are taking rides on the two rotten floorboards. What have you got to tell us about when you grow up? Come up to the front and face the class," said Teacher Preim. I walked up to the front of the class and stood next to teacher Preim. He pointed his whip at me, "What would you like to be when you grow up and leave school? Please, do not whisper or murmur. Do make sure that everyone can hear what you have to say."

I looked at him, pointed both my index fingers at him and shouted loudly, assertively and clearly, "Sir, I want to be a teacher like you!"

Teacher Preim was shocked and taken by surprise by my answer. His eyes lit up, his face flushed and a very big smile was followed by a loud burst of laughter. He hugged me up in delight. The children also laughed at me saying, "You… a… teacher!" When the class quietened down, he sent me back to my seat. Then he walked to the teacher of the class next to our class, which was Standard 2. Teacher Preim told him what I said. He was still smiling. The Standard 3 teacher joined in and the three of them were looking at me and laughing.

I felt embarrassed. My answer was spontaneous and immediate. I did not think of what I had said. It was like an automatic reflex. Teacher Preim returned to our class still smiling. He said to me in a warm and prophetical manner, "You are not going to be a teacher like me, oh no! You are going to be a much greater teacher than me. You are going to be a teacher of teachers!" He went on, "I will be keeping this blackboard record of all of you to see where you all are in the next ten years from now. And as for you, Usati, I will be keeping my beedy eyes on you." He called me up to his desk and said that they would be promoting me directly to Standard 3. "When you leave my class, you will be going into teacher Grant's class. You will be getting plenty of homework, quick-fire quizzes and lots of compositions to write. Do remember to do plenty of reading aloud at home." This advice served me well throughout my schooling.

Teacher Grant put me to sit in the front row directly in front of his desk. "I am going to keep a close eye on you," teacher Grant said. He and teacher Preim live in San Fernando and come to school by taxi. Teacher Grant is also a pleasant and kind teacher, but unlike teacher Preim he does beat us in class for misbehaving. He is a short person so his nickname is "Shorty". He said to us, "I don't believe in beating you all if you get a sum wrong, or if you spell a word wrong. I will go over everything with you so that you understand how to work out your sums and how to spell the words correctly. But everyone must pay attention and concentrate fully on the lessons. Ask me any questions you may have regarding your work and we will sort them out together. These are my ground rules," said teacher Grant. I enjoyed being in his class as well.

It is Monday and I am dreading to go to school this morning. What will the children say to me? I am feeling ashamed at how I am looking. Over the weekend on Saturday morning Mr Bryna came to clip the mule's hair. He comes every month to clip the mule's hair. Nana supervises the clipping and ensures that the mule is well groomed. The fourteen grandchildren were looking on at the mule-clipping process. When Mr Bryna finished his job, Nana shouted and asked, "Wey dat buaye dey, bring dee buaye foh me." Nana was looking at me while he was asking. He came up to me and held me, bent my head down, and said, "Now Bryna, clip out aal ye hair. Dis buaye too bad. Ye too harden." I was standing while my whole head of hair was clipped off. Nana kept saying to me "Doh shake, doh shake." It was almost a clean shave Bryna had given me. I simply cannot understand why and how I am so badly behaved that I have to be punished in this way. I get beaten regularly from Nana for writing with my left hand. I work with Brother as well as I can, I carry out my daily chores like Brother, and yet I am told that I am too bad, and too harden. I cried throughout the weekend fearing Monday morning. Nanny soaked my head with coconut oil. It was only last Wednesday afternoon we helped Nanny to grate the coconuts to make three gallons of home-made coconut oil. "Doh cry, bayta, ye go grow back soon," Nanny comforted me. At that moment her comment was not much comfort to me. I was thinking of Monday morning in school.

We arrived early, and Brother went to play with his

friends. Tom and Henrik stayed with me as I was crying. The small children like myself came and surrounded me, not knowing whether to laugh at me or to sympathise with me. When the bigger children saw my head, they started laughing and clapping. Then the chanting began, "Clean head baba, penny cassava. Clean head baba, penny cassava."

The chanting grew and grew, and the chants reverberated throughout the school playground. The teachers heard the chants but did not come out. I did not know where to hide myself. Even the little children joined in the chanting. It was good fun for them but not for me. Thank the Lord that the school bell rang. They added, "Saved by the bell, saved by the bell."

When we got into our classes after the routine lining up and inspection, teacher Grant held my hand and went on stage in front of all the classes. He tapped the bell three times to draw everyone's attention. He put his arm on my shoulder and addressed the children.

"I heard a lot of chanting outside this morning. I gather that it was aimed at this boy. Yes, do take a good look at him. He is no clean head baba penny cassava. He is a bright boy, brighter than all you boys in the school. Do you know why? I will tell you. He has cut his hair very short to prevent him getting any head lice. The lice have no place to hide in his head. Even the eggs and nits cannot cling on his hair. He is a healthy boy with no infestation of head lice. Furthermore, his head will be kept cool as the wind blows through his head. For your health I suggest that all you boys take a leaf from his book and do cut your hair as he has done. From now on we do not want to hear any more chanting or taunting. I'll leave it to you all to come and say sorry to him."

On one afternoon teacher Grant said, "We are now going to have a quick-fire mental arithmetic test. The questions are straight equations and worded problems so you must listen and concentrate well. OK?" After a range of twenty-four questions on addition, subtraction, multiplication, division, squared and square root and angles, he paused. "We will have one more question and do listen carefully. If it takes three minutes to boil one egg, how long will it take to boil six eggs?" I quickly wrote down my answer as: "Three or eighteen, depending on your method used." My answer created a very lively and heated discussion in class, some children arguing in favour of three and others were clamouring for eighteen because they had chosen only one of my answers. Teacher Grant seemed to enjoy the arguments and remained smiling and silent.

The other classes stopped their work and were looking at us and wondering what was going on in our class. Teacher Singha came over to find out what the commotion was about. I don't know what he said about the last question and our responses. They both looked at me, teacher Grant said something about me, and teacher Singha said to me in a very fierce tone of voice, "When you come in my class I will see how bright you are." Teacher Grant said that I would skip Standard 4 and go into

Standard 5. Teacher Singha is in charge of three classes – Standards 5, 6, and 7. Teacher Singha frightened me with his remark. It sounded more like a threat than a welcome. His face was fierce-looking. He did not smile. His eyes had a steely look. I could read anger in them. It was the very first time that I had come so close to him since I had been going to school. Those words pierced me like a dagger. I got scared. I would have to face him in the next class. I could not escape his class or escape him because he commands the last three classes. He was notorious for beating children mercilessly.

On several occasions, parents had come into the school with sticks and cutlasses to beat him or chop him up for beating their children. Their missions had all been thwarted and failed by the diplomacy and effective communication skills of the head teacher. If I should go home and tell Nana that teacher Singha beat me in school, Nana would not ask why I was beaten. He would get out his leather belt and start walloping me as well. Then he would speak, "Ye [it is] good foh you. Wey you eh larn you lesson good. Dee teacher hah a damn right to beat you backside." The school has a reputation of getting good examination results because of teacher Singha. He is responsible for all the examination classes. The whole village knows this.

CHAPTER 6

I AM TEN YEARS of age and Brother says that I have entered the scorpion's nest and that I will be wrestling with "Mr Scorpion." A few teachers have been given nicknames. Mr Singha's nickname is Scorpion, because his whips do sting ten times more than ten scorpion stings. Interestingly, this nickname was further consolidated and fully registered in our village record book. It happened when a large black scorpion was hiding in one of his shoes, and lay waiting for him. The scorpion stung him when he slipped on his shoe. One further characteristic of Scorpion is his Friday attire.

He rides to school on a Raleigh ladies' bicycle. Every Friday Scorpion wears a test cricketer's outfit. His all-white flannels, cap and shoes make him stand out from the other teachers. In reality, he is a mere pseudo-cricketer. He is tall, thin-framed, partially bald and in his late thirties. Scorpion is brown-skinned with light-brown eyes, high cheekbones and an oval-shaped face and with a hungry look. He loves singing and leads the school in the singing classes. He cannot read a bar of music but has a good ear for it. He prides himself on his baritone voice.

He also directs the school gardening activities and exploits this to punish the boys. He would send them out in the garden to work instead of keeping them in their classes. As a result the boys miss out on their schoolwork and no one goes over it with them. How are they expected to learn it? Sometimes the boys are sent out in the mid-afternoon heat. I have been subjected to this exposure on several occasions during my years in Standards 5, 6 and 7.

One teacher who comes from Marabella always goes to the next village for his lunch in a country rum shop. He buys a petit quart of puncheon rum with a bottle of lemonade and calls it his shandy. The rum costs twelve cents. Every lunchtime he orders the same drink. He is nicknamed "Twelve". The entire school population calls him "Twelve". Teacher Grant and teacher Preim come to school by taxi. They live in San Fernando. Teacher Jackson and his wife, teacher Cecilia Jackson, moved into the village from Rio Claro. Teacher Nick, the local schoolboy taken on recently as a Monitor teacher in the school, has been transferred to Cedar Hill. At home none of the adults in either of the two houses ever asks us about school, or about the teachers or about our lessons. But they are always asking or reminding us of our morning and afternoon chores and plans for the following day.

Scorpion blatantly practises favouritism among his

pupils. He unashamedly and embarrassingly mollycoddles the big girls. If a pupil is in favour with him, he or she can do no wrong. None of his favourites ever gets as much as a light smack from him. For one boy he has a particular pet name. He calls the boy "chat-tree". Scorpion is the most senior teacher next to the head. However, he wields more power than the head. He runs the school and the headmaster is a nominal figure, using him for the ratification of rules or routines.

The overall standards of Sunnyvale CM are well above the national average. In cases of discipline the school is considered as one of the best. The Pavlovian principles are applied daily. The number of times that the bell is tapped together with its velocity do produce the appropriate responses from the whole school. School inspectors and other visitors are warmly impressed by our system. Discipline is enforced by the use of the whip. It is the decisive tool.

At home all of us enjoy playing scooch, three holes, jail, rounders, sixty-yard sprint races, skipping and cricket.

Brother and I make our cricket bats from dried coconut branches and bacando roots and pieces of board. Papa made six bamboo root balls for us. Nana seems to enjoy seeing his grandchildren playing and having fun. One of the balls went by him. He picked up the ball and examined it. "Wey are you buaye get dis white baal? Wey kind ah baal is dat? Ye [it is] so light an ye white like chaak," Nana said.

Brother went up to him and in a proud manner said

to him, "My Papa made six of these bamboo root balls for us and you not having any." Nana was in a pleasant mood when his favourite grandson spoke to him. He looked at Brother, shook his head and said, "Ah go get better bat an bole dan dat." Brother pulled away the ball from Nana's hand. "Are you buaye finish you wok?" Nana asked. Brother nodded and walked away. Then Stamford and Sam came and joined us. Nana told them, "Are you buaye nah know how to play bat an bole, man." Sam replied, "Bass, we dee larn nah." Sam ran with a hop-and-drop and Nana laughed at him. That was the end of Sam's game.

A few months later Stamford and Sam came to work on a Sunday morning. Stamford had half a sugar bag of mangoes. He has many different kinds of mangoes around his house. He selected two of the loveliest mangoes and told Sam to hold on to them for him. When he poured out his bag of mangoes he began calling out the names of the mangoes as he held them up. "Dis is a lang mango, dis one, a tin mango, dis is a Julie mango, dis is a hag mango, dis one a turpentine, dis is a doudouce mango, dis one a calabash, and dis one is a rose mango. Eat how much you want." Then he took the two mangoes from Sam and said, "Wey dee gyal dey? Ye is me child." Rani was in the kitchen helping Nanny with the cooking. One of my cousins sped up the steps to the kitchen and said to her, "Stamford wants you right now." Stamford said to Rani, "Ah bring dis two mango specially for you. Ah pick it wid me own han.'" It was the biggest calabash mango among the lot. The other was a doudouce. It was the smallest mango. Rani showed them to Nanny. Nanny said to Rani, "Yea gyal, dat Stamford an Sam like you too bad." Following this, the work of shelling corn started in the large shed and near to the cocoa-house.

Nana, Stamford, Sam, Brother and I rolled out six barrels of grains of corn from under the cocoa-house. There were sixty barrels of corn remaining. We filled twenty-four bags and Nana sewed them with his souja (a very long sewing needle) and twine. Nana would be taking the corn to the Port of Spain market early on Monday morning. This is the most pleasing job that all of us enjoy doing. Our cousins join in filling the bags. The reason is simple. When Nana returns from the market he usually brings at least two big baskets of cakes, buns, sweet bread, biscuits and chocolates. He would call out, "Are you buaye, come here and gi Nanny dis." We know that he is referring to Brother, so he runs off to collect the treats. We all surround Nanny like cobos round a carcass. This is our regular reward for our hard work. When it's my turn to get the treat, Nanny says to me, "Ah have ah mind not to gi you none, caz you too lazy." My other name is "Boh king lazy". Nevertheless, I do get my share, and I don't care what names she calls me. On this occasion, while we were eating and lapping up the bits and pieces in the yard, Nana called out again, "Are you buaye, come here."

Again, Brother went up to Nana, "Dis is foh you aal to play real bat an baal." Brother tore up the parcel excitedly and found two cricket bats and a red cork ball. He simply looked at Nana, did not say thank you Nana, but walked off with a broad smile. Nana warned him, "Now doh study play an forget you wok nah!" Brother did not answer Nana. We were the only boys in the village who had "store bats", and thus there was envy for them. Other boys used to come in the yard to play with our bats, but Nana put up a large gate to keep them out. We would be playing cricket for hours and hours, and sometimes forget to do our evening duties, particularly attending to the mule. Nana shouted and quarrelled with us on a number of occasions about playing and forgetting our work.

One afternoon Nana bawled and started quarrelling again, "Are you buaye like to play too much. You eh doin you wok, you study playing aal dee time." Then he shouted again, and this time he was referring to me, "Are you buaye, come here." I went up to Nana trembling in my boots. "Go an bring dem bat an baal foh me." I hurried upstairs for the two bats and the cork ball. Brother and I had oiled and rolled our bats with linseed oil. I slowly came downstairs only to see Nana waiting by the big chopping block with his razor-edged sugar cane cutlass in his hand. "Gi me dem bat. Stand up right here." Nana took one of the bats and "whap, whap, whap, whap" went the sound of the cutlass blade on the bat. "Gi me the adder one," he said. I handed him the second bat, which ended with the same result. "Wey dee baal dey?" he asked. Frightened, I reluctantly took the ball out of my pocket and handed it to him. The ball ended up in pieces. Nana said, "Take up aal dem piece an throw it by the choolha to bun. Are you buaye too harden. Are you buaye doh do you wok an only want to play. You only study play." Brother was nowhere to be seen when that incident took place. Crying and with tears running down my cheeks, I slowly picked up the pieces of the bats and took them into the kitchen for Nanny to use as firewood.

For several weeks I had nightmares over the incident. I reflected on the scene many times. I wondered why Nana did not want Brother to see him chopping up our bats. Why did he want to torture me by witnessing that vile act? If Nana could chop up the bats into pieces could he chop me up in the same way? The way Nana arranged the block, how he placed each bat to lie on the block, how the cutlass came smashing into the bat making a clean cut with each stroke, how the pieces fell on the ground one by one in a heap, was a most horrible, frightening feeling in my head. How could he make me endure such an act? The bats were still while the blade came down on them. But I would have moved away had it been me on that chopping block. Soon the pieces would turn to ashes in the fireside when Nanny is cooking our food.

I told Brother about it. He was distressed for some time but not as much as I had been. I had to stand there and endure the chopping up of the bats until it was over. He said to me, "Keep quiet, let me handle this from now. You do just what I am going to do." Every day we managed our work on time. We played no cricket. We were sitting and scraping off corn grains from the cobs after we finished organising the mule for the night. Nana would come to inspect the mule, and would see us behind our graters until it was dark. We would not leave the graters until Nanny would come to fetch us. Sometimes, Rani would come and call us. Nana would ask, "Wey dem buaye an dem? Wey dem doing in dee dark?" despite knowing our whereabouts. Our scheme went on for a couple of months and Brother decided that he would make his next move.

"Moye, tell Nana to buy back our bats." Nanny listened and said nothing. We emptied six barrels of corn and Nana sewed the bags with his souja and twine. The truck was there at 4.00am to load the twenty-four bags of shelled corn. When Nana returned, we had the regular treats, i.e., cream cakes, buns and sweets and chocolates. Nana called out again, "Are you buaye, come here." Brother went to him and was given two bats and a red cork ball. Brother never said thank you to Nana, he simply smiled with joy. "Doh study play only, do aal you wok too." We laboured over our treasured bats, applying linseed oil and rolling the bats with a full bottle of water. Papa was happy to see us with our bats when he passed by. We would call him to play with us but he would decline. It was not many months which passed by and we lapsed in our work. Would you believe that I had to go through that same process of Nana chopping up the second set of cricket bats all over again? It was a very painful reminder of the first instance that Nana chopped the two bats he had bought.

I had to carry the pieces into the kitchen again for firewood. This second occasion Nana gave me a sound beating on my bottom and legs before he chopped the two bats. He said, "Are you buaye like to play too damn much. You study play, an you nah dah do dee wok. Are you buaye too harden. You nah dah listen." This second act was doubly painful. I could not stand up properly but Nana made me stand up and watch him. My bottom and legs were sore. Tears were streaming down my face. I could not see clearly, but the sound of the cutlass on the bats was loud and clear. Each chop resounded against the nearby rice box. I reflected on this event and asked myself, "How can Nana be so brutal and cruel? Does Nana dislike me so much? Brother was not here to witness any of this chopping up. Can the chopping up of the bats be deemed criminal damage to our property?"

The pain was not so severe the second time. I knew what to expect. However, the loss of our bats was extremely devastating to Brother and me. It would never happen for a third time because it was too awful for us to bear. I would rather not have any bats and be happy in the house than to endure this torture again. Despite all this amount of beating I received from Nana, I believed that Nana thought that I was worth a penny or two. I saw this at weekends when he had the workmen and Atta in his company.

When the workmen gave Nana the number of rods that they did for the week he would always call me to calculate the number of tasks each person completed and how much must be paid to each of them. He always shouted, "Wey dee buaye dey? Tell ye to come here now." He never called Brother to do the calculation. Everyone knows that Nana is referring to me when he makes this type of call.

Nana regularly invites his friend Atta Roberto the overseer of a large cocoa estate to come over and spend time with him. His plantation spans twenty-five to thirty acres of cocoa and coffee. Stamford and Sam would also join them. Nana would shout out again, "Wey dee buaye dey? Tell ye to come now." This time it is for me to read the newspapers for them. When I am through with this Nana would tell them, "Man, you eh see dee buaye dah read, yeah man, dee buaye could read." He would treat his friends and workmen with rum, whiskey and coconut water. I am the one to fetch the coconut water and jelly coconuts for them. I am a monkey among those coconuts.

There are twelve coconut trees around the two houses. I am the climber of coconut trees. I would climb one tree and pick one or two bunches of soft-jelly coconuts. On one occasion I climbed a tree with a squirrel ahead of me. It made two leaps up and looked down to see how far away I was. As I got closer to it, the squirrel made another two or three leaps up and looked down again at me. It was teasing and challenging me. Its non-verbal taunts lured me and led me into its deadly trap. The climb went on like that until I reached the top among the coconuts. The squirrel came very close to me and looked at me. I stretched my hand out to hold it but it disappeared and I was suddenly on my way down to the ground. I felt light and was floating through the air as I came down and hit the ground with a solid thump. I was unconscious. They bathed me, put me to lie in the breeze until Uncle Jhan came to take me to the hospital. I was silent until I was halfway to the hospital. I grunted, mumbled, and made some incoherent sounds. I heard myself muddling those sounds. Uncle Jhan said, "Thank God, the boy will live." I was hospitalised for one week and sent home with 75% recovery. I kept my arm in a triangular bandage for three weeks.

Everyone said that it was a spirit which lured me up the tree and that it was no ordinary squirrel. Mr Daniel said that the evil spirit from the silk-cotton tree was transformed into a squirrel and its evil and deadly charm was leading me to my death. He also said that at night time the spirit can change into an owl and would keep on flying in front of you. If anyone attempts to shoot it, the gun will backfire and shoot that person instead. I never climbed another tree since that event. Nana got a long bamboo rod to pick the coconuts after that.

The unrelenting garden work continues daily. Nanny brings the lunch for us so that we do not have to come home to eat. In every field Nana has built a shelter where we can have a cool rest. He calls it his marai, or ajoupa. It is covered with carat (palm) leaves, the same as our house. Nanny would dish out the food for us and then remain with us until it's time for us to come home. It means that Rani is all alone at home. She cleans the house, washes the clothes on the scrubbing board, and gets the evening meal ready for us when we get home. The most back-breaking job is for Rani to scrub the dirty clothes and sheets on the scrubbing board. She tells Nanny that her arms and back ache after the day's scrubbing. Then Nanny will give her a thorough massage with coconut oil. On many days she is left alone in the house all day to do all the housework. She will have to prepare the lunch for everyone including Stamford and Sam. On Saturdays, Nanny and Rani have to cook for all the workers, because they will be coming for their pay.

Nana treats all his workers very well and does not have any difficulty recruiting them. Some feel disappointed when he tells them that there is no work for them for the time being. Nana would give them lots of strong puncheon rum containing prunes that have soaked and been allowed to mature. The drinks go down nicely with coconut water. I was the climber of the coconut trees until I fell. They would be given small bonuses in their wages every week. Nana's generosity is well appreciated.

The men go home in a drunken state following a few hours of consumption of the potent drinks of alcohol, hence they do look forward to Saturday afternoons. When the vegetables are ready to pick, they are regularly given supplies of tomatoes, aubergines, peas, cucumbers, sweetcorn, bodi and ochroes to take home. Nana has built three long bunk beds each three tiers high. These nine shelves accommodate the tomatoes. Tomatoes are picked three times a week and Nana goes to the market on Tuesdays and Fridays as a wholesaler. All hands are needed to pick the range of vegetables.

Rani is the houseworker. All her jobs must be completed by the time we come home for lunch. After eating, we have to sort out tomatoes and the other vegetables for the market, and for storing them in the bunk shelves. During the week, Nana organises his Saturday payout for his workers and puts the money in his drawer. That is the usual routine. My services do come in handy to calculate the wages for the workers. Nana does not ask Brother to do the calculations.

CHAPTER 7

On Saturday 18th, Nana went to his drawer as usual for the money to pay the men. "Who take dee money from dee draah?" Nana bawled out as loud as he could. Stunned, shocked, horrified and angry he went to Rani, "Who take dee money from dee draah?" Rani got very scared and was shocked to hear this.

"I don't know, Nana," she said.

"Who come in dee house?" he asked.

"Nobody Nana," Rani said.

"Wey dee money gaan?" asked Nana again.

She said, "I don't know, Nana, I haven't seen any money at all, Nana."

"But ah put dee money in dee draah, dey, right dey!" Nana exclaimed. "Aal dee money gaan. Ah come to pay dee woka an dem and the money gaan from dey."

Nanny questioned Rani, "Baytee, wey dee money gaan, gyal, you dee take dee money, gyal."

Rani replied, "Nanny, I never saw any money, I don't know where the money was in the first place. I don't know anything about any money, Nanny."

Nanny said, "Bu you alone in dee house aal day, gyal. Who dee come in dee house to take dee money den?"

Rani replied, "Nanny, nobody came into the house, and I never saw anyone coming inside the house."

"So wey dee money gaan den?" asked Nanny again. These questions kept being repeated several times and each time Rani gave the same answer. Nana's shouting was very loud that some of the villagers heard distinctly what was going on in the house.

Aunty Jenny heard Nana shouting and asking about the missing money. Mussy on the other side of the road also heard. Both of them came and joined in the questioning. Aunty Jenny asked, "Gyul, Rani, did you see any money in Nana's room?"

"No Aunty, I never saw any money nor did I see anyone coming into the house. I have been doing my work all morning and having to get the lunch ready for them. I don't know anything about Nana's money. I don't even know where Nana's money was. I am telling you the God's truth, Aunty."

Now it was Aunty Jenny's turn to repeat previous questions, "Did you see anyone come into the house, any time or any day, Rani?"

"No Aunty, no one came into the house. I am alone in the house, and I get on with my work. You know that I have to finish all my work before they come home."

Aunty Jenny asked her, "When last did you see your father?"

Rani said, "Aunty, I have not seen him for about two weeks. The last time I saw him is when we were playing in the yard, and we ran to see him by the roadside and he gave us some Prasad."

Mussy also asked, "You eh take no money, gyal?"

"No Mussy, I never took any money, Mussy, in the name of the Lord God above I did not take any money," answered Rani.

Brother was listening and said nothing up to this moment. Then he said, "My sister says that she did not see nor handle any money. I believe her. All of you must leave her alone and go and look for the money. You cannot keep on having a go at her when she has told you that she knows nothing about any missing money. She is honest and is speaking the truth. I am telling you so."

Rani said, "Maybe Nana mistakenly put the money somewhere else, and forgot that he did so. Perhaps Nanny and Nana should go in their room and check all the places where Nana puts money to see if the money is found in another place. Nana could have forgotten that he put it in a different place." Nanny went and told Nana about Rani's suggestion. Aunty Jenny said, "Moye, I'm coming too." Mussy said, "Moye, I want to come an sarch dee room an aal."

Nana, Nanny, Aunty Jenny and Mussy went into Nana and Nanny's bedroom. Nana said, "Ah put dee money right dey, right dey, self. An dee money eh dey. Ye gaan. Wey dee money gaan from dey?" Aunty Jenny, Nanny and Mussy searched through all the drawers. No money. They looked under the mattress, no money. Under the bed, no money. They looked into the cupboard, top shelf, nothing, middle shelf, and there the money was hidden behind some clothes. No one could see it unless you went searching at the back of the cupboard. It was a great relief.

Nana belched out aggressively, "Who dee ass put dee money dey? I put dee money right dey in dee draah, right dey, man ah say. Ah put dee money right dey. Who move it from dey an put it over dey. Me eh dee put no money dey."

Nanny told him, "You must ta forget you put it over dey dis time."

He said, "No man, ah tell you ah put dee money in dee draah, right dey. You tink ah goin mad? How dee ass dee money waak over dey?"

Mussy said, "Dee money eh lass, an nobady eh tief it."

Nanny came out of the bedroom and told Rani, "You Nana put dee money in dee cupboard an ye forget dat. Dee money dee hidin behind dee clothes." Then Nanny went on, "Baytee, child, you smart too bad. Is dee fus time you Nana make dat kind ah mistake. You Nana na da forget so easy nah, gyal?"

Rani said, "Nanny, I am relieved you found the money. I've been very worried because nobody ever came in the house. I am here all the time doing my work. So how could Nana's money have gone missing?"

The crop season is in full swing. Brother and I go

with Nana at 4.00am to load cane on the mule cart. By 6.00am Nana takes the first load of cane to the sugar cane factory. Both of us cut our bundle of grass before coming back for breakfast. The mule pen is cleaned, we have breakfast, and shell two barrels of corn before going to school. When Brother is turning the mill we finish early, but when I have to turn the mill we get to school in the nick of time, so we don't have any time to play. On some occasions we have to run to school in order to be on time. It will be Nanny's job to sit behind the grater during the day to grate off the remaining corn grains from the cobs. During the day, Nana would carry two more loads of cane to the factory. There is always a very long queue of bull and mule carts waiting to have their canes weighed before the crane lifts the loads off their carts. On Tuesday and Friday mornings we have a reprieve from loading cane, because Nana goes to the market to wholesale a truckload of vegetables. We finish our work early and we do get time to play at school before the bell rings.

CHAPTER 8

S TANDARDS 5, 6 AND 7 were merged together as one
class. Sometimes each class is set separate work by
Scorpion. But on most occasions, we seem to be doing
the same work. I question this in my mind. How can
we be doing the same work and yet they call themselves
Standards 6 and 7? Would not the older classes have
covered the Standard 5 work already? They have the
advantage over us Standard 5 children.

Scorpion stresses the importance of what he calls,
"The Three Rs". We would be doing these three Rs every
day and sometimes mornings and afternoons with short
breaks for other subjects. Rote learning is the order of
the day. We must memorise almost everything that we
are to learn about, so that we must be quick when asked a
question. Thinking time spells trouble for us. The whips
shower down on our backs. Scorpion is a merciless beater
of children. He is the most feared teacher in the school.

This reputation is known throughout the village. The peasant farmers accept that the teacher will beat children when they do any wrong, or if they don't know their school work. What they do not envisage is the severity of the beating by Scorpion. It is savage, it is brutal, it is criminal. It is the children who are exposed to such beating who feel the pain and fright from Scorpion's stinging and painful whipping. I happen to be one of these children.

On one occasion I was severely beaten by teacher Singha for not knowing how to work out a compound proportion problem. My back was sore and painful. I asked Scorpion to go over the sum because I was not in class. Scorpion had sent me out to whitewash the stones which border the front flower garden at the front of the school. I must say that it looked very beautiful indeed. I was told to do this job because the inspectors were due to visit the school on the following week. This difficult problem of compound proportion was explained to the class while I was doing hard labour outside.

He went over the sum hurriedly and moved on to another topic. My thoughts were on this problem trying to understand the method of working it out. I turned to ask the boy next to me to see his working. Scorpion saw me and whacked me on my back again. "Pay attention when I am talking," he said. When I got home, I told Nanny. She told Nana. Nana took out his leather belt and gave me several more belts on my already painful back. "Dee teacher right, you must larn you lesson good. Den dee teacher eh go beat you foh nothin. Are you buaye too harden." Since I received this treatment from Nana, I never again told Nanny when I got beaten in school.

A typical compound proportion question goes like this:

"If it takes 7 men 5 days to complete 17 tasks, how long will it take 23 men to complete 64 tasks?"

There will be variations to this problem. For example, it may be required to find out how many men will be needed, or how many tasks can be completed by x number of men in y number of days.

I believe in learning the principle of working out the sums, because I understand it better, retain it longer, and can apply the principle at any time in the future. It will amount to a learning for life. As we are forced to memorise information, I tend to remember it for a short time. If I don't use the information for a few months I tend to forget how to work out the problem. However, this is teacher Singha's teaching technique: rote learning. We are robots rather than individual critical thinkers. This is advantageous to teacher Singha because I tend to forget something learnt six months ago and not used since. It gives him the opportunity to wield his whips severely on our backs. If I am lucky to escape his whips I will be sent out to clean and tidy the flower garden.

It has a two-feet-high croton hedge enclosing the garden. There are roses, palms, periwinkles, ixoras and orchids, maintained by the bigger pupils. There is the vegetable garden and two large mango trees at the back of the school. These provide welcome shade and fresh air for outdoor classes. When I moved up to Standard 5, Alex left school to become a policeman.

He will be the first policeman the village will produce. I have often held the view that one day Alex would come into the school as a police officer and lock up Scorpion for beating young children so severely. That would teach Scorpion a lesson. What is the attraction in being a police officer? Alex says, rubbing his hands together with a broad gleeful smile, "I like the uniform. It makes you feel big and important. And the people will be more scared of you than respect you." Alex's aim for being a police officer is for personal achievement and fulfilment. It has very little or nothing to do with maintaining law and order in society.

The sugar cane crop season is coming to an end, the vegetables are finished and the rainy season is approaching. That means rice planting. Aunty Jenny and Uncle Jhan have other plans, which they have discussed with Nanny and Nana. They want to have Rani married and to get her out of the house. They do not want her to become pregnant while she is at home. They do not want to have the family's respectful reputation to be tarnished in any way. It would bring shame and disgrace to the entire family. Then she will be left unmarried because no man will want to marry that kind of girl. The quicker they marry her off the better it is for Uncle Jhan and Aunty Jenny's greedy motives.

It is Aunty Jenny's idea which sparked this affair. She quietly told Nanny that, "Rani is getting big now. We must find someone to marry her off. Don't let her go back to school because the boys will be looking at her."

Nanny replied, "Gyal, dee headteacher dee come las week, an ask Nana to sen ye back to dee school. Ye tell Nana dat ye have a jab for she. She go be a teacher in dee school. It go be good for dee gyal. Dee headmaster say dat we eh have nobody who is teacher in dee family."

Aunty Jenny said, "But, Moye, she will still be in the house with you. You know how dem boys and dem fast. You can't trust dem young boys these days. Moye, we don't she to get pregnant an have child in the house. Dat go bring so much shame for all of us. She will disgrace to the whole family. We don't want dat to happen eh."

Nanny insisted, "Buh ye Nana done tell dee headteacher, yea. Dee gyal go start to wok in dee school from next Monday. Nana say, dee headteacher beg, an beg, an beg ye, and den Nana ley dee gyal go to teach. Ye tell Nana dee gyal go make a good teacher an he go mind ye heself."

Aunty Jenny replied, "But Moye, when she put on all her nice dresses she will attract the boys in the village. They hang around the standpipe with their tins and box carts either waiting for water to come into the pipe, or waiting for the girls to come with their buckets to fetch water, or to moless the girls when they pass by." Aunty Jenny's wish is to keep Rani at home, treat like a Cinderella and then marry her off to some well-to-do cane farmer. This must be done sooner rather than later.

There is regularly an acute shortage of drinking water

in the village because of the limited supply from the village standpipe. The water comes in the pipe for four to six hours on some days and is turned off for three to four days every week. Water shortage is worse during the "crop time", that is, when the sugar cane is being harvested and taken to the sugar cane factory. No one can predict when water will come into the standpipe. When the water comes at night there is utter chaos in the community. There are no street lights so we depend on flambeaux to guide our way. Additionally, there are several potholes along the road, causing problems with the box carts. There is unnecessary spillage of this precious commodity.

The slogan "WASTE NOT WANT NOT" is posted at several places in the village. When I look at this slogan I always remember our principal and his one cup of water. This slogan drives home the message of conserving water and using it wisely. In college, during one assembly morning the principal held up a cup of water in his hand.

"Look," he said, "do you see this cup of water? I can have a complete bath with it." The entire assembly giggled. "This is no laughing matter," he shouted. "It goes to show just how far a cup of water can go. Don't waste it in these difficult times. Heed the slogan everyone," he said. His technique of having a bath with a cup of water continues to intrigue me. It is the importance of conservation of this precious lifesaver that he is driving home.

At night time, the flambeaux are the mobile street lights in the village. Each box cart and bull or mule cart carries its flambeau to guide the cart from the potholes on the road. It is not so scary, but the villagers' dogs are the scary ones. These dogs will chase after us as we are running with our box carts. Some of us keep long sticks to ward them off. Despite these setbacks the box carts roll on.

Nana did not see his friend Atta Roberto for several weeks. While Nana was busy with the cane and vegetables Atta was busy picking cocoa and coffee in his estate. His workers are regulars. They have been working on the plantation for years. They are indeed a happy family of workers.

One Saturday Nana, Brother and I went up to Atta's home and then for a walk about in the cocoa-estate, or so I thought. It is a six-acre block of cocoa and coffee in Pay Shay. Nana allowed Brother and me to have the freedom of the land. We ran through the large thick bushes and played hide and seek in the smaller bushes. There were three-feet-long slim birds' nests hanging from the tall trees. They were swaying in the breeze with their rounded bulging ends. They were firmly attached to thin branches of the giant cedar and the mahogany trees. These nests belonged to the yellow-tailed migratory birds. They would leave their homes early in the morning as one great army of soldiers heading for the front line. They would be returning to roost in the evening with their full complement of soldiers. Their timing is precise and punctual. Every morning at 7.00am they would be flying over Nana's house on to their destination. Every evening at 5.30pm they would be flying over Nana's house when returning home. Their timing is similar to that of the Zeppelins flying over our little carat house on Cotton Hill.

The cocoa trees are laden with yellow and green cocoa pods. They hang out from the trunks and branches like diverticula on the colon. These ripened yellow cocoa pods are heaped up by their thousands. The workers have been picking cocoa all day. These yellow pods contain their sweet-tasting beans. The workmen are the jack-asses to transport bags of cocoa pods on their backs to the several assembly points. Fruit trees are dotted throughout the cocoa fields. There are mangoes, pawpaw, pomerac, and oranges. There is also an abundance of wildlife to feed on these fruits. Some of the wild animals are regularly killed for wild meat. Atta gives Nana deer, agouti, armadillo, opossum or wild boar when Nana comes here. Atta also brings wild meat regularly for us. Today we are taking home venison and agouti, three bags of cocoa beans and one of coffee beans.

The workers showed us how to cut and open the cocoa pods. We would split the cocoa pods in half and scoop out the slimy, creamy and moist beans from the pods. These will be dried in the cocoa-house. The undergrowth is awash with grass for the mule and plantain and banana trees. The soft and succulent water grass provides ample food for the pigs. The cocoa land is undulating giving a picturesque scenery. We see a group of deer grazing in the distance. As we are leaving the estate the mass of yellow-tailed corn birds arrived from their day's migration and stood next to their nests. What amazes me is how each one can identify its own nest among the hundreds of swinging nests. Since we got home late, Nanny had done our evening duties for us. Nanny told us that the six-acre block of cocoa was Nana's. Atta had recently acquired it for him. I could only now connect why Nana allowed us to run freely through the cocoa estate.

Next morning Brother and I were back again on the water trail. We loaded two barrels on the mule cart. There was a twenty-five to thirty yard queue waiting for water. The Daniel boys were also in the queue with their box carts. Other villagers joined the queue behind us. I told Alex and Henrik about our trip to Pay Shay cocoa estate. They had not seen a cocoa tree although West Hill has its cocoa field. Mr Daniel would not allow them to go up West Hill. They remain at Cotton Hill and in the valley, seeing the cotton, cane, the bamboo patch and the silk-cotton tree instead. The boys got their tins filled and were off with their box cart as they were ahead of us. When it was our turn to fill our barrels, we managed to get only one barrel of water. We would have to be on the alert when the water would come back again in the standpipe.

The weekend was rather hectic and I did not get enough time to do all my homework.

I tried to sit up late but I fell asleep over my book. Nanny shouted at me, took the book away from under me and told me to go to sleep. I thought I would get up early and finish off my homework before going to cut grass. There was one question remaining and I rushed through it. As usual, we completed our morning chores and we were off to school. I was worried about my work because I did not get sufficient time to do it properly and to check it before going to school. I have been beaten many times for "misbehaviour" reasons, for delaying answering, for getting wrong answers, spelling mistakes. My "behaviour" problems include folding my arms, bending my head down and keeping quiet. While Scorpion is beating me he says that I am not paying attention. I never told Nanny anything about any subsequent beatings.

One of Scorpion's favourite students is a contributory factor towards Scorpion's attacks on the pupils. "Chat-Tree", a pet name for this boy, is sent out every Friday afternoon at 3.00pm to cut a bundle of whips from the back of the school for the following week. Scorpion locks these whips in his teacher's desk at the front of the class. These will partially dry out over the weekend and be ready for use on Monday morning. The fiercest day of the week is Friday. No one has been able to explain why Scorpion likes to beat the pupils so much and so severely on Fridays as compared with the other four days. He seems highly energised on Fridays. His special outfit is always a "man dressed in white". He starts beating children from the inspection session. One boy, Karly, ducks under the desk to avoid further beating. On one occasion another boy, Faiz, fainted during his flogging. His father and two older brothers came into the school to attack teacher Singha. Faiz's father said to the head teacher, "Wey dat Singha dey? Ah go ring out ye neck for ye. Wey dat blasted Singha dey?" His eyes showed aggression and murder. The head teacher spoke to the three of them outside of the school. He was afraid to bring them into his office, or to face teacher Singha. He tried to keep teacher Singha out of their sight. Again, the head teacher calmed them, spoke softly, and promised them that he would deal with this issue with teacher Singha and to ensure that teacher Singha does not beat the boy again.

FRIDAY 18TH

This week it has been my turn. I did not see Scorpion coming behind me. Suddenly, "whap, whap, whap, whap", on my back were the sounds of the whips. The shock and the pain made me scream out loud. I felt the pain coming around to my belly. "That is wrong. The sum is all wrong," he said. More blows followed on my back. I cried out but that did not stop him beating me. Teacher Singha went to his desk with his book. He showed me how the sum is worked out. My back was very sore and extremely painful. I could not concentrate on what he was showing me. He continued beating me on my back and neck. I could not move my back because it was very sore and painful. Tears were streaming down my face. The other children were looking at me. They said and did nothing, although they felt sorry for me. A few of the whips caught me on my neck on my left side. I found it difficult to move my neck, and I was in severe pain in my back.

When I came home in the afternoon, I was very scared

to tell Nanny, because she will tell Nana. That means that I will get more beating from Nana. I tried to lie down on my back but it was very sore. I did not say anything to Brother or Rani. I did my afternoon duties with great pain, discomfort and limited movement. When I finished cutting the cane tops, I attended to the mule, gave him grass, "chop-chop" and molasses water and oatmeal. Then I came inside and sat quietly still reeling from the pain in my neck and back. I went to bed early not speaking to Brother who was lying at the other end of the bed. He did not ask nor say anything to me. That was a very long and painful night.

Brother got up before me in the morning. Rani and Dewan were also up. I slowly pulled myself up when I heard them talking. I walked slowly out of the bedroom. Everyone was in the kitchen going for his or her breakfast. "Wey wrang wid you? Wey you bend you neck like dat foh? Wey wrang, buaye?" asked Nanny. Brother and Rani looked at me, with tears pouring down my cheeks.

Brother asked, "What happened, boy?"

Rani said, "What happened to your neck, it's swollen!"

Nanny came to me and said, "Lif up you head." I screamed out when Nanny attempted to straighten my head. She stopped. "Take out you shut, an ley me see," Nanny said. I carefully and slowly and painfully removed my shirt. "Barp re barp!" Nanny yelled out. "Look how much blood in you shut. Ley me see you back, tun rung." Nanny was horrified. She put her both hands to her mouth. "Who hit you?" she asked. Crying overtook me, I could not speak.

Brother said to Nanny, "Teacher Singha beat him in school yesterday."

Nanny called Nana, "Come see dee buaye, how dee teacher dee beat ye. Ye back cut up wid dee whip. Look how dee man dee beat dee child."

When Nana saw my back, he was furious. "When dee teacher beat you?"

Brother said, "Yesterday."

Nana said, "Look at aal dem whale in he back. Aal ah dem cut up."

Nana counted, "Seben ah dem," he said. Although Nana would usually beat me also when he heard that I get flogging at school, on this occasion he was sympathetic with me. Nanny cleaned the seven weals. The wounds were all open and oozing across my back.

"Take dee buaye to see dee dactar," said Nanny to Nana.

"Caal Jhan," Nana said.

"Ah carrying dee buaye by dee dactar now," he told Uncle Jhan.

Dr Luo was well known throughout country. He was the only doctor at the time trained in both Traditional Chinese Medicine (TCM) and Western medicine. He examined me. He took my pulse in both hands, and looked at my tongue. He made his notes. He drew the shape of my tongue and identified a couple of areas. He did the same regarding my pulses. When he saw my back, Dr Luo was furious.

"Who did this to the child?" he asked.

Nana told him that it was teacher Singha.

"Nobody beats a child like that. This is totally unacceptable for any teacher to beat a child like this. This is criminal behaviour. How can any child learn when he is beaten in this way? This man must be taken to court. I will attend court if required to do so. Take this medical report to the police straight away. I would like to have this teacher prosecuted and sent to jail."

The report indicated the lengths of the weals, which were bleeding: "Three wounds are seeping out whole blood while four of them are seeping plasma fluid. There are seven (7) weals, each twelve (12) inches long, running diagonally across this child's back. He is the grandson of Surdat of Sunnyvale village. The child's neck is swollen and head is bent to his left side. His neck has a circumference of 21 inches."

That was written in bold and underlined in Dr Luo's report. A ten-year old child's neck circumference is on average twelve to fifteen inches. Antiseptic solution of Savlon was prescribed to clean the wounds.

Nana thought of Dr Luo's comments with the report in his hand. He did not go to the police to report my beating. We came home and Nanny cleaned my wounds. The head teacher came in the evening to discuss this with Nana. He read the medical report, shocked at the sight of my wounds and my swollen neck with my head bent towards my left side. The report described it accurately. The head teacher pleaded with Nana not to go to the police as the consequences would be grave for teacher

Singha. The head teacher tried to paint a good picture of teacher Singha as he gets good examination results. He said that Singha has placed Sunnyvale CM high in the league tables in the country. He used all his diplomatic skills to influence Nana that the best course of action is for him to handle the matter. He said that he would make a copy of the report and return the original. Nana agreed. The head teacher won. Two weeks later my wounds had almost healed, and my neck swelling was gradually subsiding. My head was still slightly bent to my left side. The head teacher saved teacher Singha again. I returned to school not knowing what to expect from Scorpion when he saw me. The worst of the wounds on my back was still aching.

There was not a single word of feedback from the head teacher. Nana was surprised at this but said and did nothing about it. Scorpion saw me sitting in the front row of the class. He said nothing to me. He simply pointed with his whip for me to go and sit at the back of the class on my own. I was a one-student last row. He kept away from me. The head teacher forgot about me. Scorpion's teaching carried on as usual. I waited for Friday. Scorpion's routine was unchanged. He wore his cricketer's outfit on Fridays as usual. He kept on beating pupils the same way. In the afternoon Scorpion called out, "Chat-tree, it's three o'clock."

"Yes, sir," said the boy. He went out and returned with a handful of whips, mainly guava and tamarind. I began to question whether the head teacher had mentioned anything to Scorpion about my injuries, or about the continued beating of the children. Fear returned to me that I may be subjected to more beating. Teacher Singha had his own plan for me. His plan would affect me for years and years to come.

The first week of my return to school was quiet. Teacher Singha did not say a single word to me for the entire week. Not a word! None of my work was marked or corrected. I handed in my work with the rest of the class and it was returned the same way it was submitted. Scorpion would walk around the class and look down at the other students' work. He would make little comments like, "This way", "Oh yes", "Good", or "That's wrong", followed by whips, or "Right you are." At least they were receiving some form of feedback from him. When he got to me he stayed at a distance to look at my work and quickly moved away as though I had some kind of serious infectious disease. The great relief for me was that I was not touched with a whip for a full week. It would remain this way until I left Sunnyvale CM. That was a milestone change in my primary school education – no communication, no beating, no physical pain. No tears rolling down my cheeks as before. The pain is all internal and accompanied by the external behaviour of teacher Singha towards me.

It is more painful, stressful and humiliating than the physical pain of the recent whipping. The feeling of rejection, social isolation and humiliation will remain with me for the rest of my life.

This feeling of not being wanted, of being socially isolated within a class of thirty-five students, of not being spoken to for several consecutive weeks and sitting on my own at the back of the class, deliberately forming a one-student back row, degraded and debased me. This was the gutter feeling that I experienced. That gutter feeling cannot be dug out of me. It is my permanent and lifelong companion. That is the pain which I am enduring. The pain from the physical bruises and swelling have all gone but what lives on is the pain of rejection and humiliation that I have experienced and am still experiencing. This is the psychological trauma which teacher Singha inflicted on me.

And above all, do remember that I was only ten and a half, going on eleven years of age. What a lifelong burden to bear.

We are in the examination classes. What is the effect on me in preparing for examination? How do I feel when I do work with the other students but have to mark and assess my own work? When Scorpion returns my work I have to check it over myself. Scorpion will not allow me to look at other children's corrected work.

If I try to ask another student something and Scorpion sees us, that student will get a walloping. I must have no contact with the students while in class. The only contact and normal interactions take place outside the school. The colleges' entrance examinations are soon approaching. Everyone is being intensively prepared for these examinations. The first examination day duly arrived. It was the first time that Scorpion spoke to me. It was one year since I returned following his beating.

"Would you like to go with the others to sit the first college entrance examination tomorrow morning?" he asked me.

I immediately replied, "Yes, sir."

Teacher Singha said, "I did not submit your name, because I was not sure that you would want to go." He continued, "Anyway, you can still go with the others. The exam starts at 9.30am. Make sure that you are there by 9.15am."

This was the best day for me in one year. It came towards the end of my school life at Sunnyvale. In the next few weeks we sat several other college entrance examinations. The final examination is the school leaving certificate examination. This is a state examination.

All the results of this state examination and the college examinations were sent to the head teacher. The school had a 98% success in the state examination that year. My neighbour was awarded a state scholarship. The boys were advised to go to one college so that they can support each other. Although I was pleased to go to college in September, I cannot help myself hating Scorpion for stinging me so severely, both physically, and more so, psychologically.

I was happy to give Nanny the good news. I had never told any of the adults in either of the two houses how I was treated when I returned after the severe beating. I simply couldn't wait to tell Papa that I passed for all the colleges and decided to go to one of the top two in the south, because some of the boys would be going there as well. I told Papa first before telling Nanny anything.

It's November and the rainy season is still with us but it is coming to an end. It is the rice harvesting season. I have already described the rice planting. Now three to four months later the rice is ready to be harvested. The ripe rice grains look very much like fields of wheat in late July and August harvest time. Nana makes a three-feet-by-three-feet barbecue-style wooden grill. This is mounted on four bamboo posts. Jute bags are spread under the grill and around it. The grill bars are two inches apart so that there is a wide enough space for the rice grains, called "dhaan", to fall through. Two or four men will be beating off the rice on the grill to allow the grains to fall through. There are no combine harvesters in this operation. It is sheer hard manual work.

In the lagoons, a number of men will be cutting the rice stalks from near the roots. Others will be bringing the rice for the men at the grill. This is where Brother and I are involved. We carry bundles of rice on our heads and shoulders for the men at the grill. This is very tiring because we have to walk in soft, muddy ground. The sinking ground holds on to our wellington boots, and we have to pull ourselves through to reach the grill. It is more difficult when we have to do this while the rain is falling. The grains are filled in bags. Brother and I get relief when he takes home one load of rice on the mule cart. The men would empty the bags in the cocoa-house. We would have a well-deserved interlude. The characters in this play are strong and muscular. They carry heavy loads on their backs throughout the day.

It is Nanny and I who do the rest of the rice work. We dry, fan out and clean the rice grains in the cocoa-house. Then we bring the grains and store them in two large rice boxes. We have to turn the grains in the sun to dry out the grains. We fan out bits of straw, dust or other debris from the grains. The dhaan (rice grain) is stored in at least two large wooden containers. There is sufficient dhaan to last through one year until next year's harvest comes in. During the war period Nana is never short of rice. There is enough rice to feed both houses throughout the year and still there is a surplus when the "new rice" comes.

This "nawa dhaan" (new rice) is always first cooked on Dewali evening. Prayers are offered in the name of the Lord, as a thanksgiving. Rice pudding is traditionally made on this occasion. This is the saga of the rice planting/harvesting activity during the rainy season. At the end of November and into December preparations are being made to harvest the sugar cane once more. This is called the "crop time" or the dry season. The sugar company paves the road with a large round sharpening stone like a wheel. It is mounted on a stand with a handle to turn this wheel. This is for the villagers to sharpen their cutlasses to cut the sugar cane. There we have it, where the cycle of work begins all over again from January to May.

CHAPTER 9

MY PRIMARY SCHOOLING IS finished, the rice
planting is finished and it is a foregone conclusion
that I will be starting college in September. Brother, Rani
and Dewan are all very happy for me as well. Aunty Jenny
and Uncle Jhan weren't pleased at all.

"Do you mean that he will be spending another five
years in that house?" Aunty Jenny asked Uncle. "How did
he pass and our daughter didn't?"

"Of course, they will send him," Uncle Jhan said.
Aunty Jenny mulled over this and said to him, "I will
make damn sure they don't send him. He too blasted lazy.
He always hiding from work." She added, "Jhan, I must
move very quickly before it is too late."

Brother said in his usual funny way, "Now that you are
going to college, are you still going to be the finest ladies'
man on this planet?" The four of us burst out laughing.
Nanny wanted to know what we were laughing about. I

hit back at him, "Yes boy, yes! It's books, books, and more books. These are my ladies for my future."

I told Nanny that I passed to go to college. I also told her that Lallies passed, but he did better than me. He has been given a scholarship so he will be going to college for free. He does not have to pay any fees, but I have to pay. It is $16 per term for five years. There are three terms in the year. It means that I have fifteen terms of college. The total tuition fees over the five-year period will be $240. This sounds a lot of money to pay, but it is over five years. Of course, I will have additional expenses to buy books, uniform and travel to school.

Having outlined this to Nanny, she became very angry with me. "How dat buaye [i.e. Lallies] gettin free callege and you have to pay? Why you eh get schalarship an al? Me eh go pay for you, an ah go tell you Nana not to sen you."

A huge bombshell dropped on me. Brother listened and said nothing. He remained silent. I pleaded with Nanny to give me a chance to go to college. I begged her repeatedly over the next two weeks to allow me this one opportunity in my life. All I'm interested in is gaining a good education. The chance is there before me. Brother knows just how much I want to go. He went to Nanny and asked, "Moye, please send the boy for me. Let him go to college, do it for me." That was the last plea to Nanny and it came from Brother.

Nanny looked pitifully at Brother and then at me. She slowly and painfully shook her head to deny him his request. She said, "Dee buaye too lazy, an ye too harden. Ye eh da want to wok. Ye boh king lazy, wey ye eh get schalarship too an go foh free. An he want to be head teacher? Well ley ye faddar sen ye. Me eh ha no money to sen ye. Ah tell Nana not to sen ye aready."

I persisted, "Nanny it's just one chance I am given, please Nanny, let me go to college, please." This time I was crying and begging Nanny for the chance to go to college.

Nanny looked at me and said firmly, "If you want to go, tell you faddar to send you." I was shocked. After all my years of slogging myself, working so hard, this was my reward.

We did not see Papa for several days. Apparently, he is gradually doing a little work in the garden. Papa is still regularly seen walking along the road in a dishevelled state. He would walk slowly, looking tired as if he has just moved Mount Everest. He is at times drunk and looks like a tramp on the road. No one wants to talk to him, and he does not want to speak to anyone, except us, of course. When Nanny, Aunty Jenny and Uncle Jhan see him like this, it gives them added leverage to slander him in front of us. For example, Nanny would say, "See, you fadder looking like a beggar on dee road. Wey ye na get up an ye ass an go an do some wok. Aal dee wok in dee gyarden jus so."

Of course, it is extremely humiliating for us to hear such things being said about him. He is still our father. Sometimes I wonder whether Nanny or Uncle Jhan say such nasty things about Papa for us to develop hatred against Papa. We do know how much he is disliked by them. One evening Papa was walking along the road in a drunken state. I ran out quickly and grabbed him tightly. I started crying and said, "Papa, Papa, I want to go to college, and Nanny says she will not send me. She said to come and ask you to send me. Papa, will you please send me? It's the only thing in my life that I want. I want to have a good education. I know that a good education will be the best preparation for my entire career. Please, Papa will you send me to college?" I was holding on to him. He began to cry.

He said in a sad very voice, "Son, I will sen you to callege. If I have to eat dry roti, or suck cane an mango, I go wok an sen you." It is the first time I ever heard Papa use words as the following, "Dem have so much money, an dey doh want to sen you to callege? I go ask your Uncle Cliff to help me. But to go callege, you go go by dee hook oh dee crook."

A big burden has been lifted off me when Papa said that he would support me. When I came inside the house, Brother saw my face lit up. He said, "I know Papa will send you, he is that kind of person. He will do anything for us. Papa will make the biggest sacrifice for us. We don't have to worry about all the things Nanny and Aunty Jenny say about him. I feel hurt as well, boy. But you will make it, boy."

I told Nanny that Papa will send me. Nanny was still scathing in her remark, "Ye [i.e. Papa] eh ha two penny to rub in ye backside, an ye go sen you to callege? Who go gi ye money to sen you to callege? Eh, tell me, wey ye go get money to sen you?" Nanny was almost certain that Papa would not be able to afford such expense to send me to college.

I hurriedly organised myself with a light-blue shirt, and dyed one of my brown khaki trousers in grey. Papa brought a pair of black Technic shoes for me. I never wore any shoes at primary school. Everyone went to school barefooted. The shoes were tight for me. After two days of wearing them I got blisters in my feet. I resorted to wearing crepe soles (i.e. plim soles or washy-kong). I wore the Bata crepe soles for the next five years at college. I had a haircut but not with Bryna's mule clippers. Therefore, there would be no chants of "clean head baba, penny cassava."

THURSDAY 18TH

Today is a rather unusual day to start and end the school week. It is my first day at college. It is an orientation day for all the first years. There are forms in the first year called 1A, 1B, 1C, 1D and 1E. I am in Form 1A Special. Our form is given this title because we were seen to be a rather special group. Special personalities were identified at such an early stage in our lives. It is hoped that their predictions would come to pass. We were given a detailed introduction of the course and a brief one of the college. We were shown round various departments and offices and introduced to the lecturers who will be teaching us during the year. We discussed the timetable for the term. It is a short first day and week.

Over the next five years our form maintained the "A Special" title. The most striking difference between the primary school and the secondary school for me is discipline and orderliness. At assembly everyone breaks up and heads for his class. At the end of the day when the bell goes for dismissal, students rush out like wild animals getting out of a cage. The noise level is alarming. The decibels have increased tenfold. In an instant the classroom is empty. This was never the behaviour of the children in my primary school.

My first day and first week is negotiated and ended. We are given a long weekend to digest and assimilate the forthcoming foods for thought. My pair of shoes caused great discomfort. From the following Monday onwards and until I completed my secondary schooling, I wore "washy-kong" i.e. plimsolls. They were the cheapest footwear. At weekends I would wash and scrub them. When dried, I would put Blanco on them. Blanco is a whitening powder which is dissolved in water and used to whiten the plimsoles.

When I got home Brother was still at his commercial college, and Rani and Dewan were also in school. The only one at home was Nanny. She showed no interest in my first big day, and therefore I did not mention anything. Aunty Jenny gave me a sharp look and turned away. I changed from my college uniform into my normal garden clothes.

After lunch Nanny said that we have to go and pick pigeon peas. This is the early crop. Normally, pigeon peas flourish abundantly in January to February. It is Nana's awareness of the market when peas will be scarce that we have this early crop. Nanny and I picked five bags of peas and hardly made a dent on the amount yet to pick. At least they are five bags in advance of tomorrow's picking. On mornings I do no work, but I carry out the afternoon and weekend duties as usual.

Stamford and Sam came early and Nanny gave them breakfast with Nana. Four of us will pick the remaining field of peas. We came home for lunch with about a quarter left for the afternoon session. At about three o'clock we went to pick the rest of the peas. The trees are laden with peas so it takes quite a while to do one tree. The prolific yield of pigeon peas at this time gives Nana a handsome profit as prices are high. By the end of the day we had amassed twenty-five bags of peas. Nana had made two trips with the mule cart. Brother, jokingly, keeps telling me that Tobago, the mule, works like a donkey. He also tells me that he feels like Tobago at times for the amount of hard work he puts into a day. Nana will be going to the market to sell the truckload of peas early in the morning. After completing our evening work the four of us sat out in the veranda. While we were eating, I told them about my first day at college. It is so different from the primary school life.

It is a very large two-storey building. It is crescent-shaped and assembly takes place within the crescent. The first-year intake is 160 students in five groups. I mentioned the noise and the disorderly conduct when the final bell went to signal the end of the first day. We were like visitors on an outing to an art gallery rushing out at the sound of an emergency fire bell; strange but interesting.

This is not an open-plan system like Sunnyvale. Each class is in a private room. Our class has forty students. I showed Brother and Rani my timetable for the autumn term. It is a neat booklet. They are impressed with it. This is a first for all of us to have such a timetable. By the spring term this format of timetable will be a routine item. I remembered teacher Preim when our form master told us to read very widely, both fiction and non-fiction. I wondered whether he had attended this college and got his advice from here as well, and whether he passed it on to all his pupils in turn. I had gone directly to the public library when school was dismissed for the day. I took my student ID to join the library. It is the main library in the south of the country. We have now got access to the best library service in town. Brother says that he is a bit jealous of me now that I can go to the library anytime or as often as I wish to go. I am in town five days a week and that gives me the advantage.

Brother has been doing well in his commercial subjects. He is very good in his shorthand. I read for him while he speed-writes. When I am finished reading a passage I ask him to translate what he has written. Invariably, he gets the whole passage translated from his shorthand version correctly. On one occasion he signed up to take the shorthand eighty words per minute examination.

We practised for a hundred words per minute. He did this very well. I moved the goalpost to 120 words per minute. We worked at this speed for two weeks until he succeeded in achieving this feat. Now eighty words per minute seems too easy for him. I suggested to him to opt for a hundred words per minute instead of the previous eighty words. He agreed with me. We practised for 120 words per minute assiduously to ensure that he would certainly pass at a hundred words per minute. On examination day, I said good luck for the day. He went with this intention, but when he entered the examination room he sat for the eighty words per minute test. I was very disappointed in him for doing the eighty words. I did not tell him "Congratulations" when he told me that he passed. In fact, I was still annoyed with him for what he did. It had been an utter waste of my time in drilling him at a higher speed per minute shorthand.

Since I started my secondary schooling, happily, I have no time to do any morning chores. I must be ready by 6.45am because the school bus arrives at 7.00am every morning from Monday to Friday. There are three buses and they are filled with students travelling to San Fernando. My weekly season ticket is my precious passport. It costs sixty-four cents per week. I renew it every Saturday morning. Nana has begun to miss my contribution in the garden because of my schooling.

I have a lot more homework every day so I have to spend more time reading and writing. I have been beaten on my left hand by Nana since I was six years of age up to the present time. While I am writing and concentrating on my work, Nana appears from behind me and whacks me on my left hand. Then suddenly, "Tie! Tie! Tie!" sounds are heard as either sticks, whips or belts rain down on my left hand. He has been warning me not to use my left hand since I started writing at the age of six. My poor left hand has suffered years of beating from Nana. My left hand becomes very painful and sore. I am left to gently rub and massage it with coconut oil. When we are playing cricket, Nana would be watching to see which hand I am using to throw the ball, to bowl and to bat. Consequently, I became a fully fledged right-handed cricketer. This game involves full arm movements but writing demands fine hand movements.

Each time Nana repeats this command, "Ah tell you nah to write wid dat han. Dat is a bad han. Dat is a dutty han. Dat is dee devil han. You wash you backside wid dat han. Nat to write wid da han, ah say. You go bring bad luck in dee house. An you go bring dee devil and dem spirit an dem in dee house an aal." Over the years and to the present Nana hits me on my left hand and tells me these statements. To avoid his beating, I pretend to be writing with my right hand when he is around. Eventually I am becoming ambidextrous. I would also stop writing and begin reading until he goes out.

Nana views left-handedness as a negative force, a force of evil, and a force which he must rid me of. Do remember that Nana cannot read nor write. He is illiterate. But he is an astute businessman. Because he is illiterate, and due to their beliefs, it is not surprising that he would react to my left-handedness as he does. Sometimes I have to delay my writing until late at night to avoid Nana. That also presents another problem, that is, late-night waking.

Even during my primary school days I have been blamed for burning up the paraffin in the light and using up too much pitch oil. Now that I do have to spend longer hours to do my work, Nanny is often quarrelling with me. Sometimes she catches me sleeping over my books because I have been so tired. She does not seem to understand my position. I will accept any amount of beatings or quarrels from Nanny and Nana in order to get my schoolwork done.

We work as usual over the weekend. Normally Aunty Jenny would be in and out of Nanny's kitchen everyday as an influential advisor. She makes many decisions for Nanny. These are then conveyed by Nanny to Nana, who finally decides. For example, when Nanny told me that she would not send me to college, I could not have gone to ask Nana directly. All lines of communication and requests must filter through Nanny. This is, and has always been, the case in getting to Nana.

I was surprised that neither Aunty Jenny nor Uncle Jhan asked me about my first big day. After all, I am the first one in the family to break such ground. With the enthusiasm bursting in me about my novel experience, this has been an anticlimax. I must remind you that my only direct line of communication with Nana is when I get a severe walloping from him with a stick or his leather belt.

On Sunday, Nana, Brother and I spent the day at Pay Shay. We picked cocoa and coffee, and cut water grass. I am getting really good at cutting cocoa pods and scooping out the beans. I suck the beans to my delight, oblivious of the health hazard it presents. It's similar to the health hazard of sucking sweets. It's the sweet taste of the cocoa beans which lures me into this vice. My rationale is that this is a once in a six to eight week indulgence. That would make it thirty to forty times of sucking these fresh cocoa beans in the next five years.

It's Monday morning. I'm feeling tired from the long weekend work. I am fully dressed in my uniform. I've got a very light blue shirt, grey trousers, black socks and now black plimsolls instead of the white ones. These do not get soiled as the white ones, but the weekly washing continues. I've also got my navy-blue with white diagonally striped tie and a navy-blue badge with its white inscribed college insignia. Then comes the final showpiece. I slip on my navy-blue blazer with its insignia. I feel transformed and privileged to be in this outfit. It is the uniform of one of the two most prestigious boys colleges in the south.

Aunty Jenny quickly ran over to see me. She was most impressed. Nanny saw me, smiled and said, "You lookin' nice, bayta." It was the most heartening and uplifting comment which I have received from Nanny. I had a small bookcase and had to take a couple of books in my hand. Brother, Rani and Dewan were absolutely thrilled to see me ready for school. Soft-hearted Rani was crying with joy for me. She was very happy indeed.

By 6.45am we were all out in the veranda waiting for the bus to arrive. It was prompt and off I went. In a few days the novelty had worn off. It simply became a routine activity. There was a great deal of excitement and noise in a busload of students with different uniforms. Everyone knows that mine is a privileged one. It has raised my self-esteem dramatically, but I would not allow this to overtake me. I am beginning to value the concept of selective education and elitism as I am now part of this system.

Some villagers claim that my college is the best in the south. I know that this is not entirely the case because sometimes the rival college gets better results than we do. Also, it's the real battle of the giants when it comes to the annual Inter-Col day. We do make contingent plans for this great event. Plan A comes into immediate operation when we win. If we lose on one occasion, we activate Plan B and put it into operation just as readily as we would have done with Plan A. We resound the stadium with our choral singing, and console ourselves with our chants, "Watch out, next time, watch out, next time." We issue this threat and challenge to our rivals one year in advance.

In Plan A we rehearse one of our favourite rhythms. It is sung repeatedly before and during the match, as a motivational force to our team. The team's spirit is strengthened and given added vigour to fight harder. It goes thus, "Hi, hi, hi, hi, see you there, we are going to give you beer." The sound of the word "beer" in our team's ears whets their appetite to work harder and harder on the battlefield.

Nana was getting enormous praise for sending me to college. The villagers would stop and say to Nana, "Bass, you doin' dee bes ting, man. You sen in dee boy to dee bes callege. Ah glad foh so foh dee child." Nana laps it all up and does not say a word to them. He reserves his right to silence and so he is totally non-committal on this issue. The peasant villagers talk among themselves and say how good Nana is to send me to college. I get such feedback periodically. This is the one occasion when Nana is not being honest to himself and to me. It does concern me. I only hope that Papa doesn't hear them.

At 9.00am assembly, further instructions were issued and followed by the Lord's Prayer. Today, my first full day at college, heralds the beginning of a five-year sentence of hard labour. I love the challenge of all these new subjects, particularly Latin, in which we are studying Virgil. I remember in the infant department at Sunnyvale CM, teacher Nick telling us that we can all be scientists in our own way. It was then a dream, but the reality is now dawning on me. We have languages, science and arts in our mouths. It only remains for us to chew well, digest fully without rebellious "Qi" energy, and assimilate our learning to make it characteristic of us.

By the end of the fourth day I barely knew about a quarter of the boys in the class. I sensed a rift developing among the boys. Two groups suddenly formed. The town boys stuck together, and the country boys remained together. It was not a good start for a group of forty. Matters got to a head-to-head confrontation. The discord would be settled by a Friday afternoon after-school duel:

Time – 3.30pm
Location and Venue – Paradise Pastures
Gladiators – Wide (Town Representative) vs Narrow (Country Representative)

The whistle blew and the two fighters faced each other to do battle. They grabbed each other and the tough tussle sprang into cruise control. The supporters were highly vociferous and more excitable than the fighters. The two teams' supporters were cheering and shouting to outdo one another. There was clapping, jeering and cajoling coming from the two sides. The fighters were grappling with each other, and rolling down the hill locked together. Fists were flying around in thin air from both contestants. They looked around for other aids. The fighters were running out of ammunition as the little pebbles and leaves had been used up. They both turned to the biggest resource in the pasture. Heaps of cow dung were dispersed all over the pasture. The fighters picked up cow dung and pelted and smeared each other with it. This was a one-round do-or-die, win-or-lose contest.

The battle of wits was going on. They were running all over the pasture to find more cow dung as the nearby heaps were exhausted. At 3.55pm precisely the two gladiators hugged each other. They put their arms around each other and slowly walked towards one large group of cheering and clapping supporters. "Narrow" and "Wide" were two walking heaps of cow dung. The judges unanimously declared the result of the match was a tie. The boys shook hands, went and bathed and changed into clean clothes. The follow-up, feedback, analysis, and discussion lasted one full term.

The most beneficial aspect of this event is that we got to know each other's names and backgrounds, home situations, our likes and dislikes, each other's friends and associates within the hour. We were like old friends having a reunion. This fight was the best thing that happened to the group. It was the best form of orientation among ourselves. Following this, we became a congenial and cohesive group. We became known as "The Forty".

What a fruitful end to the first week of my college life. I hurried home to relate this unique fight to my brothers and sister.

I saw Papa on Saturday just in time for him to give me sixty-four cents to renew my weekly bus ticket. The home and village life continued in the usual manner. I carried out my chores as usual. There is a continuing shortage of water in the standpipe. Some villagers use the pond water. It is boiled before drinking it. The women go by the pond to wash clothes and sheets and spread them out on the cricket ground. They take their scrubbing boards, blue or brown sopa and Oxford blue to whiten their washing. These are the only washing detergents the villagers use. Many of the girls and their mothers carry buckets or tins of water on their heads. The boys use their box carts. There has been no water in the standpipe for three days. When the water came in the standpipe Uncle Jhan and Brother made two trips with the mule cart to fetch water from the standpipe until the water was locked off. They had got four barrels of water for the two houses.

Aunty Jenny uses the water freely. She does not heed the slogan "Waste not want not". Nana is very irritated by this but he restrains himself from quarrelling with her. Aunty Jenny's concern lies elsewhere. Five years of my schooling is too long for her. If Rani becomes a monitor pupil-teacher, that's a further concern. Her life in the back house is dull. She wants to be in the picture. She wants to be noticed by the men and women for her elegance and beauty. She wants to be in the front house and pose in the veranda for the villagers to admire her. She is aware that the young men refer to her as the "model of Sunnyvale".

At present we are the ones who see and know everything that's taking place on the road. Brother, Dewan and I are regularly sitting in the veranda and see what is going on around us. Nanny keeps Rani in the kitchen with her. Aunty Jenny is becoming desperate to move into the front house. She urges Uncle Jhan to do something about it. She is also working out her plan. There is a little sibling rivalry between Uncle Jhan and Brother. Uncle Jhan is Nana's only son. Therefore, Uncle Jhan thinks that Nana must pass on everything to him. Uncle Jhan does not do any work in the garden. It is Brother who works very hard with Nana every day. Brother is Nana's favourite grandson, and the first boy grandchild in the family. It is Brother who gets the best from Nana. Nana has bought a farm tractor, trailer, and a range of ploughs for Brother to use in the garden. Nana regularly tells Nanny, "Dee buaye da wok hard too bad, nah. An ye da wok fas like hell." Uncle Jhan knows that Brother will be successor and beneficiary to Nana's estate. In fact, Nana is grooming Brother to inherit the house and land. Uncle Jhan and Aunty Jenny are quietly devising their plan.

Brother has given up his commercial course to work full-time with Stamford, Sam and Nana. Nana is losing out on my services due to my schooling. Therefore, his early investment in me as the fourth member of his permanent workforce has taken and suffered a dent. The head teacher came at least three times and pleaded with Nana to allow Rani to become a monitor pupil-teacher. He came back and asked Nana to send her to write her high school entrance examination as well. He is confident that Rani would do well in either of these two opportunities. He encouraged Nana to allow Rani to undertake these career opportunities. It will be good for Rani and the whole family. Nana agreed to the head teacher's request for both of the career opportunities.

On the exam morning Rani was dressed, ready and waiting for Uncle Jhan to take her to sit the high school entrance examination. Nana had told Uncle Jhan to make sure that Rani got there by 9.15am because the examination starts at 9.30am. Although it was a twenty-minute drive to the high school, Rani was dressed and waiting for him since 7.30am. She sat in the veranda with Nanny looking out for Uncle Jhan. At 8.40am Uncle Jhan arrived and stopped in front of the house. Nanny said, "Uncle jus come, an ye by dee road. Go now." Uncle Jhan looked at Rani and Nanny in the veranda, waited a minute or so. Immediately after Nanny told Rani to go, Rani was walking down the stairs. Uncle Jhan looked at Rani and drove off, leaving Rani on the stairs. She did not have time to walk down the stairs and he was gone. Uncle Jhan did not return until midday.

Rani was devastated. She was disappointed. She sobbed and sobbed all morning. Nanny could not appease her. Later she changed from the ugly sister's beautiful dress into her usual Cinderella clothes. Neither Nanny nor Rani could comprehend Uncle Jhan's refusal to take her to sit the examination. None of his children was doing well enough at school and were therefore unable to sit these examinations. In the evening Nana quarrelled with Uncle Jhan about his behaviour. Nana would not put up with anyone who defies his orders. Therefore, Uncle Jhan was in his firing line. Nana exploded, "You tell me don't ley dee gyal go an teach. You say ye go lok foh man in dee school. Ye eh go larn nothin dey. Ye go make child in dee school." Uncle Jhan said nothing because it would be worse for him. Nana continued, "Ah tell you to carry dee gyal to write exam, an you lef dee gyal, an you madder watchin you go wid dee car. Dee head teacher come half dozen time an beg me to ley the gyal go. An ah dee tell ye, yea. You go make me look alike a ass wen ye come back."

When everything quietened, Aunty Jenny said to Uncle Jhan, "I know he will get on and quarrel. But we have got things going in the right direction for us. There will be no teaching, and no high school for Rani." It was many years later I learnt that Aunty Jenny was instrumental in getting Nanny and Nana to refuse to send or pay for me to go to college. Rani is now staying at home with Nanny every day. She has never seen any of Nana's cane fields, or rice lagoons or the cocoa estate. Her place is always in the home. Nanny says to her, "Baytee, you da gimme ah good han. You da help me do aal dee wok in dee house. When you go get married an go away ah go miss you too bad. You da do aal dee cookin', an washin' an you da clean dee whole house foh me nah. We go look for a nice husband foh you."

Rani said to Nanny, "But Nanny, I'm not interested in marrying. I want a profession. I missed an opportunity to be either a pupil-teacher, or to go to high school. I would like to go and work and earn my own money. I do not want to depend on any man to support me. I want to be independent, Nanny. The only way I can achieve this is by gaining a professional qualification. So far I have been unable to get through with this. Aunty Jenny and Uncle Jhan are the ones who are preventing me from gaining a career. Do you remember how Uncle Jhan saw me in the veranda waiting for him and he drove off and left me?" Nanny said that she was also vexed about that. Rani put Nanny in a dilemma when she asked Nanny, "Can I go to see the head teacher and ask him for another chance to become a pupil-teacher? I would like very much to be in the profession." Nanny felt uncomfortable, because she would need to approach Nana again.

"Nanny, how many girls in this village have been given two opportunities to forge a career for themselves? How many girls' parents would prevent their daughters from going to high school, if the head teacher came and encouraged the parents to send their girl children to high school? If I can go back and ask the head teacher to take me on, this could help other girls to do the same and gain a profession as well. I do not want to be a teenage wife and mother of two or three children. What future does that hold for me, Nanny?" Rani questioned Nanny, and continued, "If Uncle Jhan and Aunty Jenny are keen to have a wedding in the house why don't they marry their daughter? She is older than me. She dresses up nicely, acts like a princess and follows her mother's footsteps."

Nanny said, "Baytee, ah dah taak but dey doh listen. Me cyant tell dem nottin."

CHAPTER 10

Rani continued her home routine. She is a very good help for Nanny. She is left alone at home more frequently so that Nanny can help out in the garden. She would always have food prepared for us when we come for lunch. She finishes the washing and the cleaning by the time the workers get home for lunch. Rani does complain that her back aches because of the scrubbing on the scrubbing board. It is sheer hard labour. When washing clothes Rani has to manually scrub down our dirty working trousers, scrub bedsheets and towels on her scrubbing board. She runs through several bars of the blue and brown soap during the course of the week. The Oxford blue makes the white washing brilliant white. It is hardly surprising that she complains of backache. Nanny would give Rani a massage and tell her to have a rest.

This rest is usually cut short when Nana shouts, "Wey dee gyaal doin? Dee food eh ready?" Rani will sprint out of bed. Nana is served first downstairs, then Stamford and Sam. Brother and I eat in the veranda. Nana is pleased to get a little help from Nanny. On Wednesday after having lunch Nana went upstairs to change his clothes. He stormed out, red in the face, anger in his eyes, leather belt in his hand, and Nanny in the kitchen facing him.

"Wey dee blasted money gaan again from dee table? Who take up dee money from dee table dis time? Ah put dee dam money an dee table dis marning, an dee money no dey. Ah ha to pay dee man an dem dis Saturday. Who tief dee money from dey?" Nana ran to Rani, "Who tief dee money from dee table? You tief dee money from dey?"

Before Rani could open her mouth to answer, it was leather belt upon leather belt upon leather belt on Rani. In his ferocious temper Nana was merciless, pounding Rani with his belt. Nanny intervened and got several belts as well. She tried to restrain Nana by holding his arm. Nana stopped beating Rani. "Dee gyal da tief dee money. Aal day ye in dee house wey ye da do? Look foh money?"

Nanny asked, "Baytee, you dee take dee money?" Rani shook her head. "No Nanny, I did not go in your room today. I closed your door and did the rest of the house. I said that when you come home I'll go clean your room. Nanny, I never went in your room today. Nanny, I had so much dirty clothes to scrub down and wash this morning. I did not have time to clean the whole house. I'm speaking the God's truth. I did not handle nor steal Nana's money. I know nothing about it."

Nanny raised a series of questions. "Baytee gyaal, wey dee money dee go from dey den? Who go go an take dee money? Buh you alone dee day in dee house whole day, gyaal? Who go come in dee house? You eh see no bady come in dee house, gyal?" Rani, in deep tears, and in great pain from the beating, answered quietly, "Nanny, I've been in the house this morning, and then went downstairs to do the washing. I shut up the doors, while I was in the kitchen preparing the lunch for when you all come home. I have not seen anyone coming into the house at any time." Rani's back is sore and very tender from the severe belting. She told Nanny that her back and arms were hurting her. She flinched when Nanny touched her back, "It's hurting me very much, Nanny," she screamed.

Nanny took her upstairs, put her to lie on her tummy and examined her back. Nanny, being very upset with Nana, called out to him, "Come an see wey you do. Dee poh child back cut up. She say, ye eh take dee money, an you dah beat dee child like dat so bad. You must ta put dee money some whey again like dee fus time."

Nana came and saw the damage which he had inflicted on Rani. He felt guilty because he does not know who took or moved the money. The word "sorry" does not exist in Nana's vocabulary.

Aunty Jenny was observing everything from her veranda. There had been this money issue before, when Nana had misplaced the money. She came across and saw the bruises on Rani's back as Nanny was rubbing it with coconut oil. Mussy also came over because she too heard Nana's shouting. Nanny was very gentle as Rani's back was painful to touch.

"Ye Nana da over beat dee gyal too bad. Dee gyal say ye eh take no money. Ye eh know wey Nana dah put the money," Nanny told Aunty Jenny.

Aunty Jenny said, "Let us all go and search the room again. We'll make sure that Nana did not misplace the money for a second time. I have noticed that he is becoming forgetful quite a lot these days. The workmen are giving him a lot of pressure because they want their pay."

The four of them searched Nanny's room thoroughly. This time, they drew a blank cheque, "No money." They racked their brains for a solution. The villagers heard that Nana was missing his money for a second time and blaming Rani for stealing it. Rani was beginning to get a bad name in the village. This will spoil Rani's chances of getting a suitable husband for marriage, they are saying among themselves.

Aunty Jenny came up with a seemingly credible answer for the missing money. She analysed, "Moye, you know she father don't work these days. The man keeps walking up and down the road like beggar and a pauper. Sometimes, he is drunk as well. I have to ask you, where does he get money? Who gives him money? How does he feed himself? And above all, how does he pay to send the boy to college?" Aunty Jenny continued, "We know that this is his biggest expense. It costs a lot of money to send the boy to college you know. Is not this true, Rani?" Rani, feeling very much ashamed to hear such statements about Papa, and to be confronted with the truth about his expenses, can only nod her head. Nanny, Mussy and Aunty Jenny thought about Papa's home circumstances. They agreed with Aunty Jenny.

Aunty Jenny continued, "Another thing I would say is that all of us know Rani is the only one in the house all day. Everyone else is out in the garden. She must know if anyone comes in the house. Who else could have taken the money since no one else came into the house? Her father probably has little or no food in his house because he does very little work to help himself. Why doesn't he go out to do some work? It clearly stands to reason that Rani must have taken the money and given it to her father. With that money her father could pay for the boy to go to college." Nanny sometimes call Papa "a vagabond". "The truth is, the country is also having shortage of food and medical supplies from the effects of the war. Her father is not getting foodstuff because he don't have no little children to mind," said Aunty Jenny. "The shopkeeper won't give 'im any creddit nah, because he cannot afford to pay back the shopkeeper. So when you put all of this together it makes sense that Rani might be giving her father the money."

I have not seen Papa for the last two weeks and I need money to buy my weekly season ticket.

Nanny sends me to the shop for flour, sugar, salt and oil with the ration card. I bought sugar, salt and flour but there was no oil in the shop. Therefore, Nanny went local, making home-made coconut oil. This is a great fun activity. Medicine also is still in short supply and the village is feeling the effect. *Mycobacterium tuberculosis* remains the biggest threat to child mortality in the village. They do not have any knowledge of TB. The villagers firmly believe that it is the evil spirits from the silk-cotton tree which are taking away their children. Evil spells are cast on the families in the village causing sickness and deaths. Therefore, they quickly seek the witch doctors to drive out the evil spells from their children and their families. I am getting to the end of another year at college. I've got another six weeks before the end of term. Sixty-four cents drama.

It's Friday evening and I must finish all my schoolwork as usual so that I can go in the garden and not worry about schoolwork over the weekend. I finished my homework after midnight and went to bed feeling drained. I have no money to renew my season ticket in the morning. I got up early and ran up to Papa's house at West Hill without Nanny seeing me. Papa was not at home. I ran back quickly and Nanny saw me as I was coming up the stairs. "Wey you been, dis hour? You eh ready to go in dee gyarden?" she asked.

"I went to look for Papa, Nanny. I have no money to renew my weekly ticket this morning, and Papa was not home. I have not seen him for two weeks," I said.

"You fadder like to knack about too much. Ye eh know ye gat to gi you money to go to dee callege?" she said.

I made my plea, "Nanny, I have no money, can you please lend me the money, just lend me the money, so that I can renew my ticket. If I don't renew it today, I will not be able to go to school next week. I will not be able to travel at all. When I see Papa I will give you back the money."

Nanny said, "You fadder know damn good you go ha to buy you ticket an ye eh gi you no money? Well, me eh ha no money too." I was stunned by Nanny's remark. I became desperate and helpless. I began crying. I could not bear to miss out on a week schooling. I begged Nanny again and again to lend me the money. I pleaded with her in my sobbing to lend me the money.

"Nanny, it is only sixty-four cents I need to renew my ticket, please lend me it. When I see Papa I will give you back the money." I repeated this several times.

Nanny asked me again, "How much foh dee ticket?"

"Sixty-four cents, Nanny," I replied.

Brother came up at the same time and saw me crying. "What's wrong with you now, mister man? Which girl are you crying for now, is it for the two little ones lying in the riverbed?" He was laughing.

"Boy, I don't have any money to renew my weekly bus pass for next week. I did not see Papa for two weeks. I ask Nanny to lend me the money, but she would not give it to me."

Brother got serious. "Moye, why don't you give him the money to renew his ticket?"

"Ent ye fadder sennin ye, wey ye doh gi ye dee money," Nanny said.

Brother said to Nanny, "If I had $64 I would give him the lot, but I don't have a cent on me. Moye, give the boy the money. He's only asking for sixty-four cents."

Nanny listened to Brother and gave me three shillings (seventy-two cents). "Ah wah back me change, you hear me?" Nanny said to me.

"Thank you very much, Nanny, thank you, Nanny," I said, bowing down and touching Nanny's feet. This was a mighty relief for me. I returned her eight cents immediately after renewing my weekly bus pass. When I saw Papa he gave me sixty-four cents for Nanny. I headed directly for the garden where Brother, Stamford and Sam were working.

Uncle Jhan and Aunty Jenny have been discussing me regularly. I am in town five days a week. Aunty Jenny told him, "That boy will be in the house for another five years. We can't wait that long to get them out of there." Uncle Jhan said, "I love his uniform. But our daughter did not pass for high school." They discussed between themselves what to do about Rani as well. "She can't go on stealing money and denying it," he said.

Uncle Jhan and Aunty Jenny wanted to get to the root of this missing money. They discussed it with Nana. Following on from what Aunty Jenny had said to Nanny and Mussy and now to Uncle Jhan and Nana, they strongly believed that Rani took the money and gave it to Papa. But they have no solid proof of this, only mere suspicion. The Obeah men (witch doctors) can give them the proof and identity of the thief.

Uncle Jhan said to Nana and Nanny, "The Obeah man will tell us if Rani stole the money. Let us take Rani to the fellow in Muruga. He is good. Many people go to him. He can tell we for sure." Nana, Nanny, Uncle Jhan and Aunty Jenny took Rani there. The place looks dreary and frightening. There are dozens and dozens of multicoloured flags posted in front of the house. There were more flags at the back of the house. Some people come discreetly and have their flags erected behind the house. The more flags around the witch doctor's home, the more popular he is, and a greater income he generates. The black flags outnumber the other colours by a ratio of 3:1. The next most popular colour is red.

As the visitors enter the premises, an old man who was sitting in a dark corner with a dim light coming from behind, came out to greet them. He shook Nana's hand first, followed by Uncle, Nanny and Aunty Jenny. He led them into a small hut by the side of his house. It was dark, made darker by the four walls being covered with black sheets. The walls were bare and the room was smoke-filled from the burning incense. A human skeleton stood in the left-hand corner. And two skulls on poles. His library of books were on the shelf behind him. He brought a dim light forward.

"I am Dr Agu-Rum, a specialist in revealing mysteries, and casting out evil spells in sick people. I help many families to get rid of their problems." He asked Nana to sit in the front of him, and the others to sit behind Nana. He sat with six books at his side. "I see five of you here today. What have you come for?" Dr Agu-Rum asks Nana. This witch doctor is an elderly, frail-looking man. He has deep-set black eyes, grey eyebrows and a receding forehead. His hair is grey on the sides. He has two missing front teeth, an elongated chin and sunken cheeks. He is softly spoken, and at times hardly audible.

The little room was poorly lit with one candle already three-quarters burnt out. The air was thick from the burning incense sticks. The Obeah man asked which one of them was the problem. He wanted a short history of the issue.

Nana began to cough from the polluted room before speaking. "Ah lass me money dee edder day. Somebady tief it. Dem say, dee gyal take dee money an gi ye fadder dee money. Ye fadder doh do no wok. Ye da waak about aal over dee place. Ah wan to know if dee gyal tief dee money. Ah wan to know foh sure, if ye tief dee money an gi ye fadder. Is plenty ah money ah put dey to pay dee wokka an dem. Is $750 wey gaan from dee room."

The Obeah man asked, "Which one ah dem you say tief dee money?"

Nana said, "The grandchild."

The witch doctor spoke softly to Rani, "Come here, child, and show me you han'. Hold dis in you right hand. Hold dis in your left han'. Say dis after me, word for word, a'right? You an me goin to communicate wid me spirits."

The practitioner recited a paragraph from his book, which was wrapped in a black cloth. The words did not sound like Spanish, nor French, nor Latin, and certainly not English. It is clear that Rani did not recite what the man said but he carried on all the same. He got up, went into another room and brought out a dead black cobo. He also brought one of the human skulls and placed the cobo on it. He placed it in front of Rani with the cobo's beak pointing at Rani's eyes. The Obeah man was observing her reaction. Rani was certainly more curious than frightened. She quietly asked herself, "I wonder what's he going to do with this cobo."

The man began chanting, and the smell of incense continued to pollute the room. He took the bird, placed it on Rani's head, and continued his muffling sounds. They were indistinguishable gibberish. His performance was spectacular and impressive. The procedure took almost an hour. The Obeah man sat down and looked directly into Rani's eyes. The ritual was finished.

The Obeah man turned to Nana, "Ah see somethin' dey, but ah can't make it out. It like a shadow. An ah can't get nothin' comin from dee child. But somethin' right dey. Ah see a shadow but ah can't make it out, sir. Sir, dat is aal ah could say." Nana looked very disappointed. Having to come all this way and not get the result he expected, and the cost infuriated Nana. The witch doctor said to Nana, "Is $300, sir."

On the way home, Nana spoke in an aggressive manner, "Dem fella an dem, eh wot one ass, man. Dem only take me money foh nothin'. Dem woss dan dee damn tief wey take dee money." Nobody responded. Uncle Jhan was responsible for organising this day. He was keen to find out who stole the money. How could it go missing when Rani was at home all day, and all alone as a worker and a watchman for the house? Uncle Jhan said that all the evidence which they have put together pointed to Rani.

"She has to, and must know, who took the money." But the Obeah man could not prove that Rani took the money. Uncle Jhan persuaded Nana to take Rani to other specialists in this field. One such specialist was the voodoo and witchcraft practitioner, the "Shango" woman. Nana spent more money and time searching for answers and still there was no fruitful outcome. Uncle Jhan and Aunty Jenny urged Nana to visit the Shango lady to see if she could tell whether Rani stole the money.

The Shango woman lives along the Sisters Road near White Land. Her home lies behind several palm trees and bougainvillaea plants of various vibrant colours. She has a herbal garden on the left side of the bungalow. There are scores of free-range cockerels among her stock of poultry. There is an open-air shelter on the right side of the house. This is her operation centre. At one corner there is a chopping log two feet in diameter, and three feet high. This is her sacrificial altar. Her practice is an open-air ceremony performed in the glare of the public. The neighbours are used to her activity in treating her customers and so they take little notice of her.

"Hello, marning to aal a you, an welcome home. I am Modder Alma, an everybody know dat. Everybady come here wid a problem. So, what is you problem dis marning?"

Uncle Jhan said, "We had some money missing from the house the other day. We want to know if this child took it. It was a lot of money. We do want to know if she took it. She denies having any knowledge of the money."

The Shango woman began her routine. She was wearing a red-and-black striped dress reaching her toes. Her broad-rimmed hat was made of plaited coconut leaves. She was a rather obese fifty-year-old, with a gracious perpetual smile. Her white teeth are set against a black face and eyes. Her flabby cheeks and pronounced buttocks flapped up and down as she danced round a bonfire several times and chanted her gibberish. Alma waved a huge flambeau continuously as she danced round the bonfire. The Olympic torch is no match for the brilliance of her flambeau. She was shouting loud. She was becoming hysterical. She shook her head and hands vigorously while bowing to the flames.

She knocked Rani over during her dancing, pulled Rani round with her, and dropped her on the ground. The woman brought in a live red cockerel and sacrificed it on her sacrificial altar. One chop was sufficient to behead the red cockerel. As the blood poured out of the cockerel the woman fed it into the fire going round and round the flames. She continued to hold the chicken to the flames as she danced round it. Rani was lying on the ground and was included within her cyclical dance. This was a dramatic performance. Her loud singing were her prayers to summon the evil spirits to answer her. She beat her drum louder and louder as she sang. She was in a state of frenzy. Then she threw the cockerel into the flames.

She sat next to Rani, placed her hand on Rani's forehead, chanting louder and louder in frenzied mood. Alma pushed Rani and she fell backwards. She picked Rani up and danced round her about half a dozen times and collapsed in front of Rani. All her antics failed her. Rani is too strong in mind, and so she resists all the woman's attempts to subdue her. At the end of this exercise Rani is exonerated. The Shango woman said to Nana, "My name is Alma. Dis child eh tief no money." Nana was annoyed and disappointed again. Alma said, "Dat go cast you $150 today, but as dis is you fus time here ah go make it $100."

Nana's friend Atta Roberto also got involved very reluctantly. He would never imagine that Rani would be so hand-fast. He loves Rani, and considers her as his daughter. He has repeatedly told Nana that he is very lucky to have a wonderful granddaughter as Rani. Stamford also feels the same about Rani. Stamford says of Rani, "Dee gyal is mee eyeball." They both love Rani very much indeed. When Sam comes home he is usually calling out for "mee child". *Can these three men be wrong about Rani?* Nana asks himself. Nana's most trusted friend is Atta. However, to please Nana, Atta very reluctantly recommended the renowned Obeah man from Mayo. Nana had asked Atta several times to make an arrangement to see the witch doctor but Atta refused to do so. Aunty Jenny is the main driver to push

Nana to see this man in Mayo. Atta is certain and fully confident that Rani is innocent. He always considers Rani as a blessed child. This Mayo Obeah man is good at casting out evil spells from another person and putting evil spells on others. He has powers to prove a person's guilt in stealing. Many of them are satisfied with this witch doctor's results. Therefore, he takes higher fees from his clients. Only cash payments are accepted by all these Obeah men.

Atta told Nana that this is not right or proper what the child is going through. "Pusha, she is only a child, I don't like what you all are doing to her. You are only destroying the innocent child's mind. I am 100% sure that Rani would not handle any money. I am doing this because it's you and you ask me many times to help you. So, I have arranged for you to see this Obeah man on Friday 18th at eleven o'clock in the morning. Let's hear what he has to say.

"Pusha, to tell you the truth, you must have wasted three to four times more money behind these blasted Obeah men, practitioners, see-ah-man, witch doctors and pundits, call them whatever you like, you have spent more money on them than the money you lost or stolen or simply went missing. So, Pusha, I'm putting it to you, what sense does it make to go through all this, and make your grandchild suffer so much, and you get nothing for it? I would never want to do such a thing to my child, it does not matter how bad she may be. This damage you are doing to the child will cause her to hate you for the rest of her life. Pusha, you don't want her to hate you like that. Now that I have spoken my mind to you, think it over, and if you decide to cancel this appointment do let me know. Yes, Pusha, if you do decide to cancel this appointment, I would be extremely happy indeed. Do remember, I am only thinking of little Rani, my child, OK? I do not want her to go through this ordeal. That is my firm view. Or, if you are going ahead with the appointment then everything remains in force."

"But Atta, you da make good sense man. Wey you na taak to me like dat befoh eh. Me eh dah spen so much money nah. Man, ah done spen it aready. Ah kyan't get it back now. Foh mee self, man Atta, ah go caal it aff man, Atta. Me too eh wah me child to suffer dis kind ah ting. Bah de gyal [Aunty Jenny] wey wan me to take ye [Rani] by dee man. Ley me ah taak to dee buaye, [Uncle Jhan] nah, an ley me hear wah ye go ha to say nah."

The very first of these practitioners to whom Nana had gone to find out about the missing money was Pundit Dhaykha. He is a well-respected Hindu priest in the remote village of Poole. This rural community has a thriving cocoa and coffee industry. You also can hear the howling monkeys in the distant forest. It is hardly surprising that the nearby village is called Monkey Town.

Pundit Dhaykha, well into his sixties, is poor in material things but he is rich in heart. He is generous, kind and helpful towards anyone who comes to him. His mandir (prayer building) sits alongside his home. He told Nana that when he looked into his book he saw a bright vision. He knew that Rani did not handle any money. He accepts no money from anyone. He had a lengthy conversation with Nana. He told Nana that he has a blessed child. Nana decided to stop going to visit anyone else after hearing what Pundit Daykha said about Rani. It was Uncle Jhan and Aunty Jenny's persistence which caused Nana to go to those Obeah men.

Nana, Nanny, Uncle Jhan and Aunty Jenny took Rani to the Mayo man. They entered a dark room. They have grown accustomed to seeing such an environment. The Mayo practitioner welcomed them and introduced himself as Dr Namhaebo. He carried out his consultation, had his diagnosis, and now it was time for him to act. He led Rani into a private, dark room with a single candle lighting in the far corner. Nana, Nanny and Uncle Jhan can hear the conversation, but they cannot see anything. Aunty Jenny was peeping from behind the door. The smell of the incense was intoxicating. Nana began coughing. A cock was crowing in the room. A bell was ringing. The witch doctor was speaking "in tongues". The language was alien, Rani thought. Skulls and reptiles were suspended from the ceiling. The reptiles were live; they were moving and crawling in one corner. Rani was scared. She wanted to run out. It was a gruesome and scary-looking room in which to be.

The room suddenly got quiet. Moments later, Rani screamed out very loudly, "Nanny, Nanny, Nanny, come, come quick." Uncle Jhan rushed into the room before Nana. The man was trying to pull back up his trousers quickly. Uncle Jhan saw the Obeah man's trousers halfway down. Uncle Jhan grabbed hold of him, kicked him in his testicles, punched him in the face before the man could retaliate. Nana took a piece of wood and chased him round the house. The man stumbled and fell. He was at Nana's mercy. Nana showered down blows on the old bitch. Nana was going to kill him, but Uncle Jhan stopped Nana. "This blasted man was going to rape the child!" Uncle Jhan exclaimed. This Obeah man was left savagely beaten in the drain. He was an awesome sight – blood red.

Nanny was holding Rani like a baby. Rani was trembling incessantly. Her tears were dried out, her teeth chattering, and fright was overwhelming her. She did not want to let go of Nanny. Nanny comforted her all the way home. This experience shattered everyone. Aunty Jenny felt guilty about the incident because she was insisting that Nana should take Rani to this witch doctor despite what Atta had told Nana. Nana thought of Atta. He regretted going to this man. It was too late for regrets. He told Nanny, "If ah dee listen to Atta an take ye advice, dis ting woun dah happen to dee child today nah."

All four adults, Nana, Nanny, Aunty Jenny and Uncle Jhan knew that they had done a terrible injustice to Rani, but they could not climb down to say sorry to her. They are too proud to do so, particularly Aunty Jenny. This humiliating and degrading experience which Rani suffered will haunt her for the rest of her life. The offenders could never be forgiven for their actions, not even by the Lord

God Almighty. No compensatory gestures can amend or obliterate the psychological damage inflicted on Rani. This is the dire result of an unknown sum of missing money in Nana's house.

A week later Nana did puja with Nanny and Rani sitting for it. Nana does his "Hawan" himself under the avocado tree every two months. He is his own pundit. We have to sit and listen to his prayers and hold the "Jhandi" (flag on a bamboo pole) together while he puts it up. There are lots of tulsie plants growing around the avocado tree. Nana and Nanny call it "the zaboka" (avocado) tree. The "tulsie" plant and the "paan" are plants for religious Hindu functions and ceremonies. The paan is a tree climber like the climbing ivy plant. It adheres to the trunk of the zaboka tree like the parasitic leech clinging on to my lower leg.

Uncle Jhan and Aunty Jenny took it upon themselves to seek other witch doctors to find out who stole Nana's money. They went as far as Rousillac, where Nana's cousins live, Siparia, Sangre Grande and Mayaro, seeking help from the Obeah men. All the while Uncle Jhan and Aunty Jenny were spending a lot of Nana's money on these additional enquiries from the Obeah men. Nana was becoming very angry with them and said to Nanny, "Dem buaye an dem [Uncle Jhan and Aunty Jenny] spendin' me money like *gobarr* [cow's dung]."

At last Uncle Jhan turned to our local "Mr Know-all" witch doctor, Ganti, in the village. He lives in the west side of the river and a quarter of a mile from Nana's house. He is the most flamboyant character you will meet. He masks his face, but his eyes are unmistakeable. Once you've seen them you will always remember them. Both of his eyes are cock-eyed. He suffers with gross nystagmus. When you think that he is looking at you he is not. He makes up his eyes with red, blue and black eye make-up. The cut-out around his eyes is large so that his eyebrows are visible. He paints them green. In fact he looks ghastly. He looks like someone in a carnival masquerade. He is skinny and short and about thirty or thirty-five years old. He has 365 flags posted around his home. Each one represents a day in the annual calendar. On leap years he puts up an enormous flag containing a patchwork of 366 individual multicoloured pieces of material. Every flag is sewn around its perimeter with cotton balls. Of course, the cotton is freely available at Cotton Hill. There is a rivulet running at the back of his house. It enters the Guaracara river two miles further down from the bridge. Ganti sees the two fair-haired, fair-skinned and blue-eyed girls lying there at the bottom of this stream. He visits them and communicates with them regularly. At least once a week Ganti is seen coming out of Nana's cane field. He goes to the silk-cotton tree to invoke the spirits.

His advertising board in front of his house reads, "Your Professor Ganti. I profess to know everything. And I profess to tell you everything. Tel: 018 0018. I give you 18 years of experience."

"Hi Jhan, long time no see, man. I hear about your

father missing the money. How you doing so far? Any luck yet? What your father going to do about that silk-cotton tree? The cobos doing plenty mischief around the place. Well, what can I do for you today man? Are you still going for it?"

Uncle Jhan said, "Well yeah, Gan, so far nothing has come up and we still don't know who took the money. We can try and see what you could come up with."

"Come inside and sit by the candle," he said. His business room has one door and no windows. This room is under his house. It is poorly lit and suffocating with the smoke of the burning incense. There are several creatures suspended from the ceiling. He has two cobos, two goat skulls, a chicken head, one barn owl, two squirrels, three huge rats, and four black scorpions. There is a python pinned on the wall. Ganti said, "When I invoke the spirits one or two of these creatures become live." He goes around chanting his "prayers" and touching them to see which ones will be activated. It is the first time that Uncle Jhan has entered this room. He finds it rather gruesome and frightening. When he thinks of some of these creatures coming alive, Uncle Jhan is trembling in his guts, but he is trying to put on a brave face. Ganti senses this, but says nothing to him.

Ganti selects one book from his bookshelf and reads silently while Uncle Jhan continues to gaze around the room at the creatures to see which one may come alive. Suddenly one of the cobos opens its beak as if it is having a big lazy yawn. Uncle Jhan got frightened. There was a squawk from behind him. Uncle Jhan looked round but nothing was there. He wanted to run. Ganti continues his reading silently. There was another louder squeal which came from behind him. This time Uncle Jhan saw the cobo looking at him; it stretched its neck while it slowly closed its beak. Uncle Jhan forced himself to look up at the ceiling. He almost fainted when he saw the python slowly slithering across the ceiling. Uncle Jhan was shaking and chattering with fear. Ganti put his hand on Uncle Jhan's shoulder to allay his fears, but Uncle Jhan jumped up.

"OK, Jhan, I can see how scared you are but you did not run out of the room. Now, I want you to go home and check out when it is going to be the full moon. At midnight, I want you to kill a red cock – blood red – and bring the head to the cemetery. I'll be waiting over there for you. Don't disappoint me. If you want to change your mind, tell me two days before so that I can revoke this whole process, otherwise it will fall on you and finish you. Dat is how dis thing work."

Uncle Jhan pondered at what he was told, debating whether he should or should not go ahead with this procedure. After all, it is he and Aunty Jenny who want to prove that Rani stole Nana's money and gave to Papa. The previous Obeah men were not able confirm this. But Ganti has the power to prove or disprove whether Rani stole the money. Nana and Nanny refuse to see any more Obeah men. Nanny says that Rani has suffered too much already. Uncle Jhan turned to Ganti and said, "Gan,

I'm going ahead with it. I'll meet you at the cemetery at midnight on the eighteenth. It's full moon."

He was at the cemetery promptly at the stroke of midnight. Ganti was waiting for him. He was wearing a black outfit with hat, gloves and a full-length gown. He was barefooted. He told Uncle Jhan, "I would like you to hold the cock's head in both hands and stretch them out to offer it to my team of advisors when I tell you, OK?" Ganti began his chants and after eighteen minutes Uncle Jhan saw figures coming out of one of the graves. These bizarre seahorse- and praying mantis-shaped figures were walking from side to side. There were eighteen of them. Suddenly, a big black cobo arose from one of the graves and started hovering over the figures. Then another seventeen arose and followed the first one. After several minutes of this performance it was time to move forward. The cobos continued to fly over the figures as the figures slowly and deliberately headed towards Uncle Jhan.

Uncle Jhan was amazed at Ganti's power to invoke the evil spirits. As they approached Uncle Jhan, he got scared, hoping that they would turn back. But they kept coming slowly and slowly towards him. The cobos disappeared. The eighteen morose figures came up very close to Uncle Jhan to receive their offering. He was scared out of his wits, screamed out, dropped the cock's head and started running for his life. He stumbled over, got up and continued running until he reached home. The two dogs, Bulla and Clara, were barking frantically and running up and down the yard as if they were hunting down a fox or a wild mongoose. They were seeing the spirits and chasing after them. Uncle Jhan slouched in the veranda, breathless. He remained there until he could catch his breath. Bulla and Clara gradually quietened and eventually lay on the warm yard.

Chapter 11

THE WATER SHORTAGE CONTINUES to cause serious problems in the village. We have to be grateful for the pond, but this water level is getting low. The water truck supplies the village with water twice a week, but the amount we get is rationed to two tins per house. That's why we are reminded of the slogan "Waste not, want not". The pond has plenty of fish and alligators. There are two-feet-long "wabeen" and six-inch-broad "cuscurub". The four- to six-feet-long alligators bask on the sunny bank while the women wash their clothes on the opposite bank. They spread their washing on the outer cricket field to dry out. The guava trees line this bank. The sweet smell of the ripe guavas makes us salivate. The girls carry buckets or tins of water on their heads with their mothers from the pond to their homes.

One of them is B. She is the prettiest girl in the village. This is the general view of the boys. B has long, straight, black waist-length hair. She has a round face and sparkling light brown eyes. Her cheeks are red from the heat of the sun. She wears a charming radiant smile. She shows off her prowess in carrying the water on her head without holding on to the tin. She sways her hips from side to side to show off so that the boys can look at her. The other girls try and do the same as B to attract the boys' attention. Their mothers walk behind them.

The boys stop playing their cricket to allow the women and their daughters to pass across the cricket field. This gives the boys the chance to have a good look at the girls as they pass by. The girls are quite conscious of this as they make little glances at the boys. The cricket practice continues when they have gone. We do get further interruptions when we hear Lutchman's mother shouting and screaming from the top of her voice, "Boye-wah, Boye-wah, go an cut dee bundle ah grass foh dee animal. Ah say, bring dee bundle ah gass quick. Den come an see bout dee animal. You hear wat ah say?" The cricket practice will be adjourned but the talk about the girls will continue. Who would we say demonstrates the best style in carrying their buckets and tins of water on their heads without holding on to their buckets? No one talks to any of the girls, because both parties will land themselves into trouble. It is safer to look at the girls and remain quiet. When they come to the standpipe to wait for water the boys get a chance to talk to the girls. They will be the ones trying to attract the girls' attention by making jokes and laughing loudly together. However, the girls do not come out to the standpipes at night. On most occasions the water comes in the standpipe at night.

This Friday evening (17th) I must complete all my schoolwork so I am free for the weekend. "You Nana gwain Pay Shay tomarrow marning to pick carn an cocoa," said Nanny. "Are you buaye [brother and I] go ha to get up awley to go, you hear?" I had pre-empted another busy weekend for us. Following my evening duties I buckled down to my work. It was just past 8.30pm. I was tired, but I must get my work done. I worked until it was past midnight. Brother woke up and said, "Come get some sleep, we have to leave early for Pay Shay." He went back to sleep. About fifteen minutes later Nanny came into the sitting room. "You still waking? Like you go sleep right dey? You better go to sleep now. You gat to get up awley in dee marning." She blew out the kerosene lamp and sent me to bed.

"You bunning too much pitch-oil in dee house every night," she said. I trotted off to bed. Brother was asleep again. I did not disturb him. I crossed over him carefully and went on my side of the bed. Moments later I was in the "arms of Morpheus" as Scorpion used to say to me at school. In the early morning hours Nana woke up from the noisy box carts with their empty kerosene tins on the road. Some boys were already going to fetch water from the standpipe. Scorpion says, "Empty vessels make the most noise." It is 3.00am this morning. Nana said to Nanny, "Ye gat wata in dee pipe. Ley dem buaye an dem [Brother and I] go an get two barrel ah wata wid dee mule

This large copper was used for water for the villagers, that is communal use. It was maintained by everyone to ensure that when water comes in the only one standpipe the copper will be kept filled. When the standpipe water was locked off this water was used. The pond water was used for washing clothes and watering plants. It was also boiled and then used for cooking or drinking.

On a lighter note the pond, the copper and the standpipe served as meeting places for the boys and girls when they came with buckets and tins to fetch water. B was the one girl who attracted all the boys' attention. She was very conscious of that. She would show off and make style with a tin of water on her head. She would not hold on to the tin, would balance it and sway her hips from side to side as she walked home. The copper pictured is from the early 1900's sugar cane factory. When the factory was operational in the village these coppers were used for the mules and bulls to drink water. The animals would be led to the coppers. They would stand around the coppers and take their drink. The copper pictured is owned by Habib Jahoor. Usati's nana had two such large coppers. He and his brother would fetch barrels of water from the standpipe on the mule cart and brought to fill the coppers.

kyart." Nanny woke us up. Brother saw me very drowsy and ready to fall back to sleep. He left me, harnessed the mule, loaded two barrels on the cart and went to fetch the water. At 3.30am there was a long queue of people and box carts waiting for the water to come in the standpipe. At about 3.45am the water was gushing through the pipe. The news went round quickly. "Dee water come! Dee water come!" they were alerting the villagers.

Nana heard people saying, "Water come! Water come in dee pipe!" "Dee buaye an dem gwaan foh dee wata aready?" he asked Nanny.

"Yea," she said to him. Brother returned at 5.00am with two barrels of water. Nana was downstairs getting ready to go to Pay Shay. We would have to go later because of the water crisis. When he saw only Brother coming in with the water and mule cart he was instantly enraged. He shouted at Nanny, "Wey dat buaye dey?" He was referring to me.

Nanny said, "Ye still sleepin."

Nana said, "You mean to say, dee buaye [Brother] gaan an ye own for dee water, an dat one still sleepin'? Wey ye dey?" Nana shouted. "In dee bed?"

Nanny said, "Yea, ye dey in dee bed. Ye nah dah get up yet. Ah dee wake ye up, an ye gaan back to sleep."

At 5.15am Nana took up a long piece of wood and banged it on the step. "Ye too damn lazy, ye eh want to do no wok." He banged the wood on the step again as he was coming upstairs for me. His footsteps were heavy. He was in a terrible mood shouting, "Wey ye dey, wey ye dey?" as he sped upstairs. He pushed the bedroom door open. I jumped out of the bed. I heard, "Whap! Whap! Whap!" on the empty bed. Nana thought that I was still there in the bed. But he saw me fly through the interconnecting door into the next bedroom and out of the front door, through the veranda and down the stairs. I turned around only to see Nana chasing after me. I ran as fast as I could and he nearly caught up with me. I made it to the cocoa-house. I ran round and round the cocoa-house as Nana was chasing me. I went under the cocoa-house, into one of the aisles among the stacked steel barrels of corn grains. The three aisles were too narrow for Nana to come through. He saw me in the middle aisle. He couldn't get in. He kept beating the barrels in anger. It was quarter past five in the morning.

He ran outside to see if I would come out at the other end of the cocoa-house. I went between the barrels in a corner. He could not see me. He banged against the wall. I tried to move out because I had got stuck between the barrels. Nana saw me as day was clearing. He pulled out a board and got in. He cornered me there. He landed blow after blow on me. "You too damn lazy, you too damn lazy," he said, as the blows fell on my back, on my legs and on my arms. He was merciless. Whatever part of my body he could reach, he hit me. I bowed my head, put my arms on the back of my neck and protected my head from the heavy stick. I was in terrible pain. I was screaming, crying and bawling but Nana continued to beat me. The morning got clear at about 6.30am. Nana left me in the corner. He said, "Me eh finish with you yet. Wen you come in dee gyarden ah waiting foh you." He was getting late to go in the cocoa estate.

I was in severe pain. My back, arms and my legs were very sore and painful to touch. I could hardly move out of that corner. I stayed there for what seemed to be ages. I began thinking and thinking and thinking hard. I began to reason with myself. I remained under the cocoa-house thinking and reasoning. What was I thinking and reasoning?

I have been severely beaten under this cocoa-house this morning of Saturday 18th of April at 5.15am, at this same hour of the morning when I was born. That morning was a beautiful sunny Sunday morning, Mama had told me. When I ran under this cocoa-house at 5.15am, it was warm, dry and dark. It is now belting down with torrential showers of rain. It was falling "bucket a drop" Nanny would say. I got beaten for not getting up at four o'clock in the morning to go with Brother to fetch water from the standpipe. Why should I face more beating in the garden?

My body is very painful. I am regularly accused of being "too lazy" although I feel that I do my fair share of work here. Neither Nana, Nanny, Aunty Jenny nor Uncle Jhan cares about my education. Nanny and Nana refused to send me to college. I must be one of the workmen, yes, one of the permanent gang of four. I do not want that ever. I will never be a part of this group in the way they want me to be. I have this one opportunity of a lifetime to receive a decent education and no one, I am saying that no one, is going stop me from achieving my goal.

I remembered how I had to beg Nanny to borrow sixty-four cents to buy my season ticket to travel to school. She made me pay her back the money. Many thanks to Brother who pleaded with Nanny to lend me the sixty-four cents, I am working here doing all I can reasonably do, and what do I get in return? Do Nanny and Nana really love us as their grandchildren? Do they care anything about my education? Or do they have us as their workforce twenty-four hours a day? Are we mere manpower and economic resources to foster Nana's business? Above all, what disturbs me most, is that Nana gets praise from almost all the villagers in Sunnyvale for sending me to college. It amazes me to see how he laps it up. I simply cannot digest that most of all. None of the villagers knows the truth of the matter that it is Papa who is sending me to college. They would not think that he is able to afford it.

Papa is regularly seen drunk and walking along the road. He does not speak to anyone when he is in this state. No one would talk to him. He does little work in the garden. He does not work for anyone to earn money. I often wonder how he manages to get money to support himself as well as to support me to go to college. So far, Papa has been able to give me my tuition fees of $16 dollars per term, and sixty-four cents per week to travel.

The only thing I receive from Nana and Nanny is board and lodging. There is plenty of everything at

Nana's house – food and work and punishment. I can get board and lodging elsewhere without punishment. What I want, Nana and Nanny are not giving me. I cannot take any more beating. I will not, and it is time that my body gets a rest. I will not take any more beating. It is too much for me to bear. Therefore, I am not going in the garden this morning nor at any other time ever. I am not going to get any more beating from Nana. He is waiting for me in the garden but I am not going. The rain has been falling since 6.30am. It is now 7.30am. I am under the cocoa-house. No one has seen or heard what happened to me this morning. Only Nana and I know. And heaven has seen and heard every word and everything. He is the witness to all of it. My mind is made up under this cocoa-house, this morning.

I am going away from here. Yes! Yes! I am leaving now. Not an hour longer! I am leaving Nana, Nanny and my siblings. I will never come back here. My table is turned. There's no turning back. No! My final whistle is blown.

I crept slowly and painfully out of the corner. I walked out of the narrow aisle. The rain was still belting down. That special morning of Mama's funeral, there was sunshine before the great storm and then followed by sunshine again. Mama left us on that morning. She was dead. It is the same thing happening this morning. We have dry weather and a shortage of water. This is followed by the terrific downpour of rain, and I am leaving this morning. But I am alive. I walked through the heavy rain from under the cocoa-house to the sitting room. I was drenched because I was not able to run any more. My body was still in too much pain.

Is it not ironic that I have been so severely beaten because of the shortage of water and now the heavens are wide open? The torrential rain is bucketing down and soon the two massive coppers and the dozens of barrels will be filled to capacity. There will be excess water flowing away because there is too much water for both houses.

I slowly bundled up my books together, packed my book bag and wrapped up the rest of my books in a plastic sheet and a sugar bag. I picked up my uniform and put it in another bag. I never stopped crying. Brother, Rani and Dewan watched me doing this. None of them knew anything. Brother spoke, "What are you doing? Come and get ready to go in the garden." I simply shook my head because I could not speak. I was overcome with physical pain and emotional grief. When Brother saw that I picked up my uniform he became serious, "Where are you going?" he asked. Still no word from me. They saw me crying continuously, not knowing what happened to me. I picked up my bookcase and the rest of my possessions. I put some under my arm to hold everything together. Then I walked into the kitchen. Nanny looked at me. I spoke for the first time to them, "Nanny, I'm going," with tears flowing non-stop from my eyes.

"Wey you goin?" she asked.

I said, "I am leaving, and I am going away." When Rani and Dewan heard "leaving" and "going away", they started crying. Rani could not stop crying for me and probably with me. Nanny seemed annoyed with me. She asked me, "Wey you goin'? You tink you fadder go mind you? Eh, you fadder eh have two penny to rub ye backside, ye go mind you? Ye eh dah do no wok. Aal dee wok in dee gyarden jes so. Wey e go get money to mind you?" Everyone, including Nanny, knows that the only place where I can go is at Papa's house. I have no other place to go.

I plucked up courage. From where it came, I did not now. I said, "Nanny to answer all your questions and remarks this morning, it is with sadness, grief and utter despair that I am handing you back your own words. It is the phrase which you have said to me so many times over the years whenever I say something or ask for something. Today, to answer all your questions and remarks I am simply saying, 'kutch nah bole.' I am leaving." Shock, raised eyebrows, stunned silence and disbelief from Rani and Brother, and even more so from Nanny resulted from the utterance of this phrase and at this moment in time.

I turned to go, and Rani grabbed hold of me, "Don't go, please don't go," she cried bitterly. Dewan also began crying when it got into him what it meant by my going. Brother looked utterly distressed, his eyes were dull, his face was sad, but no tears flowed. I can see that his tears were suppressed and he also was crying in his heart. Nanny was firm and angry with me. I saw her expression. Her face indicated no sign of sympathy or sadness at my going away. She made no attempt to dissuade me, or to ask me not to go. She remained in the kitchen, and as I turned around to face Brother and Rani, Nanny said to me, "You gwain today, an doh badder to come back wen you gaan." I said nothing. Brother was standing at the kitchen gate which leads down the stairs. He was blocking me. I faced him with tears pouring down my face. He said softly, "Where do you think you're going? You better put those books down and get ready to go in the garden. Come and eat something and then we will go in the garden."

I was too weak to push Brother away from the kitchen gate. I stopped in front of him, looked at him, and shook my head and I said, "No, boy, I am not going into the garden ever again. Don't stop me, please. I cannot take any more beating, boy."

He asked me, "What happened this morning? I heard Nana quarrelling."

I said, "Brother, boy, Nana beat me very badly under the cocoa-house. He hit me all over my body except on my head. This was at 5.15am. It was because I did not go with you to fetch water from the standpipe. Nana is waiting to beat me when I go in the garden. I am not going. I am not going into that garden. I am going away and I am not coming back. Nobody is going to stop me. If you knew what I suffered there under that cocoa-house, if you only knew… I cannot say any more. It is too painful for me to recount or talk about what I went through under that cocoa-house this morning."

Brother took away my load. He said, "Let me see, let me see." He saw my arms, and raised my shirt to see my back. He looked shocked. He gave me back my load of books and uniform. He said nothing and slowly moved away from the kitchen gate to allow me to pass. This gate was to prevent the dogs from entering the kitchen or the house. I slowly walked down the stairs for the last time.

The rain continued with torrential showers. It was 8.30am, Saturday April 18th when I walked off the last stair and out into the heavy rain. I never looked back but kept on walking towards the cocoa-house at the back. I passed Uncle Jhan's house and Aunty Jenny and her children were in their veranda looking at me. Within minutes I was drenched in the rain again. I passed alongside the cocoa-house and went through the sugar cane field. I went at the back so that no one would see me. I came up from the back of Papa's house. He was not there. All my clothes got soaked in the rain while coming to Papa's house. I changed into one of Papa's trousers and a shirt. Today marked the turning point in my life. I have left a house of plenty and come into a house of near emptiness. This is the most significant change I will experience. I will be living in abject poverty from today onwards. The other significant change is that there will be no more beating, no more beating in this house. We were very poor in Cotton Hill. I have returned to poverty in West Hill. Brother and Rani know it only too well.

I know that I am going to suffer serious hardships here with Papa, but I am prepared to live with it. I will certainly have the opportunity to do and to work for what I want. I want to have my education. My education is the only goal I want to pursue. I am confident that

Papa will support me throughout my education. Surely Papa can get some food from the garden. He can plant tomatoes, bygan, karailee, eddoes, and pigeon peas. That's plenty for us. He has two big mango trees at the back of his house. The neighbour has their orange trees on their boundary edge. I can ask them for a few oranges. With this simple plan, I am hoping that we can manage such sustenance. Papa has three acres of sugar cane to harvest at crop time. This could provide my school fees, books and travel money. I am hoping that Papa might just make a little change in his way of life, now that I am living here with him. I am hoping that he will agree to implement this plan for our benefit. I can also plant a few roots of bodi and ochroes and corn at the back of the house.

We have been told that in unity there is strength. I have broken away from my siblings. Therefore, our bond is now weakened. I know that they will always be thinking of me, because of Papa's home situation. While we were with Nana and Nanny, they did not want us to come at Papa's house. Brother is also worried that my studies may be affected by our separation and by the lack of food in Papa's house. He devised a plan to help me. It involved all three of them.

Brother told Rani to secretly wrap up some food, give it to Dewan to bring for me. Rani and Dewan must not allow anyone to see, because our cousins and Aunty Jenny are regularly in and out of both houses. Dewan must pass through the cane field at the back of the house and bring the food for me. By doing this Dewan made his track easier and easier to walk through the cane field. Later on he would run through his track to reach my new home in five minutes. Rani must send food for me once a week without fail. That was Brother's orders to Rani. He would ask her from time to time if she is managing to send a weekly food supply for me. Rani would send sufficient food to last me at least two days. I have to find food for the remaining five days. Sometimes, Brother would bring the food himself to see me and to find out how I am doing. Dewan gave me weekly updates of what was happening at Nanny's house.

It was on one of these visits, when he brought the bowl of food, when he told me that Aunty Jenny and Uncle Jhan came over and told Nanny not to let me come back into that house. They could not stop me from going to college. They were the ones who told Nanny and Nana not to send me to college.

On one of these visits I told Brother in detail about the cocoa-house beating. He was shocked and could not have imagined it. He was fully aware that Nana and Nanny treated me badly. I was the scapegoat in the family. I told Brother, "Boy, you know very well that I do not like the hard work. I tried to hide from it whenever I could." He knew that I never liked it. Rani and Dewan sent food for eighteen months, but then food supplies stopped arriving. Brother did not tell me the reason for it.

Aunty Jenny had run over to Nanny to find out why I had left. Nanny relayed the water issue to her. Aunty Jenny saw me walking away. She did ask me where I was going but I did not answer her. She asked Nanny, "So has he gone to his father for good? If so, why would you want him to come back? He's gone already, let him go. Don't let him come back in the house again."

Aunty Jenny discussed me with Uncle Jhan. "Jhan, this is a surprise. One of them helped us out by himself. We did not have to do anything to chase him out. You make damn sure he does not come back. I was worried about him staying for five years. You know how much I want to live in the front house. I want to sit in the gallery and look out. I cannot see anything that's going on in the front. Jhan, Rani will have to be the next one. Look for somebody to marry her. I know she does not want to marry. But she can't rule us. She will have to obey Nana's orders."

Uncle Jhan came over to Nanny and told his mother, "Don't let that boy come back here. He's gone already, let him go. Let him go on his own way from now. He is too lazy. He is not much help here anyway." He continued, "Moye, we have to marry off Rani and let her go from here. That is the next thing we have to do. I talked to two fellas already about it and they from nice family. We could fix up everything."

Uncle Jhan had blocked Rani's opportunities twice in the past. Now it is her time to be out of Nana's house, like me. Nanny repeatedly reminded Rani how helpful she is in the house. Nanny has a lot more time to rest while Rani does the housework. Rani would rub down Nanny's legs and back for her as well.

One day Nanny told Rani, "Baytee, gyal, ah gat dee sugar." Rani did not understand. Rani sent me a note with Dewan asking what is the meaning of the statement.

I replied, "My Dearest and most beautiful Rani, it's lovely to hear from you. Thank you for your note. At least I am happy to see your lovely handwriting once more. And above all, thank the three of you for your weekly food supply to help keep me going. It is a much-needed support and I fully appreciate it. I cannot repay you for this. You and Dewan are really helping me to survive with the amount of food you all are sending me every week.

"Regarding Nanny's medical condition, it is called 'non-insulin-dependent (type II) diabetes mellitus'. It's a very common worldwide disease. Asians do present a high risk of developing it. It is due to insufficient production of the hormone insulin. This hormone is produced by the beta-cells of the islets of Langerhans in the pancreas. The hormone goes directly into the blood stream to control the blood sugar levels within normal range, that is, 4–8 millimetres per litre of blood. Diabetics usually have blood sugars well above or below this range. You must observe Nanny for the extremes of these levels. They are hyper- and hypoglycaemic states, i.e., too high or too low blood sugar levels respectively.

"Be particularly vigilant regarding the hypo-states. I am sending you some notes on these two states. Do read them and have them handy for reference. The hypoglycaemic state is more dramatic. One can quickly go into a hypo-state and can also quickly get out of the hypo-state. Always have a fifty-gram glucose drink readily available to give Nanny should she happen to go into a hypoglycaemic state or coma. You can also give her two tablespoons of brown sugar mixed in water if the glucose is not readily available.

"The aetiology of this condition is multi-factorial. Lifestyle contributes heavily to causing type II diabetes. This nasty condition affects all the organs in the body, particularly the eyes, kidneys and heart and blood circulation. A poorly maintained condition may cause blindness and peripheral neuropathy. So, do try and keep a check on Nanny's blood sugar levels by testing her blood regularly. Tell Brother to take her to the DMO at least every week or two weeks, or go to the clinic in San Fernando. It is also very important for her to take her anti-diabetic medication every day. You stated that two of Nanny's toes are black and hard, and that she does not see very well. I'm sorry to tell you that her toes have become gangrenous. The toes are deprived of an adequate blood supply so the tissues there have died and are in a bad physical state. One problem with her eyes is that she may have developed or be developing cataracts. The other common problem is a probable age-related macular degeneration taking place. The radical solution is a possible lower limb surgery. But Nanny may not want that.

"There are some other simple but effective measures we can take, and I am so sorry, it will be down to you to implement them. Firstly, Nana has plenty of bygan [aubergine], tomatoes, karailee, pumpkin and corn to sell in the market every week. These foods are very good to help to control blood sugar levels. Bygan is a natural way to treat type II diabetes mellitus. So too is the karailee. They are natural hypoglycaemic agents. It is possible to get karailee in tablet form in the pharmacy. You must encourage Nanny to have these foods every day, to help reduce and regulate her blood sugar. You may reduce her intake of too many starchy foods. Carrots, tomatoes and watercress are also quite beneficial for her condition. They also help to reduce cholesterol levels and improve her vision. Always cook food with plenty of garlic, onion and coriander. My dear Rani, do avoid giving her sugary foods. Keep a list of these helpful common foods handy, and everybody can eat them every day too. These foods will be helpful for Nana as well. You need to explain this very simply to Nanny to get her to accept this approach. Tell Brother to get some anar fruits [pomegranate] from Pay Shay and give them to Nana and Nanny everyday. They are foods to help with blood sugar and blood pressure maintenance and memory problems."

CHAPTER 12

IT HAS NOW BEEN six months of walking down and up West Hill on my way to and from college. This morning, the 18th May, I accidently noticed B, the most beautiful village girl, who lives at the bottom of West Hill, peeping out of her bedroom window. The boys in the village regularly talk amongst themselves about how pretty she is. As soon as she spotted me she disappeared from her bedroom window. The next morning the same thing happened. This continued for a few weeks. Then B stayed a little longer, about ten to fifteen seconds, before she disappeared from her bedroom window. I became conscious of this girl's actions as it was occurring every morning when I walked down for my bus.

Her presence at her window became noticeably longer, and soon she actually stood there and looked at me for about twenty seconds before she went away wearing a serious expression. One morning she stood there for about half a minute, and she gave me the first very brief smile before she shot off from the window as she usually does. Up to this point B and I had never spoken a word to each other.

We fear being seen talking to each other. It is a risk that would ruin my career and she would receive a thorough beating from her mother. Then the next step would be for me to marry B straight away. I simply cannot entertain such a thought, because my education is my top priority. Discreet non-verbal gestures must suffice for the time being to preserve this relationship. I do hope that B shows a similar understanding. I thought of B's smile on the bus all the way to school. It was a beautiful and charming smile. The smile radiated from her eyes to her cheeks and lips. There was a warm feeling within me. I will remember this first smile from B for my lifetime. That is how I feel about B's smile. I am looking forward to getting more of B's smile.

At the beginning of the next term I looked up at B's bedroom window but no one was there. Two mornings later B appeared, smiled and waited for a while. I smiled back at her then she went away from window. Such morning greetings continued for three to four weeks gradually developing into exchanges of broad smiles with each other. I noted it down in my diary. I was certain that B and I were affectionately connected to each other over these past months. B would be at her bedroom window in the mornings and afternoons waiting for me to come for my bus in the mornings or coming off the bus in the afternoons. We would exchange smiles and wave goodbyes with each other. She would move away from her bedroom window to carry on with her work.

I asserted myself and initiated my first written communication to B. It was a short note of compliment on her beauty, and her smile. I ended by telling her of my keen interest in her. I hid this note in the hibiscus hedge which is at the front of their house. I stuck the note between a forked branch in the middle of the thick hibiscus hedge. No one could see it from the roadside. The note read:

"Oh my dearest B, my love, my sweetheart, you are the love of my life. I am absolutely ecstatic and deeply overcome with joy and happiness. Knowing that I now have you, the most beautiful girl in the village, as my true love, makes me feel so very privileged indeed. These are my first words to you to let you know how much I am deeply in love with you. I would like to know how you feel about me. I would love to hear that our feelings are mutual. I am sending you my first few lines of poetry, and there will be hundreds more to come if you'll agree.

"I think of you at your bedroom window,
Although we've never said a word, you seem to know
That your glistening eyes, and radiant smiles,
Make your beauty shine for a million miles.

You are my sweet sixteen
Nowhere the world has ever seen

Such beauty is all pervading
You reign supreme as my belonging."
B, you are sweeter than honey to me. Cheers my love."

When B looked out of her window I smiled, looked in the direction of the note and pointed to it. B seemed to have understood my gesture. She smiled briefly, gave me a short royal wave and moved away. She went off directly in search of the note in the hedge. I saw the bushes shaking about. B held the note tightly in her hand and ran quickly upstairs. I caught my bus and I was off to school.

I was having ambivalent feelings regarding my note to her. I kept on guessing in my mind as to what type of response I would receive from B. Will it be an approval, or a rejection? My mind was wavering one way then another. The longer she delayed in replying the more negative I felt. B did not come to her bedroom window for the next four days. I began to feel that my note was not approved of. Did I spoil my chances with B? As each day passed by without a sighting of B, I thought to myself, *Damn it!* I had hit the rejection button.

The following week, B was at her window smiling very broadly at me and pointed to my original spot in their hibiscus hedge. My heart skipped several beats, and it was pounding hard against my chest. My pulse was racing. Although B had given me a brief smile, I was having mixed feelings about her reply to my note. I found her note in the same forked branch I had used. On the outside of the note there were two bold Xs. Relief hit me. I instantly knew that she approved. I would be reading the note with delight. It was a very happy moment to open up the folded piece of paper to read its contents. That would become our regular note hiding place. It was the beginning of a very happy, affectionate, warm, friendly, and long-lasting love affair between us. Three notes per week on average were exchanged between us successfully and secretly throughout the years ahead. In one of the notes I included my road map to her. It went down badly. More of this will come later on. Now I will read B's first note replying to mine. It went as follows:

"To my one and only love, U, I am so happy and thrilled to receive and read your precious letter. My darling, U, I also think of you day and night. You are the first person who has captured my heart. I feel that I am drowned in love for you. Whatever I am doing I am thinking of you. I have the same warm feeling burning inside me. Sometimes I forget myself and call your name. My mother heard me on a few occasions. Then she asked, "Wey you say jus now, gyal? Who you callin'?" I jumped a little as I caught myself. I said to her, "Nothing Moye, I am just talking to myself." U, you are my first love, and I will treasure and save my entire body for you. I love the poem you wrote. You are a great poet. Please, please, do write me more, plenty more. I am going to write one to you, but I am not as good as you. It comes from my heart...

"My heart yearns for you, day and night,
Darling, U, you are my burning light,

I long to feel and kiss your lovely skin,
Without committing any awesome sin.

"There we go. I hope that you will like it. U, my sweet love, I can't wait to receive your next letter and poem. You make me love you more deeply the more I read your notes and poetry. They thrill me. I read them over and over and over before I fall asleep.

"U, it is a good thing that my Mama and Papa cannot read or write so my love letters are safe in my room."

The bond between us is getting closer and stronger as time flies by. We expressed a mutual feeling in our letters and notes. We feel totally lost if we do not see each other every day. It was becoming a compulsion. B and I had still not yet spoken to each other. Yet we were never bored writing our notes/letters/poems to each other.

One afternoon B was at her bedroom window absorbing a fresh breeze and reading aloud to herself one of my letters and poems. Her mother heard her and came into B's room. "Who you talking to, gyal?" her mother asked.

B replied, "Nobody, Moye, I am just reading. Moye, do you mean that I can't even read for myself?"

Her mother said, "Ley me hear wey you reading. Ah see you dah come by dee window plenty now. Which man you dah look for, gyal?"

B said, "There is no one here, Moye, just me alone." Her mother came to the window and looked out. No one was there.

232

"You see for yourself, Moye. I am only reading and breezing off."

"You fadder go marry you and you go go from here," B's mother told her.

B said, "Moye, who told you I want to get married? I am not ready for that yet. And you know I am just sixteen years old."

Her mother said, "Gyal, you dah have too much mout' dees days, but you fadder de talkin' dee same ting dee edder day. Ye say you big now. Is time to married you." B's mother went out of the room.

B pondered on what her mother told her. Her father would arrange her marriage to some stranger she has never seen, nor heard of. B thought of a plan. It was in her next note to her nearest and dearest, U. It read:

"My darling, U, I would like us to get married now. I can't wait until you qualify and start working. It will be too late. My father is already looking for someone to marry me. If we get married now my parents can't do anything to me. U, I know how poor you are, and you are still in college. I will live with you in your old, leaking carat house. I don't mind living like that because it will only be for about three years. That time will fly. We can even live like a brother and sister and I will let you concentrate fully on your studies. U, my sweetheart, I will never distract or disturb you from your work. I want you to succeed in your exams and I will do all I can to help you succeed. I promise you.

"My dearest U, if you don't want me to live with you

in your house, I can stay in my own room at my home until you qualify. We can still see and talk to each other every day. We will have no need to leave notes for each other anymore. We will be together for the rest of our lives. I know that this is what we want so that we can live as husband and wife for the rest of our lives. Isn't that so, my sweetheart? U, let's get married now before my father marries me off to some stranger. I do not want to lose you. I am patiently waiting for your reply. I am sending you another poem:

> *My Darling U, I'll eat you for my breakfast, lunch and supper,*
> *You are my diamond, gold and silver,*
> *This treasure is my prize so rare,*
> *Such fortune, my precious, I'll treat with diligent care."*

Our secret notes to each other continued to flow relentlessly and with greater endorsement that we are a perfect match for each other. I replied to B's verse with these lines:

> *"Dearest B, I fear, I need no cannibal in my life.*
> *But I'll own you as my loving wife.*
> *And I'll look into your eyes some day*
> *To prove the truth of what you say.*

"Here is a special gift from me: (1) the *Holy Bible*, (2) the *Bhagavad Gita*, (3) the Hanuman Chalisa, and (4) the

Gayatri Mantra. Do read them everyday for your daily prayers."

I now responded to her suggestion of marriage. B knows my home situation well. For two people so much in love with each other it is most highly unlikely that we can live together in my house as a brother and sister. We know that we are already married, therefore it will be very difficult for us to behave as a brother and a sister. B living at her parents' as a married person, waiting for me to complete my studies, is an equally bad idea. There may come someday that B's mother may shout or quarrel with her and tell her to go to her husband. She would be married so she should be in her husband's house. Sadly, I had to turn down B's suggestions. I told her that neither scenario would work. My position is that I am barely struggling to support myself at school and I am making many sacrifices to gain my education. I am better off as a single person to achieve this. Although B was upset with my reply to her, she came round to see my view. Our note exchanges still flowed smoothly.

B and I exchanged ideas for a road map for us to follow as husband and wife. Some of her thoughts were inspiring and practical. For example, we would use local hardwood from West Hill for furnishings. B was happy that her surname would not change, only her title, after we are married. My next letter contained our road map.

"Dearest B, I have at last been able to put things together for our road map – our plan for our life together. I believe that it is the best for now but I do not want to prejudice your view. Tell me what you think. B, there is one task in the road map which will contradict what you said about your parents' illiteracy. Them being illiterate only holds good for the immediate purpose. I am looking at the broader issue. It is one of my strongest desires. I aim to make every single adult in the village become a literate person. Plans are already in progress for this ambitious project. Details of this will be made public in the not-too-distant future. Your help is needed to push through the programme. Now it is time to look at our road map i.e., our plan for the present and future:

Education: indeed, this is my first love, and it will always be my first love. I pointed this out to B. There are no ifs or buts about this. I made my first love absolutely crystal clear to B with all my reasons and explanations and justification to follow if needed.

It's education first, education first, education first. This is the priority in my life. Education matters, and matters most for me. Nothing nor anyone will stand in my way of achieving my education.

On qualification, I would seek to become a teacher. I would be an educationalist. This would entail further studies abroad. I wanted to learn, develop and apply theories in education for the benefit of all children and adults

I would make Sunnyvale a literate and free village.

House – I will build a comfortable four-bedroomed house with an integral garage at the brow of Cotton Hill on the same spot where our old carat house was situated.

There will be a hibiscus hedge at the front and croton hedges on the sides and at the back. There will be palm trees dotted around the compound.

Family – We will aim to have three children. We wish for one boy and two girls. We will be content with any children given to us.

Car – A convertible with our private number plate. We would drive through the village on evening and night drives.

Faith – We would lead a good Christian lifestyle and live for the truth and by the truth. We would be devoted, loyal and faithful towards each other throughout our lives. We will be practical and realistic under the fountain of idealistic values. We would read the *Holy Bible*, the *Bhagavad Gita*, and recite the Hanuman Chalisa and the Gayatri Mantra and the Lord's Prayer.

Health – We would manage a health-conscious lifestyle.

Furniture – Solid hardwood will be used from West Hill forest.

The Big Day – our Wedding Day. This was jointly planned between B and me. For this big day there would be a small number of people. We will have two guests to sign the register and the pundit to conduct the wedding ceremony. Marj and my friend the President will be the two guests. The ceremony will take place in our home. The wedding photo shoot will be taken outside, in the cotton field amongst the snow-white cotton. B's brilliant white wedding dress and a dazzling silver tiara will be handsomely complemented with the natural beauty of the cotton trees. We would pick cotton fibres and blow them towards each other. This symbolises truth, love and purity, which we offer to each other.

Following a small reception, the wedding party of three will leave us. The President would make his speech as usual. Knowing the President as I do he may very likely open up in poetic style with something reading like this or not far off:

> *A wedding unites a man and a woman (or a man and a*
> *man or woman and a woman),*
> *It is so nice to see B's Can-Can,*
> *She is young, strong and a sheer beauty,*
> *Today, Marj and your President sign their wedding*
> *treaty.*

At sunset, B and I would tie a couple of small cans to the back of our car and drag them on the road. We will drive through the village. B in her white wedding dress and long white gloves will wave regally to the villagers like the Queen of Sunnyvale while I drive our convertible car slowly along. When we return home in the late evening after sunset we would refresh and B will wear her light pink fully see-through nightdress. Finally, the hour has arrived when we must retire. From then on, no words would be spoken between us. B and I will share our glasses of mauby together with our arms entwined in each other. We will use the power of non-verbal communication to convey more than a thousand messages towards each other. We will use eye contact and gaze, smiles, waves, soft gentle touches and inviting sensual gestures to drive home the intensity of our love for each other. We will offer our virgin bodies to each other as our wedding presents in bed. This would be the "ace" of our road map. The End."

The road map was given to B in the usual manner. I carefully placed it in the forked branch in the middle of the hibiscus hedge making sure that it was not visible from the road. B was already waiting at her bedroom window for me to come for my bus. We smiled and waved to each other. B watched me going to the hedge where I placed the note. When I came out of the hedge, B had gone. She quickly ran down their back stairs and then ran to the hedge. She quickly dived into the hedge, picked up the note and ran indoors. It was all done in a flash. Some minutes later my bus came for me to go to school. I could confidently guess where B would have gone at that moment. On my way to school, I was imagining B's reaction if she approved of the whole letter. She would take it and press it hard to her and give the most charming smile. She had told me in an earlier note this is how she reacts whenever she receives a note from me. Where does she go to read my notes? That's an interesting question. On one afternoon I came off the bus as usual. For the past two weeks B had not come to her bedroom window. On this occasion she was there, not smiling, but she just pointed to our note hiding place and went away.

CHAPTER 13

I PICKED UP THE note. B's vexed manner worried me.
I might have mentioned something of which she did
not approve or was not happy about. *What could that be?*
I wondered. Her note read thus:

"How dare you treat me like this? How dare you?
Who do you think I am? And what do you take me for,
a fool? I will never ever take second place. You are my
first, and do you expect me to be your second love? I'm
not having it, and I will never accept second place in your
life. I ought to be number one, the first, the first one in
your life. Everyone and everything else will have to take
second, third, fourth, etc. place if I am going to be your
future wife. My mother and father think the world of
me. I am their eyeball. Even the President told me how
beautiful I am. He said that I am the prettiest girl in the
village and that made me blush. But I do not like him or
any of the boys in the village. All my love is for you. You

240

are my number one, my nearest and dearest, so I must take my rightful place in your heart and in your life.

"Now, I like everything else in our road map, especially the wedding day speech by the President. It is a very nice idea. It will go down quite well."

There is a degree of logic to B's series of questions and in her last statement of assuming number one position. B's view is primarily subjective. I allowed a couple of days to pass by. My reply contained two significant words with a longer than usual note. They were for her to undertake an "objective evaluation" of the correspondence. It read thus:

"B, I am sorry to have hurt your feelings so badly by putting you second place in my life. It is true that you will be the other half of my life. Yes we will be equal halves combining to complete the whole picture. It is like yin and yang, two halves creating balance for the whole. It would enable us to fulfil our dreams. However, we must consider our priorities and put them into perspective. I must say that you will be playing the most important role in my life. Your support is invaluable to our success. I recognise and appreciate this immensely.

"All my life I have had to struggle and fight my way for education. This is one thing that I have always sought to achieve. Today, I have won a partial battle and am on that road to gaining my education. Under no circumstances would I want to slip off that road. I see education as the key to unlock any door for life opportunities. Education is the bedrock on which my foundation is to be built.

Education is power, the power for greater life choices and opportunities. Education facilitates earning power, and therefore provides a better and healthier lifestyle. With your support, my dear B, I will gain added impetus to advance my education, and prepare for a better life for us. This is my justification to claim education as my number one priority. Dearest B, I'm asking you to allow the status quo to prevail for the present. We'll follow our road map. As for your parents arranging your marriage, I do have the confidence that you will be able to tactfully dissuade them from a forced marriage, or an arranged marriage to a complete stranger."

Four days later I received B's reply:

"Why do you always have to be right? Eh? You, my loving BJA? [With a smiley face drawn.] You are my one and only. You have convinced me and won me over. I love you for that even more now. Yes! Yes! I will not have it any other way! My dearest loving BJA! OK? You have all my support to complete your education and become a distinguished professional. I am with you all the way. This is my big smiley face to let you know how happy I am and I am writing my special name for you. My sweetest and most loving BJA. I will always cherish you with all my love. U, it's just that I am thinking so much about our wonderful future plans I tend to get carried away and wish it can all happen overnight.

"But my darling, U, do you know something, I love you for being level-minded and you keep me on the right track. I am thinking of our road map. It truly inspires me. For example, I wish we could go driving through the village in a car this minute. I feel so excited only thinking about it. I could borrow some money from my mother, and you could rent a car for a half-day. What do you say? I'll wait for your answer.

"U, This comes from deep inside my heart to you. I write:

My love for you is on solid ground,
Strong and sweet it has no bound,
It lives within my heart and head,
I'll live for U, until I am dead.
I'm yours indeed,
To plant your imperishable seed.
For this is my promise to you
That if you love me as you do
I will be there with you
In every thought and deed."

I replied: "B, your words of poetry thrill me very much indeed. Do you sincerely mean all of it? I have the same feelings for you and only you. Regarding the rental of a car this is a mighty problem. I can see how excited you are about our future plan. It's going to be one hell of a time for us when such a moment arrives. My love, you know that I cannot drive, I don't have a licence, not even a provisional one. Above all it is illegal for me to drive a car as I am not yet eighteen. I haven't even sat behind the wheel of a car to learn the A B C (accelerator, brake, clutch) of it. My answer to your suggestion is a definite NO. Let us bide our time."

B replied: "U, forgive me. Oh my God! I never thought of those things. You are right again! My big, dearest and most thoughtful BJA. U, I must tell you that I feel that I can't wait to go driving down the village in our car. But it's better this matter is closed. Case compromised! We both won this time because you can't keep winning every time!"

CHAPTER 14

Our secret notes lasted a few years during my schooling, thus bringing us closer and closer together. There came a time when we could not rest until we saw each other even for a fleeting glance. In the mornings, B would stand at her bedroom window looking at me until I boarded the bus. She would come out in the afternoons as well. That was a welcome bonus. We were seeing each other, smiling and waving with each other twice a day. On one afternoon I came off the bus as usual and my dearest love was already at her bedroom window looking out for me. B knew at what times the morning and afternoon buses would be arriving at the junction. Before I could look up at B, I heard a very familiar voice. It was friendly and pleasant in tone.

"Hi, hi. Hey man!" shouted my second mother, Madam Daniel. "Ah cyan't believe ah seeing you. Lang, lang time I eh see you, man." She was loud, cheerful, and was in her usual charming manner. She came up briskly to me and gave me the biggest hug. She smacked two kisses on both my cheeks. "Well, well, is so nice to see you today." I did not get a chance to say a word as yet. "But look at you, man. You is a big man now! Wey! You lookin' so nice, man. But you is a real man now."

I butted in, "Thank you, Madam Daniel. I am just coming from school. I travel by bus every day."

She said, "Look here, man, doh caal me Madam Daniel again. You make me feel ole, man. Yea, you make me feel like dem ole, ole ooman an dem. Caal me Marj from now. You know me name a'ready, ah doh have to tell you dat. Dee whole village dah caal me Marj. An' you is a big man now. Yea man, you is a big man. Doh caal me Madam Daniel again nah! You hear dat? Man, look at aal dem book an dem you dah hah to read nah! Wey Papa yoh! How lang ye go take you to read, ah mean to read aal ah dem book, man?"

Marj held on to both my shoulders and shook me. "You see you have brad shouldars. Like a real man." A few of my books fell out of my hand with her strong shaking. She helped me to pick them up. Marj said, "When you comin' to see me, man? Glory and Alex go be so glad to see you, man. Come soon nah. Come Saturday. Aal ah we go be home nah. Danny an aal comin' Friday night from wok. Ye wokin' in dee sea deez days nah. Ye still da wok in dee night an aal. Danny dah still wok shift, since dee lang time now. Come home by we nah man on Saturday. Ah say, aal ah we go be home eh!"

"Marj, I'm sorry, I wouldn't be able to come on Saturday, because I am in the middle of exams. When they are over and I get some free time, I'll come. I'll let you know. I'd love to come up to see our cosy old mud house at Cotton Hill."

"Man, dee ole carat an mud house break dong lang time, man. An ah big cotton tree grow up right dey. Wen you come you go see it nah. Ah say, Alex and Glory go like to see you an aal," she said.

"Sure, I'll let you know when I am able to come over," I said to her.

B was standing at her bedroom window throughout my interaction with Marj. She saw every single movement, every gesture, and how Marj held on to me and kissed me on my cheeks. She heard every single word that was said. She developed mixed emotions. She looked sad, mad, angry, and jealous yet with a little satisfaction. She became calm, and gradually regained her warmth and love. She has known Marj all her life to be this cheerful, happy-go-lucky, outgoing and extraverted character. Marj has not changed. She hugged me again and said, "Ah goin' now, but doh forget to come an see we, you hear dat? An you is me saviour an aal. Wen ah dee pick you up in me arm an show you to Danny he couldn't beat me again. Ah never forget dat eh. You dee save me so much ah time."

I said to Marj, "I'm pleased that I proved to be a human shield for you during those days. OK Marj, bye for now."

Marj looked up at B's window and called out to her. "Hi, nice gyal, you watching out to catch fly? Oh you breezing aff? Gyul, you is dee prettiest gyal we have in dis whole damn village, from Cotton Hill to Wes' Hill. Ah dah tell aal dem young buayes how nice you is. You an me Glory go pass like two sister. Ah bin by Jenny dee adder day, an we dee taaking bout you and Glory. Ah tell she you is dee prettiest ting we hah in dee whole village ah Sunnyvale. Gyal, wen ah tell she dat, Jenny get mad an she stan' up an say, 'Well wat about me? All the young boys an dem have their eyes on me. Marj, my love, if you want to know, I have always been the most attractive and sexiest woman in this village. After all I am a town girl and little B is only an ordinary simple country girl. Marj, if you go around spreading that kind of news about B, I have some news for you. She would not be the prettiest girl in this village for much longer.'"

Marj, being so naïve and simplistic did not read the wicked, spiteful and hidden agenda in Jenny's intent but went on to tell her, "Jenny, gyul, ah tell dee child, ye [B] jes doh badder wid no bady nah! Ye fadder go get ah nice man to married ye [B] eh! Ah tell ye, doh forget nah gyal, ah go come an put on dee saffran pan tap ah ye wen dee day come eh. An ah tell ye, 'You go look more pretty den. An you go have plenty ah nice chiren too.' The gyal dee smiling too bad wen ah tell ye dat."

Indeed, B was smiling all through Marj's comments, but she was steaming hot inside her. She wished that Marj had gone away much earlier, only to leave me alone. B gave Marj a gentle royal wave and said, "Bye Marj, see you later," and she disappeared from her bedroom window. I could feel B's displeasure by the way she spoke to Marj. The tone of her voice did not reflect her gentle words. I hope that I will see her in her true frame of mind when next B comes to her bedroom window. She may have cooled down.

However, while travelling to school I noticed that Aunty Jenny would walk to the junction to wait for a particular taxi driver. This happened on several occasions and I wondered why this particular taxi driver among all the other taxis passing by. Aunty Jenny loves flirting around with the young men in the village. She is brazen-faced about it. Such gossip flies around the village very quickly. The President wasted no time in coining up his scathing jingle:

> *Ole Jenny is a foreigner,*
> *She come all de way from Muruga*
> *Telling we she come from Couva,*
> *An sayin' she from Arima*
> *She's honey sweet and sexy,*
> *Jenny's lying in dee taxi.*
> *She gone to Ganti to make a deal*
> *The effects of which will make you reel.*

Aunty Jenny had her sights set on B via the taxi driver, and was rather disturbed about the lovely comments Marj had made on B. She befriended the taxi driver, encouraged, coaxed and even paid for him to do her dirty work.

During all our years of a warm and loving relationship, B and I have never got physically close enough to touch each other. We have never spoken to each other. All our communication so far has been via secret note exchanges and through the non-verbal gestures. B and I have always been at a distance of a minimum of ten yards from each other. That is the distance from her bedroom window to the road, where I stand and wait for my bus, and from where she would smile and wave to me. Hence, it is hardly surprising that B would instantly react jealously when she saw how Marj was holding and hugging me up directly in front of her. I am aware that B felt she should have been the one to hold and hug me. However, B realised that Marj's greeting was purely neighbourly and maternal. She knows that Marj used to look after us when Papa and Mama went into the garden to work. Marj is a second mother to me. As a child B used to come with her mother to pick cotton on Cotton Hill. As children we used to run through the cotton fields playing and picking cotton. Now B no longer goes up there. I received a note from B as normal. This time her note was terse and seemingly fraught with anger and jealousy. It read:

"My love, I heard and saw everything that went on between Marj and you this afternoon. Tell me, did Marj fall in love with you or what? The woman wouldn't leave you alone. Look how she was hugging you up like that. I know that she is like your mother, she helped to mind you when you were a child, but I am still vexed to see you and her hugging up like that in front of me.

"Well, I want to tell you this, my sweetheart. I don't want you to go by Marj and them on your own, you hear that? When we get married we will be living opposite to them, then you and I can go to their house as often as we wish. That is my point of view, and I don't want you to tell me 'no.'

"My sweetheart, U, I couldn't sleep well last night. I was twisting and turning practically all night, because I was thinking of you and Marj carrying on outside my bedroom window. I have never yet touched you, but Marj rough you up and hug you up, and even kissed you on both cheeks. She caused some of your books to fall out of your hands by the way she roughed you up yesterday. That hurt me most last night.

"I want you and me to be a virgin man and a virgin woman when we are married. OK! I want you to promise me that. Furthermore, it is I who must give you all the kisses you want. You will get all the most romantic, the sweetest, the tastiest, the deepest, the longest, and the most loving and sexiest kisses you need from me and only me. I will give you any amount you want. How about that? But I don't want anyone else to ever kiss you or rough you up like what Marj did to you. This is my poem to you to end my letter. To my dearest love:

Love brings sweetness, love can cause pain.
Yesterday, it almost drove me insane
To witness another woman's gain,
I say, my jealous poison must not reign."

B was obviously jealous of the fact that Marj was making such fun with me. Marj is totally illiterate, but she is a very kind and caring person, and she got on extremely well with Mama. They behaved like sisters towards each other when we were living at Cotton Hill. I told B that I put forward a plan to the boys to help people like Marj to learn to read and write properly. The boys were to think about this idea then we can meet formally to discuss it. The general feeling coming back is that it is a good gesture. Once this general principle has been established, the details can be worked out. I said to her that she will have to help out in this project.

CHAPTER 15

M Y AIM IS TO make every adult in the village become a literate person. I sought help from the boys of the two clubs, one a cultural club, the other a sports club. The President of the cultural club will take a lead role in this project. He has been president of the club for eighteen consecutive years and wealds great influence. A joint meeting of both clubs was arranged. The President called the meeting to order.

"Boys, the President speaks, shut up all of you. The message for tonight is – boys beware of the evil deeds you do and warn the women folk as well. Do you know why? Listen to this statement. 'The evils that men do live behind them, but I say, the evils that women do live in front of them.' Just look at all them heavily pregnant women going to antenatal clinic. I rest my case. Secretary Usati, I hand over to you."

"Boys, you know a lot of us have been helping out

over the past few weeks to carry out a survey in the entire village on illiteracy and violence. Here are the results: 83% of the women cannot read or write because they did not go to school; 35% of the men cannot read because they left school early or defaulted, very poor school attendance; 100% of children suffer abuse, child labour and corporal punishment with no sign of abatement; 76% of the women experience domestic violence from their husbands; 81% of the villagers believe in black magic or Obeah. They believe somebody has worked Obeah on them. That is why the villagers quickly run to the Obeah men for help. In the process they cause so much more sickness and disease within the family. 97.8% of the villagers agree to support this venture.

"Our aim is to enable every adult in Sunnyvale to be able to read and write. We are going out together on this project. Learning is a change in behaviour. Our objective is: if we can change and improve the life and well-being or behaviour of as little as *one* adult member in the village in eighteen months we will have achieved our objective.

"The plan is as follows: Cotton Hill, The Valley and West Hill will each have two days of teaching per week. Each day it will be for one hour only. This project will be for eighteen months. We will have formative and a summative evaluation. Boys, you will be given teaching plans and visual aids and handouts as teaching packs. We will work throughout this period to cover the whole village. We will adapt our teaching plans to suit every single home. We will use a very calm and supportive approach, apply positive and negative reinforcement and extinction principles in the teaching/learning process. We are mindful that they are all adults who will be learning. We will use adult learning principles. We will apply further motivational theories of learning as we go. This is the outline plan of the project. Thank you all in advance for your help and participation. I'll hand you back to the President."

"Well done, Mr Secretary. Boys, I am sure that you are not surprised at these results. These results give us the proof which nobody can deny now. This is the first venture of this nature that we are undertaking for the entire village.

"I, the President, will lead this project. When the President speaks, everyone obeys. When the President takes on a task, the President does not fail to deliver success. You boys, the President speaks. OK? We have painstakingly expounded the merits of this venture to every adult in the village during the survey period. We will be going into every home in the village to carry out our teaching. Many of the boys and girls who had to leave school early by the age of eleven or twelve years to help their parents work, will have a second chance to learn to read and write properly.

"Boys, you've often heard it said: 'Eat little and live long.' Usati said that we are attempting give our villagers a little food for thought, not to endanger them, but to motivate, stimulate, and enhance their quality of life.

They can live longer and happier. We hope that this learning, which we are conducting for the next eighteen months, will spur further learning in some of our men and women. We hope that some of them will go and attend formal adult education evening classes after this project. This could be a good foundation on which they can build. This village will be a fully literate one. This is your President speaking.

"This job we are taking on is already halfway done. All the villagers agree and are willing to co-operate with us. Some of them said that this is so good, why did we not do something like this before. Now we have a good chance to finish the other half. We have thirty-seven boys in White Rose and Sunnyvex here tonight. Tell the other boys to come and join us in this venture. That is the President's orders.

"The President speaks again: now, this is for our mothers' and fathers' and brothers' and sisters' own good. So, let us turn this into a great success. We will start and finish the job as we promised them. We start next week on the 18th. OK? It doesn't matter that it's a Tuesday. The teaching packs are in print and we will have them ready in a day or so. We will go over them at our next Saturday meeting."

The President speaks again, "We not doing this for foreigners, you know. Ey you big shot, over there. You hear me? Yea you, Lutchman, you hear what I said? We not doing it for foreigners, eh! Unless you fadder is a hit and run foreigner."

The President says, "I close the meeting. See you on Saturday evening."

I chose to teach the Daniels, because of our longstanding close relationship. They trust me and feel most comfortable with me coming in their home every week on Mondays and Tuesdays from 6.00pm to 7.00pm. I grew up with Marj in my early days at Cotton Hill. She was a mother to us. Mr Daniel and Alex were happy to join in and help Marj and Gloria. Their support has been immense. Mr Daniel showed a good deal of patience in teaching Marj. She needed to have words and phrases repeated to her before she got hold of them. Mr Daniel would give her a pat on her shoulder, or a slight peck on her forehead and say, "Damn it dum dum you got it at last," with a smile on his face. As the weeks passed Marj and Gloria progressed very well. Alex gave them added help in their reading and writing. My teaching plan followed the same structure throughout so it was easy for them to understand and follow.

The structure was: assessment, goals, objectives, planning, visual aids, handouts, implementation, evaluation, and the next week's lesson in advance.

Every one of the boys followed this structure for the next eighteen months. Every home in the village got a dictionary and almost every adult was taught how to use it and to be competent at using it. Everyone was encouraged to have it by his or her side while reading and to look up new words. This would help to increase his or her vocabulary and to understand the text.

B was rather disappointed that I did not come to her home when we focussed on teaching the residents of West Hill. She was expecting me to come to teach her parents and be happy to sit with us for the hour's lesson. I felt that it would be more distracting and counterproductive. It would be better if two other boys went there, one of them being the President.

We all received feedback from each other as to our progress with the families. Because the teaching was done in the comfort and safety of their homes, no resident felt threatened. We made use of their experiences to put them in a formalised learning context. Their learning was more meaningful and relevant because it was structured to suit each person's home environment. The adults were able to connect with the things around their homes. It was easier for them to remember names on the large flash cards which were stuck on to the various objects around their homes. B was actively involved in encouraging and teaching her parents to read and write. The President thanked B every week for her help. In some of B's notes to me she would let me know what went on during the teaching session. She would relate some of the jokes that the President would make so that her parents would laugh and feel more relaxed.

For example, one such joke is as follows: Old Mr Flood down the road has a farm with a lot of animals. Mr Flood brought his animals together for a contest. He put his most stinking messy pig in a room and closed the door. He told the other animals, whoever goes and spends the longest time with the pig will win a big prize. The animals started going into the room with the stinking dirty pig. The sheep went in and was out in two minutes. The dog went in and was out in one minute. The duck went in and flew out after three minutes. The horse went in and was out after five minutes. Then the gobbler turkey entered the room and went straight into action. The gobbler began to pick at the pig. The pig ran round and round the room. The gobbler kept on picking at the pig until the pig could not take any more. He headed for the door and the gobbler chased him out of the room. The turkey gobbler stood at the door, stretched its neck, gobbled away, fanned out its feathery tail and flapped its wings at the same time. The gobbler was victorious. The End.

CHAPTER 16

THE DAILY GREETINGS AND note exchanges between B and me flowed smoothly, silently and happily. In the evening, I came down to the shop and also to catch a glance of B. She was in her hammock singing sweetly and loudly. It was our favourite song. She was swinging vigorously and smiling broadly while singing. I stood looking at her and listening. I smiled. I enjoyed the moment. I knew that she was singing for both of us. Both of us loved this song, "So Hani Raat". I had not heard her singing so loud before. She was swinging in the hammock so vigorously. She looked very happy and smiled lovingly with me. When the song was finished, she sang it all over again. It was my best birthday present from B. I was delighted and slowly walked home as her echo faded away. My evening was complete. I was excited and thrilled to bits. I could see in my mind B singing and swinging in her hammock. As soon as I got home I quickly grabbed my pen and started to write my note for B for her to receive next morning. It went like this:

"B, thank you so for singing our song for me. Your voice is sheer melody and charm. You can give the nightingale a very tough run for its money. I was hungry, but now I'm filled with the thought of you and your singing for me. I have just coined this short verse for you:

Today is my birthday, my sweetheart sang for me,
'Sohanee Raat nadal chookhay,'
So sweetly sung to fill my heart,
And echoing in me is your work of art."

This joy is running through my veins and I am waiting patiently for the morning to come so that I can place this note for B. I completed my homework by midnight. I was lying on my bed, which was the floor. I could see the moonlight through the holes in the roof of the house. I was able to see just one bright star. It was shining directly over my head. I thought of the night when Jesus was born and a bright star shone over the manger. That must be a good sign for B and me. The star comforted me. I thought of B and her singing. It filled me with great joy and happiness and I fell asleep easily in such frame of mind.

The following morning there was breaking news in the village. My next-door neighbour, Lutchman, shouted out to me. "Neighbour, neighbour, you eh hear what happen las' night dong dee road, man? Is aal over dee village."

"What has happened?" I asked.

"Ruction, ah say, ruction dong dee road, man! Ruction dong dee road, man," he repeated.

I insisted, "Well go on and do tell me what's happened."

Lutchman said, "You go dong dey, and see for youself, man. Dee man an dem havin panchait by dee roadside, man," he shouted out again from his veranda again, "Man, go dong dey an see wat ruction goin'on. If you goin' now ah go come wid you." Lutchman and I walked down to find out what was going on. He took his cutlass with him as he was heading to cut a bundle of grass for their animals.

It is true that several villagers were out on the roadside seemingly worried, or angry, or concerned, but talking quietly to each other. As we walked down the road I could not hear the neighbours' conversations. When we got to B's house I noticed several people under the house. I took no notice of that because this was fairly normal for villagers to gather in each other's home and chit-chat. This was regular communal-style living, particularly in rural communities like Sunnyvale. The village was peaceful so where was this ruction, I wondered?

We popped into the shop, and guess who was there? The President and two of the regular boys, namely, Tan and Kel. This was unusual for them to be gathered down here so early in the morning. The President lives two miles away from this junction while the others live nearby. There are no phones in the village, so why was the President down here this early? The boys all had a rather gloomy look about them, and were not saying much.

Our greeting was cold. Why were they in such a frame of mind? The regular boys are jovial and usually mucking around with each other. There is fun and laughter among us, but not this morning.

I said, "What's going on, why are you looking so sorry for yourselves? Cheer up boys and who is treating me to a drink?"

The shopkeeper passed me a glass of mauby. The President then said to me, "It's not me, I have nothing to do with this! Don't blame me, you hear, I say don't blame me for anything, OK?" The President looked at all the boys to see if anyone would address him.

I said to him, "What the hell are you giving out about? Was there some crime committed during the night that you all are keeping quiet about? You said don't blame you. What's gone wrong that you are telling me not to blame you? Just tell me what is going on down here. This man, Lutchman, said that there is 'ruction' down the road. And look, President, what the hell are you doing here so early in the morning? This is not our usual liming time. So, there must be some kind of ruction overnight. Put me in the picture." Liming in this context is a group of boys having a quiet social drink accompanied with generally light-hearted gossiping. They may also take a gentle stroll along the road while passing the time, they may go out for a drive.

Tan said, "And you don't lie, playing this Mister Innocent! Don't pretend you didn't hear, nor you don't know anything."

I said, "Why are you all in a hump this morning, you eat fowl backside or what?"

The President remarked, "No, man it's real breaking news, and I am surprised that you, you of all people, didn't hear or don't know anything. Well, we too, had a big shock when we heard of the disappearance of you-know-who. All of us have been blaming you for it. It could not have been anyone else who would do such a thing. I got another surprise when I saw you walking in here just a few minutes ago. So, it is big ruction, and very big ruction as well. All of us still in shock, that's why we are in this mood."

"What happened?" I asked him.

The President replied, "Come on man, don't play dumb nah. You! I was 99% sure that you were the chief architect behind this. To tell you the truth, when we first heard, we blamed you straight away. We just said among ourselves, that what a bleddy rotten bastard you are to have done such a thing like that. There are other decent ways to get a woman if you want one without shocking anyone. That is the news spreading around first thing this morning. We thought that we won't see you for a week until your honeymoon is over." The President paused for a moment and said, "You too damn slow."

I said, "You still haven't filled me in as yet as to what has happened."

Tan, Kel and Lutchman said together, "Look over the road, what are you seeing up there? They are tying up the loose ends together right now." They were pointing at B's home. There was a group of villagers gathered under B's house.

The President said, "Well, boy, I don't know how to break this to you. Take a seat, man. Barman, half a dozen beers please." He quietly said to me, "She's gone. She eloped last night, the 18th."

I asked him, "To whom are you referring?"

He replied, "B, it's B, boy! She ran off with Havio last night. Both sides of the parents and relatives are below B's house this minute. Look across again and you will see them. They are getting married. Their wedding will be over in the next half hour. And that's it, signed, sealed and delivered. Done and dusted. On Monday morning they will be going to San Fernando Warden Office to register the marriage. I will be seeing them and will be the Registration Officer in the office to register the marriage and issue them with their marriage certificate. B's gone, and B is going to be the most beautiful bride you will have known. This is the shocking news we are on about, that is, the elopement of your B."

The President continued, "It was only on Wednesday that we had our weekly teaching session under their house. Everyone was happy – father, mother, son, and B. B's parents were pleased that they were gradually able to read and write. B has written and posted at least fifty large flashcards all around their house. She helps me in the teaching programme by reminding her parents to look at the flashcards and read them aloud every time they pass by an object in the home. During the week she sits with her mother and gets her to write down words and phrases. B seemed very satisfied with her parents' learning. She was also relaxed and comfortable last Wednesday."

Shock, sadness, horror, rejection, desertion, deceit and depression filled and overwhelmed me. These emotions are mixed up inside of me into a "callaloo" ready to boil and overflow after hearing the shocking news that B has eloped. How could she do such a thing to me? Last night she sang for me. She looked so happy. How could she suddenly dump me for that boy? Was B telling me huge lies all along? Could B be so deceitful, unfaithful and disloyal to me, and yet make such promises? How could B ever be so cold and callous yet pretend to be very warm and loving? Questions were hitting me from all angles. Why and how could B have done such a thing to me?

What about our road map? Would that have caused it? Treating her as second best, and having to assume second place in my list of priorities; would this have brought such a reaction in her? She knows that I have another eighteen months at school before I sit for my final examinations. Were the next eighteen months too long for B to wait? I wonder whose time was running out. Whatever the reasons may be for B's decision to run off with another man in this manner I may never know. The news of B's elopement began to spread throughout the village. By midday the whole village was talking about B's running off with a man. There was a mixed reaction. B's name was ringing in their ears. Some villagers accused her of bringing shame to the family. Others called her a "bad" child, but some others were sympathetic towards her. Some others said that her father was going to marry her to a stranger so she ran off with the man she liked.

I asked myself, "Was B taking me on a long fruitless journey only to demonstrate what a fool I am? Would she ridicule and mock me with her husband later on? Would B tell her husband about our secret notes or show them to him? Then would both of them laugh at me? How embarrassing that would be for me to see the both of them together. Why would B want to write to me again? She must be very happy with Havio! I will not be able to see her again. I may never know why she ran off so suddenly with Havio. Was B secretly having a relationship with Havio as well as with me at the same time? It is customary that the woman's place is in the home. Now she is Havio's property. B would be washing, cooking, cleaning, and bearing children. She would be living with her extended family and have all the domestic work to do. She will always be in the company of members in the family. Havio's family is large. Her entire life is now re-patterned. She has made her choice."

Maybe it is pure speculation that B has eloped. It was probably no fault of B's to have ended up that way. Could there have been some element of abduction which sealed her fate? This is most uncharacteristic of B to have done such a thing. While I am very hurt and humiliated and terribly mocked, I am keeping an open mind on this issue until the truth is revealed. It may simply take years to come out. I have confidence in B to tell the truth. At present, I cannot fathom that B would do a thing like this to me, bearing in mind that she sang so sweetly for me the previous evening.

In the meantime, I do have to reconcile myself that I will be seeing a vacant bedroom window from now on, and for the foreseeable future. There will be no more note exchanges left in the hibiscus hedge. There will be no more smiles and waves from her bedroom window. On the other hand it may turn out that she has done me a favour. I can concentrate fully on my studies and would not have to think about B anymore. It seems to me that this is the end of another chapter in my eventful life. I must focus on my own home situation, living in our old leaking carat house. Papa hasn't got the money to repair it as yet. He continues to walk aimlessly and is usually drunk. One blessing for me is that he is able to support me in college.

I have been concerned about his mental state. He is not the happy smiling Papa we used to know when we were living at Nana's house. Since Mama's death he continues to walk along the road aimlessly and is often drunk. This is Nanny and Aunty Jenny's main criticism of Papa. I can hardly talk to him at the moment. I am fully dependant on him to support me through my schooling. There is probably nothing I could do to help. I felt that if I could manage to get him to talk a little it may be just a start in the right direction. It is extremely awful and sad to see him walking and wandering around aimlessly and not saying much to anyone. I wish I could do something, anything, to get him out of this state. Will a touch of gardening do? If he sees me doing something of this sort, it may well trigger something in him. I planted some vegetables at the back of the house and have been looking after them for several weeks. The tomatoes and ochroes are beginning to develop flowers. I am helping myself to grow a small amount of foodstuff. In a few more weeks I shall be reaping my own tomatoes and ochroes. Perhaps, this may spur Papa to do some gardening, and on a larger scale than mine.

CHAPTER 17

ONE EVENING PAPA CAME from the garden with some tomatoes and bygan and bodi. He said, "Dee tree an dem jus beginning to bear. Dey have plenty ah flowers an some small small bygan only."

"Did you manage to plant all of these vegetables in the garden?" I asked him.

"No, dey from dee man in the odder gyarden. He have plenty in he gyarden an he gimme some till mine start to bear. Ah see you tomatoes flowerzin an aal. Dat good." We got talking about his cane and the ensuing crop season. This season he may not get a good crop because the land was left unattended. I seized the opportunity to ask him about my burning issue, that is, Mama's death. From his reaction, it seemed that this was Papa's most painful issue.

I said, "Do you remember the day of Mama's funeral?" He looked at me, seeming to be shocked at this question.

He changed immediately; he became very sad. I could see his eyes were filling up with tears. He nodded. "Can you tell me more about how Mama died? I remember the funeral morning very vividly. I do remember the whole of the morning activities which took place under Uncle Jhan's house. You did not say anything. You were crying all the time. Aunty Jenny said that she died in childbirth. But the details I do not know. No one has told me anything. When I was by Nanny, no one would dare mention Mama. I don't know if it were too painful for them to talk about her. One day I mentioned her name and Nanny shouted at me and told me not to ever mention her again. Would you please tell me Papa? I would really love to know. How did Mama die?"

Papa remained silent for a long while. His face changed. He got serious. He bowed his head. He was almost in tears. All the memories of that funeral day flooded him. The mental load was back on him. I knew that I had put him in a very awkward position. I did not want to change the topic because I may not get another opportunity to ask this question. Then he spoke in a very sad tone.

"Son, you remember dat day good. Ah go tell you everything. Me an you Mama de bringing a bag ah corn from dee gyarden. She dee gone in dee gyarden wid me, but she eh do no wok. Ah go carry dee bag ah corn meeself. When she come down from dee bull cyart she dee going up dee hill. She slide an fall down. Ah drop dee bag ah corn and try to hold she but she roll an roll down dee hill a good bit before ah catch she. She bleed for so.

"An Nana take she in the haspital. Dee dactors gi she blood, an me eh know wey happen. Dey say dey couldn't save she an dee baby. Son, ah can't get it out ah me head. Ah tink about it every day, since she dead. Ah kyan't wok, me can't do nothing. Dat wey happen. Ah lass everything today. She was dee bes in dis whole wol, ah tell you. Dis is dee fus time ah taak about she since she dead."

I said, "You have spoken an awful lot today. I am glad that you were able to do so. You will see that from now on you will begin to feel a little better. And also, I am now better informed of her death. If you want to talk about her at any time just talk. It will help to relieve that heavy burden you've been carrying for all these years."

I said to Papa, "You are still not the same person you normally are. Now I do understand why you are so extremely unhappy. Considering what you are going through it is not surprising that you are in this state. If I am to be more accurate, I'd say that you have been very depressed for all these years. What's worse is that you have not had any help from anyone. That is, you received no medical help nor any social help. People ignored you or said bad things about you because no one seems to recognise what you have been going through all these years.

"The fight with Uncle Jhan made things worse for you. You lost out on us as well They drove you out of the place and you were only allowed to see us for a few minutes by the roadside. This was a double blow for you. No one seems to understand this. Nanny and the others have been remarking on your conduct without considering what's going on with you. None of them has any understanding of the damaging effects that losing Mama as well as all of us will have on you. I'm so pleased that you told me about Mama's death.

"I do have a suggestion, and I would like you to consider it really seriously, and to take it up. You need a lot of medical and professional help. Dr Luo is the best person to help us. Both of us will go to Dr Luo and we'll talk with him. I'm positive that he can help you. You do know how very understanding he is. We will see him tomorrow, Thursday 18th. Just as you have told me about Mama today, do tell Dr Luo everything. Tell him exactly how you have been feeling these years gone by. He will certainly be able to help you to feel better again. Dr Luo, as you know, is very reasonable. We'll get ready and go early tomorrow."

The next day, Dr Luo sat at the table opposite to Papa. He said, "Put your hands on this small cushion." Dr Luo took the pulses on both of Papa's hands. He recorded three pulses from each hand. He said to Papa, "These pulses in your left hand are the heart, the liver and the kidney. The ones on your right are the lung, stomach/ spleen and pericardium. Now can you stick out your tongue for me please?" He drew a rough shape of Papa's tongue and began adding on shaded areas to the tongue diagram. He explained to Papa what he observed from Papa's tongue.

"The tip of your tongue represents the heart, the sides on the left and right are the liver and gall bladder, behind the tip is the lung area, the middle is the stomach and spleen, and at the back of the tongue is the kidney area. Your liver and gallbladder area is redder than usual. The kidney area is pale, and your heart area is red. Your tongue is red with a thin coating." I found that to be very interesting and fascinating indeed.

He took a detailed history of Papa's mental state. He formulated his diagnosis in TCM (Traditional Chinese Medicine). Dr Luo told Papa that from a TCM perspective Papa presents with a complex pattern of an excess and a deficiency condition. It is to do with Qi stagnation and liver fire and kidney yin-deficiency. He told Papa that he had two options for treatment, either he could take antidepressants or he could go for TCM. I asked Dr Luo, if he would not mind, could we go for the TCM approach instead of the antidepressants. He agreed and said that he would also suggest it. This would involve Papa taking acupuncture and Chinese Herbal Medicine for several weeks.

The first treatment of acupuncture started immediately. I had never heard of acupuncture or the letters TCM before. It is out of sheer curiosity that I suggested this line of treatment for Papa. Dr Luo is rather special. He is so patient and understanding. He explains everything he is doing. He shows Papa the various sizes of the acupuncture needles and inserted one needle on my arm for me to experience what it feels like and how painful it is. I felt a slight prick on my arm, but when he twiddled and twirled the needle I felt a bit of pain. The needle pain settled and it was relatively pain-free for the twenty minutes. I was intrigued by the way this form of treatment is administered. There are no drugs in the needles. So how do they work?

Dr Luo inserted needles on Papa's feet, arms, and back. He said that since this was Papa's first experience of this type of treatment, he would insert only six needles on his hands and feet. He recommended three treatments per week for two weeks, and two treatments a week for another two weeks, and one treatment a week for two weeks. I looked carefully at the sites where the needles were inserted and began memorising them. I went over them several times so I could learn them well. There is one needle I cannot forget. This is the one on top of Papa's head. Then inserted a needle between his big toe and first toe. I said to myself, *Oh! Top and toe.* This was the most striking feature of the series of needles inserted. Dr Luo kept the needles inserted for twenty minutes before removing them. On subsequent occasions he kept the needles in for twenty-five to thirty minutes. I said nothing to Papa on our way back, because I was concentrating on the sites where those needles were inserted. As soon as we reached home I quickly jotted down the sites of the inserted needles. Dr Luo told Papa not to expect any dramatic change in the way he was feeling following the first session.

We needed to go back in two days for the next

treatment session. I told Papa of my plan. I said, "Papa, if I stick my pen where the needles were inserted would they have any effect whatsoever? I am only applying pressure on the sites with my pen point. You will feel some pain but not like the needles. Let us give it a go this afternoon."

Papa said, "But you don't know where to press." I said that I had memorised the sites and I had written them down. He smiled. This was the first time I had seen Papa smile for years. I wondered whether the needles did some magic on him.

Several weeks later he said that he had felt that a heavy load has been lifted out of his head after talking about Mama with me and with Dr Luo. Each time we went to Dr Luo he would encourage Papa to talk about Mama and that awful day. It was a nightmare to him. It was a good thing that Dr Luo got him to open up and release the mental burden he was carrying. As more needles were added I had more memorising to carry out. From the second session, I walked with a pen and paper to write down the needle sites, because there were more sites used. One particular needle was inserted at the top of Papa's head bang in the middle. Dr Luo said that that needle would bring clear yang to the brain and relieve stress. He said that they are acupuncture points or acupoints. That was another new medical terminology I'd learnt.

Between treatment days Papa and I carried out our version of acupuncture with my pen. Papa also remembered the sites where the needles were inserted and began doing it himself. He was also given a herbal prescription to take two times a day. It contained blood-cooling and nourishing, liver-soothing, and kidney-strengthening ingredients.

Papa began to feel well in himself after four sessions of acupuncture and one week of the herbal medicine. He started going into the garden more regularly. He was applying himself to his work for longer periods. I felt that to be a positive indicator. The good thing which came out of this acupuncture treatment was that Papa and I learnt some acupoints which we could do on ourselves. This is a good example of rote learning, memorising what I saw, without knowing its significance. This was the method of learning at my primary school. We had to memorise almost all our work.

I went into the library and asked the librarian to help me find some information on acupuncture. She raised her eyebrows. "What's that?" she said. She also had not heard of such a word. We went through the reference catalogue to find diagrams of acupoints. I copied down almost all the acupoints Dr Luo used on Papa. Each point was described by name, location and function. That gave me an idea about the use of acupuncture to treat patients.

Papa and I became some sort of practitioners to treat ourselves. We stopped going to Dr Luo. We practised acupressure on most of the points which Dr Luo had used during Papa's treatment sessions. I learnt those acupoints very well and could do them from memory. I used them throughout my schooling not knowing the benefit that I may derive from them. I knew that I would not be harming myself in any way whatsoever. If it has benefitted Papa, I was sure that the acupressure on myself must benefit me also.

CHAPTER 18

PAPA HAD BEEN FEELING better within himself and was working harder in the garden. He said to me, "Son I eh have no money to give me to travel to school. The tomatoes and bygan and peas eh ready to pick an sell to get some money. So, ah ask dee boy dong dee road to carry you for truss an ah go pay 'im by the end ah dee mont. Den dee provision go be ready to pick an sell. Den ah go pay dee boy. Ah tell he to carry you every day an bring you back till you finish you callege. Dee boy say dat he carry he bredda an al to dee callege." I asked Papa who is the fellow coming to pick me up. He said, "Dee boy dong dee road nah, he living by dee school. You get ready and he go come for you."

On Monday morning at 7.00am the taxi driver pulled up in front of the house. There were two passengers in the car. My heart jumped hard with severe palpitations when I looked at the driver. I did not know what to do or say. I was reluctant to sit in the car but I had no choice in the matter. I walked to the car with my head bent down to avoid any eye contact with the driver. His younger brother who was sitting in the back seat opened his door to let me in. His sister was sitting in the front seat. I was mute. The taxi driver said, "Hi, get in, you will be travelling with me for the next eighteen months. Your father and I arranged it for you." He paused for a moment and said, "Fancy that, I have to put up with you for so long. Don't worry nah, we'll make it."

I sat quietly in the car extremely ashamed and embarrassed at the same time. I said hello to his brother and sister. I am wondering what this driver was thinking about me. Is he laughing silently at me. Is he saying to himself, "Look what a fool he is. Why did his father ask me to carry him to school every day? Does his father not know that it was I who eloped with his B? I ran off with her and carried her to my house. I am married to B." It was a very strained eighteen months of travel to and from school with Havio.

This travelling with Havio daily to and from school was embarrassing, humiliating, belittling, and extremely unpleasant for me. It made me quite withdrawn and reduced my self-esteem to zero on the scale of nought to ten. I would feel ashamed of myself to talk to Havio. He would have been told everything that went on between B and me. I felt that he would make me a laughing stock. How would any person feel when he or she has to depend on the person who has stolen one's loving partner? Such was my predicament.

One thing that I noticed was that Havio was always early in the morning to take me to college. He was never late even once in the morning for the full duration of the eighteen month period of travelling with him. I fully appreciated his gesture, more so because he was taking me to and from college on credit. This scheme for me has been to "buy now pay later". Papa paid him at the end of each month. Sometimes I wondered where Papa had got the money to pay Havio. I dearly wanted to thank him for always coming early every morning, but I felt very ashamed to face him. I would sit in his car and simply say "Hello," and remain silent for the whole journey to and from school. I carried on like this for the next eighteen months until I finished my schooling.

My return journey after school was in stark contrast to the morning journey. Invariably I would come to the taxi stand and have to wait for hours for Havio. I had to wait for him because I had no money to travel with any other taxi driver. Some evenings I waited until 7.30pm or 8.00pm at the taxi stand for Havio to take me home. School was dismissed at 3.15pm every day. On those evenings I would not be home until 8.00pm or 8.30pm. I had no choice at all but to endure my lateness in reaching home. I did not question him at all for fear that he might stop taking me on credit. That was the big problem of having to depend on the one person to bring me back from school. I prayed and thanked the Lord for the last eighteen months of travelling with Havio.

My schooling had been rough and tough, but

rewarding. Burning the midnight oil can produce a few happy moments. These can come with their side effects, however short-lived these side-effects may turn out to be. On one occasion I happened to be a good target for the form master. Although the form master had us for one year he knew a mere handful of the boys.

CHAPTER 19

MONDAY 18ᵀᴴ JULY. THE end of term and year examination results are usually sent out in the holidays. Results are not given to us in class. On this occasion our form master decided to break the rule. He came in. The boys stood up.

"Good morning, boys," he said.

"Good morning, sir," we answered.

"Take your seats."

He began to talk about the overall performance of the whole class. He looked annoyed and unhappy. There was no indication of an imminent smile coming from him. He checked his notes quietly in front of the class. This was completely out of his usual cheerful, friendly manner. He remained standing. He was rather short and obese, in the forty to forty-five age bracket. His voice was calm and welcoming. This morning he seemed to be out of character. The class remained silent. We could hear a pin drop. Tension built up in the class. *Something must be amiss*, I thought to myself. *For how long are we going to be silent? Who is going to break the silence?* I questioned myself. It felt as if we were in a psychiatric group therapy session.

At last, our form master looked up, gazed around and said, "Where is...?" (a deep pause) "and..." (a further pause) "who is..." (a longer pause) "Usati Harri Ram?" in a deep strong voice. If the tone and the sharpness of his question could speak, they would tell us that he was in no mood for reconciliation but for confrontation. Thirty-seven hands stretched out pointing with their index fingers like poisoned arrows at me. They pointed from the front, the back and the sides, straight at me. The two boys sitting on my left and right turned to look at me. Our form master was in no doubt that it was me.

"Stand up," he yelled at me in an angry voice. I stood up. "No, stand up on your chair," he ordered me. There was no "please" or politeness or "will you kindly" in his command. I thought for a moment quietly within myself, *Are we in an army training camp this morning?* I stood on my chair. He looked at me again and said, "No, that will not do. It is too low. Stand up on your desk, so that everyone can see you properly."

I could not take this any more so I opened my mouth, "Sir, if you didn't mind, I'd rather not stand on my desk."

His reply was quick and sharp and in one word, "Why?"

I said calmly to him, "Sir, it is because, the higher I go, the harder I'll fall."

He came back at me, "That's precisely my intention. So, get up there now."

I stood up on my desk.

"Take a good look at him, you boys. Do you see him? Take a good look at him again. Yes? He has failed! Do you hear me? I say, he has failed to gain *one* mark! Now, take another good look at him once more, OK? I say to you boys that, he has failed to gain *one* mark…" (pause) "to…" (pause) "make…" (pause) "100 marks."

The whole class resounded in a chorus of "Oohs". This was followed by spontaneous cheering and clapping. After the boys settled down, the form master came up to me and shook my hand. He was his usual self again.

He said, "Will you kindly take your seat, my boy? Well done chappy!" With his acting over, the status quo was restored.

"Sir, what about our results?" the boys asked.

He said, "They be will posted to you during the holidays as usual."

CHAPTER 20

AUNTY JENNY IS NEARING her goal. She is the person providing the domestic duties for Nana. She cleans, cooks and washes Nana's clothes. She doesn't like doing these jobs for herself, particularly washing and ironing. Here she is doing the work for Nana. She has full access to the house, but she is not allowed to sit in the veranda to look out. Nana does not allow any of the womenfolk to sit at the front to look at people walking up and down the road. They must always be in the back. This does not suit Aunty Jenny. The whole idea of wanting to occupy the front house is to pose in the veranda and to look at the men and women passing to and fro along the road. She wants to notice others and to be noticed by others.

She is urging Uncle Jhan to do something. She has no more ideas to float, neither does he. For all her efforts in doing so much work in the house, she is not receiving her just rewards. One can sense that her frustration is building up. The fact that she has access to the house, and that she is in control, what more does she want? Nana is thinking of bringing in a lady to help out, but he is dissuaded from doing so by Uncle Jhan. He told Nana, "You can't trust anybody coming into the house, these people are too hand fast these days. They will pick up anything from the house and walk out. You wouldn't know when and where they've gone. So, don't take that chance."

Brother has been taking Nanny and Nana to the DMO to have their blood pressures and blood sugars checked fortnightly. Their blood sugars and blood pressures appear to be nicely maintained. Rani continues to provide balanced meals daily. She also ensures that they have freshly squeezed carrot juice and tomato juice every morning. She carries out her usual routine with the washing, cooking, cleaning the house and the yard. Nanny says to her, "Baytee, you dah wok so hard every day, and you dah give me a good rest. Now dee steam food dah taste good. Me gettin' to like dee food. Me foot nah dah hut me too much deeze days. Ah could wahk good now. Tomorrow ah go go in dee gyarden, and help Bredda an Nana to pick tomatoes and bygan. Ah know you go get everything ready foh we wen we come."

I have been receiving my weekly bowl of food with grateful thanks to Rani and Dewan. This is a welcome relief from my burnt roti with tomatoes. Rani is an excellent cook. Since she was five years old Rani has helped Nanny to cook.

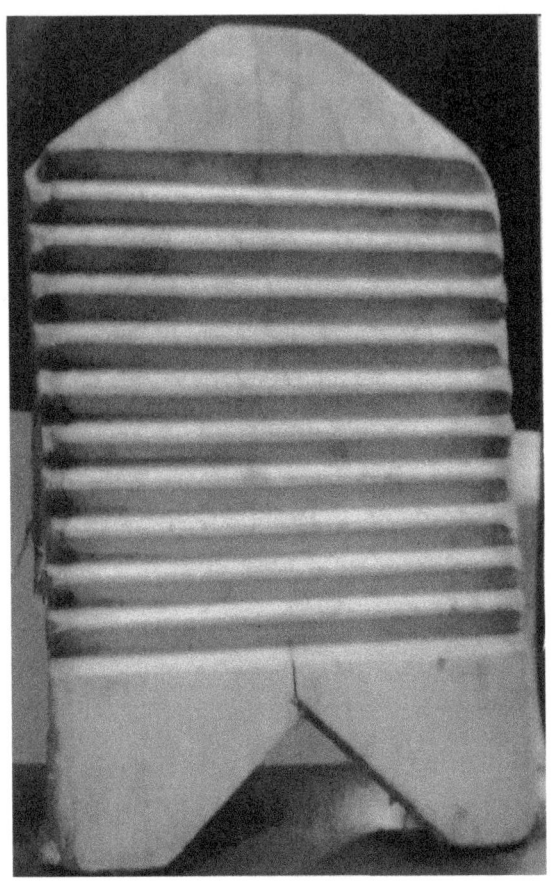

Every home in Sunnyvale had a scrubbing board to scrub and wash clothes and bedsheets. Bars of blue and brown soaps were used as washing detergents. There were no washing machines in Sunnyvale. The scrubbing board was placed in a tub at an angle of 45 degrees. The top end rested on the tub. From the age of six Rani was washing and scrubbing clothes on Nanny's scrubbing board. Every day she would be scrubbing a large bundle of clothes belonging to all of us. Nanny was relieved of the washing, cooking and cleaning. The scrubbing board eventually became Rani's scrubbing board. That was a tedious back-aching daily chore for Rani. The scrubbing was made of solid hardwood mahogony. That is a very durable wood. The scrubbing board pictured here is a 1950s solid hardwood tool. It is owned by the author's cousin Vishmati Roopchand and it is still in current usage. With kind permission.

Friday 18th March. The workers will get their pay on Saturdays as usual. Nanny and Rani have to cook for all of them. Nanny, Dewan and Nana came home for lunch. They left Brother, Stamford and Sam to finish a small section of cucumbers, tomatoes and bygan, and Brother will bring the full cartload with him. Nana had his lunch and took his afternoon siesta for a couple of hours. He went into their bedroom. Seconds later Nana's shouting and quarrelling could be heard up at Cotton Hill. He is flaming mad at this moment. When Nana is in his most enraged mood he could kill anyone. He bawled out again, "Wey dee blasted money gaan from here? Who take the money again? Dee dam gyal is a blasted tief! Ye take dee money again, an gi ye fadder dee money?" Nanny ran into the bedroom where Nana was still searching for his missing money. Nanny asked Nana, "Wey you dee put dee money dis time?"

"Right dey, right dey man. Ah lef dee money right dey dis marning an den ah gaan to wok. Ah now comin here an dee money gaan. Dis is dee tud time now, dee money gaan. No bady know wey dee money dey, oh wey dee money gaan from dey."

Nanny said, "Dee gyal alone de dey home aal day today till we come back." Nanny asked Rani in a very calm and sympathetic manner, "Baytee, gyaal, you dee take dee money dis time?"

Rani replied, "No Nanny, I never took any money, I am totally innocent, Nanny. I have always told you that I have no knowledge of Nana's money, none whatsoever. What more can I tell you, Nanny?"

Aunty Jenny heard Nana's shouting and quarrelling and quickly ran over. She retorted, "You mean Rani stole the money again and give she father the money? Moye, ah keep on telling you, marry her and get her out of this house. How much more money she going to keep thieving and giving to she father. The man don't work, he always drunk and walking up and down the road." These words inflamed Nana to his limit. He became red in the face. This spelled danger of murder. He ran for his thick leather belt, and raced into the kitchen and began beating Rani.

"Tie! Tie! Tie! Tie!" the leather belt sounded as it showered down on little fourteen-year-old Rani. Nana kept on beating her mercilessly, all over her body with the belt. Then he pulled Rani by her long black hair, out of the kitchen, and downstairs into the yard. He got a stick, and continued pounding her until Nanny ran in front of Nana. Nana hit Nanny as well for stopping him. Nana shouted, "Go an bring aal ye clothes here in dee yard."

Mussy and Aunty Jenny ran upstairs, collected all of Rani's clothes and a couple of pairs of shoes and threw the clothes under the umbrella-shaped tree. There were no red flowers. They put the clothes on the exact spot where Mama was lying, and where the four of us crossed over, down and under her seven times on that morning of her funeral. Nana shouted, "Bring dee tin ah pitch oil, bring dee tin ah pitch oil, I say." Two of our cousins ran and brought the ten-gallon tin of kerosene, or paraffin. Nana poured the tin of paraffin on the heap of clothes, saturating them. Nana shouted again, "Bring dee bax ah match." The boys ran into the kitchen for the box of matches.

Rani was crying and sobbing profusely. No one could console her. She was weak, her legs were weakened, and nobody would support her. She collapsed in pain and suffering from the beating. It reminded me of the morning when I was beaten by Nana under the cocoa-house. No one had seen me, but Rani was in full view of all of them. They saw everything and only Nanny did come to save Rani. Nanny sat down with Rani and cuddled her, to comfort her.

The boys brought the box of matches and gave it to Nanny. "Gimme dat match here," said Nana, and he snatched it away from Nanny. He struck one matchstick, and the wind blew it out immediately. He struck another, with the same result. Nana went nearer to the paraffin-saturated clothing. He struck the match and quickly threw it on the clothes. A huge blaze erupted as the clothes started burning. Nana shouted again, "Bring dee edder tin ah pitch oil for me." The flames continued raging. Nana pulled Rani away from Nanny and poured the tin of paraffin on Rani. She was drenched from head to toe. She smelt of paraffin. The paraffin was dripping off her hair and off her clothing. "Wey dee match dey? Who take dee match an gaan wid it? Bring it here ah say," Nana commanded. They handed Nana the box of matches. Nana struck one matchstick. It went out with the strong wind. He struck another matchstick and as soon as he attempted the throw, the lighted match it went out. As he was attempting to strike another match, an eighteen-feet-long black snake appeared in front of Nana. It raised its head like a cobra and was going to pounce on Nana. He ran for a stick to beat the snake. When Nana turned around the snake had disappeared. Nana searched the croton hedge but there was no snake there.

Then he went back for the box of matches. Nana was about to strike the match, and Brother came in racing the mule cart as he saw the fire in the yard. He sped up the mule directly onto Nana. The mule trampled over him. Brother jumped off the cart and ran directly in front of Rani. The smell of her paraffin drenching was intoxicating. Brother pointed to Nana, "No! No! No! You can't do that! You can't burn her. I say, you can't burn her. If you try to burn her, you have to burn me first," Brother said to him.

Nana looked at Brother and at the box of matches in his hand. Brother is his eyeball, that is, Brother is his favourite pet grandson and Nana will not want to do something that will displease Brother. Nana looked at the box of matches again, then dropped them. He said to Brother, "Dee gyal take dee money again an gi ye fadder."

Brother asked, "What proof have you to say that she stole the money? Who could say that Rani stole the money? You, Jenny, Soomintra – you are ashamed to use this Hindi name – Rani is a thorn in your eyes. You have been wanting to get rid of Rani from this house for a long time. How many men have you and Uncle Jhan sized up for her to marry, to get her out of this house? Today, all of you want to see her burnt alive. None of you attempted to stop Nana. Isn't that so? You, Soomintra, you only want to get her out of here by whatever means. Is that not the case?"

There was a moment of silence.

Brother continued. "If anyone of you here can prove to me, or even give me one ounce of substantial proof that Rani stole the money, you can chop off my head. That goes to you, Mussy, to you, Moye, to you, Aunty Jenny, and to you, Nana. All of you will have to pay for this one day."

Nana said to Brother, "Tell you fadder to come an carry ye from here. Me eh want ye in dee house."

Brother said, "I will go to find Papa and bring him. But I want you to promise me. You must not put your hand on my sister ever. Promise me that now. If you lay even one finger on her, I will kill you, I mean it." Nana was stunned.

Aunty Jenny was relieved to hear Nana's words. That is what she wanted to hear all along. The words had come at last. Rani would be leaving Nana's house in a matter of hours. Internally, Aunty Jenny was very happy indeed. It meant that there would be only two more siblings to clear out from Nana's house.

Brother told Nanny, "Take Rani and bathe her thoroughly. Wash off the smell of the paraffin." Aunty Jenny's daughter is a year older than Rani. She gave Rani one of her dresses to wear after the bath. Rani refused to wear it and wore one of Nanny's bodices and a long skirt instead. Brother said, "I am going to fetch Papa."

Nanny knows that she is going to be at a loss if Rani leaves this house today. She is hoping that Brother will not find Papa, so Rani will remain. She is going to tell Nana how much help she gets from Rani. Since Rani had changed her dietary regime Nanny has been feeling well. Nanny is aware of that. She does not complain of the pruritic itches, and blurry vision, and the poor sensation in her lower extremities so much these days. She will ask Nana sweetly tonight to keep Rani in the house to help her in the daily domestic duties. I feel bitter about the way our grandparents treat us. The boys, that is, Brother, Dewan and I have been slaves to Nana's garden work, and Rani is a slave to Nanny's housework.

Nanny was crying for Rani and cuddling her. Rani was wearing Nanny's skirt and bodice. Rani was in tears and in severe pain from her merciless beating. She was frightened of an unknown future when Papa comes to take her away. She could not absorb or withstand any further beating from Nana. I identify fully with Rani. I could not and did not stay there for any more beating. Now Rani is about to leave in similar circumstances. This cycle of deprivation, cruelty, ill treatment and corporal punishment on us, as children, is repeated. I asked myself, "Are these the conditions under which must we leave Nana's house?"

Confirmation and shear relief filled Aunty Jenny when she saw Brother and Papa walking in. She kept on reciting in her mind, "Another one gone, that leaves two more to go." She said to Uncle Jhan, "Darling, one by one we are emptying that basket."

When Papa came Nana was not at home. Everyone else was waiting for Brother to return. Uncle Jhan was sitting in his veranda reading his newspaper. Nanny, Mussy and Aunty Jenny and all her ten children were in the yard standing in the shade under the umbrella tree. Aunty Jenny is relieved. At last, she and Uncle Jhan would be rid of their thorn. Their previous attempts to marry off Rani had failed. This time they would see the back of Rani permanently. When I left Nana's house on that rainy morning, they also saw the back of me permanently.

Regarding me, Aunty Jenny kept on telling Nanny, "Moye, don't let him come back, don't let him cross this yard again. He's gone, let him go for good." They had issued the same warning to Papa on the day of the fight with Uncle Jhan and Papa. Will they say the same thing about Rani when she leaves? It is a fact that Aunty Jenny and Uncle Jhan are emptying Nana's household of children.

Before leaving with Rani, Papa told Brother, "Son, me children scattering like sandbox seed. It is the end of another milestone in our lives."

Nanny used to say, "Wey wan door shat anadder wan dah open," and the last time she used such a remark to Rani was when Uncle Jhan refused to take her to sit the high school entrance examination. Rani replied, "Nanny, this is not entirely true. My doors are continually closing while none is opening. On the previous two occasions the doors were slammed firmly on me by Uncle Jhan and Aunty Jenny. I'm hoping that the next one may remain open for me to enter whenever that may occur. Nanny, I'd so much wish to have a profession, so that I can work and become an independent person."

Papa told Brother, "Son, ah go carry she by Uncle Cliff. He go get a job foh she. Doh tell dee boy [i.e. me] nothin' nah, because it go worry 'im and it go affect he studying." Brother simply nodded. No one attempted to dissuade Papa from taking Rani away. Even our cousins with whom we grew up and lived like one large family did not try to hold back Rani from going. Uncle Jhan remained in the veranda as he did not want any confrontation with Papa. He observed the sombre scene taking place under the umbrella tree. He did not carry out his threat of chopping up Papa following their fight. Neither did Nanny, nor Mussy, nor Aunty Jenny attempt to drive him out as they had done and promised to do if Papa entered into the yard. The mood had changed. On this occasion, Brother who is Nanny and Nana's eyeball, their favourite grandson, was crying as he looked at Rani. He behaved like Papa on the day of Mama's funeral. Brother was slowly shaking his head as Papa held Rani while Nanny reluctantly released her to Papa. How much grief and sadness filled him as he also thought of my state of dire poverty. My three siblings were helping to keep me afloat with a weekly bowl of food, and Rani may now be in the same predicament as me. How will she make do?

These thoughts drowned Brother's heart, and paralysed his vocal cords, but lacrimation was profuse.

I took no notice of last week when I did not get my weekly bowl of food. A few more weeks went past with no food. I became concerned as to what might have occurred. My first thought was that Rani was caught by Nanny parcelling up food in a bowl and wrapping it up. If so, I am sure that Rani would get a sound beating from Nanny. Then I would be the cause of this. I know that Rani will always speak the truth, even if it means punishment for her. She will not try to cover up and tell lies. That is Rani all round. She and I hate people telling lies. I will never forget those ladies who lied to me and said that Mama was sleeping, while I knew that Mama was dead.

Several months following Rani leaving Nanny, and while I was washing my uniform and hanging it out to dry, Brother came with a bowl of food for me. I said to him, "Boy, it's been quite some time since I've seen you. I'm doing the usual weekend stuff and getting things ready for Monday morning. How have you been keeping, and how are Rani and Dewan?"

He said, "I am sure that this is the first question you will be asking. Finish hanging your clothes and let's sit down and eat something."

I asked him, "What have you got?"

He said, "One of your favourites."

"I am one of Pavlov's two-footed dogs. Just the smell coming out of the bowl is making me salivate profusely," I remarked.

We sat down to a hot bowl of Nanny's soup. Nanny and Rani make the most delicious pot of soup. I had mine in my calabash bowl, and Brother had his in his blue enamel bowl.

"I do have a couple of bits of breaking news for you. But before that, how is school going these days?" he asked.

I told him "Boy, school is not going. My school is not going anywhere, it is static, it is staying firm and solid. Not even hurricane 'Hurry' could move it. So, have you got it? I'll be going directly on the hill through Paradise Pasture to enter school."

"Well, I take it, that's all OK for now," he said.

I commented, "This soup is fantastic! But do give me the breaking news, don't keep me in suspense unless you want me to be your neurosurgeon and extract the info from your brain."

He replied, "I don't too much fancy you quack surgeons. Anyway, one is about Rani and the other is about me." He said, "I am going to get married!" He exclaimed with a loud sigh, "Nanny is finding it more and more difficult to manage the housework." He put up his hand immediately to stop me from interrupting him. "I'll tell you about the second issue after. The wedding day is fixed. The bride is already chosen although I have not seen her as yet. I'm not to see her until the wedding day. Nana and Nanny and Atta arranged it and fixed everything. Uncle Jhan wanted to tell Nana which girl I must marry, but Nana does not want him to dictate on this issue. It was Atta who decided that the girl is a suitable match.

Nana agreed." Brother is Nana's eyeball despite Brother's argument with Nana regarding Rani. "You must attend my wedding. I will see to that and arrange everything for you.

"Regarding Rani, she is now living with Uncle Cliff. He has got her a job as a teacher. You know how Nana was missing money and everyone there was blaming Rani for stealing the money. They said that she gave it to Papa, and Papa supported you in college with it. She was severely beaten by Nana, almost burnt alive, and Nana asked me to get Papa to take her away. That is the story in brief. I have written these twelve pages in detail of all what has happened at Nana's house. Dewan would also tell you more. I cannot talk about these things so I will write in detail again to fill you in. OK?" Brother loves to write and goes into great detail. He does have an eye for every detail. He could become a brilliant writer if he wishes to go down that route. My three other informers are Mussy, Dewan and Atta.

CHAPTER 21

AFTER LEAVING COLLEGE, AND half a dozen unsuccessful interviews with the Hindu School Board, telling me to "Come back in three months there will be a position for you," Uncle Cliff said, "Why don't you come over to the CM?"

I was baptised on Sunday January 18th. I attended the church services and Sunday school for the children. I enjoyed telling the children stories from the Bible. I received a confirmation letter of appointment to start teaching at Jordan Hill on Wednesday March 18th.

I made my vow to the Lord: I vowed that when I start my career in teaching I will never, ever lift my hand to strike a child, or smack, or pinch a child. I will not use any form of corporal punishment on any child.

I was filled with delight and relief. Just before sunrise the next morning I got my lota of water, put a tulsie leaf and a hibiscus flower in it, faced the direction of the imminent rising sun and chanted the Gayatri Mantra, beginning with "Om". I followed it up with reciting the Hanuman Chalisa. Then I sang myself the famous hymn which is sung at funerals. For me it was the beginning of my professional life. I sang "What a Friend we Have in Jesus", over and over. These three recitals and chants have become my daily mantra up to this day. My heart is filled with a religious joy. I offered my thanks and myself to the Lord in order to perform my duty as a teacher, a facilitator and an educator for children's learning.

I was transferred from Jordan Hill to Penal, and from there I went to Claxton Bay. I enjoyed it there and loved the crab-running season at Claxton Bay. The mangrove crabs would be running crazily everywhere, and they would be crossing the road in their hundreds. Nana would come and carry barrel loads of them. He would also take the mangrove water to keep the crabs alive for at least one week. He would feed them with dasheen bush and cassava leaves. When I used to be at Nana's, we would have callaloo and crab for lunch and dinner. We would have curried crab and roti for breakfast until the crabs are finished. The crab-running season is July to August annually.

Six months later I received another transfer. This time I was sent to Sunnyvale CM to start on Monday January 18th. I thought to myself that I had completed the circle. My education had boomeranged on me.

Several of the teachers were still there. They loved the village and its uniqueness. The villagers are kind, helpful and supportive towards each other. This simple, peasant communal living brings the community together. They share their produce and time with each other. This small village is one secret garden. The literacy programme which we carried out is paying handsome dividends. The mere fact that the adults can read and write has given them more confidence within themselves. No one can refer to them as "idiots" any more. They sit at the junction under the samaan tree and read the newspapers in the evenings. Two newspapers are more than adequate to circulate among ten to twelve of them. The villagers are more enlightened and informed of current affairs within the country as well as internationally. This little learning which they had received from the boys is giving the younger adults a huge impetus to attend the adult education evening classes at the local centre. It gives them the opportunity to build on it. Some of them are aiming to attempt formal examinations, which they had missed during their school years. The teachers adore the idyllic settings of the cotton fields, particularly when they stand on the brow of the hill where our house once stood and admire the soft, snow-white canopy of the undulating cotton field. They love the picturesque pond with water lilies in it, basking alligators on one bank, and guava trees lining the opposite bank.

The teachers are looking forward to seeing me as one of them. Since I left school to go to college, I had kept away from this place. I did not want to be reminded of my bad experiences during my years in Standards 5 to 7. Some of the boys used to return to talk to the teachers. One such person is Chat-Tree. I do not need any formal introduction to the school. Of course, it is my old Alma Mater. There are only three new teachers since I left. Teacher Preim, teacher Grant and Nick received transfers elsewhere and have been replaced by three others. Teacher Singha is still the most senior teacher. There is little or no change in his teaching style. He continues to have good examination results, and he continues to bludgeon children. Parents continue to come with sticks and cutlasses, as they did in my day, to the school to attack teacher Singha. They get thwarted away by the skill and power of the head teacher. He would be quickly on the phone to the police station. These routines have not altered.

A staff meeting is held on my first day – Monday January 18th. The headteacher says that, "It is so wonderful to see one of Sunnyvale's products return to serve his community. We hope that you will have a huge impact on all the pupils since you have been one of them. I hope that you will be a good role model to them."

"Thank you, sir," I replied. "I will try to live up to your expectations. I am happy to be on the other side of the fence from now on. We are all colleagues together with the same objectives in mind as we facilitate active, creative, enquiring and questioning minds in our children. I am willing to accept the challenge it presents."

The head of the infant department wants me to join her team. I will be teaching one of the second-year infant classes, under the direct gaze of the head of the department. She is a married lady with a young family. She is one of the nicest persons in the village, as well as in the school. She is pleasant, kind-hearted, warm and generous. She is very supportive towards me as I launch into my profession. She is in her mid-thirties. All the teachers continue to teach using their essential teaching aid, the whip, and this head of the department is no exception. I am the exception, I am the odd one out and would continue to be so. I would maintain this stance throughout my teaching career and for the rest of my life. Meanwhile, the teachers are saying among themselves, "He is still green, he will be like us soon, give him a chance and we'll see for ourselves." Some of them have said those words directly to me. I simply smiled, thought about it, and told them that I am all for this challenge. I said to them, "If Socrates, the father of classical philosophy, has shown that it can be done, why can't I take a leaf out of his book and do likewise?"

I continue to apply my theories of teaching and learning, of motivation, and needs and rewards in my class. They had been successful in teaching the adults during our eighteen months home teaching programme for them.

There are no more sand trays in the infant department. The gigger fleas have gone. The ground is covered with asphalt from the pitch lake at La Brea. Most of the school playground is paved in pitch. This has helped to clear up the gigger fleas from the classrooms. The children are using slates and slate pencils to write. This is an improvement from my infant days. Most of the other routines remain the same, i.e., the lining up, the inspection, the orderliness and military-style marching into the classrooms and of course the extensive use of the whips and rulers for corporal punishment.

Eighteen months in Sunnyvale sees me as an old head among the teachers. The staffroom is not a room. It is an open area at one end of the stage with a few chairs. We can sit and have a break there during the lunch and recess times. Now I'll be treading on very hot potatoes. Therefore, I have to choose my moments. I have to behave like the opportunistic *Mycobacterium tuberculosis* bacteria to pounce, and spread my germs when the conditions are favourable. My aim is to ban corporal punishment in school as the starting point. I arranged to have a discussion with Singha on this subject. I gave him an outline plan of the discussion three weeks in advance of our private meeting. This will enable him to think about the use and abuse of corporal punishment. Several published papers were included, so that he did not have to do any further research on the subject. Three weeks are adequate to read through these papers. He can also base his talk on his vast teaching experience.

He agreed and settled for Friday 18th November at 3.30pm. I asked him if he needed a drink. He declined. "What's this all about? Are you looking for fame? You are still a junior teacher and you want to tell me how to do my job?"

This series of questions put me on the back foot. It is

the most unexpected start to our discussion. I said, "I do apologise if it is upsetting you. I am not here to teach you how to teach. I am here for a general discussion on corporal punishment in the school where I am working. I do have the right to raise issues with any member of the teaching staff on topics relating to our job. Would you agree?"

"Yes, you do have that right," he said.

"Therefore, now we are on common ground. I wonder if you manage to give this some thought, and if you manage to read through the various papers?"

"Yes, I did browse through them," he said.

"Have you any initial thoughts?" I asked.

"Yes, I can see that you have done your homework!" he said. "I think it will be a good starter for us."

I replied and told him that I would be basing my argument primarily on my personal experience of being on the receiving end of corporal punishment.

"Are you going to attack me, personally?" he asked.

I said to him, "Singha, you were the sole weapon user on me when I was in your class. Of course, it will have everything to do with you, as far as my experience goes."

I spoke on the physical, psychological, social, emotional and spiritual effects of his beating on me, and the long-term impact they have had on me. I am careful not to offend nor to belittle his pride. He is the most successful teacher in the school as far as the examination results go. It is this point about "success" which I exploited to the fullest with him which helped to tilt the balance of the argument in my favour. I said to him, "Success can also be achieved by other means, and greater successes can be achieved by a total ban on corporal punishment."

He questioned, "How are you so sure about that?"

I smiled and said, "It's very easy to prove it, Singha, simply put it to the test. Let's give it a try, and there will be no harm done at the end of it."

He looked at me suspiciously and nodded. At the end of our meeting he agreed with me on my next move. Once I had his approval, I had already won three-quarters of my battle, because Singha has the power and influence over everyone in the school.

I pressed ahead for our next staff meeting. Corporal punishment will be the main business of this meeting. I have to gain the support from the teachers. They are happy to adopt any measures which may enhance the lives of the children we teach here.

My next move is to take the lead at a Parent–Teachers Association (PTA) meeting. It will be a convenient time for as many parents as possible to attend. Adequate notice was given to them so that they can make it possible to attend. This is to be an extraordinary PTA meeting where I will be the main speaker. I circulated flyers throughout the village. I would like them to read about the subject before attending the meeting. Since this affects the lives of so many of them I anticipate that there will be a large attendance of men and women at the meeting. The villagers were given sufficient time to talk among themselves about the topics for discussion before the meeting is held.

CHAPTER 22

FRIDAY DECEMBER 18TH. THE school organises fundraising activities, such as day trips to the Pitch Lake, the seaside, concerts and bazaars. The money goes towards getting more books for the school library. Today is the Christmas bazaar. I am in charge of the Santa Claus Stall. I picked six bags of cotton. The large tree where our house once stood produces masses of larger cotton fibres. I can easily fill at least two bags of cotton from that single tree. I do not like to leave it entirely naked. I used a guava branch as my Christmas tree. Green and ripe guavas and mangoes are part of the Christmas decorations on the tree. Then the traditional streamers, tinsel, Christmas lights and shining balls are added. The tree is snow-covered, and the ground beneath is covered with soft snow. The cotton has made an impressive show. Small gifts are tied to the tree, and the larger ones are on the ground.

I am in my full Santa outfit. Only my eyes are not covered with the cotton fibres. The children are pulling their parents to my stall to get gifts. Sales are going smoothly. The Santa songs are a great hit. The Santa sleigh is covered with the soft snow-white cotton. It is a great hit as the kids want to take a ride on the sleigh. The parents also are enjoying the fun and dipping their hands into their pockets and giving generously towards the school library fund.

My stall is the first one close to the front door. So, I get the first sale. Suddenly, there is a larger-than-life figure walking slowly up the hill with one child on each side. She is wearing a plain light-blue dress. The two children are wearing the same colour dresses. I said to myself, *I remember that dress colour very well.* They approach the front door, with this figure panting, apparently exhausted from climbing up the incline to the front door. I looked at her. My heart skipped a beat. My pulse speeded up. She smiled at me. It is a smile that I have not seen for years. It is the bedroom-window smile. I smile happily and joyously to see B. It is the first time we are so close to each other, approximately three feet apart. For several minutes it seemed, we said nothing to each other, only smiles.

She broke the silence, "Hello U, I mean, hello Santa." Now she burst out laughing. "It is my U, my dearest BJA. It's so lovely to see you, my only BJA," she said.

I replied, "Hello, B, are you still my darling B?"

B said in her soft, sweet voice, "Oh yes! For sure, I can

tell you that you are in my heart, you are in my veins, you are in my bones, you are in my skin and you are in my thoughts. You will always reside in me and you are a part of me. Do remember this."

I replied, "B, my feelings for you are the same. They will remain the same. We were born for each other despite our ups and downs."

She pulled my beard, pulled my moustache, tapped my hat and pulled my red-and-white Santa gown. She could not stop pulling at me. She seemed very happy.

"I went and bought this colour to wear especially for you today. I wanted to see if you would remember it. It used to be your college uniform colour."

I said to her, "I know that you would do something so sentimental. B, this is the first time I am seeing you since you sang for me on my birthday."

She said, "Yes, my love, but I do not want to talk about that night. Just seeing you brings true happiness in me. I see that you have not changed, you are still my handsome, charming, sweet BJA. That is the only thing that matters to me. U, my darling, I love you with all my heart, and I will always love you until I die."

I said, "But you are now married with almost three children."

B replied, "U, it is true from me what I have just said. Love is something you cannot buy and put on as we are wearing clothes. No amount of money can buy true love. No amount of persuasion or inducement can buy true love. I truly love you, and what's more, I will always go on loving you. I do want you to know that. My darling, please do not ask me to explain anything to you today. This is not the time and place for that. It is only for me to let you know that I do not love another man in this world. The only man I truly and deeply love is you."

I was going to speak and B put her hand on my mouth to stop me from talking. She said, "I know what you are going to tell me or ask me. It is not the time for me to give you any explanation. I have one request, my darling U, only one request, that you will love me as you did when we did exchange our love notes. I would dearly love to live the life we planned for ourselves. Such a life will give me all the happiness I need."

"My darling B, I do love you with all my heart. My love for you has not diminished or lessened. You are the one whom I love and will continue to love despite your marital status. One day I know that we will be together and live the married life we planned for ourselves. Bear that in mind, my darling B. Do remember that true love lives forever in our hearts," I said.

"B, my precious love, this is the first time that I am looking into your eyes at such close range. I used to see them as light brown from a distance, but they are actually hazel-greyish in colour. Your eyes are sparkling and glittering like little bright precious gemstones. They resemble diamonds. They are oozing out deep warmth and affection. Your eyes are still in love. I can feel this love and deep affection immediately transmitted to me simply by the way you are looking at me. This love is so infectious that it has weakened my heart. I am trying to cover up my feelings. Your smile is always radiant and charming. B, I thought that you would have forgotten me. Clearly, you have not."

She said, "Boy, I will never forget you. This is our first close-up meeting together. This is the first time I am seeing the colour of your eyes in all these years that we've been together. They are lovely and light-brown. They are telling me the same thing that I used to feel every time I looked at you from my bedroom window. U, I see in your eyes what I expected. You are also truly in love with me."

B said, "This is the first time that we are actually speaking to each other. We can hear our voices in our conversation. I love the tone of your voice. It is so soothing and calming. This is the first time that we are touching each other. Our touch will bind us together more strongly and keep us together for years and years. My love, do you know what they always say? They say that the old fire stick is easy to light up again, because it always leaves something smouldering inside it."

I said to her, "While that may very well be true in some instances, that may not always be the case, particularly when the old fire stick is heavily waterlogged. Darling B, I must tell you that our fire stick never did stop burning. Its flame continues to rage unabatedly."

She looked at me, attempted to kiss me but withdrew, laughed broadly, and replied, "It is my same U, my loving BJA, whom I know with your wonderful sense of humour, so sweet."

"How has life been treating you through these years?"
I asked her.

She replied, "It is not the same. And don't ask me to
say any more please."

I looked at the two girls, and at a heavily pregnant B. I
cast my eyes from the children to her abdomen a number
of times.

She said, "I know."

"What do you know?" I asked.

She said, "I know what you are thinking."

I replied, "How can you know what I am thinking?"

"It's in your eyes!" she replied.

"What are they telling you?" I asked her.

"They should have been ours!" she said smiling
broadly and lovingly. She continued, "I care for them as
though they are ours. I know what you wanted for our
children and I do whatever I can manage to do for them."

"When is the baby due?" I asked her.

"In a few weeks," she replied.

I asked her, "Is it going to be a boy or another girl?"

She said, "I don't know, and I'd rather not know until
the birth. Oh darling U, you can touch my tummy, you
know. As a matter of fact, I would love you to do so." I
touched her tummy rather half jealously and half pleased.
Then she placed her hand on top of mine. She pressed our
hands against her tummy. She said, "Now, I hope that this
one will come out just like you!" B was smiling graciously
and her eyes were looking slightly glazed and watery. She
said, "My sweetest BJA, I so wished that this one and these

two were ours." B kept our hands on her tummy for several minutes. Then she kissed my hand and said, "I wish that I could just taste those lips," pointing at mine.

I replied, "Wrong time, wrong place." I said to her, "This is the first time that we have ever touched each other like this, and what a time and place to do so. I hope that your Santa Claus will bring you that special Christmas gift safely." I continued, "I do know that you may have already compiled a list of names of boys and girls, and are putting them in order of priority at present. If you don't mind, my dearest B, would you kindly add my name to your list of boys, and give it some consideration if he happens to be a boy?"

She smiled and said nothing.

I said to B, "My dearest love, B, do you mean to say that you are still an adolescent at the age of nineteen and you are going to have three children? Darling, B, if we are to extrapolate this, by the time you are thirty-six you will have an army of twenty-three, plus or minus a few. My darling B, number twenty-three is a highly significant one in my life. My Mama died at the age of twenty-three with the fifth child in her belly. I hope that that will not happen to you since you are heading in such a direction."

B said, "My darling sweetheart, U, I have news for you. Do you remember our road map plan? We aimed to have three children. This one is going to be the last. I can guarantee you this. I will have no more children after this one. I will keep to this promise we made. I am hoping and praying that this one comes out like you.

"U, I longed for this day to arrive. Since the school announced the Christmas bazaar, I have been preparing to come so that I will meet you. I am extremely happy to see you, talk to you, touch you and look closely into your eyes. I will remember this day for many years and for many reasons."

She said, "I must get something for the kids." She got them to choose and gave me five dollars. "This is towards the school library," B said. I gave her four gifts and paid for them. "These are from me, your Santa for the day," I told her. We gave each other a warm embrace. B whispered into my ear, "I love you with all my heart. It's our Lord's truth." I looked into B's eyes. They were welling up with tears. She smiled sweetly and said, "I must have a look at the other stalls, OK? Bye for now, U, and girls, say thank you to Santa Claus," she said to her two children, and went.

A few months later, I received a note from her oldest child, Devi. It read, "FBTU, that is, FROM B TO U I am happy to tell you that Usati was born on the 18th of January at 18.00 hours. We are well."

I sent a congratulatory note to B for her new baby and thanked her for choosing my name for the baby. I said, "Congrats, my Mama B. I hope that my new namesake will give you extra joy and happiness. He is a welcome way for you to remember me. With all my love to you both. Best wishes, coming all the way from your nearest and dearest loving BJA."

Despite my long diversion from my Santa Claus role

my stall was the most profitable when the money was counted up at the end of the bazaar. My thoughts kept wavering and switching from B to my stall for the rest of the afternoon. I thought to myself, *B, you have brought me great success in love and wealth today. Is this a sign of things to come for us?* What will the soothsayers [the cobos, the curse] have to say about this?

CHAPTER 23

ATTA ROBERTO, WHO IS Nana's confidant, suggested that Nana must not allow Uncle Jhan to dictate brother's marriage. Nana took Atta with him to meet the girl's parents and to see the girl. It was Atta's approval which sealed the marriage. The girl's parents and Nana consulted the pundits for a date. Nana used Brother's date of birth, and the time of his birth, from his birth certificate. Nana also checked in what phase was the moon on the date fixed. Nana told Atta, "Dis date good, man Atta. Everytin' good. Dee moon an aal good. Ye go be two days comin' to dee new moon. Dee new moon go be on dee 20th ah dee mont, an dee weddin go be an dee 18th ah dee mont. Atta, man ah go have a new 'doolahin' for dee house on dee new moon."

Atta said to Nana, "Pusha, I'm so delighted that we are going to have a flaming June bride in your house."

The girl's parents also wanted a June 18th wedding.

There was general agreement on both sides. Brother came up to see me to give me the news.

"Boy, that is how things have developed this far. I do want you to come to the wedding. I have already arranged a taxi for you. I've paid him in advance so that he does not disappoint me. He will be coming to pick you up at 12.30pm. The 'baraat' [the wedding procession of cars] leaves at 12.45pm for the bride's home at Barrackpore. I've brought along this parcel for you. It is a new outfit for you to attend the wedding. No one in the two houses knows that you will be at my wedding."

I opened the parcel to see a new college uniform with blazer and tie. He had secretly gone to the college shop to obtain it. I was totally thrilled. I grabbed him tightly and said, "Thank you, sir."

Brother said, "I would like you to wear the complete outfit for the wedding. It is practical. You will be wearing it to go to school as well. You now have two sets of uniforms to wear."

His face changed. He looked sad. His smile vanished from his face. He spoke softly. "Rani has moved to Uncle Cliff's. She will be all right staying there. She began teaching about one month ago." He put up his hand again to stop me from interrupting him. He relayed everything in detail about Rani's ill treatment by Nana and about the behaviour of both families. "On one hand Nanny is missing her and is upset, while Uncle Jhan and Aunty Jenny are glad that she is gone. Now looking ahead, and as far as you are concerned, I will get your new sister-in-law to send the weekly bowl of food for you," he said quietly.

I told him, "Boy, the word, 'sister-in-law' sounds so odd and strange coming from you. It has always been you, Rani and Dewan."

I asked him, "Have you heard about the big PTA meeting coming up? I will be taking the lead. I do wish to change the way we live in the village. It will benefit everyone. I do have the support from the police, the inspector, and the staff. Try and make it to give me your support. During the teaching of the literacy programme I was attached to the Daniels. Marj is progressing very well. She is reading her Bible every day and has aspirations of becoming a Christian missionary. Well, boy, I can't wait to see your doolahin, and to eat some nice wedding food." He only laughed and went away.

CHAPTER 24

I HAVE BEEN INVOLVED with the Daniels since I was four years of age, and I continue to be so. Although Mr Daniel joins in the literacy programme, and enjoys reading and explaining the passages, he has not stopped beating Marj, Gloria and Alex. This happens when he does not take his tablets. His excuse is that the tablets upset him, particularly when he has to work in the sun. The DMO prescribed Chlorpromazine 25mg three times a day for him. He told Mr Daniel that he may experience hypersensitivity on exposure to the sunlight with the medication.

On one evening, they were too distressed to do any lessons. I agreed to skip lessons for the evening. We spent our teaching hour talking about their plight. Mr Daniel said that he cannot explain what comes to his head, and he said, "I just flip, get mad with them, and beat the hell out of all of them." Marj added that when he does not take his medication for a few days he gets in a violent mood, "and beat the hell out of us." They asked me to suspend their teaching sessions until they were in a better frame of mind. I suggested to Marj that she was progressing nicely, and that we would not want her to forget what she has learnt so far. The break would give them a chance to reflect on their family problem and how they can deal with it. Mr Daniel continues to work offshore with the oil company, and comes home once a month. Alex has been promoted in the police force and has two stripes.

Marj says to him, "Look at me handsome police nah man. He go start wokin an mining we yea, Glory, gyul? We eh go have to depend pan Danny foh money. He dah buy food in dee house foh we, an me eh know wey ye dah do wid dee res ah ye money. He say ye eh have no extra money to spend." Marj tells them that none of the family wants to know, or to have them, because they have their own problems. She tells them that "no man would want a woman like me, wid big children. As long as we have a house and food, why should we leave we home? It nah dah make sense!"

Marj said to Alex and Gloria, "Me eh go sleep wid Danny wen he come home. Ah have a big handsome man right here in dee house." She looked at Alex and put her arm around his waist, "Alex, ah say, you is we man from now, yea."

She continued, "Glory, you hear wat ah jes say? Ah say, Alex is we man, yea gyul?" Gloria remained quiet.

Alex said, "I am working late tonight as one of the fellows is off sick."

Marj replied, "We go wait for you and gi you you food befoh you go to sleep."

"OK I'm off now and see you later, Mama, tay ta," said Alex as he kissed Marj and Gloria. Gloria smiled and replied, "We'll see you in a bit, our really close-knit."

While walking away, he turned and said, "Look out tonight for my bite." Both Marj and Gloria have sore backs and legs from Mr Daniel's beating. Marj said, "Glory, come rub dong me back foh me an den ah go do yours foh you. Use dee coconut oil nah. Ah dee make it las week." As Gloria began to massage Marj's back, she noticed two long weals running diagonally across Marj's back. A small section of it had broken skin. This was tender and Marj said that it was painful. Gloria was careful not to aggravate the wounds. Marj's lower legs were swollen around the calf area. She gave Marj a thorough massage. Then Marj reciprocated. This would be their daily treatment from now on.

Alex was home at 11.30pm to find Marj and Gloria still awake. They served him his meal and retired to bed. The three of them slept on one bed like babies until sunrise. Marj said that it was one of the best night's sleep she has had, and it was due to the massage she had received from Gloria. After a few weeks Gloria moved back into her room. Marj continued to remind Gloria that "Alex is we man."

Alex told Gloria, "You are now sixteen, and what a

dazzling sixteen you are. You have no boyfriend as yet. Why don't you go out and have a bit of fun with the boys and girls? You are indoors all the time."

She replied, "I can't go out every day with the one dress I have, what will they say?"

While Mr Daniel is away at work Marj and Alex continue to sleep together. Gloria often hears them laughing loudly and observes a happier and more relaxed Marj. Gloria joins them and the three of them sleep soundly.

Mr Daniel came home for his week off after working for a month. Marj's plan backfired. She took a blanket and a sheet and went to lie on the settee. Mr Daniel went to bed and was waiting for Marj to join him. She told him, "Danny, ah eh go sleep in dee bed wid you. Ah sleeping right here on dee settee. An doh come here, you hear me?" This surprised him, angered him, and thought that it may be for the one night only. But the same thing happened the following night.

It mattered not at what time of the night it might be, Mr Daniel would go on to beat Marj. Mr Daniel jumped out of bed and rushed into the sitting room, pulled out his leather belt and began walloping her thoroughly. Then he pulled her into their bedroom and locked it. "You are my married wife and you have to sleep with me. I am not prepared to be a celibate." He wiped her tears, and gently coaxed her into bed for his sexual gratification. Marj unwillingly agreed to join him in bed to avoid further beatings. She hated him for this treatment and was determined to seek revenge on Mr Daniel for all the suffering they have endured while living with him.

One afternoon Alex came home with a large plastic bag. "I have got you something my dearest, Glory. Yes, go on and open it up. It's all yours." She pulled out a very nicely wrapped box with red ribbons and a red rose. Gloria's face lit up like a 500 watt Edison light bulb. Her eyes brightened. Marj was very impressed at the decorative gift box.

"This is so beautiful!" she gasped.

Alex continued, "That's only the outside of the box you see thus far, wait until you see the inside with its contents."

She went up to Alex and kissed him, "Thank you very much indeed. I even love the box on its own. It is so professionally done."

He said, "Here is a pair of scissors, open up the box."

Gloria opened the box, and her mouth opened wide. She put her hands to her mouth in shock and surprise and in disbelief. She ran up to Alex and gave him a big hug and a kiss. "It's very pretty indeed." Marj is very happy for her.

Alex said to Gloria, "Glory, the next thing is for you to try out the whole outfit."

"Yea, Glory, ley we see how you look," Marj said.

Gloria went into her room and closed the door.

Alex commented, "Marj, she is taking rather a long time to come out of her room."

"Ye mus be lookin in dee mirror for so," said Marj.

The bedroom door opened, out came the professional model swaying her hips from side to side. "Wow, wow, what a beauty. A red star is born. Glory, girl, you look like a real Coca-Cola bottle," said Alex.

She is dressed all in red – a red broad-rimmed hat, a red knee-length slim-fitting dress to reveal all her bodily curves, her shoulders, hips, breasts and buttocks. She wore a red belt, a red pair of shoes and tights and a red long-strapped handbag. She wore red lipstick and make-up. Gloria looked absolutely stunning and radiant. Marj also said, "Glory, gyul, you looking like a real Coca-Cola bottle, man. You so sweet. Aal dem boy go fall foh you wen dey see you." Gloria summed up her looks in two words, "Blood Red."

"I cannot wear this every time I go out. I will wear this complete outfit only on special occasions," she told them. She was satisfied. She ran up to Alex, "I now believe that you is we man." She cuddled him tightly, looked into his eyes, smiled lovingly and kissed him passionately on his lips. Marj said, "Glory, you see, ah keep telling you dat Alex is we man. Gi him a good hug up an a sweeter kiss dis time." Gloria is so pleased with her gift, she only needed a bit more encouragement to hold on to Alex. This time Gloria ran up to Alex, passed her hands where she shouldn't, and embraced him. Alex did the same to her. They embraced tightly and had a mighty long and deep kiss. It was Marj who said to them, "Enough now."

Gloria said, "Marj, gyul, de man make me feel drunk now."

Marj said, "Ah tell you, Alex is we man."

"Thank you, thank you for my wonderful gift. I love it immensely, all blood red."

Alex regularly walks in from the outdoor bathroom with a towel wrapped around his waist. He would sit and have his meal and then get dressed for work. Marj would pamper him, put her arm around his shoulder and say, "Dis is we handsome man, yea Glory!"

Gloria says to him, "One of these days ah go pull away that towel from you."

"Is this an idle threat?" he asked. They simply laughed. Mr Daniel also comes out of the bathroom with a towel wrapped around his waist after he had his bath. It is a common practice in the home.

One day having had his bath Alex came into Gloria's room and stood up in front of her like a statue. "Why are you standing there and gazing at me?" she said. She leaned forward and snatched away the towel from him. She started giggling at him. "Oh my gosh, what's that? It is the first time I have ever seen a big man's thing. You have hair just like me. Wait a minute." She ran for her tape measure and started measuring the length of his penis and its circumference. She said, "When it is in the six o'clock position it is soft, limp, floppy as though it's in a state of flaccid paralysis. It is a four-inch by three-inch docile instrument." Gloria is fascinated by the overall structure of his genitals.

She innocently played around with it, and was amazed at its magical transformation. It is no longer docile. It rose to a ten o'clock position, aiming directly at her. Her mouth opened big. She felt it. It was warm, hard and stiff. She thought it had got into a state of spasticity. It is not dormant any longer. It is live, live, and eager to go into action. She thought that in this state it can dish out both pleasure and pain. Alex admired her curiosity and fascination. She got her tape measure again. She said to Alex, "At the ten o'clock position it becomes a six-inch by four-inch dangerous weapon. Do you see just how it is pointing at me with its slightly curved banana shape?"

Alex said, "Maybe he is sizing you up."

Gloria said, "I cannot get this cock out of my head. From six to ten o'clock in a quick time."

Alex was going out of the room then turned around and said, "This is your first lesson in sex education."

She told Marj of her fascination. Marj burst out in a fit of laughter. "Glory, gyul, you gat plenty to larn yet." Gloria's imagination begins to stretch further, and her curiosity is growing exponentially. This is particularly the case when Alex and Marj laugh loudly and then become very quiet, just whispering to each other. When Alex is working a night shift Marj invites Gloria to sleep with her.

Gloria's wild imagination and curiosity were roused while thinking of Alex and Marj. Alex popped into her room and lay beside her. He fell asleep and spent the rest of the night with her. In one night Gloria learnt everything that she wanted to know in order to appease her curiosity. For her, it was an exciting, exhilarating, thrilling and moving experience. For the following week Marj would wake her up to give Alex his late night meal. He would lock the door as soon as she brought in his food, and keep her in until morning. The initial excitement had become the most vile, the most obnoxious, and the most filthy activity she has to perform. She reflected on Marj's words, "Alex is we man," and cursed herself for being trapped. She was extremely distressed and threatened to stab Alex if he attempted to touch her. That was the only thing which kept him away from her. Her curious desires had landed her in this messy hole. She thought of running away, but she had nowhere to go – no friends, no family, and no social services in Sunnyvale. Families and friends would tell her to go back, just as they had told Marj. These people have their own problems to resolve. It happened on Friday 18th.

One afternoon when coming home from school Gloria was sitting on the doorstep and was waiting for me. "Hello, my dear Gloria, it's lovely to see you. What a pleasant surprise it is! What brings you over to this hill?"

She replied, "Just to see your gorgeous eyes and smile."

I said to her, "Oh! That's highly complimentary particularly after a hard day at school. Let's go inside." She became serious and began to cry. She looked extremely distressed and depressed. She related the recent events at home, how rotten she feels about the entire affair with Alex. She says, "I feel like killing myself to get out of this horrible mess. I am worried about becoming pregnant now." Gloria wanted to know the early signs of pregnancy.

I said, "Gloria, these are some common features — such as, tiredness, early morning vomiting or during the day, or losing your appetite. Your menstrual cycle may cease. However, in stressful situations your cycle may be delayed and you may not get pregnant. But it must be confirmed by the DMO, and it may take at least six weeks for the confirmation to be made."

Gloria fears the dreaded word "pregnant" when she goes to the DMO. I told her, "It may or may not happen. It depends on the phase in your menstrual cycle when you had sexual intercourse." Indeed, her Coca-Cola bottle shape makes her sexually attractive.

Two months later Gloria was sitting on the doorstep waiting for me to come home. As soon as she saw me she started crying. She was in a pitiful state. She held on to me with tears streaming down her cheeks. She will not let go of me but continued crying. She could not say the word to confirm the news. Gloria looked up at me and nodded. She was pregnant! I sat her on the bench, went and got her a cup of coffee. She was crying and feeling miserable and angry. She sipped her coffee.

I said, "Gloria, I know how you are feeling at this moment. That is expected in your situation especially when pregnancy is not planned nor wanted. It is certainly not the end of the world, and most importantly, not for you. Together, we all can work through this tragic and traumatic experience to bring about a positive outcome."

Gloria was angry with herself, and hated Marj and Alex for getting her into this state. She knows that the whole village will learn of her pregnancy, and the shame and disgrace she has brought to herself, her family and the villagers. She cannot walk down the road because the people will give her contemptuous looks. They would say unpleasant things to her.

Gloria is not the only one in the village who has fallen into such a mess. Those other girls would have felt the same way and they resorted to the ultimate – suicide. Gloria thought of Shareen, Josy, and Preeta. They were all also sixteen years of age at the time when they took their own lives. They had brief lives. Gloria said, "I can now understand how Shareen and Josy must have felt at the time when they learnt that they too were pregnant. I am feeling to do the same thing too and want to get away from everybody," while the tears flooded down her cheeks. Her eyes were red. She looked into her little mirror, and said, "Blood Red."

I said to her, "Please, please, Gloria, don't think about choosing their method of escape. Please do not go down that route. I would do everything I can to help you. OK? Is there anything else you would like to tell me?"

When I heard her speak so openly, and expressed such thoughts, I feared for her safety. I was also aware that the more Gloria talks about her feelings the better it would be for her mental state, and she would be less likely to harm herself. Emotionally, she was at the bottom of the riverbed. She could be lying alongside the two fair-haired, fair-skinned and blue-eyed girls. Then I calmly said, "Gloria, there are other positive options available to you to help you. You need support from your family, medication and talking to the DMO or Dr Luo. You must be with someone at all times for the time being. You can have an abortion, although abortions are illegal in the country. The exception is if the woman's life is in imminent danger. The situation for abortion is made worse if it's a teenage pregnancy, and worse still if it is due to an incestuous relationship. However, you may well be treated as an urgent and special case.

"Gloria, it would be nice for Marj to take you visit the DMO or Dr Luo, to discuss the best way forward. They are both very understanding and sympathetic towards everyone. But please, please, please, don't do anything to endanger your life. You will be curtailing your precious life. You do have an enormous amount to contribute to your family and the community. You may not think so at this present moment in time, mainly because of the way you are feeling. It may take several months or years to heal this wound, but it can be done.

"I know that you are disgusted with Alex and Marj, but they are the only ones who can help to support you and to lift you. They are instrumental in this respect. Kindly allow them to sit and be with you both day and night. Yes, I mean they will be with you twenty-four-hours. Simply sitting there with you and saying or doing nothing, means an awful lot to support you at this present moment. With your permission, we'll walk home and I'll explain it all to Alex and Marj. OK? Shall we go?"

Marj suggested to Gloria and Alex to get married

straight away. Nobody will have nasty words to say to Gloria. They can move down to Poole and stay with Henrick, and live as happy newly married couple. Both Alex and Gloria seemed to be pleased with this idea. Alex asked for a transfer but he did not get it because they are short-staffed. Gloria did not want to marry and stay in Sunnyvale for the obvious reason of the stigma on her. Failing this Marj spoke to Hazel.

Next morning, instead of taking Gloria to the DMO Marj took Gloria to the self-proclaimed uneducated and untrained backstreet gynaecologist. Hazel has no knowledge of anatomy and physiology. She is young, in her mid-twenties, slim, and very attractive. She is neatly dressed, with a white coat, and looks like a professional. She has straight long black hair, light-grey coloured eyes and prominent cheekbones. She has neatly shaped lips and a small chin. She wears red lipstick – she calls it "blood red". She listened to Marj and Gloria, made notes like a doctor, and explained the procedure to them before carrying it out. Hazel did not engage in lengthy discussion with Marj and Gloria.

She took Gloria into her surgery. The room had a trolley with a set of instruments on it, shelves with linen and disposables, and a bed. Twenty-five minutes later she came out of her "surgery" with Gloria. She said, "Do expect some bleeding for a few days. It will gradually stop. Do drink plenty of milk and take nutritious meals. You will need a lot of rest for the next three to four days. Take one teaspoon of this herbal powder twice a day for pain and the bleeding. So, it's all done. Oh yes! It's all done and dusted.

"Now, my darling, go your own way. You are free! Yes, oh yes! You are now free! Free as the birds in the sky! Free to have any number of men and boys as you may wish. You will never encounter this problem again! So I may never see you again. Therefore, go! Go! Go and enjoy your new-found freedom! Have fun!" Hazel told Gloria. Hazel looked at Marj and Gloria and smiled, then got serious and said to them, "Do you know that I was thirteen years of age at the time when my kindly gynaecologist said exactly the same words to me. I am simply passing them on to you this morning. You and I are now sailing in the same boat, free from becoming pregnant." Hazel put her arms around Gloria and Marj and began crying. She was grieving. She said to them, "Our lives have been destroyed at such a young age. Life can be cruel for some of us. Come back anytime."

Gloria suffered severe lower abdominal pain and prolonged and profuse haemorrhaging for three days. She lost so much blood that she became very weak and pale. "She is grossly anaemic," said the DMO. "I must give her a blood transfusion with three pints of blood. She is to remain in my surgery for a couple of days. I can see that she has suffered immense physical and emotional trauma already. The damage done is irreparable.

"Encourage Gloria to eat her meals regularly to help her rebuild her strength. She would also need plenty of rest. She must also take all the medication that I am going to give her. I would like her to come and see me again next week to see how she is doing."

Gloria was sitting on our front step waiting for me to come from school. Her face was pale and drained. She was sad-looking. I said, "Hello, my dear Gloria, I'm sorry to keep you waiting."

She replied, "How did you know I was coming up here by you?"

I said, "I simply guessed." We sat on the step with a cup of orange juice.

Gloria said, "Boy, I want to talk to somebody bad, bad, bad, otherwise I will go and kill myself. The only person who I could talk to is you. I cannot talk with Alex and Marj. They keep me company only. You are always so good to me."

I said, "Gloria, I will do all I can to help you. So, don't hold back, simply tell me."

Gloria began, "Boy, I don't sleep well. I am feeling very weak and I can't do anything for myself. I have lost my appetite and I don't have any taste in my mouth. I get up early every morning at about three or four o'clock and I stay awake until daylight. I just can't go back to sleep. I think of all sorts of things. My mind is so mixed up. I just feel to go and do me self. How to finish everything.

"I keep on talking to myself. But if I go and hang myself, nobody will find me in the bush, except the cobos. I can't think of them surrounding me and picking at my flesh and leaving my bare skeleton hanging. I cannot go with the two fair-skinned, fair-haired and blue-eyed girls to lie at the bottom of the riverbed. The entire village will see me. I cannot go by the seaside and drown myself. The thousands of fishes will be munching away at me to leave my skeleton at the bottom of the sea. But ah too weak, boy."

These thoughts are harboured by Gloria during her early morning waking. I listened, and recognised the depth of her depression. Gloria is suicidal. She requires urgent medical help. The DMO prescribed a trycyclic antidepressant – Amytriptyline – 25mg in the morning and at night, and to be reviewed in a week. Twenty-four-hour observation was also recommended by the DMO. It is Alex and Marj who will have to carry this out, because there are no proper psychiatric services available for her. The medication is gradually helping to lift Gloria out of her depression. She is communicating in a reasonable and rational manner.

One morning the biggest rooster climbed up onto the branch of the breadfruit tree. He walked along the branch until he reached outside Gloria's bedroom window. At 3.55am this big, handsome red yard cock started crowing ceaselessly. He did not stop until daybreak. Did he have a form of verbal diarrhoea? He helped to keep Gloria awake that morning. She broke her concentration to listen to the cock's melodious tune. Each crow was long and high-pitched. Gloria was feeling stronger and she was more alert. This is the time I told Marj and Alex to be very aware of, and to be particularly vigilant in observing Gloria. This is the time she has the energy to commit suicide. Therefore, twenty-four-hour observation is absolutely crucial, I stressed.

When the sunlight peeped through Gloria's window she thought that it was time to get up. She gently and slowly opened her bedroom window, to see this enormous ten-pounder plus, handsome prince of the yard looking at her. He restarted his crowing to show off his elegance in stature. He stood erect and stretched out his neck as he yelled a long crow. That was sung for Gloria. She smiled at him. He knew that she approved. Was it to be his final curtain? He waited for her to leave her room before he would climb down the tree. Gloria picked a large breadfruit from her window.

This morning has been a happy one for her. The morning sunshine was warm and inviting. A cool breeze swept through her hair. It was refreshing. Everything seemed fresh and invigorating. Gloria wondered whether it was because she had consumed the blood-invigorating herb from the back garden. The Chinese refer to it as Yu Jin. The Indians call it haldi, and its English equivalent is turmeric. Here, it grows and produces prolific yields. Marj had boiled the turmeric with cinnamon and a piece of ginger and given the decoction to Gloria during her "post-operative" period. Marj told me that the "harrdi go move dee bad blood and dee cinnamon and ginger go warm up she belly an take she pain away. Ah dee larn dat from me modder."

Gloria said, "Marj, I would like us to have a fantastic dinner this evening. I'm feeling great today. I was greeted by the prince of the hens. He crowed beautifully outside my bedroom window and waited until I got out. I stretched my hand out of the window and picked this breadfruit, one of my favourites for the meal. I would like us to kill the biggest yard cock we have. It will go down well with peas and rice. You and Alex catch him and I will kill him."

Alex told her, "But you have not done this in your life, you would not know where to start." The water was boiled.

Gloria looked at this gorgeous red-necked and red-feathered bird. He looked at her and made his longest crow. She bowed to him, and was pleased with his performance. She held him down with her right foot on its feet and her left foot on its wings. She held the head up and in an instant it was over. The scene was blood red. She said, "You have made your final crow a few minutes ago." Gloria went into the kitchen, "Marj, he's all yours. The handsome prince lies waiting for you. Thou, prince, shall crow no more."

Marj said to her, "Glory, ah goin to make you favourite dinner for you dis evening. Ah so glad you feeling good an you appetite coming back."

Gloria said, "I'm going to invite our good neighbour and friend, U, to come and join us for dinner. I consider him as part of the family."

CHAPTER 25

I HAD NOT SEEN Brother for a while. I knew that he would be busy in the garden. His wedding preparations were steaming ahead. I saw two men and two women going house to house issuing invitations and collecting cups of rice or flour from each resident in the village. I felt ashamed to tell them that we had no foodstuff in the house to offer them. Fortunately, they spared me the embarrassment by not coming in. They passed our house without looking at me. I wondered whether they received instructions not to come in and invite Papa and me.

Normally, every single house in the village is invited to any function which a resident may be having. Why should they discriminate against us? If this is the case then we would be the first in the village not to be given an invitation by these "Naawhz" for any village occasion. I went to see what preparations were being made at Nana's house for the wedding.

As I passed along the road I could hear Aunty Jenny calling out to Nanny, "Look, look, he jus like ye fadder." In fact, she knows damn well that I am going to one of the top two colleges in the south. Now, why should this woman, my aunt, make such a scathing and untrue remark about me? Nana had put up a long galvanised tent covering at least three-quarters of the yard, in case it rains as well as to provide shade from the sun. There was another covered area where food would be served. There was an array of huge pots and trays. They were already washed and left to dry. I give Nana great credit for his meticulous planning of the events which he undertakes. In Brother's case he would be more so, having Atta as his "right-hand man". Atta is consulted on almost any issue affecting Nana. The mid-section of the tent is well decorated with various colours of crepe paper, cotton and satin ribbons. There was the Beidi completely organised and protected for the welcoming ceremony when Brother comes home with his bride.

I got ready for the taxi which Brother organised for me. Four of them and the driver pulled up. The President of Sunnyvex was among them. Embarrassment and shame hit me again. I had to pretend my innocence and laugh with the boys. They were not wearing college uniforms. They clapped when they saw me in my outfit. I said, "Boys, this is a specific request coming from the doolaha (the groom)."

The taxi driver is the one who eloped with my dearest B. He is Havio. There were thirty cars making up the "baraat" (the wedding procession of cars) and heading for the bride's home. There was a loudspeaker blaring out the latest Indian songs, and the "tassa" (musical drums) group ringing out its rhythmic music. When we get there the bride's "tassa" team will compete with ours to outplay each other. That's the welcoming ceremony.

Hindu weddings are rather lengthy ceremonies. They may take at least seven days leading up to the wedding day. Brother's wedding is of this type. Our group stayed together and the President made a speech towards the end of the ceremony. He took the microphone and issued a stark warning.

"Ladies and men, the President speaks and when the President speaks, everybody have to obey. Do you hear that? If you did not hear that, then go back home and bring your blasted hearing aid. OK! The President speaks for the third and final time: To everyone of you present here today, and to all those absent today, the President is issuing my very stark warning: don't trust married people. We have just witnessed these two people joined in matrimony, that is, you've seen that the pundit tied a knot to join the doolaha's gown to the doolahin's gown. They walked round in a circle with man leading woman. That symbolises male domination over female in our society. They exchanged mala, that is, their garlands. But did you notice that the doolahin's mother (bride's mother) would not allow the bride and groom to see each other's faces when the malas are exchanged. This wretch of a woman did the exchange of mala for them.

Now these two bitches who just got married work like a pair of scissors. You hear that? I say that married people work like a pair of scissors. Although their two arms work in opposite directions, they will chop off anything or anyone who comes between them. So, if you ever see the two of them fighting, you run for your life. If you play brave to come and separate them, they will turn round and cut you down. Good evening."

It was a lovely ceremony. When the "baraat" was about to leave all the car horns started tooting. The loudspeaker system blasted out wedding songs and the tassa band beat frantically loud. They waited for the wedding car to lead the procession of cars towards our journey home. We arrived at 7.00pm. The welcoming party stood in the yard and the ladies at home including Aunty Jenny and Nanny threw rice grains over the wedding car and on the bride and groom. This was to wish the married couple happiness, health and wealth. With the wedding over it was back to my usual routine.

Thank goodness it's the weekend, I said to myself as I hopped off the bus to walk home. I will take a break from work this evening, and make an early start tomorrow morning. This will give me an opportunity to listen to the neighbour's radio Indian song programme. I simply sit at home and listen, because the radio's volume is at maximum. The surrounding neighbours can also hear the blaring radio. Who benefits most from and enjoys such loud music? I do, but the neighbour is unaware of this. As I approach home there is an absolutely radiant and gorgeous professional-looking model standing in front of the house.

CHAPTER 26

"Hello! Hello my dear, how lovely to see you. You are a scarlet angel to greet me." She smiled broadly, bowed and lowered her red umbrella.

"I thought that I will give you a bit of a surprise this afternoon," she said.

"It is a rather big bit of a surprise I must say. Well, what's the big surprise?" I asked.

She was dressed in an all-red outfit – a red broad-rimmed hat, a knee-length, very tight-fitting dress, belt, tights, high-heeled stilleto shoes, long strapped bag, and red lipstick. She spun around and lowered her umbrella.

"Alex bought this for me. I modelled for them and Alex and Marj say that I look like a Coca-Cola bottle."

I said, "You are ideally suited for the catwalk."

She quickly replied, "Not even a dog will look at me. This is the first time that I am wearing it. I said that I will only wear it for special occasions. Today is a special occasion."

I detected the terseness in her tone of voice when she spoke those words. Indeed, she looks very beautiful in that skin-fit dress. It clings to her body to outline her lovely breasts, narrow waist and large rounded hips and bulging buttocks. Gloria is slim and tall, beautiful, warm and charismatic at most times, but all these qualities are overshadowed by her recent trauma.

Is this physical appearance a mere camouflage for her deep-seated hidden feelings? Can she be trusted and taken on her word in her present mental state? Can she be allowed to walk the streets on her own? Her words are carefully chosen. They require detailed analysis. I do have grave reservations about her. Alex and Marj must be reminded to continue their twenty-four-hour observation. I must explain to them in simple concrete terms what I mean by this phrase.

Gloria said, "I have come to take you with me. We would like you to have a meal with us this evening. I told Marj to prepare a special dinner. Marj has been asking for you for weeks. Since she saw you coming off the bus one afternoon almost every day she looks out for you. She will be happy to see you."

"Give me a few minutes to get sorted out. Come in and help yourself to a drink. There is a little soursop drink in the calabash bowl."

Gloria is still highly suicidal. She is now strong enough to carry it out. They (Alex and Marj) must be warned again tonight.

We walk slowly and casually down West Hill. The

boys are coming to gather at the junction and at the rum-shop. This is their usual Friday afternoon "lime". They would sit under the samaan tree and read the newspaper. When they saw her they started whistling and clapping. "Happy birthday, Glory, happy birthday to you." They also chanted the local Trinidadian favourite jingle, "Rum and Coca-Cola, it good for you daughter."

They are worse than Alex and Marj. The boys love to tease and humour the girls in the village. This did not go down well with Gloria as she was in no mood for jokes. She was fuming with rage. However, she walked in a stylish manner swaying her hips from side to side as she passed them. They shouted and clapped, "Oh, gyul, Gloria, you got it."

We reflected on our early days at Cotton Hill. "You is my saviour, you dee save me plenty ah time from getting licks from Danny," Marj said.

I replied, "I was an effective human shield for you, Marj. I was a mere four-year-old at that time."

Marj said that she spent half a day preparing this special meal for us. "Ah wanted to get it just right," she said.

"Thank you all for such a delicious and sumptuous meal. I love it and thoroughly enjoyed it, especially the 'boil-an-fry' breadfruit, fried plantain and the cassava pone are always my favourites. I must make a move now and leave you to have your well-earned rest. I'm sure that you have had a hectic day in providing this lavish meal, and can't wait to hit the pillow. Thank you again, Marj, Alex and Gloria."

Gloria started clearing up the dishes and was washing them in the kitchen. That gave me the opportunity to speak to Alex and Marj to remind them of Gloria's mental state. I said, "Marj and Alex, these are dangerous times for Gloria. You must be particularly vigilant and don't let her out of your sight even for one minute. I repeat that she must have continuous twenty-four-hour observation.

"These are the times when she will use subtle devices to disguise her severe depression and suicidal intention. She will easily trick you to leave her on her own. Please do not fall into her trap. The result will be fatal. So, do be aware of this at all times. You have done splendidly thus far over the past few weeks. I thank you for that for Gloria's health and safety. Do continue to give her continuous twenty-four-hour close observation. Please, don't let her out of your sight, not even for half a minute. Allow her to carry out her everyday living activities, but one of you must stay with her and watch her movements. At least one of you must always be with her wherever she is or wherever she goes. OK? I cannot emphasise this strongly enough.

"Observe her very closely when she is taking her medication. Make sure that she swallows it with a drink of water. Then ask her to open her mouth to make sure that she has swallowed her tablet. Ask her to raise her tongue so that the tablet is not hidden under it. These are important things to do to help her. I have explained all of this to Gloria already. She has agreed to allow you all to be with her at all times. She trusts me and has confidence in me to help her get better. I can see her clearly from here. She is washing up the dishes in the kitchen. Please do remember all the things I've told you. Ah! She is coming. I must go now. Bye for now, Marj, Alex and Gloria. It has been a lovely evening. I thoroughly enjoyed the meal, especially 'the boil-an-fry' breadfruit and plantain. Of course, the barbadine and soursop drinks were absolutely delicious. The final touches were the glasses of the mauby drinks. Thank you all once more for inviting me along tonight. Goodnight, goodnight."

Alex said, "I am glad to see you, and see you later, Mama, tay ta."

Gloria added, "See you in a bit, my close-knit."

There was a pause and silence among the three of us before Gloria spoke, "U, you are more than a brother, family, friend, teacher, counsellor and a doctor to me. That says it all."

Then Marj added her piece, "An you is mee saviour from smaal."

As I was going out, Gloria said, "I'll walk you out to the road, I must." I gave her a cuddle and we walked to the roadside with arms around each other. Gloria pulled me close to her and said, "Wait a minute, I've got something to tell you. There is a gift for you. You will find it under the big cotton tree which has grown up on the exact spot where your old carat house was. It is the tallest of the cotton trees. The old house broke down and this tree grew up there. You can't miss it. This gift will be there for you in the morning. It's no point going there now, you will not find it. If you go during the night it will not be there. It will be there for you in the morning at sunrise. You will find it at the root of that cotton tree. It will be hidden under a huge pile of rubble. OK. Goodnight … and… goodbye." And she walked away. I pondered over Gloria's last few words. The manner of her expression did not sound as a pleasant goodnight and goodbye greeting. That feeling of finality hit me particularly when she stressed heavily on the last word, goodbye. Her voice came across as being more angry than friendly. It was certainly more finite in the manner Gloria expressed it. It was too late to go back to warn Alex and Marj.

Gloria went in to find Alex and Marj relaxing in bed. "Come and lie down and relax too, Glory," said Alex. Gloria replied with a charming smile, "It's all right. I had a wonderful day today. I thoroughly enjoyed myself today. It was so lovely to have our dear U with us for the meal. He is everything to me. I was in my special outfit all day. I felt happy wearing it for the first time.

Marj and Alex said, "Glory, you look like a real Coca-Cola bottle today. We so proud ah we pretty Glory."

Gloria replied, "I felt like a princess today. But I am tired from all this and I need to spread out on my bed and relax."

Marj said, "Come nah Glory, and let we hug you up nah man."

Then Alex echoed, "Gyul, me too want to hug up we Coca-Cola bottle."

Gloria replied sweetly, but very sarcastically and

disgustedly), "This Coca-Cola bottle" wants to have a bit of breathing space. I want to stretch out and relax. I want to be in my warm bed to end this lovely day. You all relax here, and I'm going into my bed for a very long rest. You will see me in the morning. Goodnight and goodbye." This was said with deep disgust, hate, and contempt for them. Gloria quietly said to herself, *I finally got my way with those two murderers.*

I got up early the following morning and at sunrise I was beneath this enormous cotton tree. The soil under our house must be very rich to produce such an outstanding tree. A huge pile of rubbish and stony rubble surrounded the root. I shifted it and down at the bottom, three-quarters of the gift was underground. I pulled it out.

There it was. A Coca-Cola bottle with a folded paper inside it. The bottle was sealed. I wiped the bottle and tried to see through it to see if I can read the note. I had no such luck. I hid the bottle inside my shirt and on my side. I held it down with my arm and went in to see Alex and Marj. Why would Gloria give me a Coca-Cola bottle as a gift? I never referred to her as a Coca-Cola bottle. It is Alex and Marj who called her so. Why would she leave a message in this type of bottle? And why would she put it under that particular cotton tree? The fact is she wanted me to convey her message to Alex and Marj.

Marj and Alex were holding on to each other in the kitchen crying. Marj was frantic and hysterical. She was bawling and walking round and round in the kitchen. Alex was holding on to her. She was bending and straightening up with her arms stretched out. She was moving them up and down. All these movements and gestures were performed simultaneously. Tears were flowing from both Marj and Alex. I thought for a moment. Are they both feeling sorry for each other? Or is Alex now sympathising for Marj? If so, for what? Her crime? I had left them in a happy frame of mind last night, and quietly issued a stark warning to Alex and Marj before leaving. I had ensured that Gloria didn't hear me. "Please don't leave Gloria on her own, by any means. Do continue with your twenty-four-hour observation on her. These are now dangerous times for her to be left on her own. She is now physically stronger and is able to harm herself. Please do remember to act on this advice. I repeat, it's twenty-four-hour observation of her. OK?" They assured me that they wouldn't leave her on her own.

In her hysteria, Marj clung on to me, wailing and screaming and bawling. "Oh Gad, oh Gad, me eh know wey to say. Dem cobo and dem come an take she from me las night. She look so pretty in dat red clothes. De las ting she say wah 'blood red.'"

Indeed, the cobos had been shrieking and squealing and encircling over the house for the past three weeks. Marj had seen our local Obeah man, Ganti, going to the silk-cotton tree, and coming out of Nana's cane field a few days ago. Last week Marj and Alex had an infestation of bed bugs on and in their bed. Their mattress was swarming with these bugs. Some fell off the bed and were running around and looking for creases in the floorboards to burrow themselves. Alex burnt the mattress and fumigated the room. Two days ago two mirrors fell from the wall and hundreds of shards were strewn on the ground. "We have a lat ah bad luck going an deez days," Marj had said. She continued, "Look how dem mirror an dem faal an break up in pieces. Dat is a real bad sign." But she could not get the cobos out of her head. They were the evil spirits which came into her house last night, Marj strongly believed. They took Gloria from her. No one can dispel this belief from Marj. "Somebody wok dee Obeah on she," Marj reiterated. "But we eh ha no enemy in dee village," she confirmed.

Alex held my hand and led me into Gloria's bedroom. There she lies, peaceful, silent and in her full regal splendour, all in red. She lies on her bed fully dressed as she was yesterday. She is wearing her red broad-rimmed ladies hat with two red ribbons hanging on both sides of her face and tied in a bow under her chin, her red knee-length dress and belt, her red long-strapped ladies bag lay by her side, a pair of red flowered tights and red high-heeled stiletto-style shoes. She is wearing her bright red lipstick, her long gold pendant earrings and her red umbrella opened above her head.

Gloria's eyes are opened with a fixed dull gaze. They are glassy, dazed and dry. Her pupils are dilated and fixed, her lips are cyanosed. Her facial muscles are rigid. Gloria lies pulseless, speechless, motionless and expressionless. Rigor mortis is firmly set. She must have died several hours ago last night, I guessed. Her mouth remained open, and some liquid has leaked out of the corner of her mouth onto her neck.

The DMO arrived. He was looking around the room as though he had lost something. He found a Coca-Cola bottle under the bed, containing a red substance. Some of it was splashed on the floor. He picked up the bottle, and slowly brought it up to his nose. The smell was highly pungent. The liquid has the colour and consistency of blood, but certainly not the pH of blood. The DMO has seen this liquid previously so he immediately recognised it. It was in the case of the sixteen-year-olds Shareen and Josy. They had succumbed to the same type of deaths, again because they were pregnant. The DMO stated that Gloria passed away about twelve hours ago. The cause of death was confirmed: suicide by poisoning.

I waited for an opportune moment to release the final bombshell. I thought that Gloria's "gift" was not for me because of the medium – the Coca-Cola bottle. Marj and Alex are the ones who refer to her as a Coca-Cola bottle. I took out the bottle from inside my shirt and handed it to Alex. He looked at it, "Another Coca-Cola bottle?" he questioned. Alex opened the bottle and fished out the note from inside it. His eyes were red with tears streaming down his face. He read loudly for Marj and me to hear:

"Alex, I killed the big red cock today… The 6 x 6 big live cock killed me tonight… signed… the real Coca-Cola bottle… BLOOD RED."

This note rocked Alex to the depth of the abyss. He is

the lock and the key in one. He is responsible for Gloria's death. He led her to commit suicide. He murdered her. "*I am a murderer,*" he said to himself. He paid the ultimate price for his sexual grooming of an innocent mind. Above all, Alex is a senior police officer at the local police station. Marj is the core of this fatal disaster. She wanted revenge on Mr Daniel for the beating and suffering of the three of them. She wanted them to join her in this revenge. They had nowhere to leave and go to, and Mr Daniel was, and is, the breadwinner due to his hefty salary. I had previously served as the human shield for Marj at the age of four when we were at Cotton Hill. This time, Gloria wanted me to serve as her postman to deliver the Coca-Cola bottle with its message to Alex.

The White Rose and Sunnyvex boys added salt and even hot pepper to the wounded soldier with their satirical humour. The tassa boys saw the crowd parading through the village. They also joined in with their tassas. A slogan was designed and developed by none other than the President. It is only the President who can utilise such wit. It reads with a lovely chanting melody:

LAWMAN MAKIN' LAW – Who say Dat? The tassa drums beat out loud and paused.

LAWMAN BREAKIN' LAW – We say Dat! The tassa drums beat out loud again and paused.

The slogan was posted at strategic locations in the village – at Cotton Hill, by the pond, and at West Hill. The boys, led by the President, waved their placards, chanted the slogan and taunted Alex as they paraded up and down the village. When they reached the front of Alex's home they stood there for about half an hour and kept on repeatedly chanting the jingle accompanied by the tassa drums. When Alex heard them and saw the slogan, he knew immediately that they were targeting and tormenting him. He was and is the cause of Gloria's death. His shame, his guilt and severe depression are eating away his body, his mind, and soul as if he ever had one. He was too ill to work. He thought of himself as the worst criminal on this planet. He needs a refreshing bath, he told himself. Will it be a help? Or will it be a hindrance?

Alex got into his swimming trunks, took a towel and blue soap and went down by the river. He stood by the bridge and looked down at the crystal-clear water below. It was cool, calm and flowing quietly. Suddenly, he saw a huge splash in the water as if someone had thrown a massive boulder into the river. The clear water turned cloudy and opaque. It looked like a barium meal X-ray image lining the oesophagus down to the stomach. Children's voices were loud with a joyous laughter coming out from the water. He can see the tiny pebbles on the riverbed, but they were there also, lying on their backs on the stony riverbed. The two fair-skinned, fair-haired and blue-eyed girls were looking and smiling at him. The more they smiled, the more his eyes were fixed on them. Alex could not have taken his eyes off these two very beautiful women. His eyes were transfixed by the two beautiful ladies. He was captured by their charm and beauty. He was hypnotised. He would obey their commands.

In Alex's mind's eye he thought that the two girls had grown up. *They are adorable,* he said to himself. They began calling him with their index fingers. That was the same way they had begun calling me. Then they used all their fingers. He was under their spell. He could no longer resist. They were thrilled. They sweetened him with their spell to join them. The two evil spirits from the silk-cotton tree had captured their victim. Alex went down into the water. It was cool and refreshing. This was what he wanted. Alex could see the girls from a very close range. They were gorgeous beauties, he thought. They beckoned him to come to them. He dived to reach the two fair-haired, fair-skinned and blue-eyed ladies at the riverbed. There was another huge splash of water as though there was a fight going on at the bottom of the river. The water became white like chalk immediately. It was as if ten pounds of blanco were thrown into the water.

A horrible scream came out of the water. There were several large ripples moving to the water's edge. The huge struggle seemed to be an endless one taking place. Large bubbles oozed out to the surface. These large bubbles gradually became smaller and smaller until they stopped. The water was becoming clearer and clearer. Eventually, it was calm and crystal clear once more. Alex was lying face down, the same way in which he had dived to reach the ladies. He was motionless. The two ladies had vanished from the scene. Gradually Alex surfaced, remaining face down in the water. He flowed to the edge of the river and got tangled up amongst the bamboo branches. He remained there until Marj and the police came to fish him out.

One hour later the sergeant from the local police station and Marj arrived at the scene. The sergeant was shocked and frightened at what he saw. There were two beautiful white marble figurines lying on the stony riverbed. They were keepingwatch over Alex. "What are they and what could they be doing down there?" asked the police officer. He looked at the two beauties once more and thought to himself, *Could they be another two pieces of the missing Elgin marbles?*

"Doh touch dem nah, dey wah spirits wey kill me child," said Marj.

It seemed to Marj that her grief, guilt, depression, and hate multiplied by a factor of one million. With Gloria's passing away and now Alex compounded her despair. She felt hopeless and helpless and utterly worthless.

Should she go and end her life as well? *What's my life worth now?* she asked herself. Marj closed her eyes, thought of the recent events, and tried to compose herself. She thought of me. Marj came and said, "You is me saviour from smaall. Tell me wey to do. Ah doh know wey to tun. Ah lass aal ah dem chiren. Dee devil kill mee an mee whole famaly. Look how dem cobo dee flying round dee house foh about a mont, nah. Ah didn't tink dey go come foh me chiren. Ah go tell you Nana to cut dong dat blasted silk-cotton tree wey dem spirit dah live. Is a big big cuss on dee village."

It is very difficult to dispel Marj's strongly held view that the evil spirits do live in the silk-cotton tree and caused the deaths of Alex and Gloria. The silk-cotton tree is the biggest evil curse on this village, she repeated. Generations of such beliefs cannot be erased from her and from the villagers whilst the silk-cotton tree exists here in our village of Sunnyvale.

I said to Marj, "One day, Nana decided to cut down that tree. He took his razor-edged glittering sugar cane cutting cutlass to do the job. The cutlass reads – 'SHEFFIELD STEEL MADE IN ENGLAND' on both sides of the sharp blade. Nana made one tremendous blow at the tree. The cutlass rebounded from the tree like a rubber ball. There was no impression made on the spot where the cutlass struck on the tree. Nana did not even scratch the tree, but this time he gave a much harder blow at the tree trunk. The cutlass swung back at him to cut him below his left knee on the lateral side of his lower leg. The wound was deep and bled profusely.

"Nana used his belt as an above-knee tourniquet. Atta took Nana to Dr Luo said who said to Nana, 'Oh my! Oh my! Two *He Sea* points involved – Yanglingquan (GB 34) and Zusanli (ST 36).' He sutured the wound, gave Nana a Tetanus injection and antibiotics, and analgesic for pain. Nana went back in a week to see Dr Luo. This time he explained to Nana that, 'Yanglingquan (GB34) is a special acupoint – one of the eight Influential points, and this one (GB34) is the Influential point of tendons. It may just take a little longer to get well on the move again.'"

I told Marj, "For this reason, it is rather dangerous to tackle that silk-cotton tree."

Marj said, "But U, dat damn silk-cotton tree is a real curse on dee village. Dee spirits da come from dey an take away me children, man. Is a damn curse man. I see old Ganti dah go dey every week to pray to the devil."

I said to Marj, "For all my scepticism, Marj, I do wonder if evil spirits really live there, seeing what happened to Nana when he attempted to cut down that tree."

Atta told Nana, "Pusha, it is best that you keep well away from that blasted silk-cotton tree. Let those bastards live there. But, Pusha, when you decide to share up the land and house and the cocoa estate, who will get this piece of land with the silk-cotton tree? Whoever gets that land he will have to do something about the silk-cotton tree. In the meantime we do have to live with this curse on the village."

I visited Atta regularly. He gave me wild meat such as venison or agouti. He would give me all the details of what was taking place at Nana's house. It is one of the main reasons for visiting Atta. My other informers were Brother, Dewan and Mussy.

I listened and listened and listened to Marj pouring out her grief and guilt, and her feelings of worthlessness. We went to the DMO who prescribed antidepressants and sleeping tablets for Marj. I suggested to her to take them as prescribed and not to take more than the prescribed dose at any time. Marj and I revisited the DMO frequently for her own health and safety. Mr Daniel is also taking his medication regularly. I advised them not to miss out on taking their medication. I reminded them to have regular meals. They have one surviving son who lives at Poole. Little is known about Henrik.

Alex was Mr Daniel and Marj's stepson. Alex's biological mother was a promiscuous and attractive woman in the village. She flirted with several boys and became pregnant. She died in childbirth. No one knew who the father was. Mr Daniel brought the baby Alex home to mind him and bring him up as their own child. Marj was pregnant at the time and was due to give birth within a few weeks. That was when Gloria was born. Marj brought up Alex and Gloria together and told everyone in the village that she had twins. Mr Daniel and Marj were proud to tell the villagers that Marj had twins. The villagers thought that Marj had in fact delivered a pair of twins, namely Alex and Gloria. From a baby Alex was bottle-fed whereas Gloria was breastfed. Being a boy in the home meant that the Daniel's name would be passed on to future generations.

As Alex grew up to be a handsome man, Marj had no issues in referring to him as "Alex is we man." She became infatuated with him. Alex was never told anything regarding his biological parents. This was a miscalculation on the part of Mr Daniel and Marj not to disclose the true identity of Alex. Had Gloria known that Alex was not her biological brother she would be more comfortable to marry and live with Alex in Sunnyvale. Alex would not need any transfer.

Marj was sitting in her veranda as Atta was passing. "Hi, hi, Atta, man, wey you going dis hour?"

Atta replied, "I am going down to visit the pusha. We are going to have a drink and a little chat."

"Man ah would have come down too for a drink, but I am taking tablets. The DMO tell me not take any alcohol while I am on the medication. Tell the bass that he have to do something about dat silk-cotton tree. Is a bad cus on the village, man."

Atta told her, "I'll have a word with him concerning this curse."

CHAPTER 27

NANA AND ATTA WERE making arrangements to divide up his estate as he was getting older and feeling weaker. He was not able to work as hard as previously. Nanny has been receiving help from Brother's wife who replaced Rani. I started getting my weekly bowl of food because Brother organised it. Atta agreed with Nana, Brother will own the mule, the new farm tractor, the front house and cane fields, including the cane field with the silk-cotton tree. Brother has two sons and Nana is thrilled. His name will live on for generations.

Jhan will have the six-acre cocoa-estate, and will have the rice lagoon because he does not do any gardening. Uncle Jhan will also have the cocoa-house, their back house and all the land behind their house. Uncle Jhan was not happy with this arrangement. He wanted much more than that, because Uncle Jhan is Nana's son and direct heir whereas Brother is Nana's grandson. Nana is suffering from hypertension and angina. He is being treated by Dr Luo. He prescribed GTN for the angina and told Nana to take one tablet and put it under his tongue when he gets a severe chest pain. Brother attends to Nana's and Nanny's health needs. Nana gave Uncle Jhan instructions about how to divide up the estate as mentioned above.

One day Uncle Jhan took Nana to Mr Richards. The lawyer made out the transfer of assets document according to how Uncle Jhan itemised it. Nana is illiterate. He refused to take part in our literacy programme. Therefore, he is unable to read or write. The lawyer asked Nana, "Do you really want to transfer everything this way?"

Nana said, "Yea, ah dee tell dee buaye [Uncle Jhan] wat to do."

Mr Richards said, "If that's the case I will have it ready in a few minutes." The lawyer's secretary returned with the typed document. Mr Richards said to Nana, "Sir, will you kindly sign this document?"

Nana said, "Me nah know to read an write, man."

Mr Richards said, "OK, will you kindly put your fingerprint here on this document?"

Nana placed all ten fingers in the ink and on to the document. "You want me foot an all?" Nana asked the lawyer.

"No, we don't need them, thank you, sir," replied Mr Richards. "It's all done. That's pretty straightforward to do these days. Good day, gentlemen," and he opened the door for them.

Uncle Jhan came home, sat in his veranda, and slouched in his large wicker rocking chair. Atta and Nana had bought a set of wicker basket armchairs and rocking chairs for both houses. They were Atta's choice and recommendation to Nana. Aunty Jenny brought him his lunch. She cooked dahl and peas and rice and "shataigne".

"How everything went?" she asked.

"Just as we planned," he replied. "Pa printed his ten fingers on the paper," Uncle Jhan told her. She only smiled.

One afternoon Nanny was sitting with Aunty Jenny who was doing a bit of sewing. Nanny started slowing down and was looking dazed. Her speech was slurred, and she was not responding straight away. Aunty Jenny was totally unaware of the present situation. She kept on sewing and rabbiting away.

Had Rani been there, urgent and immediate action would have been instituted. In fact this situation would never have arisen, because of her alertness and knowledge recognising Nanny's impending hypoglycaemic states. Rani would have run to the kitchen, poured out some milk or water and added at least three spoonfuls of sugar and spoonfed Nanny with it. This action would have restored Nanny's consciousness dramatically.

Aunty Jenny was speaking to Nanny, but not looking at her. She was concentrating on her sewing and speaking with her head bent down. Nanny stopped talking and fell back on her chair. It was only when Aunty Jenny looked up at Nanny that she found her seemingly lifeless and unresponsive. She did not know what to do. Although she claims to be educated, Aunty Jenny has no knowledge of diabetes. Therefore, she did nothing to help Nanny. She put Nanny to lie down, and checked her breathing. She needed Uncle Jhan to rush her to hospital, but he was not around. Nanny remained there and passed out in a hypoglycaemic coma.

Brother came home from the garden late in the evening. This was several hours after Nanny collapsed. Nanny was cold and stiff. Brother ran up to see Nanny. He held her hand and passed his hand over Nanny's face. He called her, "Moye, Moye, it's me, Moye." Miraculously, Nanny opened her eyes, looked up at Brother and closed them again. Now they would never be opened. Brother and Nana and the pundit led Nanny's funeral procession to the cemetery. Nana's business was going smoothly and suddenly another disaster had struck him. On this occasion it was Nanny who had left him. Although Nana is strong and battles well through the vicissitudes of his life, the loss of Nanny is too traumatic for him. Nana did not feel like facing the garden any more. He stayed at home and Atta kept him company almost every day. This proved to be a highly effective support for Nana. Atta gradually weaned Nana back to his usual routine after nine months. Atta was the only person in whom Nana could confide. He spent a lot of much-needed time with Nana following Nanny's death.

Papa had no one with whom he could talk and who could empathise with him following Mama's death. There lies the difference between Papa and Nana in coping with bereavement. Brother managed the gardening and the corn activities admirably. He would give Nana and Atta daily feedback on the day's proceedings. All Nana was doing was paying out the workers on Saturdays. Brother's wife took over Nanny's job of cooking for the workers on pay day.

Aunty Jenny is steadily losing her favour with Nana because Brother's wife is getting a firmer grip in the house. She does the washing, cleaning, cooking and is maintaining the house very well indeed. Nana's bedroom is clean and well organised. All his clothes are nicely laid out for him and his bed is made up with clean sheets twice a week. Aunty Jenny sees all this when she pops over to see the house. She is concerned that her chances of moving into the front house are diminishing every day. Brother and his family are cementing their hold in the house, exactly the way Nana planned it. Nana is pleased with his grand-daughter-in-law and his two great-grandsons. It is interesting to note that Nana did not play with us when we were that age, nor did he play with us at all. Now he is playing with the two youngsters regularly. They in turn are getting close to him. Aunty Jenny sees all these dynamics confronting her. She is becoming rather envious of Brother and his family. She discussed this with Uncle Jhan. He pondered over his next move. "It is time to act, and act decisively," said Uncle Jhan.

Wednesday July 18th. Brother had come home for lunch. While he was relaxing on the bed with his two boys, he heard Uncle Jhan shouting at his boys. "Why the hell you taking so long? Hurry up, man." Three of his sons were armed with sticks and Uncle Jhan was with a cutlass. He hit the cutlass on the step. The bang was very loud and frightening. The others hit the banisters. They marched up the kitchen step and Uncle Jhan shouted out, "It's him or me today! Not a day more!" He smashed the cutlass on the tall iron bedpost. The "cling" rang out at fifty decibels. Brother's two little boys screamed and hugged him tightly. They were extremely scared. The four big men, armed with weapons, surrounded the bed. Brother lay still. There was no space to get out of the bed. He was pinned down. Uncle Jhan showed him the cutlass.

"See this, sharp like a razor. Sheffield Steel will make mincemeat with you today. Get out of the house right now! If you don't get out and leave this house today I am going to chop up you and your children. Get out now! Now I say! Not a minute longer in this house. This house is mine, mine, mine. This paper proves it." Uncle Jhan showed him the legal document, but did not allow Brother to read it. Nana was below the house. He said and did nothing. Uncle Jhan and his boys came out of the house and waited to see what Brother was going to do. Brother asked Nana quietly, "I thought you said that you are going to give me the house?"

"Ah tell Jhan dat you go have dee house an dee cane land. Jhan go take dee rice land and the back house and dee cocoa house." Nana said. "He make dee paper wid dee laiya. Dee adder day."

Brother told Nana, "Uncle Jhan said that he owns this

house, the back house and all the cane land. They came and drove me out just now. They threatened to beat me and chop me up if I don't leave today."

Nana was silent. He was shocked. The paper was signed by Nana. Ten fingerprints were firmly stamped at the bottom of the two copies of the documents. That was what Brother was shown when Uncle Jhan had said to him, "See this." He pointed to the fingerprints. Brother knows that Nana cannot read and write so Uncle Jhan must have got him to apply his fingerprints as evidence of the signature. Within the hour, Brother and his family drove away in the farm tractor, with the trailer and plough attachments. They were at Papa's home in five minutes.

Three months later Dewan and his family received a similar threat from Uncle Jhan and his troops. They also followed Brother and headed for Papa's home at West Hill. All of us, Papa's four children, returned to him, but in untold miserable circumstances. Brother and his family moved out into his own house. In the mean time Nana was thinking of bringing a lady into the house to do the cooking, washing, cleaning and to be a companion for him. He spoke to Uncle Jhan about this idea. Uncle Jhan gave Nana a negative feedback on the issue, Uncle Jhan did not approve of the idea at all especially if a strange person were to come into the house. One cannot determine the motives of people no matter how far or how close they may be to someone.

Nana listened and thought that Uncle Jhan was probably right. People are out to get what they could.

Strangers cannot be trusted. Nana knows that well. Nana seems satisfied in not bringing a strange lady into the house. He discusses this with Atta, his only confidential friend. Atta advises Nana that a strange lady may have outside interests and simply use Nana for the beer.

Uncle Jhan sees Nana and Atta in deep conversation. Both of them are having their brandy and coconut water. Coconut trees surround both houses. "How dee, Jhan," Atta called out to Uncle Jhan.

"Hello, man, doing a good job with the old man, you know. I don't know how he would have coped had it not been for you today. He would have been at such a loss," Uncle Jhan told Atta.

Atta replied, "That's what good friends are for! I'm sure that he will return the favour when my time comes. I agree with you regarding the advice you gave the pusha about bringing a strange lady into the house. She will give him some comfort, but she may give him some discomfort as well. Look how much money the pusha has lost already, and we don't know who has taken it. We don't want him to keep on losing money like that. He worked damn hard for it. We just can't trust anyone these days, boy. The pusha can get on with his life as he is."

Nana went off to work as usual. He does not work as hard as in his younger days. He has to look after his health. Brother reminds him to take his medication every day. He reminds him of his heart medicines and to have them within easy reach. Nana continues to have weekly monitoring of his blood pressure and angina and ensures that his dietary regime is maintained. While Nana feels well he will take himself to the garden. It gives him exercise as well. Today is Sunday and he is off with his cutlass.

On his return from the garden he walked upstairs to change. As soon as he entered there was a tall, able-bodied figure standing in front of him. The figure was dressed in an oversized black gown. It was wearing a floppy, black broad-rimmed peaked hat. It wore thick black gauntlet gloves and a black mask with two small eye holes. Nana could not see the feet, because the gown was touching the floor.

The hands were holding a handful of banknotes. Nana was shocked. He got a very sharp chest pain. His chest was tight. Nana bent over in pain. The figure brushed passed Nana and pushed him onto his bed. The notes got scattered as the figure dropped the notes and sped out of the room. Nana forced himself up and stretched for his GTN and placed one sub-lingually. He remained on the bed until his pain eased. His scattered notes were all around him. He reflected on the figure and recalled, "Dat big, big, black ting wid dem eyes, dem eyes, dem eyes," Nana was repeating to himself. Nana thought that he recognised those eyes, but he is not certain about where or when he had seen them. The eyes continue to haunt Nana. He seems to be seeing them everywhere. Nana reaffirms, "Ah see dem eyes a'ready." Nana remained confused about the big figure behind the mask.

He has seen the thief at last. He told Brother to go

and bring Rani. He wants to make sure that the eyes were or were not Rani's. Brother told Nana, "Nana, if you want me to bring Rani, you better go and bring her yourself. But you have to take an aeroplane and fly to England to get her. She has gone to further her studies. She left eighteen months ago."

Nana told Atta that he saw the thief, but all he could see were two eyes. He said to Atta, "Atta, ah know dem eyes, ah see dem eyes a'ready, but ah doh know wey ah see dem. Dee ting dress up in black, man. Ye drap dee money right dey, an ye push me an ye gan out ah dee room. Atta, ah know dee child eh take no money. Dee buaye [Brother] say dat dee gyal gaan to England eighteen mont' now."

Uncle Jhan sat down coolly with Nana and Atta. Atta said, "Take a drink, Jhan, even if it is only coconut water." He poured out a tall glass of the coconut water. "Good day and good health for all of us," said Atta, and they went down with their drinks. Uncle Jhan said to Atta, "Since you two are so close friends, why don't you take the old man up at your place? You can have plenty of wild meat to eat every day if you like. You know how he loves his deer and agouti meat. Take him and keep him with you. That would be a nice change for him, and it is good company for the both of you."

Atta said, "That would not work out, because he has to see about the land and the cane."

Uncle Jhan said, "Don't worry about the land and the cane. I will take care of everything. He needs a good rest since he has been working so hard."

"The pusha will not feel good if he doesn't go in the garden, you know that very well," said Atta.

Uncle Jhan said, "You see, Atta, the cane and the land is not his anymore. I am putting it to you, sir, everything you see here is mine, yes, it's all mine now. I can put you and him out of this house right now. Nothing belongs to him any more. So, don't worry about the cane land. I will look after that myself."

Nana had listened to the conversation between Atta and Uncle Jhan.

Atta said, "But I don't understand you, Jhan, do you mean that you can really drive your father and me out of this house? Jhan are you going crazy or what? What the hell you got in your head? First you said that I can take the pusha home by me, and now you saying that you could drive us out of this house."

Uncle Jhan said, "Atta, that is just what I am saying. I have the paper to prove it, man. This is a legal document I have here. He [Nana] himself agreed to it and put his ten fingerprints on it. That is confirmation, Mr Atta Roberto, not so? See for yourself, man." He showed Atta the document. Atta read it to Nana.

"Atta, who say dat? Who make dat paper? Me eh say dat, man. Me tell de buaye [Jhan] wat to do. Me nah gi ye everything, man."

Atta said, "That is what the paper says and you put your fingerprints to say you agree to it."

Then Nana listened to Atta reading the document again, "My entire estate is transferred to my son, Jhan, with immediate effect." *How can his son do that to him?* Atta was thinking.

Nana said to Atta, "Wey ye mean by dat?"

Atta said, "Pusha, you agree to give him everything, and he can drive you out of the house anytime."

"Me eh tell ye dat, man," said Nana. "Ye go drive me out ah me own house, wey me build?"

Atta nodded. "Pusha, I know what we both agreed on how you would share up your house and land, but Jhan changed everything, assigned it all to himself and gave it to the solicitor, Mr Richards. That is what you agreed to by putting your ten fingerprints on the document. Pusha, there is little or nothing you can do about it now."

Nana remained silent for five to ten minutes thinking of the signed paper. He got up slowly, walked slowly to the back step, and picked up the glittering sugar cane cutting cutlass. It has a razor-sharp edge and broad dazzling blade, stamped "SHEFFIELD STEEL MADE IN ENGLAND". Nana slowly walked back to Atta and Uncle Jhan. He raised the blade over Uncle Jhan's shoulders and, before Uncle Jhan could blink, down came the cutlass.

"Whap!" sounded the blade across Uncle Jhan's neck. A clean cut!

He put down the cutlass and sat on his chair. Nana said to Atta, "Man, ah cyant truss me own son today."

All major anatomical structures were completely severed – the third and fourth cervical vertebrae, the internal and external carotid and vertebral arteries, the internal and external jugular veins, the superior vena cava, the spinal cord and the pyramidal tract fibres were all given a clean cut. Blood poured out of the vessels. The scene was messy. It was blood red.

Atta was stunned and remained silent. Nana also remained silent. It was a death scene. Atta was the prime witness, and the only witness. Nana told Atta that he would not allow Uncle Jhan to be buried near to his or Nanny's grave.

"Me eh want to know ye as me son, man me cyarnt truss me own son today," said Nana.

Our village Obeah man and witch doctor, Professor Ganti, seized this opportunity to advertise his "powers". He erected a big noticeboard outside his house. It read:

WARNING! WARNING! WARNING!

Do not follow the path of Jhan,

When he came to me, he made a pact with the cobos.

He did not follow it through.

When you come here, you also make a pact with the cobos

To follow it through, or else their spells will fall on you,

Until they finish you. You see what's happened to Jhan?

After Uncle Jhan died Nana refused to have food from Aunty Jenny. Aunty Jenny did bring food for him but Nana did not eat it. Brother's wife resumed cooking for Nana and Brother would bring the food instead of getting his children to do it.

Aunty Jenny would do the washing for Nana, to prevent him from bringing any lady into the house. This is Aunty Jenny's biggest concern. This would ruin her chances of getting the front house. She knows that Brother won't be coming back because he has his own house. For several months there is peace and quietness in Nana's house. He says his puja with Atta, Stamford and Sam. His other grandchildren do not participate in the prayers. Nana makes the prasad himself. He prefers to do everything himself. He has become a proper DIY man in these matters.

Nana said to Atta and Sam, "Ah hear dee buaye [meaning me] go ha meetin' after tomarrow. Wey ye go taak 'bout?"

Atta said, "He wants the whole village to stop all violence and punishment. He says that he will tell the people how much beatings he has had from you and teacher Singha when he was small."

Nana said to Atta, "Man Atta, me eh 'fraid ye man. Dee buaye [i.e. me] could say wey ye want. Ah could come dey an gi ye two plan ass in ye backside."

Atta said, "Pusha, you going too far, man. The boy only wants to do something good for everybody in the village. So, the big day is in two days. Plenty of people agree with him, man, Pusha. Some residents are not in favour because they feel that discipline will be lost, children will get out of hand and become uncontrollable. These dissenters aim to maintain what they call the status quo. Pusha, just cool yourself man and let us go and hear what the boy has to say. Let us go and even support him because he is fighting for a good cause."

CHAPTER 28

"HELLO EVERYONE, GOOD AFTERNOON. Hello to the inspector of schools, the head teacher and the staff of Sunnyvale CM, the local police and my fellow villagers. Hello and welcome to you all. Thank you all for sparing the time to come out in such large numbers this afternoon. I hope that it will be well worth your efforts and therefore amply rewarded. I am delighted to see so many of you here this afternoon. Thank you for your wonderful response to our request.

"We are here today to talk on a very hot issue. It is an issue which is burning in all of us. I am going to make this a very personal one. It is primarily about me, yes, about my personal experience of receiving corporal punishment, and carrying out child labour. I will refer to these as CP and CL. The other issue which burns inside of me is domestic violence. I have seen and experienced it since I was a child. I'm calling it DV. The fourth major issue is child abuse and I will refer to this as CA. Child labour is taken for granted by our parents. In short, my focus will be on CP, DV, CA and CL.

"I will relate my short life story from four to thirteen years of age. Many of you will be hearing it for the very first time.

"As a four-year-old child, I was beaten up by my father on several occasions for hitting my younger sister. My hands and feet were tied up with a rope, and then I was tied to the foot of the bed. I was to remain there without food, my father said. I was saved by my Nanny who unexpectedly turned up later that afternoon. At four years of age, I had to look after my younger sister and brother until my parents came home from the garden. I had to give them their food and was supervised by the next-door neighbour, Madam Daniel, or Marj as we all know her.

"As a four-year-old child, I was also a frequent human shield for Madam Daniel to protect and prevent her from further beatings from Mr Daniel. She and her children were regularly brutally beaten by her husband. She would somehow escape and run over to pick me up and show me to Mr Daniel. Mr Daniel would not hit her in case he happened to hit me. Wherever he attempted to hit her she would position me there. I was in the front firing line. How did I feel to be moved about facing a man with a big stick? This happened on several occasions, when we were living at Cotton Hill. Mr Daniel could not risk hitting her because he might accidently hit me. Today, she refers to me as her saviour. Yes, folks, I was a human shield for Marj at the tender age of four.

"When he raised the stick to hit Marj I got more frightened and bawled out as if my guts were coming out. Mr Daniel would look at me, shake his head and look at Marj belligerently, before dropping the stick. Today, that fear still lives within me. Now, when I talk about it, I get goose pimples on my arms. I can see the hairs on my arms standing up straight. This is what I am living with today.

"As a six-year-old child growing up with my Nana I had another very traumatic experience. My Nana ordered Bryna to clip off my hair from my head, after he was finished clipping the mule. There was nothing like cleaning or disinfecting the pair of mule clippers. My Nana called me, and told Bryna that I was too harden and to give me a clean shave. Bryna went straight into action and clipped off all my hair. I was teased and humiliated at school, when the children saw my shaven head. They laughed at me and chanted, 'Clean head baba, penny cassava, clean head baba, penny cassava.'

"There was no place for me to run and hide. I had to stay there and face that torture and embarrassment from the school children. Again, at the age of six, I was thoroughly beaten by my Nanny. Why? Why, ladies and gentlemen, why? Nanny told me to pound freshly roasted cocoa beans in the okhree and moussar. I kept on pounding those beans until my arms were aching me. I rested them and continued pounding the beans. Nothing happened. How will those beans become moist and soft,

I wondered. I poured water into the beans and Nanny came down shortly after. When she saw what I did, it was blows and blows and more blows on my backside, hands and legs for spoiling the beans. She drained out the water, and redried the beans. She said, 'Study pong dee bean an ye go get saft by yee self.' Up to this day, my friends, no one has told me by what mechanism those beans became moist and soft and malleable to shape them into small rugby balls by the sheer pounding.

"At the age of ten years, I was mercilessly beaten by Mr Singha. There he is, sitting next to the head teacher. Why did he beat me? Because I did not know how to work out a sum called compound proportion. If a child does not know how to work out a problem is this the child's fault, I ask you? Or is it the fault of the teacher? Tell me now, whose fault is it when a child does not know how to work out a sum?

"In my case, fellow villagers, this teacher Singha here, all the children know him as Scorpion. He had sent me outside in the afternoon sunshine to whitewash the stones in the front flower garden. The inspectors were coming to visit the school, so teacher Singha wanted the place to look neat, clean and tidy. It was during that time when I was outside that teacher Singha taught the class how to work out the compound proportion sum. I could not ask anyone because he would beat me for talking and not paying attention. My back and neck were bruised and swollen. I could not straighten my head because of the swelling in my neck. I was in severe pain.

"My Nana took me to Dr Luo. He was shocked to see my condition. Dr Luo wanted teacher Singha to be prosecuted. He gave Nana a long medical report to take to the police station. But Nana came home and called the head teacher instead. The head teacher read the report and pleaded with Nana not to go to the police station. He told Nana that he would handle it himself. He would see teacher Singha about it.

"The head teacher promised to make a photocopy of my medical report and return the original to Nana. Nana never saw the medical report nor heard from the head teacher again up to this day. Today, my villagers, today, I have the medical report in my possession. Here I am waving it to you. It was well kept by the head teacher for the past ten years in one of his confidential files. He kindly allowed me to have it back.

"Now, my villagers, it is no longer going to be a confidential document. It is my medical report, and I am now going to have it on public display. If anyone wants to read it you are very welcome to do so after I have finished my talk. You will see for yourself the enormity of the suffering which was handed to me as a ten-year-old child. Would you like your child to suffer this same punishment? I was thoroughly beaten by my Nana for not getting up at 4.00am one morning to go and fetch two barrels of water from the standpipe. I was threatened to get more punishment when I went into the garden at 8.00am. I was cornered between the steel barrels and took a severe hammering from my Nana. Nobody saw or heard what

I went through under that cocoa-house. I was thirteen years of age at that time.

"I regularly got beaten on my left hand from the moment I started writing. I never knew from where my Nana used to appear with a stick or leather belt and smack me on this left hand. If only my left hand could talk it would tell you the suffering it endured from the age of six when I started writing until I left Nana's house at the age of thirteen. Nana called me a devil's child and accused me of bringing bad luck into the house if I continued to use my left hand to write. He told me that my left hand was my dirty hand because I washed my backside with it. I was forbidden to eat with my left hand because it was the dirty one. I had to pretend to use my right hand when Nana was around or switch to reading to avoid using my left hand. When I was sure that he was not around I would use my left hand.

"Nana is illiterate and refused to take up the offer to learn to read and write. What does Nana know about the dominant hemisphere in my brain and my left-handedness? How many world leaders and famous cricketers are left-handed? Can they all be the devil's children as Nana told me? Villagers, I am saying to you, if you see your baby, or infant or child using its left hand please encourage him or her to do so. Please don't do what my Nana did to me.

"That, fellow villagers and colleagues, is a brief outline of the series of beatings and punishments I've received from four to thirteen years of age.

"What are the effects the punishment has had on me? Some people, like my Nana, would say, 'No effect whatsoever, he too harden.' Others may say I must have deserved such punishment.

"I will tell you the effects the punishments had on me:

Number one – pain and more pain – physical, psychological, social and emotional.

Number two – humiliation.

Number three – rejection.

Number four – social isolation.

Number five – low self-esteem and loss of confidence.

And the very big one, number six – fear – fear of the men who beat me, fear of the rod which fell on my back, arms, legs and buttocks. Fear to get a sum wrong and fear to go back to school. This fear subdued me to become a total recluse.

Number seven – depression and becoming withdrawn.

Number eight – I became unable to concentrate on any studies. This was another key factor in preventing my academic progress.

"Villagers, despite these hindrances, I ploughed and fought my way through relentlessly to get over the line. It took a lot of doing, I tell you today.

"These are my personal feelings and responses to the punishment dished out to me up to the age of thirteen. Pain. Pain. Pain. The physical pains, the bruises, the swellings, the scars and cuts are all gone. My wounds are all healed up. There is no evidence now of any such scarring on my back, buttocks or my arms and legs. No one would imagine or believe me when you see my body now. But what remains in me, villagers, what remains is a lifelong endurance.

"It is the mental trauma and scarring which lives within me. This psychological, social and emotional effect will never leave me. This effect in me is as fresh as the morning dew, and as fresh as the pond lily. It is so vivid in my thoughts, I feel that it is paining my body this minute. This psychological pain will never disappear from me. Villagers, think for a moment what a mental burden I have to carry for the rest of my life.

"Villagers, this is exactly what you do to your children when you beat them at home. It is exactly the same as what the teachers inflict on your children when they are beaten at school. The children will carry this pain throughout their lives, just as I am carrying this pain today. Husbands, this is exactly the same thing you are doing to your wives when you perform such degrading and grotesque violence against your wives. That is the psychological burden they will bear for the rest of their lives.

"Now is the time to think seriously, and think deeply, teachers and parents – is this the pain you want your children and wives to bear for the rest of their lives?

"This is the biggest injustice which we are inflicting upon them.

"Parents and teachers have their ammunitions with

them, such as sticks, belts, whips or rulers, but what have the children got in order to defend themselves? They simply have their soft, delicate tissues and bones to weather their storms. Our children's skins are mere blotting papers. They have extremely high absorbency values. That is what their ammunitions are. As parents and teachers, how proud are we to realise this?

"What Mr Singha did to me is unforgiveable. Today I have the permission to speak out openly without recriminations. Do you deserve a medal for your charitable handouts to your children? To be grouped with my teaching colleagues, villagers, I feel utterly disgusted and ashamed to be called a teacher. It is the most undeserving trait in us in such a noble, respectable and rewarding of professions.

"From the age of four I was doing child labour. Do you remember the opening words of this saga? They were 'Doh fight, doh hit your sister.' I was looking after my two younger siblings. That was my responsibility. I was only four years old at that time. I had to make sure that they got their food and cared for them until my parents came home. Marj, our next-door neighbour, would supervise us.

"I am saying to you all this afternoon that it is absolutely scandalous, it is morally unjust, it is pitifully shameful, it is extremely dangerous, and above all, ladies and gentlemen, it is totally illegal to leave a four-year-old to look after two younger siblings. Yet my parents got away with it. Today, how many other parents have also done the same thing to their eldest sons and daughters here in Sunnyvale? We deprive them of their growing childhood and education, but we give them unlawful responsibility.

"From the age of six, I was old enough to wake up at 5.45am and leave the house at 6.00am to go with my brother to cut a bundle of grass, and bring it on my head. Then clean out the mule pen, and shell at least one barrel of corn, before going to school. In after-school hours going to the garden is a normal duty. Parents, haven't your children been doing the same thing today? Reflect on this now. Your children are part of the family income generation. That is what our lifestyle is today. Is there an opt-out clause in all of this? However, this early rising each morning has become a very good habit indeed. I like getting up this early as it allows me sufficient time to carry out my usual routine.

"Well, one afternoon I quietly sneaked away and went and cut my bundle of grass for the following morning, and thought that I would win my Brother. It all backfired. I hid the bundle of grass and covered it with dry cane trash. You all know it as 'lappai'. When I brought it in next morning my Nanny was waiting with a stick for me. She asked, 'Wey you get dat bundle ah grass? Why de grass lookin' quail an ye eh ha no dew pan it?' Before I could answer sticks were raining on my hands and feet and backside. Villagers, my plan did not work on that occasion and I paid a heavy price for trying to be smart.

"Our children must obey all instructions. Oh yes! It's

100% compliance. If they don't they know all too well what will follow. I was never allowed to answer back. My Nana and Nanny would tell me that I was too rude. Is that what you tell your children too, if they happen to answer you back? How often have they as little children heard the words 'Shut Up!' from their parents? Their thoughts and ideas are suppressed. Yes, folks, in our case here in Sunnyvale, the teachers and parents are the oppressors against the meek and helpless oppressed.

"These messages are telling the children and the wives one thing, 'You have no rights! No rights whatsoever. No rights to open your mouths, to speak out, to criticise, or to give your views.' That was my experience while living at my Nana's house.

"That is the message we send out to the children we care for, the children we love, the children we bear and the children we teach.

"I will return to our children, but let us look at the way our womenfolk are treated. Worse than our children, I would say. I have observed the brutality and the cruelty that our neighbour Marj suffered at the hands of Mr Daniel. It was not for one day, it was not for one week, it was not for one month, it was for years and years, my fellow villagers. What did she do so offensive to deserve such degrading punishment? I have witnessed her beatings. No one has to tell me about it.

"As a child, witnessing these scared me to death. I cried to see it. I was feeling so sorry for Marj. I was her human shield on several occasions, folks. She would warn him, 'Doh hit dis child nah, ye fadder go kill you.' That warning stopped Mr Daniel from beating Marj. Can you imagine how I felt being in the front line of their fight? Oh yes! I was four years of age at that time of the incidents. She took revenge on Mr Daniel and paid a heavier price for it. Everyone in the village knows the full story. She said that it was due to one word: illiteracy. She said, had she the knowledge at the time, nothing of the sort would have happened. Today she is a fully literate person and is aspiring to become a Christian Missionary.

"Today, there is no such phase as 'childhood' in our village. This social concept does not exist. From a baby, we become a toddler, and then become adults, or young adults. We are treated like adults, we work like adults, we are punished worse than adults, yet we are only between the ages of five and thirteen years. This is mass exploitation on an astronomical scale. The Education Act states that it is compulsory for children to be in school between the ages of five and fifteen. Our village falls short of this.

"Today I am making a proposal to my fellow teachers and to the community at large. I would like to turn our table round 180^0. This is a dramatic change I am determined to institute in school and throughout Sunnyvale. The teaching staff, the school inspector and police here, are all supportive of the scheme. Today, I look forward to gaining your support.

"We are going to have a *total ban* on CP, DV, CA and CL in this school and in the entire community.

"This is the most opportune moment this afternoon to make a firm decision on this, because we have so many of our residents present here this afternoon. I say to you all, let it resound again and again and again throughout Sunnyvale!

"No more corporal punishment in school or at home.

No more domestic violence.

No more child abuse.

No more child labour.

"I say to everyone, search your hearts, search your minds, search your consciences, and search your very souls. Think of these young innocent minds, and think of the love you have for them. Show them the love for which you brought them into this world.

"Let us have our village free from these afflictions. Allow our children to voice their feelings. Allow them to be questioning and creative. Give them a hearing. Husbands, treat your wives with respect, they make a valuable contribution to the home. Do recognise that and treat them as equal partners in the home.

"Today our literacy programme has improved the lives of so many of our residents. It is so gratifying to see groups of young men sitting under the samaan tree and reading the newspapers together. Some of them are attending the adult education evening classes resulting from the literacy programme. This is very encouraging indeed. We hope that they may go on to gain further education in future.

"Today, we have an opportunity for change. Today

we have this opportunity to liberate this village to live a pain-free life, a life of pleasure and enjoyment, a life for free expression without any recriminations; and a life where attitudes are changed for the better in this village of Sunnyvale. Today let us create, let us build and live in our little Sunnyvale utopia. This heralds a new era for us in Sunnyvale. Today will be remembered for when freedom reigns supreme, but certainly not the type of freedom for which Hazel, the self-proclaimed unqualified gynaecologist and the village backstreet abortionist advocated.

"Therefore, villagers and colleagues, let us vote with our mouths and our hands to make this a reality. Let us shout loud across the village saying, 'No more, no more, no more punishment!'

"Today our table has turned 180^0.

"Give ourselves eighteen months of freedom, free from punishment and oppression and free from reprisal.

"We roll out this scheme from today. We will have formative evaluations at the PTA monthly meetings and a summative evaluation at the end of the eighteen-month period.

"I thank you for accepting and taking this major step forward.

"Thank you for your support, and thank you so much for coming out today. You can have copies of this speech here now. If you don't get one then you can get them at the next PTA meeting."

CHAPTER 29

AFTER A FEW WEEKS of daily life in the village, the community is settling down and the villagers are keeping their promise. The women are going around looking happier. They are voicing their opinions in a friendly manner and seeing their husbands as their equals. They do remind their husbands to exercise restraint during the trial period. The men are co-operating and beginning to appreciate the women's contribution in the home. The atmosphere in the homes is quiet. Over 80% of the women can now read and write to an appreciable level. B's parents are happy that they are able to read and write. She gave the President good support during the teaching programme.

Marj is also very grateful for her ability to read and write. She reads her Bible every day. She reads the daily newspapers as often as she gets them.

Marj has dedicated her life to serving the Lord. She

attends classes in Christian missionary work and is aspiring to become the village missionary. She goes to everyone's house, and prays with them, and asks them to turn to the Lord permanently. It does not matter what language the villagers use, they will be praying to the one God, to the same God Almighty. She encourages them to follow their own form of worship which they are accustomed to practising. The main thing is to bring God into their hearts and to have faith in the Lord.

She tells them that she is the biggest and worst sinner in this whole universe. By turning to serve the Lord she gets the strength to do so. She tells them that she is no longer afraid nor ashamed to admit her horrible sins, because she knows that the Lord God Almighty is forgiving her. She can feel it in her heart. Her pain is lifted from her. Her guilt is lifted. She continues to pray every day and ask the Lord to forgive her.

She tells them that she understands Mr Daniel better for the way he used to beat all of them and prays for him. He is a mentally sick man. She has come to recognise and accept his mental ill health. She reminds him to take his tablets every day. She is his nurse. There is one section of the Bible which Marj reads to herself every day. She also reads the same verses to all the villagers. It is taken from the Gospel of St Luke, Chapter 23, verses 39–42.

"And one of the malefactors which were hanged rail on him, saying, If thou be Christ, save yourself and us. But the other answering, rebuked him, saying, Dost thou not fear God, seeing thou art in the same condemnation?

And we indeed justly; but this man hath done amiss. And he said unto Jesus, Lord remember me when thou comest into thy kingdom. And Jesus said unto him, Verily I say unto thee, Today, shalt thou be with me in paradise."

Marj tells the villagers that if Jesus did save that wretched sinner on the cross, when he asked Jesus, she is confident that Jesus can save her as well. She tells the villagers that she gets strength from reading this passage every day. Marj follows it up with the Lord's Prayer (in the Gospel according to St Matthew Chapter 6:9–13).

Marj is called Mother Marj, the village Christian Missionary. She visits the villagers in their homes and spends time with them. She reads the Bible for them, she helps them in their housework, and encourages them to read. She says to them, "Girl, read for pleasure. I never knew what I was missing until I learnt to read and write in my ripe old age. I get so much joy and satisfaction in reading my Bible every day."

CHAPTER 30

I HAVE ALWAYS WANTED the chance to go abroad to further my education, but I did not have the money at the time to support myself. When given the opportunity, I would like to visit the county of Kent which is called the garden of England. I would like to visit the apple orchards and the hop fields. I would love to see the snow-white country lanes of Dorset and the stalagmites and stalactites in the caves of Cheddar Gorge. I had studied these in my geography class. Of course, everyone wants to see Buckingham Palace and Trafalgar Square with its pigeons.

I would be walking on London streets which are paved with gold, as we are told. I will love to see the famous Tower Bridge opening over the River Thames. Of course, I will love to see Big Ben and the Houses of Parliament. Since I was a child I have been dreaming of such adventures.

My early dream is now a reality. I am leaving my beloved Sunnyvale to visit our mother country. The whole village knows it, because of my links in the community and teaching in the school. B's oldest child, Devi, came up to me and said, "My mummy said to give you this." She handed me a small packet wrapped up with brown paper. It felt soft. I put it in my pocket and said to Devi, "Thank you very much indeed, and tell your mummy I say thanks a million for her present." I thought that I will open the gift on the day I'm leaving. That was a very pleasant surprise coming from B.

One week before leaving, I went to see Nana to tell him that I am going away. I was very scared to approach Nana. Since my beating from him, and leaving his house, I have not spoken to Nana. I never went back to Nana's house. It was all a one-way traffic. So, too, it was with Rani, Brother and Dewan. In my case it was and it still is fear of Nana. Fear repels me from going anywhere around Nana's premises. It is very difficult for anyone to envisage the extent of my fear of Nana. I have grown up, consider myself as an adult, but am still afraid of Nana. This is the only reason that I did not approach Nana earlier to inform him of my leaving.

I plucked up all my courage. I climbed up the kitchen steps. Those were the last steps that I had walked down when I left Nana's house. I went through the old familiar sitting room. The table and kerosene lamp which I had used for studying were in the same corner of the sitting room. The alarm clock which I had used to set the time to wake up to study was still working. The same curtains were washed and hung up. The calender was for the current year but the mirror was missing from the sitting room. The sitting room decor was the same as when I was there. I walked slowly to the front veranda. Nana had built another kitchen at the front of the veranda. He was sitting there and having a rest. He did not see me. I stood in the veranda and instantly remembered how the four of us siblings used to sit there and look out at those passing along the road.

My heart was thumping heavily. My pulse was racing. I began to perspire. I was frightened to say "Nana". I was about five feet away from him. I said timidly, "Nana, I've come to tell you that I am going abroad." Nana quickly glanced at me, and turned away. He waved me away and said, "Go way, go way. Mee eh want to know. You now come to tell me dat. Dee whole village done know aready and you now coming to tell me, go, go, ah doh wat to hear." Nana walked away to the far end of the kitchen and looked out of the window. I was so scared to say another word to him. I stood there for a while with Nana's back towards me. I could not open my mouth to say another word to him due to my fear of him.

I walked away through the veranda and sitting room and went down the kitchen steps. It was only at that moment I realised how hurt Nana must have felt by my not telling him earlier. He must have felt rejected at that time. The news was circulating through the village that I was leaving. I spent a great deal of time serving the community. It was my biggest mistake not telling Nana earlier. Fear of him prevented me from doing so.

I regretted this very much indeed and would now have to live with it. I may never see Nana again. Apart from the harsh treatment I received from him, it was Nana who brought us up as young children following Mama's death. He and Nanny built our foundation. We have to be very grateful that Nana took us and brought us up. I was just five years old when Mama died. It is not my ingratitude but it is my fear of Nana which caused me not to go to him earlier. Nana doesn't know and he will never know that. He may pass away with my unfinished business with him. It is so regrettable. I must add that Rani has the very same fear or even more so for Nana.

Meanwhile, the villagers are organising themselves to invade the Piarco International Airport with their presence. It will be the first trip there for most of them. Nana has been hearing how the villagers are preparing to come to the airport to see me off. Nana would have told Atta about my going away.

The village is enjoying its freedom from punishment and oppression against children and women for the next eighteen months. A number of homes were not participating in the project because of the attitudes of the menfolk. Almost the whole village came to the airport to see me off. This can be interpreted in another way, that is, they were pleased to get rid of me, as spoken by the President. The President speaks, "To you young man, why don't you haul your ass and get out of we country.

We ain't want no blasted European foreigners here. You are no longer one of us. So get the Hell out of we land." He continued, "Oh! I forget to tell you, happy riddance." Now that's our President for you.

Mr Daniel has been trumpeting all the time. The tassa drums were beating to a happy dancing crowd. Even Marj was singing, clapping and dancing to the tunes of Mr Daniel's trumpeting. "Come and dance with me," she said. I had never seen Marj in such a very happy mood. They were encouraging Papa to join them. Brother and Papa were trying to get to me to say their goodbyes. I weaved my way through the crowd, which was tapping me on my shoulders and shaking hands with me as I moved through.

I held on to Brother and Papa. They were so happy for me that they were crying. I started crying as well. Then Papa gave me his broadest smile. All he could say was, "Son, ah glad for you today." Brother said, "Good luck, boy, and best wishes for a brilliant career." The music and dancing continued. Then I saw one section of the crowd moving from side to side. The Sunnyvex and White Rose boys were hysterical. They said, "Hail to our President and away to you." Then they erupted in a chorus of shouting, "For he's a jolly good fellow... and so says *none* of us." More laughter and clapping followed.

I opened my gift by tearing off the brown paper. There was a cotton ball and a note folded up just the way I used to pick it up from the hibiscus hedge. It read, "FBTU Best Wishes." In the middle of the cotton ball was a beautiful heart-shaped 18-carat gold tiepin with its inscribed letters "UB". I pinned the tiepin on my tie across my chest. I wished B were here to see me at the airport. I would proudly show her the tiepin being worn. I would give her the biggest loving embrace and whisper softly in her ear, "I do love you with all my heart." That did not happen. I imagine that B would be at home looking after her children.

There was a loudspeaker announcement for all passengers for the 12.30pm flight to London. There was more pushing and shoving among the crowd. I heard a loud voice shouting out, "Are you buaye gaan? Are you buaye gaan? Wey you dey?" More pushing followed as the voice got closer and louder, repeating the same words, "Are you buaye gaan? Wey you dey?" I ran, pushed my way through the dancing crowd from one side to the other side, to the shouting voice. This is a voice so clear, and the expressions rather unique. It can only be one person who would speak in this manner.

I grabbed on to Nana, and started crying and crying. I held on to him very tightly. Tears were pouring down my cheeks. I don't know why I was crying, but I could not stop crying. Then I fell on Nana's feet and kissed his feet. I said to him, "Nana please forgive me, forgive me for all the wrong things I've done." I stood up and Nana said, "Are you buaye goin', are you buaye goin', me eh go see ye again." I screamed out more when I heard Nana saying those words. They shocked me. Then Nana said, "Atta bring me, look ye dey. Look ye dey." I turned to Atta and gave him a big hug and said, "Atta, thanks a million and more for bringing Nana. You have truly made my day complete." I held on to both Atta and Nana before I said goodbye to them. Atta said, "Good luck for the future."

The loudspeaker blared out, "One passenger is missing. This is the last call for Usati Harriram, the last call for Usati Harriram."

I ran towards the waiting aircraft. The stewards and security pulled me through the crowd. Marj rushed out and held on to me. The two officers looked at her. She said to them, "Man ah have to give him a kiss before he go away. He is my saviour." Marj held on to me and kissed me on both cheeks, just as she had done once in front of B. She said, "Good luck, me saviour, good luck to you." She patted me on my shoulder as the officers took me to the steps of the waiting aeroplane. I climbed up the steps and waved to the crowd before entering the plane to take my seat. I looked out of the window and the crowd was still waving, particularly those from the waving gallery. The Sunnyvale carnival was over as the plane took off in the brilliant midday sunshine. After an eighteen-hour flight via New York and Preswick we landed in the London October cold.

Six weeks later I received a letter from B. It read, "My dearest U. I hope that you had a safe flight and now you are beginning to settle in your new home. You will have to get used to the weather over there. I hope that you have got your snowman's outfit to brave the cold. You can write to me if you feel like it or when you have some free time. You know Jasodra who runs the village post office?

She is my confidential friend. I can trust her. Whenever I come to my parents I go and visit her. I have told her all my problems so that I can free my chest. I have asked her not to tell anyone, and to keep any letters coming for me safely, securely and secretly. She agrees to keep them for me until I visit her. I can count on her for this. U, you must not write my name on the envelope. Do address all my letters to: "Jasodra, B." When she sees this, she will know that the letter or card is for me. OK, do remember it. Of course, the B refers to me. I'm sure that you will have already guessed it. Oh, by the way, just to let you know, the villagers are still talking about you, and they are all praising your Nana for your success, but I do know that is not entirely correct."

CHAPTER 31

I T IS OVER FIVE decades since I left my homeland. I am
returning there for a well-earned holiday, and perhaps
for a family-and-friends reunion. I do not imagine the
quaint Cotton Hill to be the same in its idyllic setting.
It may be unrecognisable. I wonder whether the dreaded
silk-cotton tree, the plague, the scourge and the curse
of the village, is still existing. Societies change over
generations and so the communal life of the 1940s and
50s in the village may have all gone. However, the natural
contour of the land should remain the same. I'm looking
forward to sitting by the pond, picking ripe guavas and
looking at the alligators on the opposite bank. It would
be a good time to reflect. I will meet with the President
with his army of children and grandchildren. Above all,
I would love to meet B and her family. I contacted her to
give her the news.

"Hello, B, it's me."

She said, "It can never be anyone else but you, U, my darling, and how are you? It's been a long time…"

I said, "Yes indeed, just to let you know that I am coming down for a holiday in the next few months. I've already booked my flight. I'm so busy these days and it's the best time when I can make it."

She replied, "I am quite sure that it will be on the 18th on your birthday." (Pause). "However, there is one thing that I would like to tell you. Boy, I don't know if I'll be around."

I asked her, "B, what do you mean by that?"

There was another longer pause. She replied, "Boy, the doctors have given me three months to live." (Another long pause, and I could hear her crying quietly.)

I asked her, "B, well, why? What's the matter, B?"

She said, "U, my darling, I'm very sick, I've got cancer." She started crying louder and said, "Three months," and stopped. I'm shocked to hear this.

"U, the doctors showed me the series of test results they have been doing while I was undergoing the different types of chemotherapy. They said that the CEA, the CA 19-9 and the CA 125 levels are consistently high. They appear to show no signs of coming down despite the changes in my treatment. The doctors are maintaining my pain level and are trying to keep me as pain-free and as comfortable as possible. They said that I can go to Dr Luo to see if Chinese medicine would help. They do not want to mix Chinese medicine with the chemotherapy because of the risk of drug interaction.

"Dr Luo said that he has been arguing for several years

with his medical colleagues to embrace Chinese medicine with the conventional Western chemotherapy in treating cancer patients for a better patient outcome. The doctors argue that Chinese medicine is not properly scientifically researched. Further, they are not TCM qualified and they do not want to take any risks in combining both treatments. One doctor told Dr Luo that he had one bad experience using Chinese medicine and that he will not recommend it to any of the patients in his care. Dr Luo said to me, 'This debate of integrating both aspects of treatment for cancer patients continues at present, and may continue for several years to come.' Dr Luo looked at my medical reports, shook his head and said, 'The doctors are right, there is only one thing they can do for you now, that is, to continue with keeping you as comfortable and pain-free as possible.'"

I said, "Oh my, B, I'm so sorry to hear this. Why didn't you mention this to me before? What type of cancer is it?"

She replied, "I've got pancreatic cancer. They say that I've got an aggressive form of this cancer. They have tried every possible treatment and they have not been able to help me. The doctors say that they have exhausted all their options. My body is not responding to the treatments. They can't do anything more for me, so they sent me home. I suffer a lot. I have a great deal of pain. All my hair fell off because of the chemotherapy. I don't want to eat. I am usually sick when I eat. I tend to vomit almost everything. I am feeling weaker and weaker. U, my dearest, I say, I don't know if I will be around by the time you are here. U, I so want to see you. I do want to hold you. I have been waiting for you all these years until today. I know that you will come back. We will work through the plan we made for ourselves.

"U, darling, you know that I do not believe in black magic, or Obeah, or whatever they call it. Old Professor Ganti came to see me about five times and said that someone did a strong Obeah on me. He said that the spell is so strong that even the doctors cannot cure me and it has lasted more than fifty years on me. He said that he is going to do what he can to revoke and cast out this evil spell, but he does not want any money for it. But I have to agree to it first.

"My daughter told him that there is confirmed medical evidence of my illness, and it is nothing to do with Obeah. Ganti argued, 'The doctors don't know anything about spiritualism, or Obeah, or voodoo, or black magic. I am the expert in this. You know how many people I helped out already. I can help your mother but you have to agree first.' We know that many people do come to him to get help from him. On his last visit he said to me that Havio had come three times to him and asked him to work some Obeah on me so that I could run away with him. He and Havio went to the silk-cotton tree and Ganti invoked the spirits and he did the Obeah on me. Ganti said that when the evil spell came upon me I would feel very very cold. He also said that he gave Havio a specially made potion to mix in a drink for me. After drinking the potion it would make me run off with Havio. Ganti said to me that Havio wanted me for himself and that was the only way he could have got me. Ganti went on, 'I knew that the spell and the potion would make you run off with Havio.' Ganti also said that Jenny gave him big money, $750, to do that Obeah for Havio."

B continued, "Devi, my daughter, told him that I do not believe in that. She said to Old Ganti, 'What you did over fifty years ago for one sinister purpose, can you realistically tell me you can undo that today? Also, the potion which you made for her to drink would have been completely expelled from her system after forty-eight to seventy-two hours of taking it. Ganti, you cannot help my mother today. I suggest that you are the one who needs help now. Kindly go to our village Christian Missionary, Mother Marj, and let her pray for you for all the wicked and evil deeds that you have done to people through the years. She turns no one away, and you may find much solace there. So, you are not too late. Consider yourself to be lucky today, and I'll tell you that "Luck beat back Obeah." My mother will go along with the doctors and her medical treatment. There is substantive scientific and medical evidence to prove that her illness is indeed a physical one. Could it be that the potion you gave her contributed to her illness? Could it be that the potion had been carcinogenic and you yourself would have no knowledge of that? Only medical science could prove it. Now, if you will excuse me, sir, I do have a rather busy day ahead of me. Thank you for your offer, old Ganti, and good day to you.' These last two sentences were said in a deep, forceful, scathing and contemptuous tone of voice. We did not hear from him again."

I said, "My dearest, B, I am pleased that you have not entertained Old Ganti with his various antics. He is a bleddy fraudster. Your illness is true and genuine as investigated and demonstrated by modern medicine. You are indeed right to listen to the doctors and accept their views on your medical condition.

"I do understand how you are feeling. I do recognise the depth of your illness. I know that you are a fighter and a very good one at that. Oh yes, we will work through our road map. B, the doctors are highly skilled professionals. They are treating many patients like you every day, and could guess, only guess how long you will live based on their knowledge, skills and their experience. The doctors must also recognise and accept that every patient will respond in a unique manner to the same medical condition. However, they are not prophets.

"So, do have faith in the Lord. He will answer our prayers. I do know that you are reciting the Hanuman Chalisa every day and that you are also praying fervently to the Lord asking for health and strength to carry on. I am also praying for you. Our joint prayers will be answered. You will have the strength to fight on. Continue with chanting the daily mantra and throw your water every morning. Remember to recite the verse from the *Bhagavad Gita* when you throw your water. It is chapter 9 verse 26: 'I accept a leaf, a flower, a fruit, or water from the disciplined person, who with devotion, offers me that loving offering.' (*Bhagavad Gita* 9:26). Follow it up with the Lord's Prayer.

"B, I am hoping to see you when I come, and as you said, you will look into my eyes and you will tell me what messages they are giving you. The eyes do speak the truth. They tell us our moods, our love, and our likes and dislikes. We will accomplish our plans which we made. Do keep strong, try to eat a little at a time. We will meet when I come down. I will ring you again. Do keep well, and bye for now."

B has been going on steadily for a couple of months, and it is possible that we will meet and greet each other shortly. B's oldest daughter, Devi, rang and said that her mother would like to talk with me.

My day arrives and in hours B and I will be together again. However, I do have a few bits of last-minute shopping to do. When I returned home the green light on the answer machine was flashing. It said, "Hello, this is a message for Usati." There was a long pause before another voice echoed, "Hello U, guess who, yes, you are right, it's me. Call me please."

I rang B, "Hello, just returning your call."

B said, "Oh yes darling, thank you very much for ringing me back. I thought that I'd talk to you before you arrive later today. Boy, I've got so much to tell you, that I hope time does not run out on me. I'm so looking forward to seeing and meeting you. I can't wait for you to be here, so I thought that I'd start from now. Having said that, I don't know where to begin. You must have changed unrecognisably over the past fifty years. I'm much the same barring my medical condition. I thought that I'd do a bit of reminiscence, recollection and reflection.

"Do you remember how I used to look out for you from my bedroom window every morning and afternoon when you were at college? We used to smile and wave to each other and then I would disappear from there so that no one would catch me? Do you remember how we used to hide our love notes in a forked branch in the hibiscus hedge? Do you remember the day when Marj saw you coming off your school bus and she gave you a big hug up? You and Marj had a long chat together. I heard every single word. We had never done such a thing during all our years together. Do you know how vexed and jealous I was, seeing this old lady hugging you up like that in the open public, and in front of my eyes as well?

"I still love the notes we used to leave for each other hooked up in our hibiscus hedge just outside my bedroom window. Do you know that I have kept all our love notes which you have written me? No one else has seen them. I hid them in a special purse deep within my personal clothes and jewels. The small case remains locked at all times. I read them when I am lying down in bed at night. They are my secret treasures. My Papa cut down the hibiscus hedge after I left. Do you remember our secret coded greetings at the top of every note which we exchanged? They were FBTU and FUTB, from me and from you respectively. Do you know that our secret codes remain our secret up to this day? Do you remember your detailed road map for your career and our future? You said that I will not have to change my surname, only my title. I remember the key words of the road map, 'Education first, education first, education first.'

"When Havio started to take you to college on credit, and your father paid him at the end of the month, I knew that you had no money to buy your season ticket for the bus. For those last eighteen months of your college, I used to make certain that Havio went very early to pick you up every morning to take you to school so that you will always be on time. I made sure that he had his breakfast by 6.40am so that he could pick you up by 7.00am. Then I would send him to pick you up. In this way I made sure that you received your education.

"I remember that the road map also stated that, when we had enough money, we would have our own house. We would have our own car, with our own private number plate reading: 'Private UB 18 OH'! Yes! That's our private number plate.

"It will be a Triumph convertible car. We will drive *triumphantly* through our village, from Cotton Hill through the Valley to West Hill, on to Happy Hill and to Cedar Hill. There, at Cedar Hill, we will admire the gigantic cedars and picnic under their shade. Today, it still fills me with immense joy. Now it has turned out to be a most beautiful dream. It was too long to wait for you. Impulse was one factor that had got the better of me and my life changed on that night of your birthday when I last sang for you. The biggest factor is yet to be told.

"Do you remember that I sang our favourite song for you on your birthday? I swung vigorously in the hammock, and smiled broadly at you. You stood up and listened and smiled back at me. I sang it twice, one for you and one for me. It was 'Suhani Raat'. Then, you went home. My heart was filled with love and happiness as I swung and sang for you, my one and only true love. Later Havio came home and my life changed.

"U, I would like you to believe in me, and do believe what I am going to tell you today. This is the truth and nothing less than the truth. I live for the truth and I will die for the truth. I have been in love with you throughout my entire life. I have never loved another man but you. I have been through so many hardships and difficulties during these years, yet I have never stopped loving you. I have lived my life for the Lord, for my children and for you. I wanted so much to live the life we planned for ourselves in our road map. I know that you will return one day and we will be married and live the life we planned."

I said, "B, I believe you, and I know that I will hear the truth from you. I trust you wholeheartedly, and I will trust every syllable you utter."

"U, you will now hear the truth about that fateful night after I sang for you. That night Havio took me away. I remember it as if it were only yesterday. It's so vivid in my memory. My darling, I was doped, I was tricked, I was drugged, I was robbed, I was cheated, I was trapped, I was beaten, I was violated and I was imprisoned all in one night. My virginity was stolen from me during the night. I fought and fought Havio in the room to prevent him from doing that to me. I begged him not to have sex but he would not listen. He continued to manhandle me until I could not restrain him anymore. I was too tired to keep him off me. He held me down and did what he wanted to do. I did not sleep all night. I cried and cried and begged him to let me go but he refused.

"Now, Havio came home by us after I sang for you. He brought two bottles of mauby. He gave one to me, and shared the other one with Mama and himself. The mauby tasted nice and cold. I drank all of it. About fifteen minutes later I began to feel sick and headachy kind of sick. I vomited some fluids and food. Havio said that he would take me to the doctor straightaway.

"Havio tricked me into drinking the bottle of mauby in which he put a potion and mixed it up in the mauby. Ganti told me that he had put the curse on me and made up the potion for Havio to give me. Ganti said to me that it was that woman Jenny who befriended Havio, paid the Obeah money for him, encouraged, persuaded and influenced him to run off with me so that my character would be ruined. He said then I would no longer be the most beautiful girl in the village. The bottle of mauby which Havio shared with my Mama was not doped, so they were fine. That was the first and only time I was ever doped with some kind of potion in a drink. He knew that I did not need to go to a doctor, and that was how he tricked me. I have never loved Havio. I would never forgive him for what he did to me. And for that old woman Jenny, from what I've learnt now, I'll leave her in the hands of the Lord God Almighty.

"Havio took me into his car and drove me directly to his house. The moment he touched me I felt cold, and this coldness was running through my veins. It was a very strange type of coldness in me. Havio threatened me not to open my mouth. He squeezed my mouth very tightly, took me into his room, and locked the door. When his hand was over my mouth it felt like he placed a block of ice on my mouth. Such was the cold feeling which came upon me when Havio touched me that night. He slapped me several times during the night when I tried to scream. He fought me for sex. I have never fought so hard in my life to prevent this man from hurting me. Again, I cried and begged him to let me go. He slapped me hard and put his hand over my mouth to stop me from shouting.

"He said that from that moment I was his wife and tomorrow we will be married. He said that I must convert from tomorrow, that he doesn't want anyone with a different religion in the house. I had no say whatsoever. I bluntly refused to convert. I told him that he can kill me if he wants, but I will not convert to his religion.

"The following morning Havio and his brothers and parents went to my parents' home and they married me to Havio. When they got back, they put a lot of pressure on me to convert. I refused. I told them, 'Kill me, if you want, but I will not convert. You maintain your faith, and I will maintain my own faith. I have my holy scripture and you have yours. I must tell you that there is only one God and only one God to whom we all pray. We pray in our own way to the same God Almighty.' They said, 'In this house all of us must be the same.' Then I said, 'Havio cheated me and forced me into this house. He violated me, and now you have married me to him without my consent. I had no say whatsoever and now you also want me to convert!'"

B continued, "Havio's father told me, 'Dis is a strong and devout family house. As long as you is living in dis house you have to obey by my rule. You cannot tell me what you want to do. So, you must convert now.' U, I told him that I would never convert and he could send me back to my parents. Havio said, 'You are my wife, and you are staying right here, even if I have to live with you as my non-convert wife. You are not going back to your parents' home. I will treat you as a non-convert but you are not going back.'

"Since then someone was always watching over me. His mother was the main person. I have three children but they were born from fighting and forcing me into the sex act, and sometimes after taking a few drinks. Each time it happened I felt that it should have been yours and not his. I brought them up just how you would have done. I tried to give them the education that you would have given them.

"Every year I sing on your birthday. I have been doing so through the years. Of course, it's always 'Suhani Raat'.

"All these years have passed and I have kept this

incident a secret from you. I knew how much it would hurt you if and when you heard it. I did not want you to bear this pain together with me. I did not want the both of us to suffer. I bore this pain myself throughout my life. I suffered in silence through these past decades. Thanks to my confidential friend, Jasodra, I was able to unburden myself to her. My married life with Havio was a very sad, difficult, and unhappy one. There was no love between us. I was a tool in their house. The only real love that I have and feel is my love for you. It lives in me and gives me comfort.

"It is my happiness to know that you achieved the education you so desired. I quietly supported you. I was indeed so happy to see you at the school Christmas bazaar. I did not want to leave you. I wanted to stay with you all day, but it was not possible. The children were beginning to feel tired and they wanted something to eat and drink. It is my happiness to know that you are coming back today.

"I have heard all the nasty, evil and wicked things that the villagers have said about me. Oh yes, I know and I have heard those nasty names that they have called me. I am sure that you will have heard them too. They were not easy for me to stomach. I quietly endured them. For example, I was a bad girl. I eloped with Havio. I shamed and disgraced the family. I ran off with a man in the middle of the night. 'She is a nasty little wretch', 'She too hot for man', 'She running down man'. I listened and stayed quiet about it. Their minds were already made up. There was no point trying to correct them or argue with them. It would have inflamed matters even more if I had tried to defend myself. I'm sure that you have already heard all these various slanders against me. I also heard that Havio did work Obeah on me to make me go with him. Havio would never admit to it.

"No! No, he would never admit to anything which he did to me. He will deny everything I say. No one would listen or believe my word. Their minds were already made up to think that I was a 'little piece of trash'. Can you imagine those words coming out of Havio's mouth when I refused to convert? He is the one who robbed me and violated me and cheated me. Further, I could not say a word to Havio's family because they simply shut me up, just as your Nanny used to tell you, 'kutch nah bole.' It was pointless arguing with any one of them to let them know how I got into their house on that fateful night.

"I thank you for fighting for freedom for the village. There was freedom, independence, and no violence for the eighteen-month period. That day you left for England, that day I also left Havio and went to live with my parents with my three children. I never looked back. On that day, nearly the whole village went to the airport to see you off. The village was deserted. It was extremely peaceful. It was as if the light had been put out. You were that light and you showed it to me. You paved the way for me to take my leave. There was no one along the road to talk to me or to question me and asked me, 'Where are you going, B?' There was no one at home to watch over me. That was how I managed to seize the opportunity to start a new life as a single parent and gained my freedom. I divorced Havio on the grounds of ill-treatment and incompatibility.

"I have remained as a single parent from then on to this day. From then I have lived the life that you had planned for us. I lived for you and I knew that one day you will come back. We will be married and live as husband and wife. No man has ever touched me since I left Havio and came to live with my parents. I know just how wonderful and fulfilling it is to be a free, independent and private individual. I make decisions on my own and remain accountable for them. I got a job in one of the large department stores in San Fernando and worked there until I retired. I did not depend on Havio any more. He gave the children whatever he wished. My boy Usati is kind and very helpful. He is a teacher like someone I know so well. It's no point telling who that person is.

"Today, it is my children who are caring for me. They are seeing me through my final days, which are now moving into hours. However, I wait to see you now in my final minutes when our marriage bond will be made. Mother Marj has been extremely kind and helpful to me and my children. Since she heard of my illness, she has been coming to see me and stay with me every day for the past eighteen weeks. She helps me with showering and dressing up. She reads the Holy Bible every day for me. She reads Psalms 1 and 23 and follows them up with the Lord's Prayer. She says that you are her saviour and she regularly reminds me of that. She tells me that I must also recite my own prayer. I do say my daily mantra and Hanuman Chalisa every day and follow it with Psalm 23 and the Lord's Prayer. I keep on saying my prayers three to four times a day while I am awake and not in too much pain. When the pain is too severe, I cannot concentrate well. I know that you are praying for me as well.

"My dearest U, when you arrive at my side, I will look once more into your eyes and read what they are telling me. I know that they tell the truth. I live for the truth, and I live by the truth and I will die for the truth. You have said this in so many of your love notes to me. Truth gives me peace of mind and a clear conscience. Truth breathes integrity in me, you have said to me. The truth lives an everlasting life. I will look at your smile to see how truthful it is, and will wave to you once more, just as I used to do from my bedroom window. You will be here in a matter of hours. Today is the happiest day in my life. Today you are going to be with me. You said that when you come back we will get married. I have my white wedding dress, my crystal tiara and my light-pink see-through nightie hanging on the rack in front of me. All the other wedding plans are already also in place.

"My dearest, U, today is your birthday again. This time I will sing for you through the phone. It is the most fitting time to do so before you arrive. I sing our favourite song every year around your birthday. Just listen, OK!"

B started singing, 'So Hani Raat'. It was the most

moving and touching sound. She sang it with deep expression. I said to her, "B, my love, your voice didn't falter a tiny bit. It was a sweet, charming, melodious and a romantic rendition of our favourite song. The sound of your voice which was coming through the phone next to my ear was sheer delightful music. Thank you, thank you, thank you, my darling, I love you so much."

B said, "I just wanted to sing it for you again. I will tell you the rest when you come. I have so much more to tell you. I've been waiting this long for you for a second time, my most beloved friend, U, my sweet and dearest BJA. I am feeling very weak and tired. I need a long rest but I am waiting to see you within hours. However, if for any reason, I do not see you, or we do not meet today, then we will meet in paradise.

"U, my true love, my deepest and most sincere religious inspirer, my one request is that you will continue to wear our tiepin across your chest. It will mean so much to me that I am residing above your heart. I am sure that you will also like to learn that I have always kept our secret hidden within me from everyone up to this minute. I have never told Havio or any of his family about my true love and faithfulness to you. The one confidential friend we have is Jasodra at the post office. She kept our letters, notes and conversations tight-lipped to this day. I know that you will have liked me to keep it this way as well. She knows a lot about my life, because I had to talk to someone to relieve my internal burdens. I confided in her through the years. She has been a source of comfort and help to me.

"Today, I have taken out my precious treasures from my jewellery box. These have been the most secretive from anyone up to this minute. These are our secret notes we used to exchange and hide in the hibiscus hedge many years ago. I used to read them quietly from time to time and put them away safely. I feel that I am with you sitting next to me as I read them. Now I have brought them out and spread them all around me, many hundreds of them. My darling, U, they are in your very own teenage handwriting. They have been my secret companions for all these years. You will see them today when you arrive. I will now reveal one more secret to you.

"My dearest, you always told me that I am a true fighter. I wanted to give up the fight against Havio and his family because there are so many of them against me. I thought of you and your word 'stickability.' I stuck it out. Therefore, from that night when Havio took me away, I have been fighting an internal battle throughout my life between two diametrically opposing forces – the forces of bondage and freedom, darkness and light, dusk and the dawn of a new life, diversity and unification, insecurity and hope, hatred and love, lies versus the truth, deceit versus the righteous, the cursed versus the blessed, immorality and fairness, wickedness and justice, and the forces of evil versus good. U, my darling, my sweetest and most loving BJA, today, this my internal war is all but over. You are my guiding light and my true friend and spiritual inspirer. You are with me throughout this battle. Our combined forces of good have won the day.

Very soon my transport will be here to take me to the victory podium. Yes indeed, they are going to be an army of eighteen white-winged horses pulling their mighty golden chariot to sit me on the winner's rostrum. From there the fanfare of Danny's trumpet and saxaphone, the local bamboo flutes, the river conch shells, the church and school bells, the calabash shack-shacks, the local tassa beaters "the scrap iron Indian orchestra" and Nana's steel drums will blare out in an amazing harmony. They will produce a glorious and the sweetest piece of music that we will ever hear. It is the sound which you and I have always known, 'Suhani Raat.' With the majestic grandeur of this unique ubiquitously-resounding fanfare over from the intense practice of your 'Big C,' it is time to change charioteers. You and I are going be our own charioteers. We will pull on our reins riding triumphantly through the village, passing two old, haggard, decrepit, pathetic-looking, destitute, despicable, homeless, lean and hungry beggars, the perpetrators of their evil curse put on me, Ganti and Jenny, at the bridge. They live under the bridge. They are holding out their filthy and empty calabash bowls, begging for whatever scraps of food someone may throw at them from an anti-social distancing. *Hmm, You nah dah even treat ah dag like dat, Hmm, nobady eh go even feed ah dag like dat,* the villagers are repeating scornfully and murmuring silently to themselves. The irreversible silk-cotton tree village curse has fallen upon Ganti and Jenny. They read the sign on the golden chariot 'No Beggars Today' and bow their heads in shame. These two repugnant and repulsive vagrants will live in bondage for the rest of their lives, their karma. They design their own destiny by their choice of avenue.

"We ride on towards our home, our quaint, three-shaped, carat-roofed, mud-walled, detached bungalow situated in the idyllic settings of the cotton fields at the summit of the mount. We are free to live single-focused following the routes to Yoga. The day turning into night awaits no croaking toad or whistling kiss-kee-dee, awaits no man or woman. Our Elysium awaits us. I wait for you."

I said to her, "B, our waiting will soon be over. B, my darling, thank you so much for revealing your long, deeply-held secrets to me today. I have learnt so much more now of the love and support you gave me particularly when I needed it most in order to complete my schooling. All my doubts are now dispelled. I knew that I could count on your loyalty. We have devoted our lives for each other and for the Lord God Almighty, our 'Bhakti Yoga'. The fire of love rages exponentially within me on hearing your account. We had taken divergent paths but we are now zooming in and converging onto our single path. We are getting close to touching distance as I prepare to fly out today. Although we may be still thousands of miles away from each other, it feels like we are mere micro-metres apart. I am beginning to feel the warmth of your carbonated air which you exhale from the depths of your alveoli. We are stretching out our hands to see if and when they will touch. Our fingers are almost within reach but the synapse still exists. Our neurotransmitters have gone on momentary lockdown. Therefore, conductivity is seriously compromised. Perhaps, we may return once more to use our pens to communicate."

"U, I have been writing you small notes just as we used to do when you were going to college. I remember those days so well. The notes are in four-line verses. I have written them over the past three to four weeks whenever my pain eases up. Together, these verses become my poem to you. I will read it to you now although I am feeling tired. Reading the poem gives me strength to keep awake and wait for you. It goes like this:

"My Dearest U, I am gliding through my ailing
   eighties,
Eagerly looking forward to wearing my see-
   through nighties,
By that time I may need bionic eyes,
And failing that, I'll be waving my goodbyes.
Live and enjoy this present moment
That Nature has rented to us,
Leave no regrets for the morrow
In this world, my world of sorrow.

As I look at my growing old,
I see external changes manifold,
Greyness, baldness, slowness are all to bear
As well, the pain of my Cancer will never clear.

Therefore, my advice to you, is strive for good health,
It's the greatest prize we amass as our wealth,

It's not the quantity, it's the quality,
So, beware of those seeking vanity.

These are the thoughts of your dying B,
I've gone through the worst, that you'll never see.
Paradise awaits this lonely soul,
And longing to meet you, is now my only goal.

The Angels are gathered all around me,
It's time, but for no one else to see,
Yes, they're calling, 'B,' calling, "'B, forget us not,'
My Darling U, I'm riding in their golden chariot.

My dwelling place abounds in grace,
Sweet fragrance from around delights my face,
Eternal Peace and Rest consume my soul,
But meeting you remains my only goal.
We'll dwell together in our Paradise,
Forever partners in full disguise,
Oh! What joy it is which fills my soul,
Meeting and greeting you achieve my goal.

Alas! Alas! My most trusted friend, you are with me!
With Angels singing, chanting, 'Hello U and B.
OM Shanti OM, Shanti OM, Shanti, Shanti,
    Shanti.'

"I have managed to read through the whole poem for
you. My eyes are feeling tired and weak. I will rest for
a while and wait for you. All plans are in place for our

wedding as soon as you arrive. My white wedding dress and light-pink nightdress are hanging in front of me. I shall keep on counting the remaining seconds as they tick away. I would repeat that this is the happiest day of my life. Before I end this message, I will sign my name, as I have always yearned and dreamt of signing it, not as 'Miss Basdai' but as 'Mrs Basdai…' Oh yes! Indeed! As 'Mrs Basdai Usati Harriram.'" The phone went silent. Stunned silence and the phone was cut off.

Later on, the phone rang. It was Devi, B's eldest daughter, crying, "Usati, Mama passed away. I will tell you how she died. It was half an hour ago. I am sorry, I can't hold back my tears, forgive me but I have to let you know.

"She has lived her whole life for you. You are her true love. Today she has been very happy all day. She was talking about the lovely times you shared together even though you both never held hands. Her face lit up and her eyes sparkled as she talked about you. She seemed to be pain-free all day."

Devi said, "She was smiling broadly while she was signing her name. As soon as Mama finished signing her name, she put a full stop. Then her fingers froze. The pen slipped from her hand. It rolled off the bed and fell on the floor. The sheet of paper rested on her chest. Her eyes were open wide with a dull glaze, her pupils fixed and dilated. Her mouth was open as though she was in the middle of a sentence saying something inaudible, and declaring an unfinished business. She remained smiling and happy as she passed away.

"My Mama was silent, pulseless, motionless and speechless. She was in a state of flaccid paralysis for a while. Her lips and the tip of her nose were cyanosed. She was becoming cold to touch. In a matter of hours rigor mortis would set in. Death was certified – 18th June at 18.00 hours. There would be no delay in the funeral arrangements."

Devi rang once more to update me. She said, "My mother, B, was cremated by the Temple in the Sea, near Waterloo. Mr Daniel and Mother Marj led their group of Christian mourners at one section of the cremation site. The pundit was at another section offering the last rites in Hindi. He was chanting his prayers and sprinkling a few drops of water on B and on the wooden pyre. He had a lota of water in one hand and used a mango leaf to dip and sprinkle the water with the other hand. He went round the pyre five times offering his prayers and sprinkling the water on it at the same time.

"The next step was to prepare the wooden pyre for burning. Large blobs of cotton wool from Cotton Hill were dotted around the pyre. The wood was arranged in the shape of a square, layer upon layer. This afforded breathing space for the breeze to sweep through the pyre. The cotton wool blobs and the wooden pyre were soaked in vegetable ghee. One soaked cotton blob was placed in B's mouth. Then Mr Daniel played 'Amazing Grace' with his saxophone. The whole crowd was witnessing the last rites. The pundit finished his prayers but the singers carried on. It was time for the final act.

"The sun was shining brightly. The cool sea breeze

was blowing strongly. The crowd surrounded the wooden pyre in which B was placed. A more powerful gust of wind blew and as it eased away a long black snake lay stretched out on the top of the pyre. Its head was above B's head. It slowly slid down the pyre and stood over B. Moments later a flash of shimmering light came where the snake was standing and it disappeared."

There were two such miraculous sightings previously. The first was at Seeta's funeral, the second was when Rani was going to be burnt alive, and today's event.

"Mr Daniel said, 'This is the holy spirit of our Lord Almighty in the form of the celestial serpent being present here with us today. It appeared once for protection, and twice for ascension. We are in no doubt whatsoever that today B's soul has ascended into Paradise. What remains now is for her physical body to be purified by fire.'"

Devi continued, "It was B's son, Usati's arduous task to carry this out for his mother. He placed the first flame to light up in B's mouth, where she was lying in the middle of the pyre. Then the other blobs of soaked cotton were ignited all around. The flames raged high aided by the strong sea breeze and the interlacing layers of wood. The fire produced intense heat for at least one hour. Marj and her mourners continued to sing throughout the burning, until there was just a heap of ashes remaining. The microphone chipped in with the public address system. It played her favourite song, 'So Hani Raat'. The crowd fell silent as this song was played out for B. It felt like a national anthem being played.

"The villagers got buckets of sea water and washed

the ashes into the sea. B's body turned into ashes was left to float away into the wide open expanse of water. The brilliant sunshine all through the process gradually faded. Dark clouds gathered over the cremation site. The heavens opened with a flash of lightning and the rumble of thunder. The rain poured down 'bucket-a-drop', the people were saying. They sought shelter by running into their cars or sheltered under the shaded trees. All of B's ashes were finally washed away into the wide expanse of the open sea."

Devi said, "Several days have passed by, and the villagers were still talking and saying how beautiful my mother, B, looked. She was smiling in her sleep. She looked very much alive and happy."

At the eleventh hour, while sitting in the plane, the announcement was made. My direct London Gatwick to Port of Spain non-stop flight was being delayed. It would be another eighteen hours before taking off.

EPILOGUE

WHAT IS OUR DESTINY? Is it pre-ordained or can we create or design our own destiny? How could B and U, two true lovers, design such a destiny for themselves? They did not hold hands but for one occasion at the school Christmas bazaar, yet they remained so deeply in love with each other to the end. U and B planned for and dreamed of a life which they wished to have. Did the village curse contribute to it? Although they remained true to each other they were not destined to touch each other. Living for the truth, living by the truth and dying for the truth resulted in their everlasting life. There was the unusual phenomenon where the celestial serpent appeared on three occasions, one for the protection and the other two for ascension. Innocent Rani was about to be burnt alive by Nana. The snake appeared and was about to pounce on Nana causing him to withdraw and allowing time for Brother to intervene. At the two funerals of Seeta and B the Holy Spirit in the form of the celestial serpent escorted their souls to paradise. The village curse was used to charm and harm B and destroy her life. Was it guilt which caused Obeah man Ganti to come to B to ask to undo his evil curse he put on her? Is that possible after more than fifty years? Did he take Devi's advice to go to seek help from Mother Marj?

It was the pernicious, jealous and monstrous nature of Jenny which led her to harm both B and Rani. It was Aunty Jenny who had sexually befriended Havio. She paid Ganti $750 to work a very wicked, evil curse on B for Havio to run off with B to ruin her character, and be ridiculed by the villagers. Jenny could not bear the thought that another girl in the village was more beautiful than she. Where did she get so much money to pay Ganti?

Corporal punishment in schools and in the home is prohibited today, thanks to the Education Acts and the Children's Act.

Could the lives of young Alex and Gloria have been saved? Could they have gone on to enjoy a happy married life had Alex been told the truth about his birth? He was no blood relation to Marj and Gloria. Mr Daniel and Marj were tight-lipped on Alex's birth and his biological parents from the moment that Mr Daniel brought Alex into his home. They had been telling the villagers that they were proud parents of twins. This resulted in a disaster due to non-disclosure of the truth. How could they possibly retract their original statements and declare that Alex is not their true son at such a late stage? Usually, adopted children would go in search of their biological parents. In Alex's case it was so different. There were no formal papers to show that Alex was adopted. He was told nothing about his birth. It was convenient for Mr Daniel and Marj to tell the villagers that Alex was one of the twins because Marj was about to give birth to Gloria within weeks.

Exploitation and greed can have devastating effects, particularly in the hands of an illiterate Nana. Uncle Jhan met his fate by taking one step too far. He was urged on by his wife Jenny to make a false document to deceive his father to inherit the estate.

Integrating Chinese medicine with Western medicine in the treatment of cancer has taken a very long time to be embraced within the NHS. Acupuncture is practised in many pain clinics and maternity departments. However, Chinese herbal medicine is not yet fully integrated into mainstream practice. This debate continues in the present day.

Water shortages in the rural villages such as Sunnyvale continue to be a serious perennial problem to this day. There are no village standpipes any longer. Although the homes are kitted out with their own pipes and water lines, the mains water supply is generally locked off for two or three days a week. Some villagers do buy water from the water trucks. Water supply comes at night for the villagers, just as it used to be in the 1940s and 1950s. The villagers have huge water tanks which they fill up when the water supply comes.

Today the village of Sunnyvale may be considered to

be modern. There are no bull carts nor carat-roofed mud houses. The houses are huge brick-painted, beautifully-designed, burglar-proofed and fully fenced with guard dogs. On average, there are two vehicles per home and the houses are fitted with modern appliances. The one village school, Usati's Alma Mater, still exists. The educational standards are comparable with any in the western world. The silk-cotton tree is long gone but its legacy, the villagers' beliefs, lives on in their minds. Some of them still seek out the existing obeahmen for cure of an ailment.

The number eighteen kept popping up on events throughout the book. What is its significance? The first of these events was the death and funeral of Usati's mother. It occurred on his birthday. Several other events occurredon the eighteenth. B sang for U on his birthday on two occasions. Two disasters followed. The Holy Spirit removed the innocent and the truthful from the cursed village. Finally, Usati's faith stands firm and rock solid in the face of severe hardships. He devotes his entire life to his Holy Scripture which has seen a war lasting eighteen days. However, and most significantly his Holy Scripture contains eighteen chapters.

References

Baker, Jack, Contracts Assistant, kind permission granted to quote from the English Standard Version of the Holy Bible as follows:

"Scripture quotation [(Marked ESV)]are taken from the Holy Bible, English Standard Version, published by Harper Collins Publishers, 2001 Crossway Bibles, a publishing Ministry of Good News Publishers, used by permission. All rights reserved." The Gospel of St Luke Ch. 23, Verses 39 – 43, Psalms 1 and 23, and The Lord's Prayer St Matthew Ch.6, V 9 – 13.

Johnson, W.J., (1994), The Bhagavad Gita, A new Translation, ISBN 9780199538126 , Oxford World's Classics (Academic). Oxford University Pres. Kind permission has been granted to use and quote from The Bhagavad Gita, Chapter 9, Verse 26.

Vethakkan, Anita Mercy (ELS-CHN), Senior Copyrights Coordinator – Copyrights Team, Elsevier Ltd., with kind permission granted to quote 5 excerpts : The quotation is as follows:

"This book was published in Integrating Conventional and Chinese Medicine in Cancer Care, ISBN – 13 ; 9780443100635 by Tai Lahans, They, the excerpts, are CA 125 on page 196, and CEA and CA 19-9 on page 231. Copyright Elsevier (2007)."

GLOSSARY

To the reader,

I would strongly recommend that the glossary be read through first, to become aware of and familiar with the terms and phrases. Some of the expressions may appear to be foreign. The pronunciation in brackets may help in understanding the dialect and the dialogue between the characters. This will give a flavour of the tone and the emotion conveyed.

Terms and expressions with pronunciation in brackets followed by their meaning

Aloo - (pronounced as ah- luu) potato.

Baraat - (pronounced as bar- rart) the bridegroom with his procession of wedding cars going to and leaving from the bride's residence after the ceremony.

Bhajan - (bha-jan) a devotional song.

Bier - (as beer) a stand on which a coffin rests. In this context the bier is made from the local village bamboo and decorated.

Blanco - it is a whitening powder mixed in water and used to make the plimsoles brilliant white.

Bodi - (as in Bow bells, boh-dee) this is a thin, long, green string bean which grows on a vine, similar to runner beans. It can grow from twelve to eighteen inches (thirty to forty-five centimetres) long.

Buaye or Buaie - (bwa-I) boy, or boys, or you boys. It can also refer to someone directly.

Bygan - (a local dialect, pronounced as by-gan), aubergene. Also locally called melongene or egg-plant.

Choolha or chulha (pronounced chool hah) earthen fireside

which is built with a mixture of mud and cow dung. The single fireside is called "aykaila (ache-aisle-lah) and the double burner is called a doowaila (do-wile-lah). The villagers of Sunnyvvale had one or both choolhas.

Cobo - a vulture, or a black crow-like bird. It represents evil.

Deeya - (dee-yah) similar to a tealight. It is a baked earthen container, used in prayers and functions. Often seen lit up in Dewali celebrations.

Dhaan - raw rice grains with the shells.

DMO - District Medical Officer. The local GP.

Doollahah - (do-lah- hah) a hindu wedding bridegroom.

Doollahin - (do- lah- hin) a hindu wedding bride.

FBTU - from B to U.

FUTB - from U to B.

GTN - Glyceral Trinitrate. A sublingual tablet of spray which is used in an angina attack. It provides almost instant relief.

Gyal or Gyul - girl

Jhaaray - (Jhah-ray) this is a non-invasive treatment technique to drive out evil spells, or to relieve pain especially abdominal pain. The practitioner uses five or seven coconut broomsticks washed cleanly. He measures the bundle of broomsticks with the width of four fingers to his desired length. They are all equal in length to start the procedure. The practitioner goes to the patient, says his prayers and sweeps the patient from top to toes with the broomsticks. He re-measures broomsticks after the first round. Invariably he will find that the sticks are of unequal lengths. He makes all the broomsticks equal again and repeats his prayers and the head to toe sweeping. It is a procedure which is repeated five or seven times to complete one treatment session.

Karailee - (Ka-rye-lee) or Karela - bitter gourd. A rough-skinned green vegetable which grows on a vine. It has a bitter taste but it is medicinal. It can lower blood sugar in type two diabetic patients.

Kutch nah bole - (koo-ch naah bowl) shut your mouth, or say nothing, or I have nothing to say. A hindi expression. In the context of the book this phrase was frequently used by Nanny.

Liming - (as lime-in) a small group of boys sitting around, or having a quiet social drink. They go out for a leisurely walk or drive to spend the time.

Lota - (as low-tah) a rounded brass water jug with a wide open lip at the top. It is used in the home as well as in religious functions.

Luck beat back Obeah - luck overrides any form of blackmagic. In the context used, Ganti could be saved from his evil wicked deeds if he sought the village missionary. His luck will take him into paradise.

Mandir - (as man-dirr) a temple or a prayer building.

Moosar and Ochree - (as moo-sarr, and oak-ree) mortar and pestle.

Mussy - mother's sister.

No mussy - no mercy.

Nana and Nanny - (in the novel). They are mama's parents, that is, the mother's parents. Nana is the mother's father, that is, the grandfather. Therefore, Nanny is the mother's mother, that is, the grandmother.

Naawhz - (as in a pleural of now) in this instance it is one who goes out to give out invitation for a wedding. He may also prepare the central platform at which the ceremony takes place.

Ochro - it is a local name for ochra.

Oorni - a long head scarf of fine material. It is usually worn with a sari.

Paan - this is climbing plant which adheres to a tree. The leaves are used in prayers of religious ceremonies.

Panchait - (as pan- cha-it as) a group of people having a quiet discussion.

Pone - a cassava cake baked to a fairly sticky consistency.

Prasad - a devotional sweet shared out after a religious function.

Pusha - (as in poo-sha) the Big Boss in charge.

Pundit - a hindu priest.

Shataigne (pronounced as sha-tie-yin) or kataharr (ka tah harr) - this fruit is a member of the breadfruit family. The trees are almost indistinguishable from each other. They are about the same size, spherical in shape. While the outer skin in the breadfruit is smooth, the shataigne is covered with short harmless prickles about 5mm-10mm long. This is peeled off and the inner core removed. The remaining flesh and seeds are cooked in curry and fresh coconut milk. This is a very delicious exotic vegetable curry dish. It is very popular at all functions.

Souja - (as Sue- jar) a very long hand used sewing needle.

Tabeej - (as tah – beej) a blessed charm locket which is worn to ward off evil spirits. To protect someone from harm.

Tulsie plant - (as tool- see) a mauve colour plant. The leaves are used in religious functions. It is of the basil family.

Zaboka - (as zah-boh- car) avocado.

CHAPTER I

ah (a as in apple)	I
ah doh (ah dough)	I don't
go - will	(this often means the willingness to do something and preceded by a pronoun as in I will)
ah go	I will
aright	all right
all you	you all
ah go larn you	I will teach you
ah goin'	I am going
ah kyant (kia-ant)	I cannot
ah so sarry (sah-ree)	I am awfully sorry
dem	them
an dem	on them, also and them
ah good cut ass	a sound beating
ah jus done	I have just finished
ah right nah gyul (gi-yul)	all right, girl
baal (ba-aal)	ball
Barp re barp Father	oh father or Oh my God
bayta (bay-tah)	son
bawl	scream out loudly
beating we up	beating all of us

beidi (pronounced bay-dee)   prepared place for the pundit to perform prayers.

buaie (pronounced bw-i)   boy

aal you teet   all of your teeth

aright nah gyal (ah-write nah gya-aal)   ok girl

are dee larn   I learnt

are you buaie (bw-i)   you / you boy(s)

caal (carl)   call

caz (cars)   because

caz ah dah   because I do

chirren (chee-ren)   children

chookha (choke-ha)   roasted tomato or aubergene with salt,peper, onion, garlic and shandon beni (ban dhan ya) mashed up

choolha or chulha (chool-hah)   earthen fireside for cooking. Usati's mother's choolha was built on the kitchen floor. It is made of a mixture of mud and cow's dung in a incomplete circular shape. The front is open to put in the fire wood. There are two versions. One is a single burner, called "aykaila" (pronounced a-kyle-la) or a combined double burner, called "douwaila" (pronounced do-wile-la)

cobo (ko-boh)   evil spirits transformed as vultures

come nah gyul (gi-yul)	come, please come, come over, girl
dah	the
da do	do do
dahl puri (darl pu-ree)	roti made with ground yellow split peas inside it.
dat	that
datwan (dat-wan)	the local toothbrush. It is a 6-8inch length of hibiscus, guava or soap vine, which Usati and his family would use to brush their teeth. One end is chewed to form the brush and blue soap is rubbed on it to form the toothpaste. After brushing, the stick is split longitudinally in half. One half is used as a tongue scraper and then thrown away. The soap vine has its natural antibacterial toothpaste. Simply chew up one end to form the brush and it releases its natural saponins as its toothpaste. It is very soapy indeed.
dee	the
dee buaye larning (dee bw-i) larn-nin	the boy is learning
dem	these /those / they
dem chirren o	these/those children
dem man an dem	these men /those men
den dem chirren (chi-ren)	then these children
dey (day)	they, or their

dey house	their house
dis	this
dhaan (dha-an)	rice paddy in the shell
doh (dough)	please do not
doh hit dis child nah	please do not hit this child
ee	it
eh (air)	not or no, sometimes meaning 'yes'
eh go (air go)	will not
eh go stay	will not stay
fadder (fad-dah)	father
fas fas fas	very fast
foh (pronounced as foe)	for
gan	gone
gaan an hit (garn)	went and hit
gi	give
gimme	please give me
go	will
gobarr (go-barrr)	cow's dung
gyaal, or gyul (gya-al) (gy-ul)	girl
grah	an evil spell put on someone to harm the person
gyul (gi-yul) girl	
kyant (kia-ant)	cannot
kyart (kya-art)	cart
leepay (lee-pay)	a form of plastering. A mud and cow's dung mixture is made into a pasty runny consistency. A piece of cloth is used as the plastering tool. It is soaked in the mixture and

then pasted on to the walls and floor of the house. When it is dried out the house looks like a beautifully painted one.

ley dong	lie down
marning (mar-ning)	good morning
mine dem kyart (kia-art)	be careful of those carts
moye (mo-ye)	mother
nah	no / or a meaningless expression at the end of sentence
obeah (o-bee-yah)	witchcraft
obeah man (o-bee-yah man)	witch doctor
orni	long head scarf worn with sari
phooknee (phoo-knee)	a 15mm diameter lead pipe 12–18 inches long is used to blow into the fireside to ignite the firewood while it is smoking.
puffick (puff-ik)	perfect
roti (roe-tee)	a plain naan
say sarry (sah-ree)	please apologise and say sorry to her/him/them.
sarry (sah-ree)	I am sorry., we are sorry
she smaal (sma-aal)	she is small
silk-cotton tree	this is the curse of the village. The most feared infamous tree in which the evil spirits live. These spirits transform themselves into cobos (vultures), squirrels, owls and even human apparitions.
takari (tah-kah-ree)	or talkari cooked vegetables

waak fas fas fas	walk very quickly
we wok	we do work
wen	when
wey (way)	where, or what of why?
wey you saying	what are you saying?
wey you doin	what are you doing ?
wid	with
ye (ee)	he / or she
ye like dee buaye too bad	he likes the boy very much.
you dee gimme	you gave me
you go give dee chirren (chi-ren)	will you give the children
you go keep	please, will you keep an eye
you dee say dis marinig (mar-ning)	this morning you said
zeppelin	an oval-shaped wingless shiny aeroplane like a big balloon. Makes no noise. It can be guided.

CHAPTER 2

aal (arl)	all
ah goin	I am going
ah comin'	I am coming
ah does larn	I learnt, I am learning
ah doh know (ah dough know)	I do not know
ah go gi you	I will give you
are you buaye (bwa - i)	you, you boys, you all
aye aye (i, i)	hello hello

by yeself (ee-self)	by himself
bredda (bread-dah)	brother
buaiye (bwa-i)	boy
caz (cars)	because
country bookie	an uneducated country girl
cyart (kia-art)	cart
dah	do or does
dat	that
dee	the
dee bull kyart (kia-art)	the bull cart
dem	these
dey (day)	they
dey fadder go (day fad-da go)	their father will
dis man	this man
doh hit dem chirren nah (dough, chi-ren)	please do not hit these children
doh (pronounced dough)	please do not
eh (air)	will not
edder day	the other day
eh gyul (ear gy-ul)	hello girl
fadder (fad-dah)	father
foh (foe)	for
go chop	will chop
go kill	will kill
gyul (gi – yul)	girl
gyarden (gya-dn)	garden
jhaaray (jha ray)	a procedure to act as a pain relief, or to cast out spirits. Five or seven coconut broom sticks are

used. They are measured to be of equal lengths. A prayer is said by the pundit and a sweeping movement is made from the top of the head to the toes. Each time this is done the broom sticks are measured. Some of the sticks become shorter than the others. They are measured again to be of equal length and the sweeping movement is carried out. This procedure is repeated five or seven times.

kola	one section of the rice lagoon, or sometimes the rice lagoon for planting rice.
ley dem chirren (lay dem chi- ren)	let the children
marai (ma-rye)	an ajoupa
marning	morning
me doh hut no bady(doe, baa-dee)	I do not hurt anyone
modder (mud-dah)	mother
no mussy	no mercy
show off ooman (oo-man)	a woman who likes to show off her talents,

tabeej (tar-beej)   a blessed packet for the patient to wear to ward off evil spirits.

tank Gad	thank the Lord
wen ah go dey	when I do get there
wey (pronounced as – way)	please note that this

	word can have three different meanings – where, what, or why
wey dee chirren	<u>where</u> are the children
wey you doin'	<u>what</u> are you doing
wey(way) you hit she foh (foe)	<u>why</u> did you hit her
wid	with
wid licks	with beatings
who dee ass she tink she is	who the hell she thinks she is
wok	work
wuking (wok -in)	it is working
ye aalways tink ah lat bout you eh	he is always thinking a lot about you.
ye fadder (ee fad-dah)	his father
ye is dat kind ah man (ee	he is that sort of fellow
you go be	you will be
you go eat?	you will eat as question –
will you eat?	

CHAPTER 4

are you buaie (bw-i)	you, you boy
ah gi in dem	I am giving these , or I am giving them
bring dem wood	can you please bring those pieces of wood
ah waak dong	I walked down
carn hux	corn cob
cobos	evil spirits transformed

	as vultures
dee	the
dem	their
dem buaye an dem	referring to Daniel and Marj in this context.
deeya	a small earth container filled with oil and lit. It is used in functions and prayers. Similar to tea lights
dhaan dha-an	rice paddy with the shell
doh (pronounced as doe)	please do not
dong	down
eh (pronounced as air)	will not, or what did you say
eh go kill dem (air)	will not kill them
gaan	gone or has gone
ley dee chirren (lay dee chi-ren)	do allow the children
mayri (may-ree)	a raised bank to separate sections in the rice lagoon. It keeps the water within that particular section.
nah	not, does not
nah taak like dat nah	please don't talk like that
oorni (oorr-nee)	a long head scarf worn with a sari.
overdey (over-day)	out here, or over there
saah (sa-ah)	saw
seben	seven
see wey dem man an dem doin'	see what those men are doing

wey dee cover	where is the cover
wey you say	what you are saying
wok	work

CHAPTER 5

Choolha / chulha (chool-hah)	earthen fireside made with a mixture of mud and cow's dung. Cow's dung is also reffered to as gobarr
clip out aal ye hair do	clip off all his hair from his head.
doh (doe)	please do not
ghu-ghu-ree	the tawny coloured coconut residue from making coconut oil. Its taste is sweet especially when a little sugar is added to it.
moosarr or okhree (moo-sarrr, oak-ree)	mortar for pounding cocoa or coffee beans. It was also used for pounding plantain
Ye (ee)	too harden he is too stubborn

CHAPTER 6

Ah have a mind	I feel like doing something
are you buaie (bwa-i)	you, you all, you boys
are you buaie	too harden you are too stubborn, ie. referring to Usati

bacando	This tree has above ground roots. Usati's father would cut the roots to make cricket bats for him and his brother. His father would also cut and shape bamboo roots to make white cricket balls for his boys. They also used dry coconut branches to make cricket bats. Interestingly modern day short form of cricket uses white balls.
baal	ball
boh king lazy	the king of laziness
caz (cars)	because
chaak (cha-ak)	chalk
choolha (chool-hah)	fireside made of mud and cow's dung mixture
dem bat	those bats
dis	this
doh (dough) study play	I do not want you to only play, and do no work
eh(air) doing you wok	you all are not doing your work
gi	give
harden	stubborn
lang	long
marai (ma-rye)	ajoupa
smart too bad	you are very smart indeed, or you are very clever
we dee larn nah	we had learnt

wey	where, or what or why
wey dee baal dey (way dee ba-al day)	where is the ball
wey dee buaie dey (way dee bw-I day)	<u>where</u> is the boy
wey dee gyaal dey way dee gi-yal day)	<u>where</u> is the girl
wey dem buaie an dem	where are those boys
wey kind (way kind)	<u>wha</u>t kind
ye is me child (ee is me child)	she is my child
yea gyaal	yes my dear girl
you wok	you work

CHAPTER 7

baytee (bay-tea)	girl, my child
dee	the
dee draah	the drawer
eh (air)	not, did not
gaan	has gone
how dee ass	how the hell
no bady eh tief (teef) it	no one has stolen it
sarch	search
waak (wahk)	walk
wey (way)	where
ye (ee)	it, he, she
you eh take no money (U air take no money)	you didn't take any money

CHAPTER 8

ah dah taak (a as in apple, dah taa-k)	I am always talking
aal dem whale (arl dem whale)	all these weals
aal ah dem	all of these (those)
are you buaie (bw-i)	you, you are,
barp re barp	father oh father, oh my God
buaie (bw-i)	boy
caal (carl)	call
dat	that
dah	do
dee	the
dee buaie (bwa -i)	the boy
dee bes callege	the best college
dee gyaal (gia -aal)	go make the girl may become pregnant. May make baby.
dem	those, these, they
dey (day)	they
doh ley dee gyaal go (doe lay dee gya-al)	do not allow the girl to go.
fadder (fad-dah)	father
gyaal	girl
how dem boys an dem fast	how those boys are wicked
in dee gyarden (gi-ya-dn)	in the garden
lif	lift
lef	left
ley me (lay)	please do allow me

ley ye	let his
ye fadder (ee faddah)	his father
me cyant tell dem (kia-ant)	I cannot tell them anything
moless	molest, annoy or pester someone.
nawa dhaan	new rice
tun rung	kindly turn around
shut	shirt, or also to close
see dee buaie (bw-i)	just have a look at the boy
we eh (we air)	we don't
wey (way)	where, why, what
wey dat blasted	<u>where</u> is that blasted or bleddy
wey ye nah get up	<u>why</u> doesn't he get up
wid	with
ye eh have (ee air have)	he doesn't have
you dah gimme ah good han	you do give me a great help
you madder (you mad-dah)	your mother

CHAPTER 10

ah (a as in apple)	I
aal (arl)	all
beat dee gyaal(gya-arl)	too bad beats the girl very badly/severely
caz (cars)	because
cyant (kia-ant)	cannot
cobos (ko-boohz)	vultures, transformations of evil spirits

dah	does
dah tief (teef) dee money	she who stole the money
dee	the
dee man an dem	these men
ent ye fadder sennin ye	
(ent ee fad-da sen-nin ee)	Is it not the case that his father is sending him
foh (foe)	for
gyaal (gya-arl)	girl
gyaal tief dee money (gya-al teef dee money)	the girl has stolen the money
jhandi (jhan-dee)	flag with a bamboo pole erected after hindu prayers
ley me hear (lay)	do allow me to hear
ah lass	I have lost
marning (marn-in)	good morning
poh	poor
something right dey	there is something there.
tief (teef)	steal, stole, or stolen (or as a noun = a thief)
tulsie	family of basil
wey (way)	what, where, why
wey ye na taak like dat before	why did you not say this before
wey(way) dee gyaal (gya-al) doin'	what is the girl doing
wey ye doh gi ye	why doesn't he give him
you eh know wey	do you know where Nana put the money

455

zaboka	avocado

CHAPTER 11

ah dee wake ye up	I did wake him up
ah gat dee sugar	I am suffering from diabetes mellitus
awley (ore-lee)	early
bunning	burning
bredda (bred-dah)	brother
cuscurub (cus-cu-rub)	fresh water fish
dee buaie an dam gaan foh wata	have the boys gone to fetch the water?
foh (foe)	for
gaan (garn)	has gone
gyain (gwa-in)	going
kutch nah bole - (koo-ch naah bowl)	shut your mouth, say nothing, I have nothing to say. A hindi expression. In the context of the book this was frequently used by Nanny.
ley dem buaie (lay dee bw-i)	let the boys
wen	when
wey (way)	where
wey dat buaie dey (way dat bw-I day)	where is that boy
wey ye dey (way ee day)	where is he
wey you goin' (way you go-in)	where are you going

CHAPTER 12

dee edder day (dee ed-dah day)	the other day
deez	these
gyaal	girl
moie (mo-yee)	mother
mont	month

CHAPTER 14

ah dah tell	I tell
aal ah we go	all of us will
aal dem	all those
cyant (kia-ant)	cannot
doh caal me (doe carl me)	please do not call me
gyaal	girl
lang lang	a long time ago, very long
ooman	these women
wen	when
wokin (wok-in)	working

CHAPTER 17

ah tink	I do think
bag ah corn meself (bag ah corn mee self)	bag of corn myself
carn	corn
cyant (kia-ant)	cannot
dat	that
fus	first

gyarden (gya-dn)	garden
taak	talk

CHAPTER 20

baytee	girl
dee food	the food
edder (ed- dah)	other
foh (foe)	for
gaan (garn)	has gone
gimme dat match (gi- me dat match)	give me that match

CHAPTER 24

ah eh go sleep wid you	I will not sleep with you
Alex is we man	Alex is our man. He is ours
an doh come	please do not come here
dee res	the rest of
gi you	give you
ley me see (lay)	let me have a look
mama tayta	fish
we eh go (we air go)	we will not
wid	with

CHAPTER 25

baraat (barr-rat)	wedding car procession
doolaha	bridegroom

jus like ye fadder (jus like ee fad-dah)   he is the same as his father

tassa   a type of musical drum beaten with two sticks

CHAPTER 26

ah goin (ah go-in)   I am going

ah lass me chirren (chi-ren)   I have lost my children

cobo (koh-boh) vultures   Evil spirits transformed.

dem   those

look wey happen to me   just look and see what has happened to me

me eh goin back (me air go-in back)   I am not going back there

CHAPTER 27

dem eyes   those eyes

drap   dropped

dee buaie   brother

dat   that

dee   the

gyaal   girl

gaan (garn)   has gone

wey ye go taak'bout man?
(way ee go ta-ak bout man)   <u>what</u> is he going to talk about?

CHAPTERS 30 & 31

are you buaie goin?' (are you bw-I go-in)   boy, are you
really going away?

look ye dey (look ee day)   look, there he is

me eh go see ye again

(me air go see ee again)   I may not, or I will never
see you again

wey you dey (way u day)   where are you?

 **Matador**

For exclusive discounts on Matador titles,
sign up to our occasional newsletter at
troubador.co.uk/bookshop